WALKER

For Mum, and in memory of Dad

M.S. & J.S.

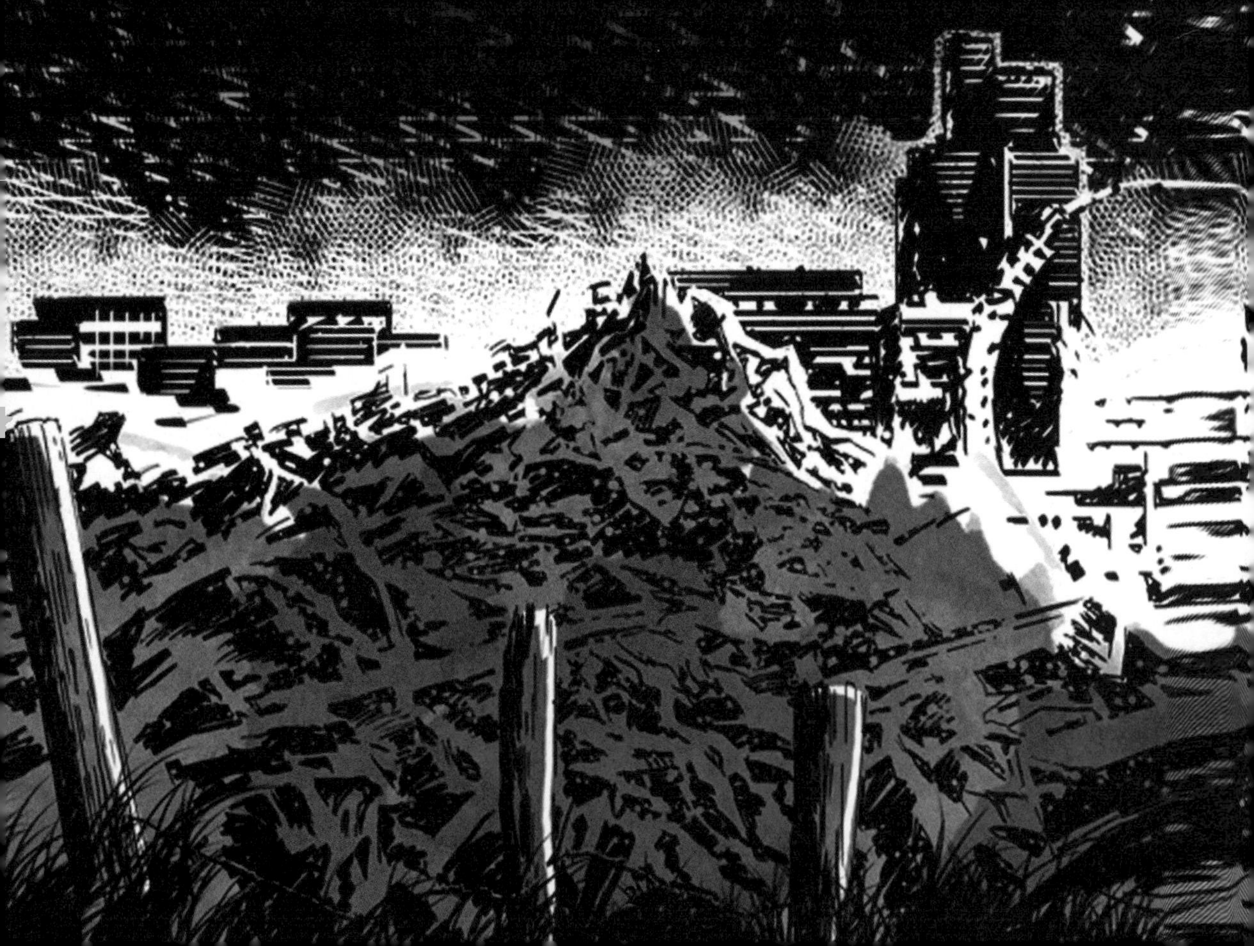

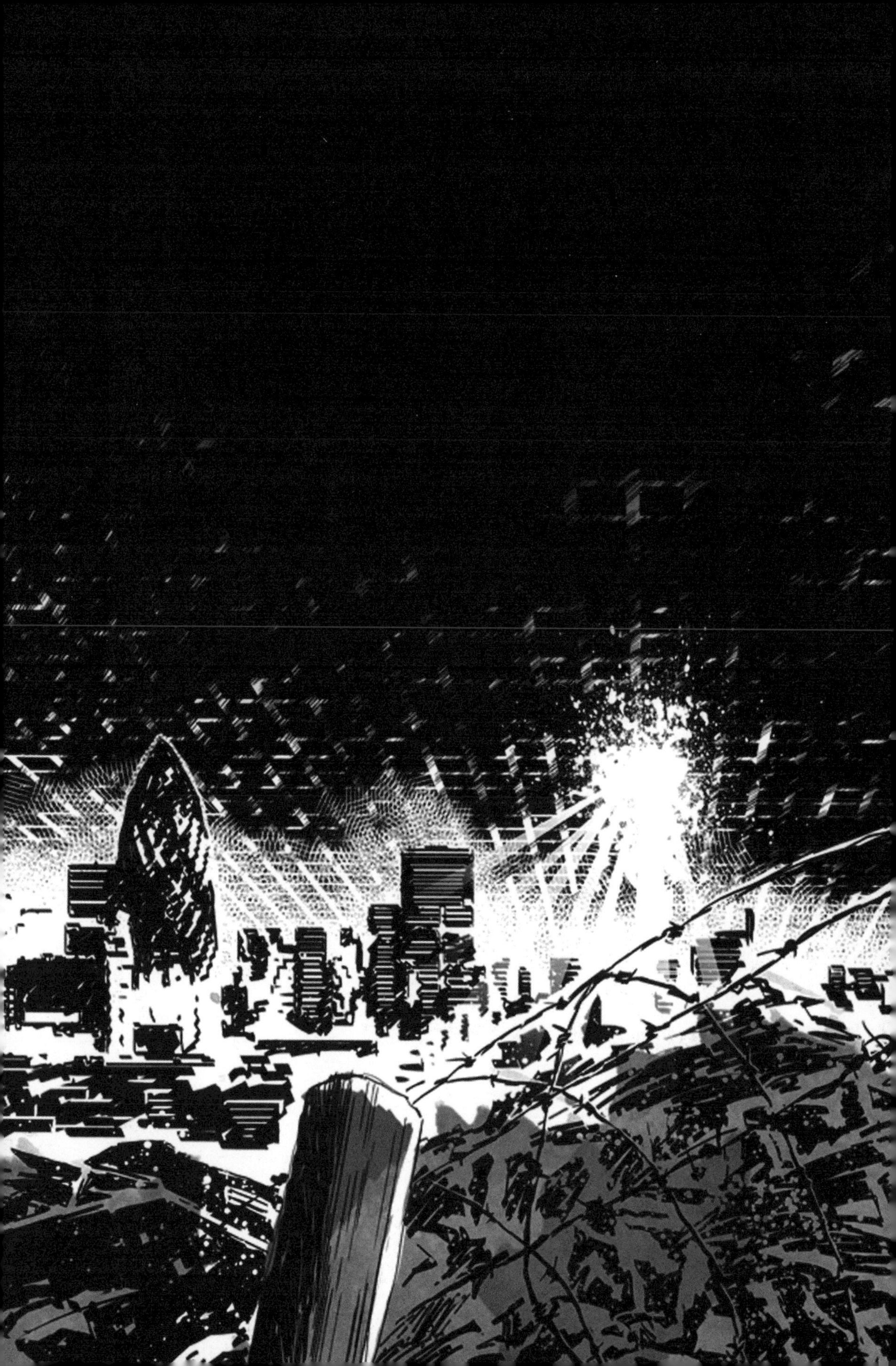

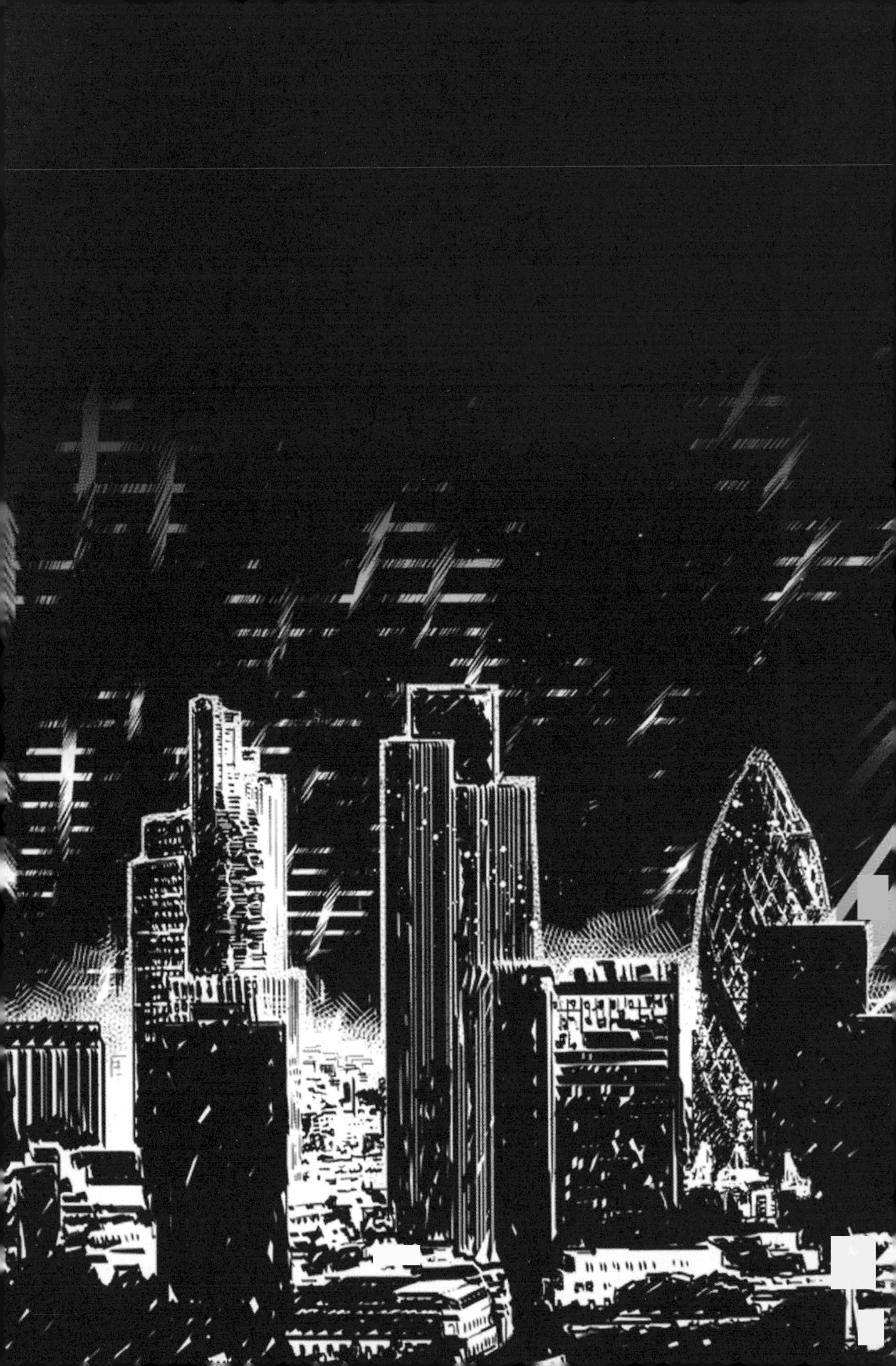

The sleep of reason brings forth Monsters

Francisco Goya

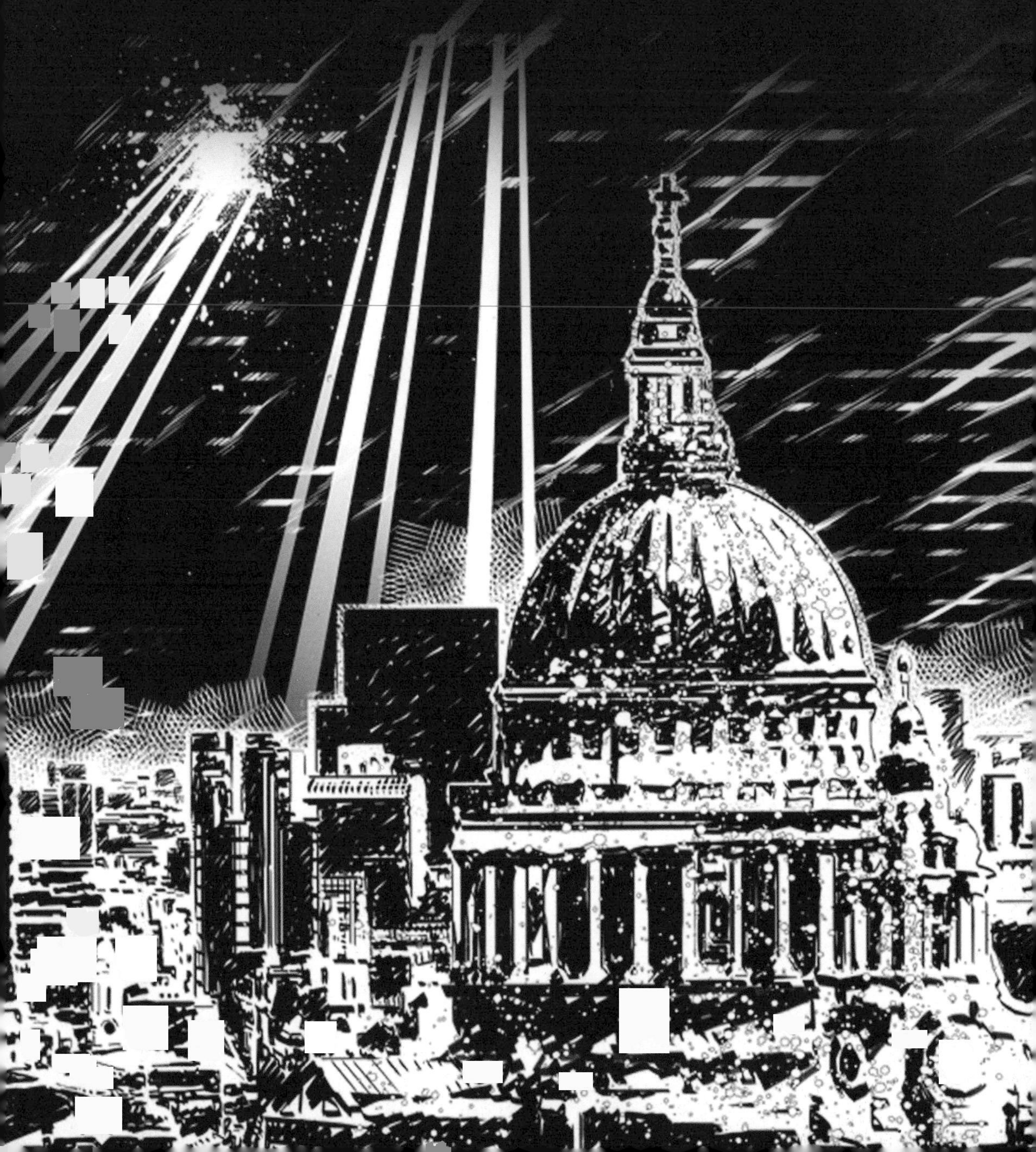

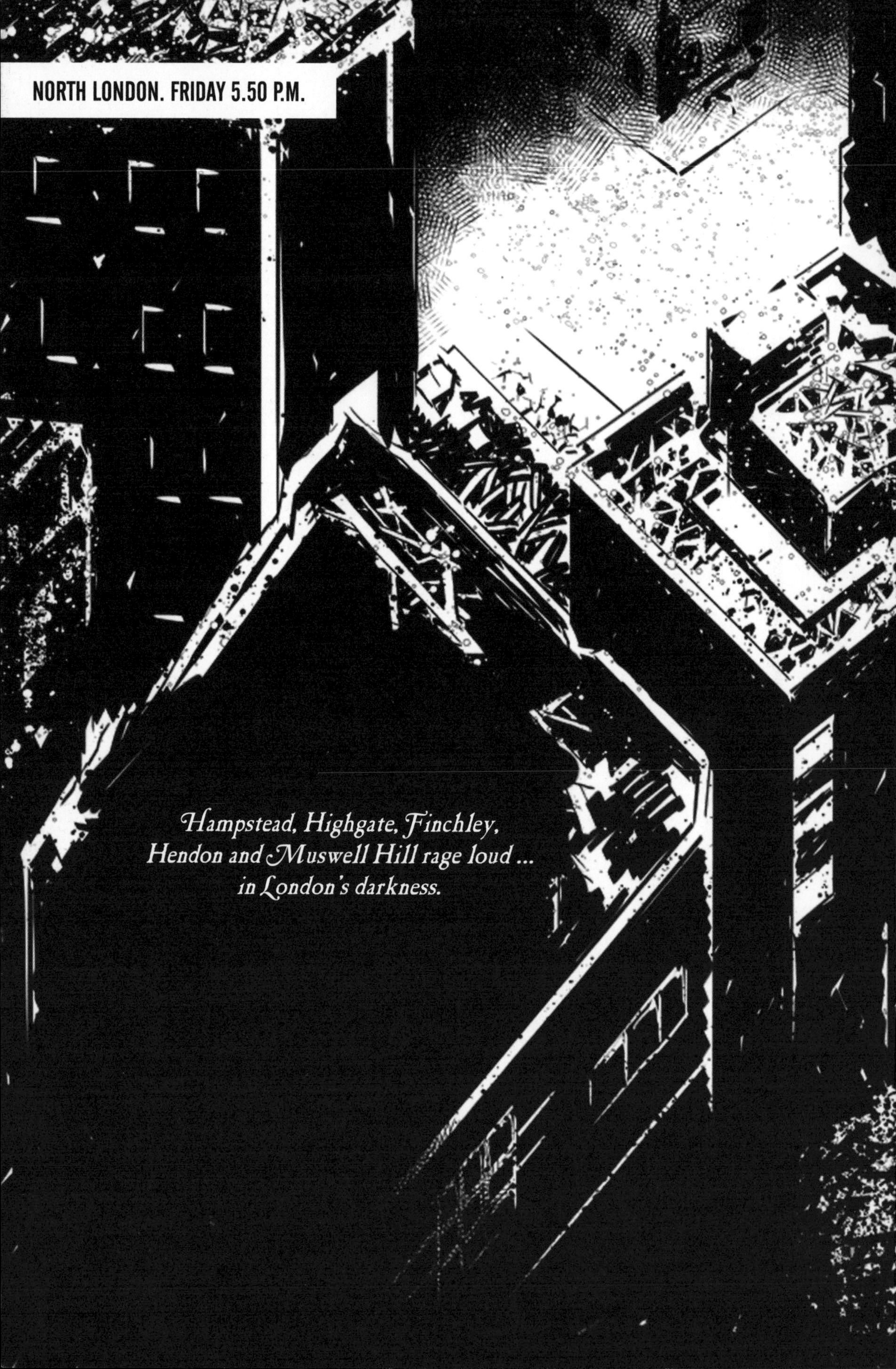
NORTH LONDON. FRIDAY 5.50 P.M.
Hampstead, Highgate, Finchley, Hendon and Muswell Hill rage loud ... in London's darkness.

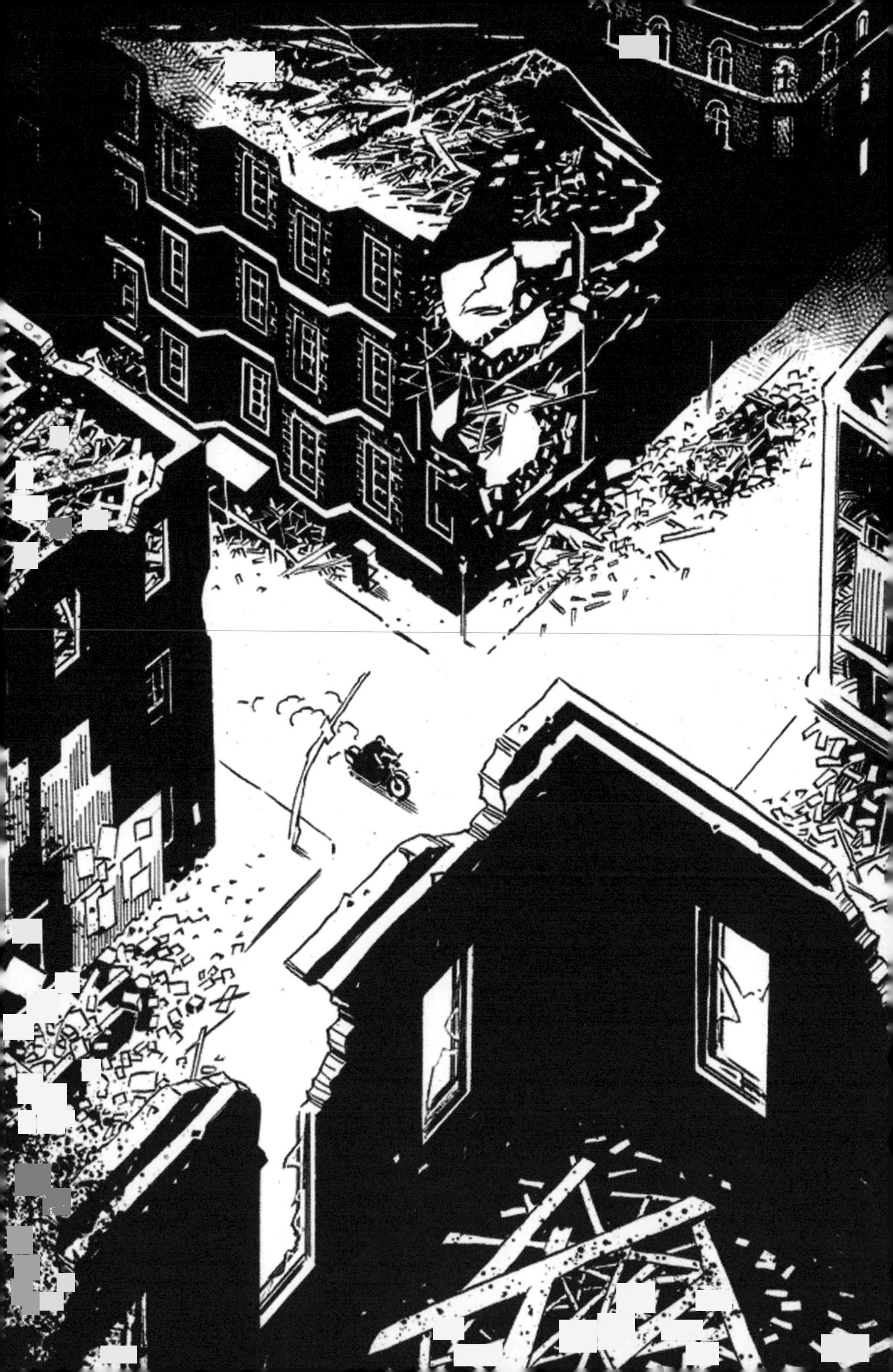

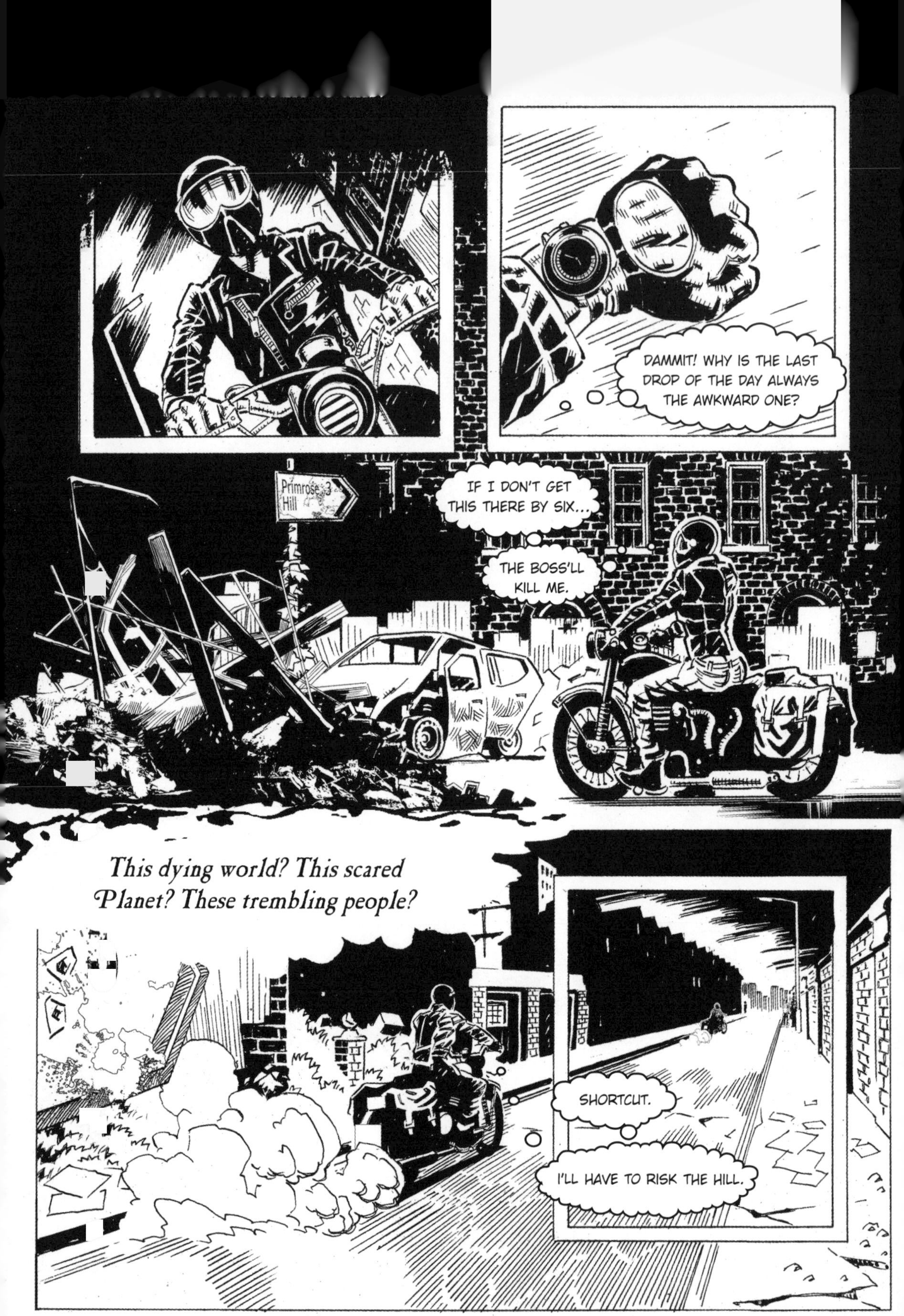
DAMMIT! WHY IS THE LAST DROP OF THE DAY ALWAYS THE AWKWARD ONE?
Primrose Hill 3
IF I DON'T GET THIS THERE BY SIX...
THE BOSS'LL KILL ME.
This dying world? This scared Planet? These trembling people?
SHORTCUT.
I'LL HAVE TO RISK THE HILL.

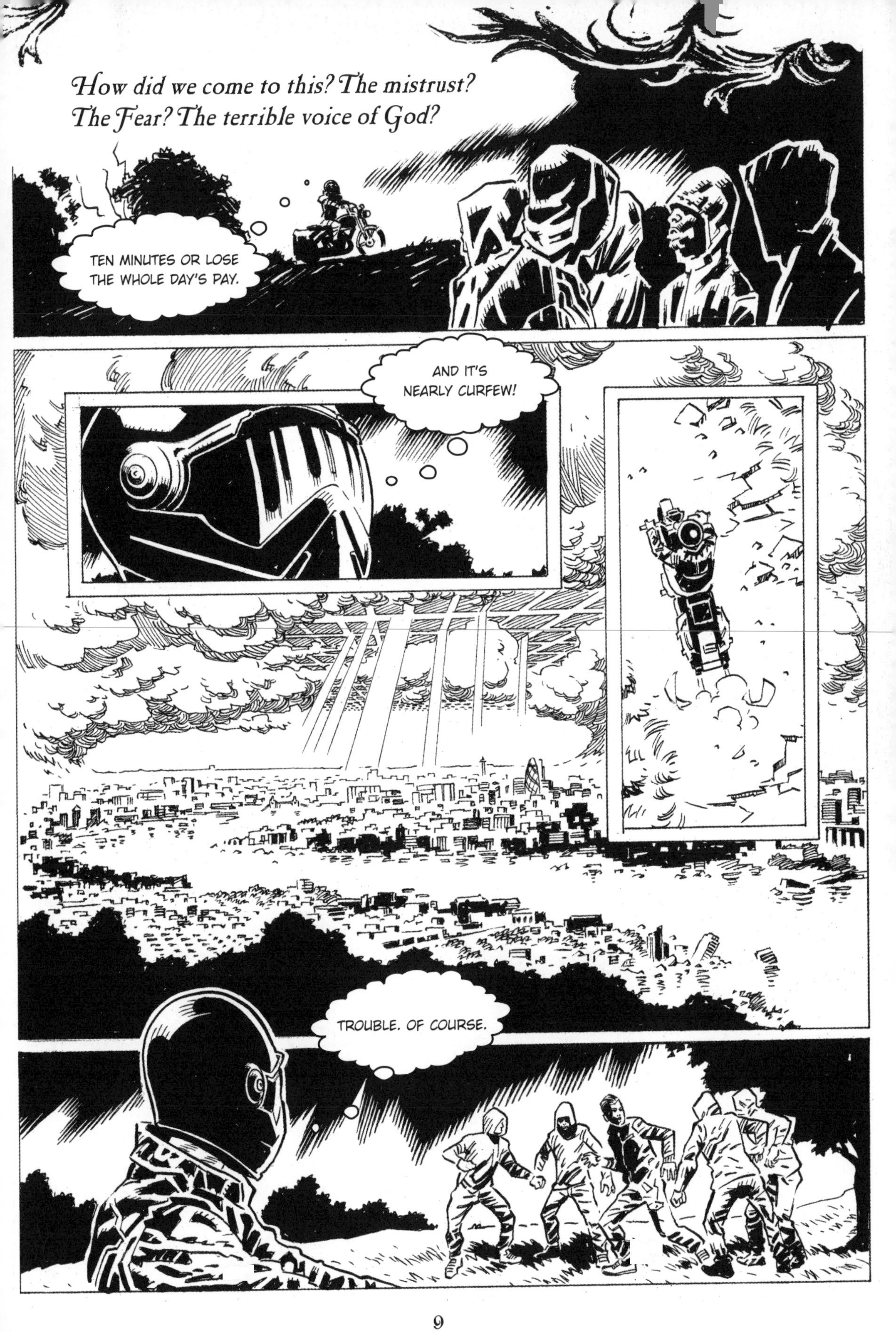
How did we come to this? The mistrust? The Fear? The terrible voice of God?
TEN MINUTES OR LOSE THE WHOLE DAY'S PAY.
AND IT'S NEARLY CURFEW!
TROUBLE. OF COURSE.

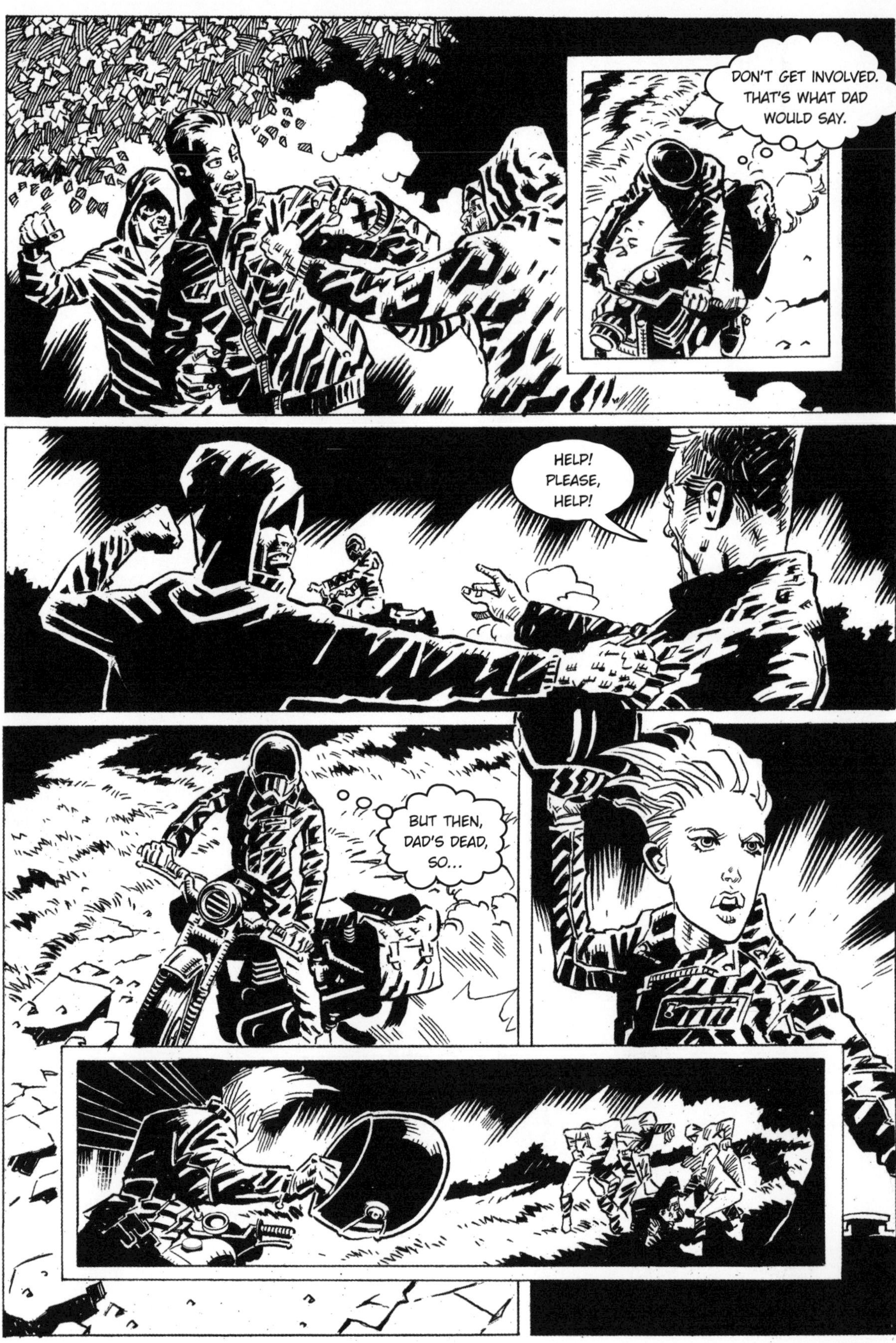
DON'T GET INVOLVED. THAT'S WHAT DAD WOULD SAY.
HELP! PLEASE, HELP!
BUT THEN, DAD'S DEAD, SO...

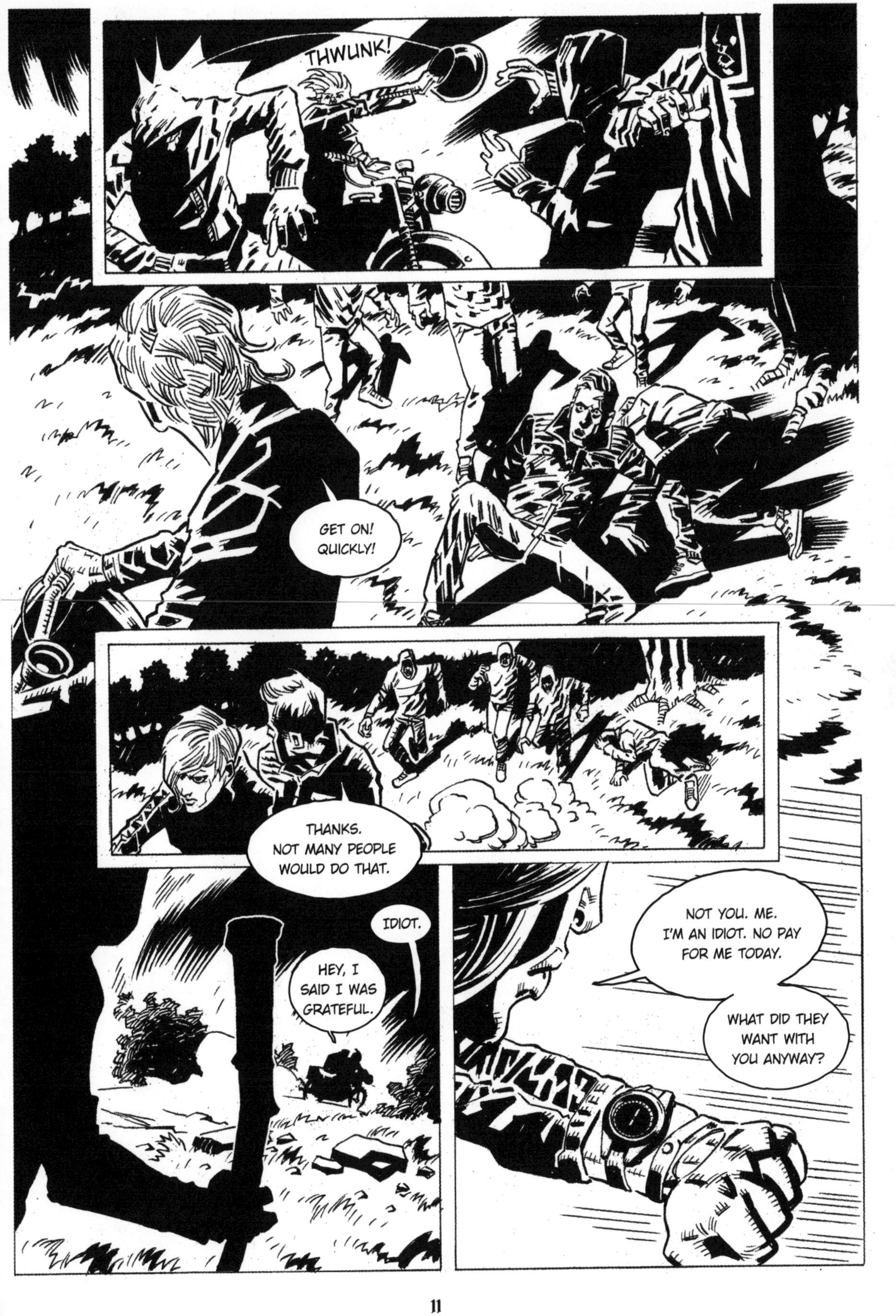

THWUNK!
GET ON! QUICKLY!
THANKS. NOT MANY PEOPLE WOULD DO THAT.
IDIOT.
HEY, I SAID I WAS GRATEFUL.
NOT YOU. ME. I'M AN IDIOT. NO PAY FOR ME TODAY.
WHAT DID THEY WANT WITH YOU ANYWAY?

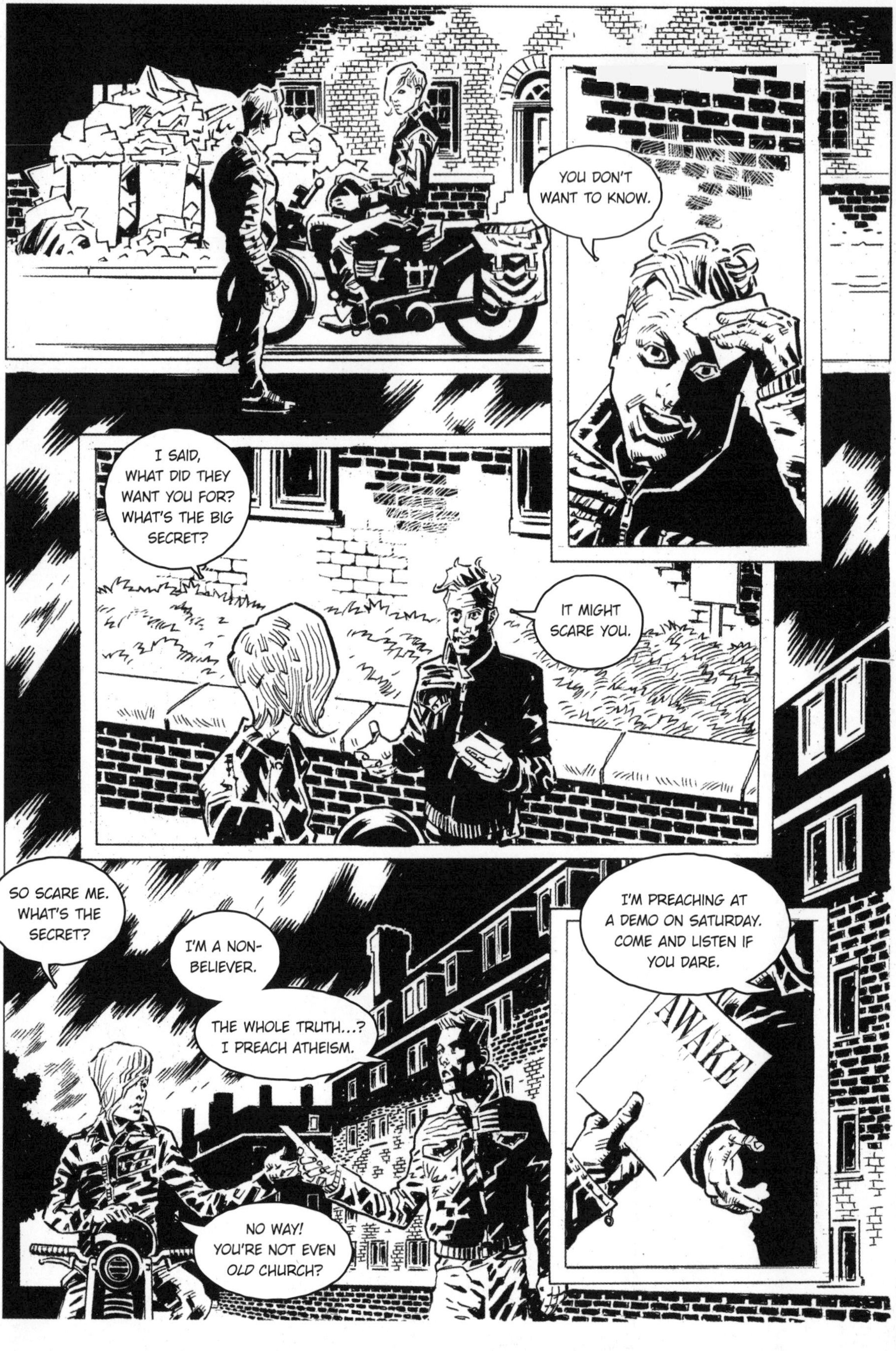
YOU DON'T WANT TO KNOW.
I SAID, WHAT DID THEY WANT YOU FOR? WHAT'S THE BIG SECRET?
IT MIGHT SCARE YOU.
SO SCARE ME. WHAT'S THE SECRET?
I'M A NON-BELIEVER.
THE WHOLE TRUTH...? I PREACH ATHEISM.
NO WAY! YOU'RE NOT EVEN OLD CHURCH?
I'M PREACHING AT A DEMO ON SATURDAY. COME AND LISTEN IF YOU DARE.
AWAKE

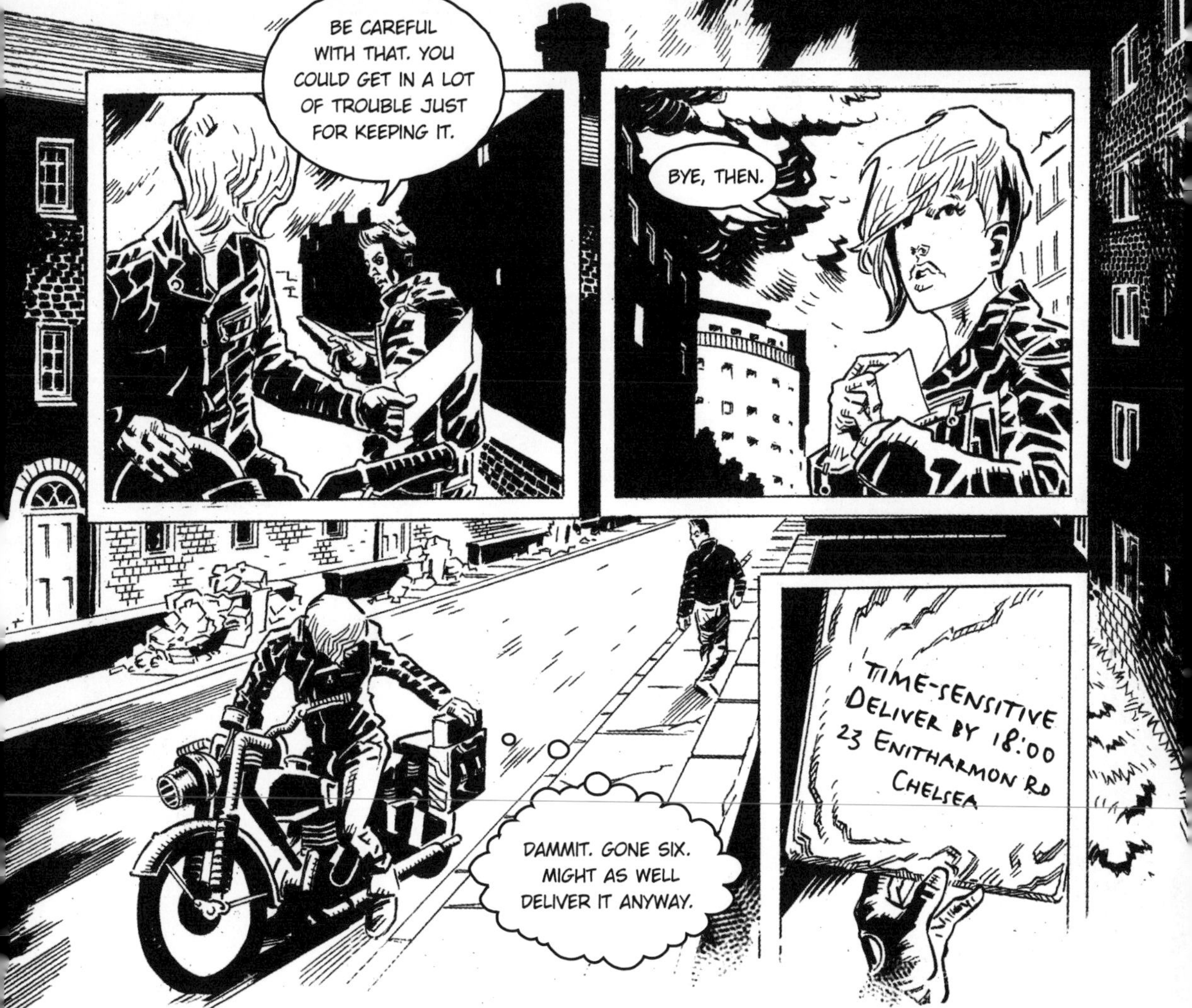
BE CAREFUL WITH THAT. YOU COULD GET IN A LOT OF TROUBLE JUST FOR KEEPING IT.
BYE, THEN.
TIME-SENSITIVE
DELIVER BY 18:00
23 ENITHARMON RD
CHELSEA
DAMMIT. GONE SIX. MIGHT AS WELL DELIVER IT ANYWAY.

Now London moulders beneath the Uncertain seasons and the Lethal Rays of the Sun – protected only by the vital Space Mirrors overhead. Thank God.

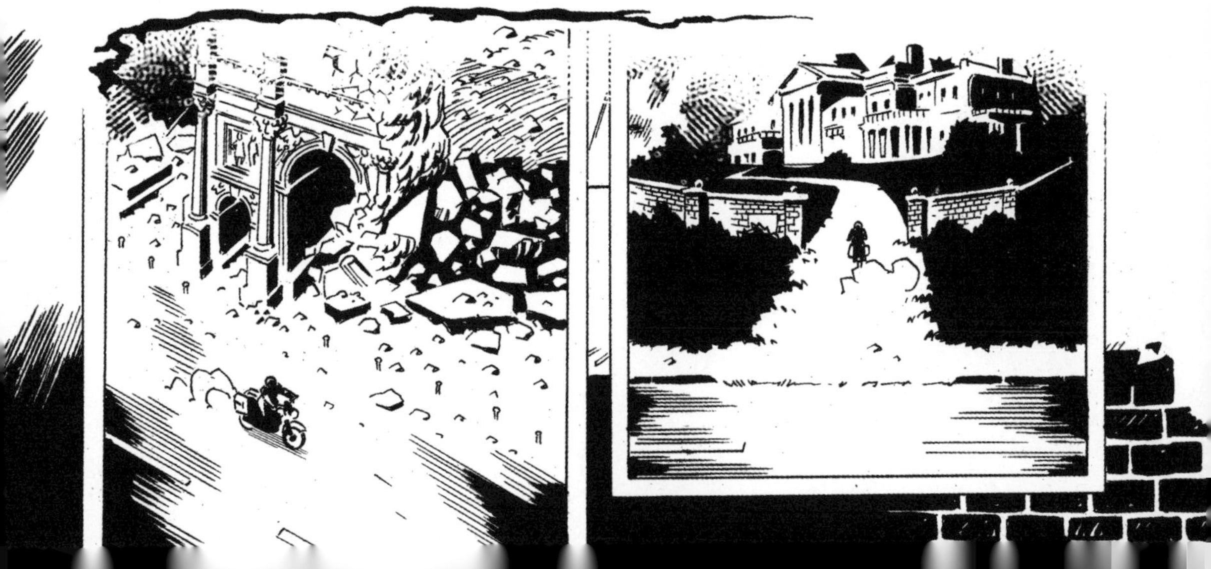

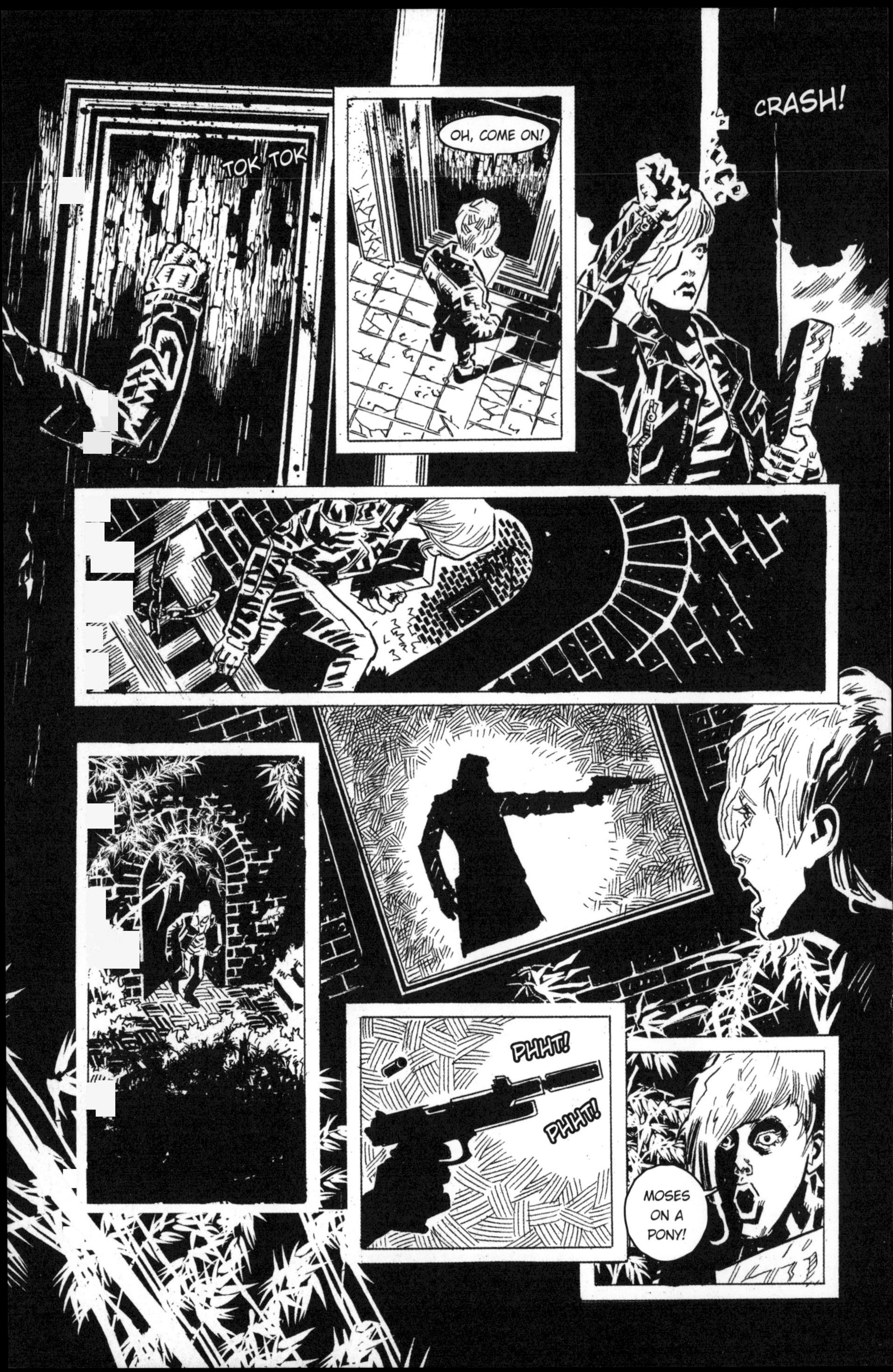
TOK TOK
OH, COME ON!
CRASH!
PHHT!
PHHT!
MOSES ON A PONY!

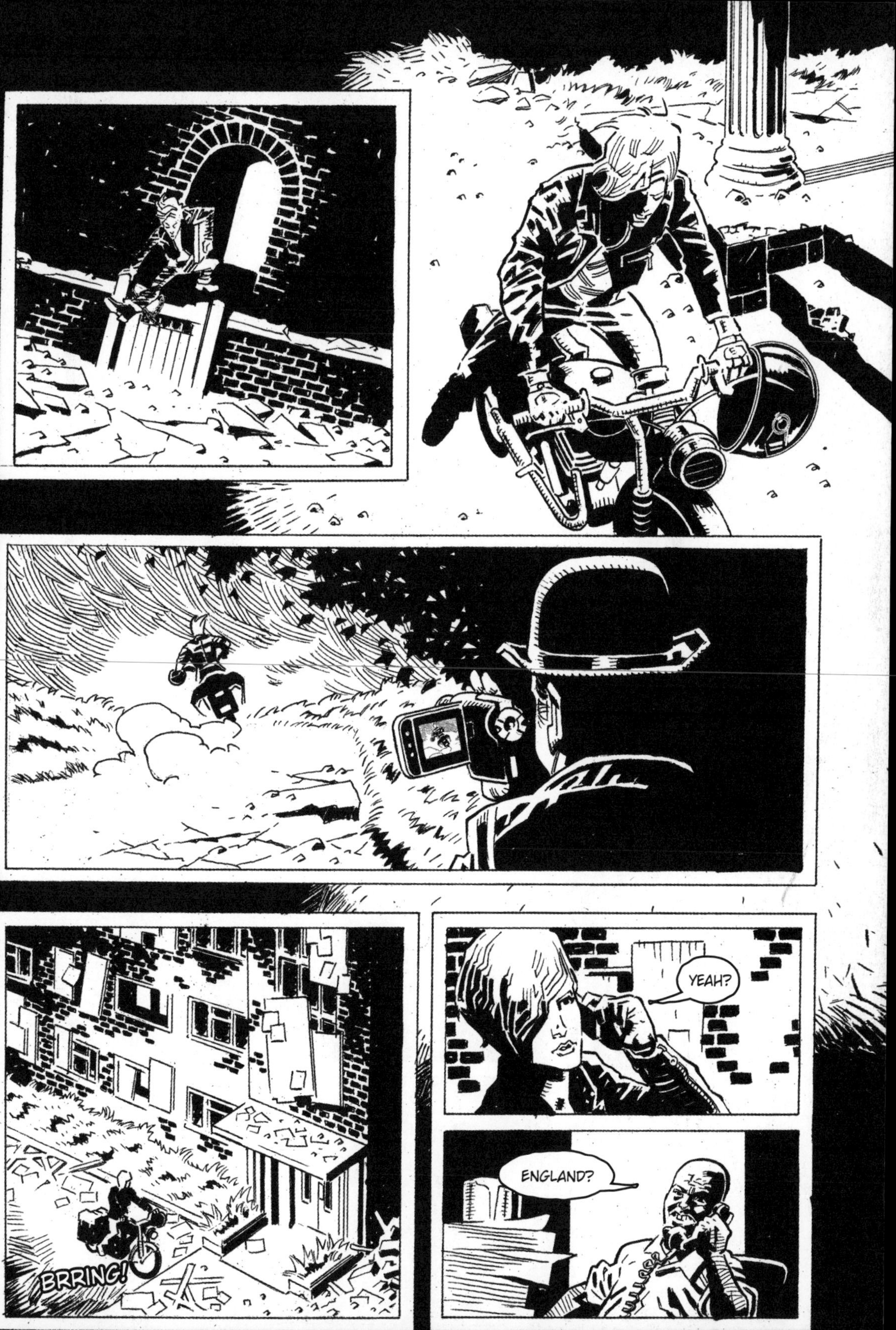
BRRING!
YEAH?
ENGLAND?

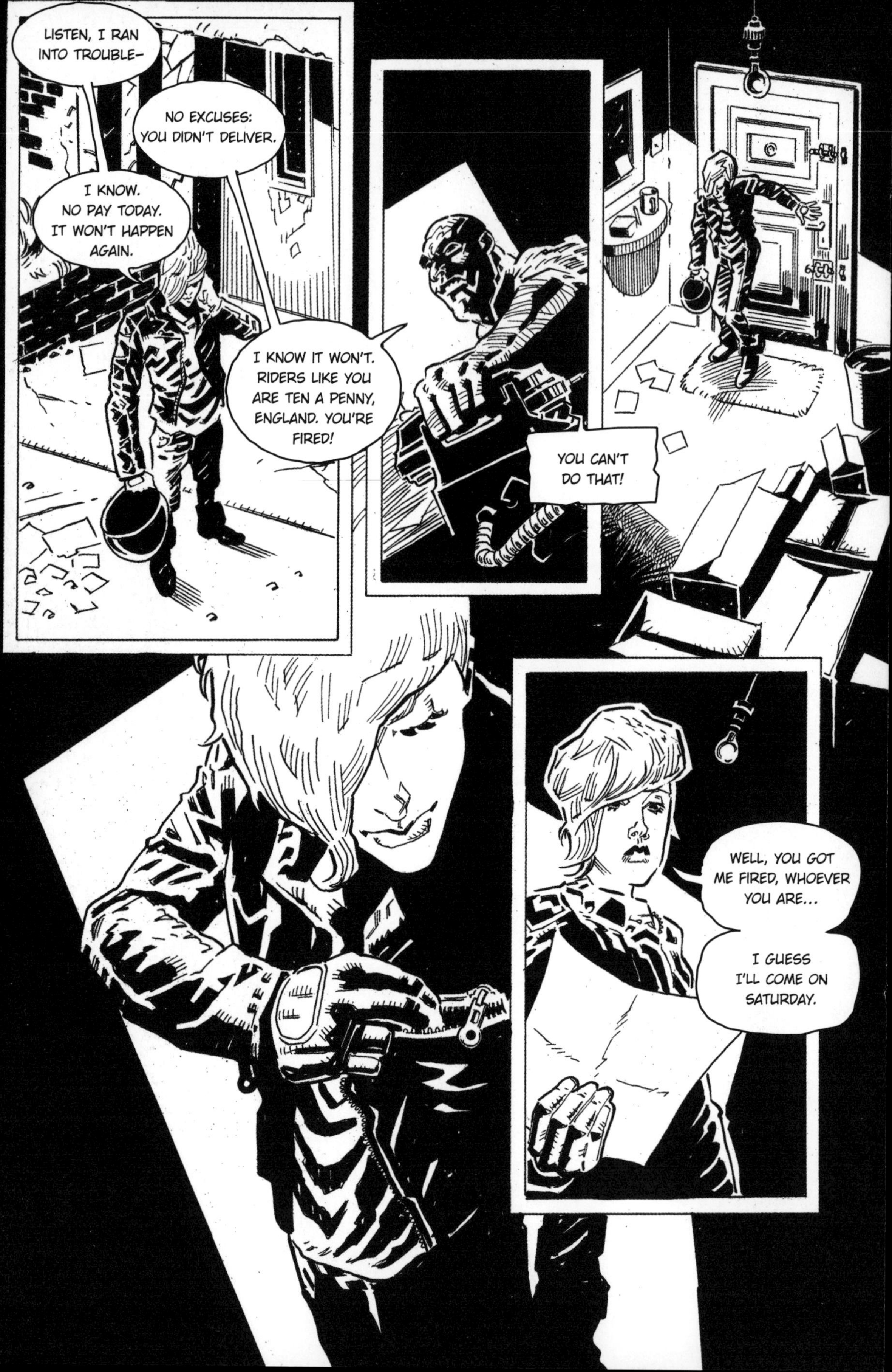
LISTEN, I RAN INTO TROUBLE-
NO EXCUSES: YOU DIDN'T DELIVER.
I KNOW. NO PAY TODAY. IT WON'T HAPPEN AGAIN.
I KNOW IT WON'T. RIDERS LIKE YOU ARE TEN A PENNY, ENGLAND. YOU'RE FIRED!
YOU CAN'T DO THAT!
WELL, YOU GOT ME FIRED, WHOEVER YOU ARE...
I GUESS I'LL COME ON SATURDAY.

It has begun.
And a Miracle
is coming...

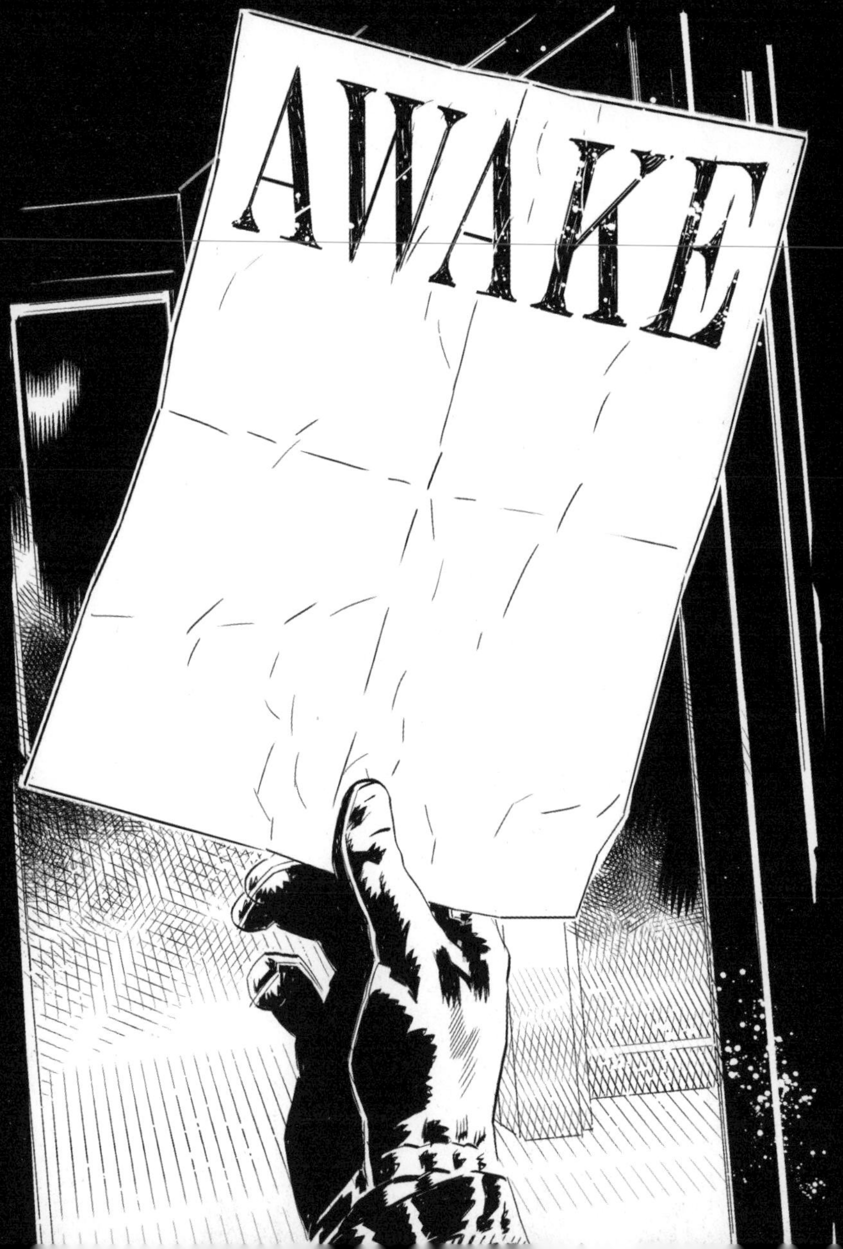
AWAKE

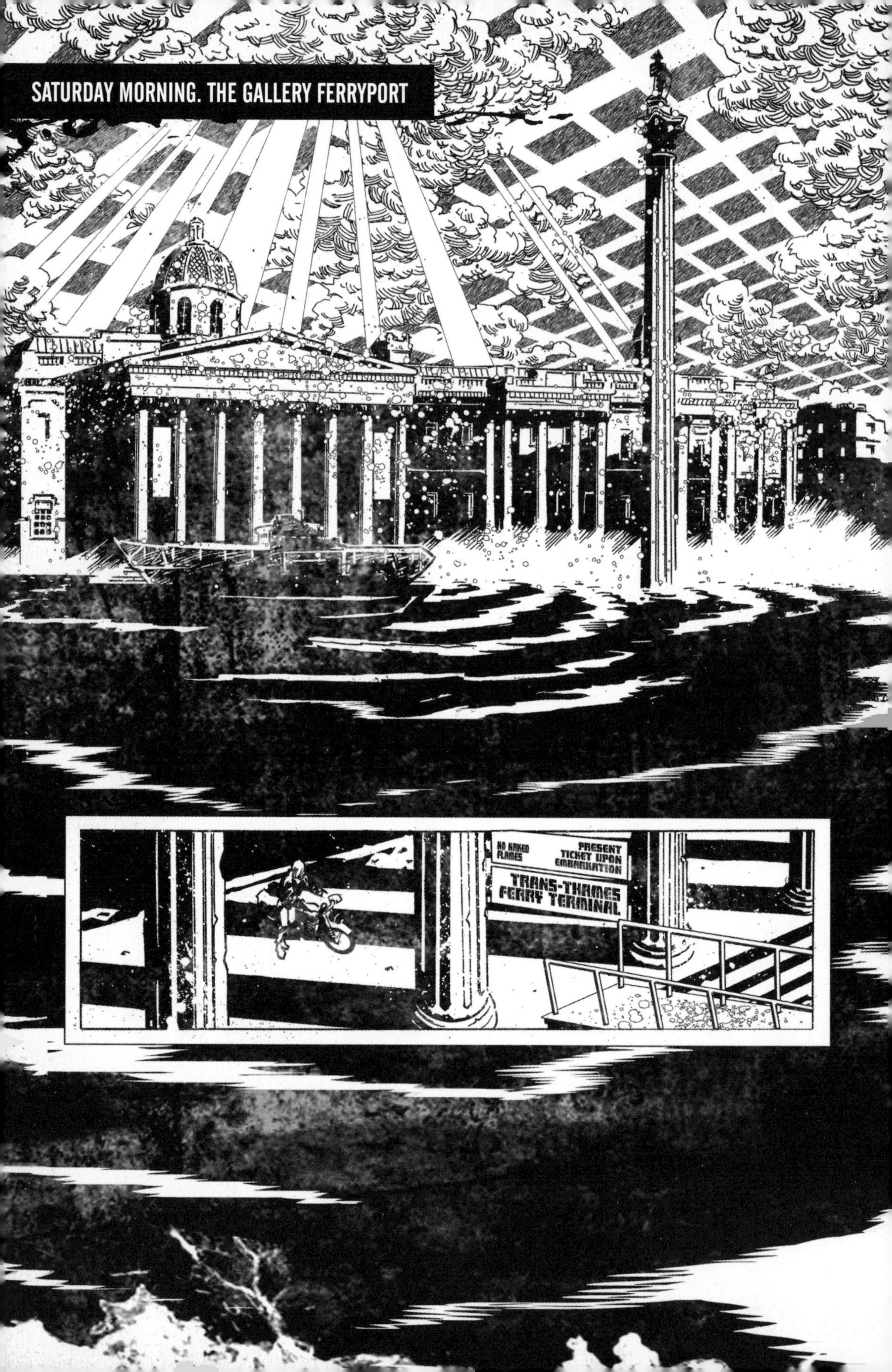
SATURDAY MORNING. THE GALLERY FERRYPORT
NO NAKED FLAMES
PRESENT TICKET UPON EMBARKATION
TRANS-THAMES FERRY TERMINAL

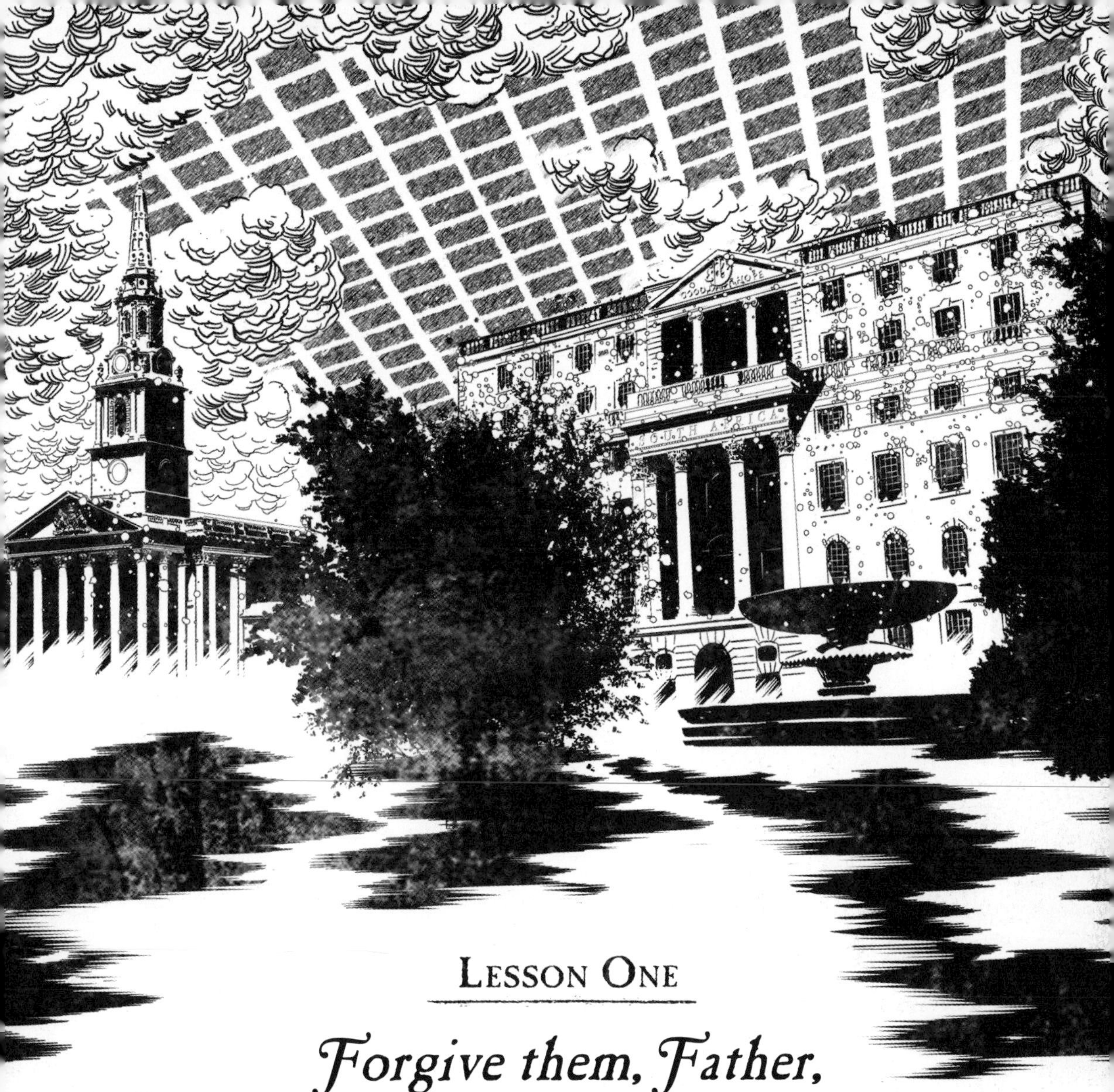
SOUTH AFRICA

Lesson One

Forgive them, Father, for they know not what they do

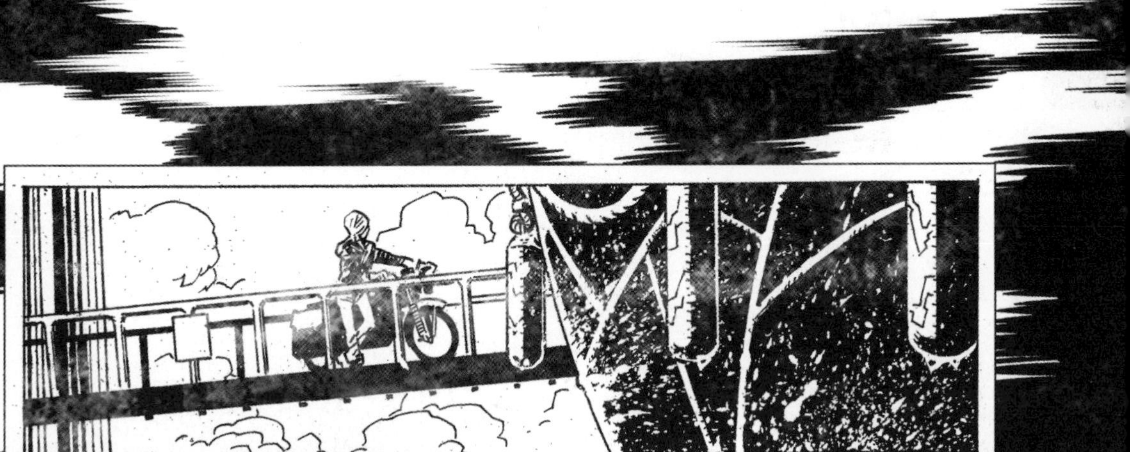

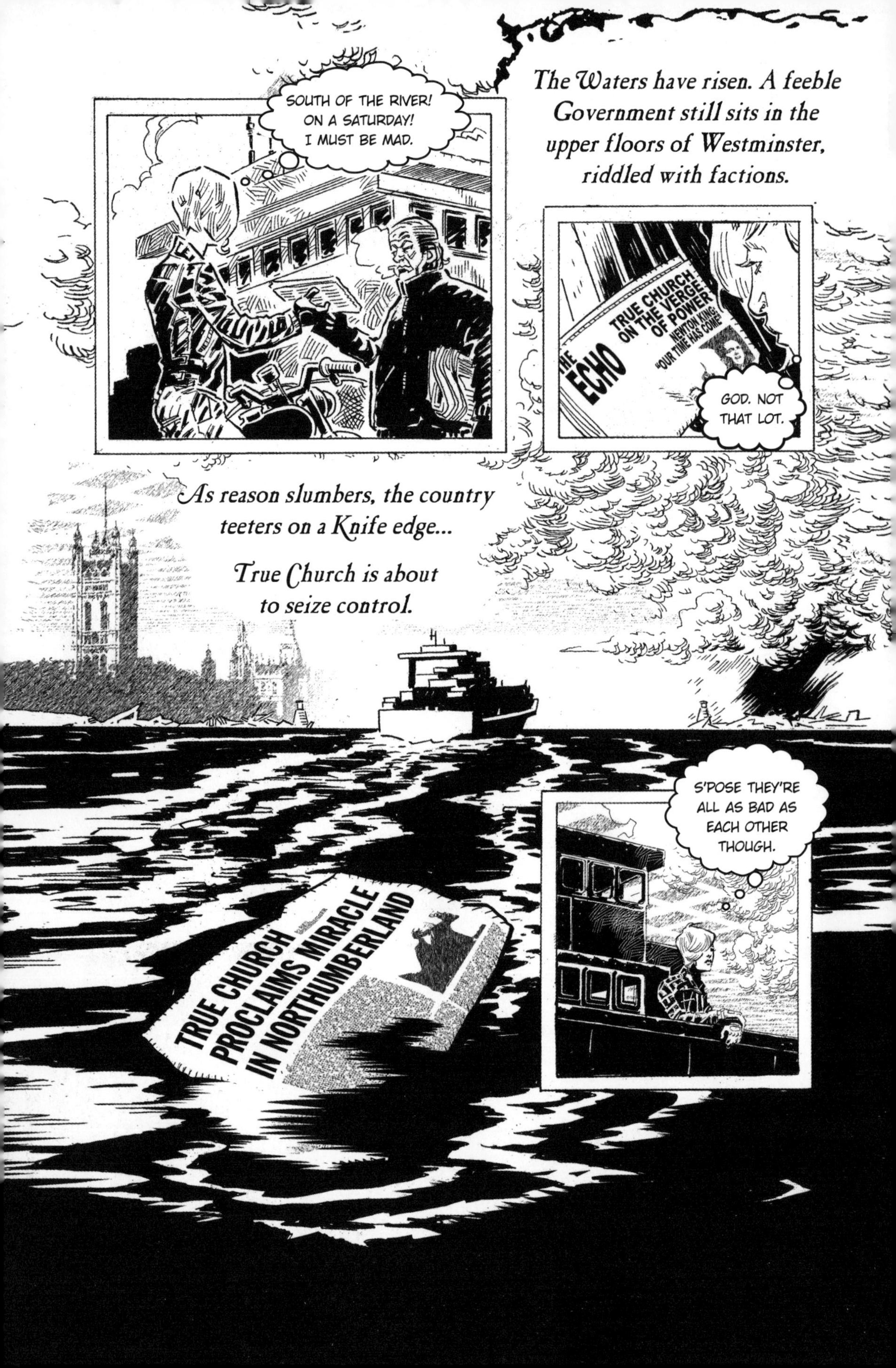
SOUTH OF THE RIVER! ON A SATURDAY! I MUST BE MAD.
The Waters have risen. A feeble Government still sits in the upper floors of Westminster, riddled with factions.
THE ECHO
TRUE CHURCH ON THE VERGE OF POWER
NEWTON KING: "OUR TIME HAS COME"
GOD. NOT THAT LOT.
As reason slumbers, the country teeters on a Knife edge...
True Church is about to seize control.
S'POSE THEY'RE ALL AS BAD AS EACH OTHER THOUGH.
TRUE CHURCH PROCLAIMS MIRACLE IN NORTHUMBERLAND

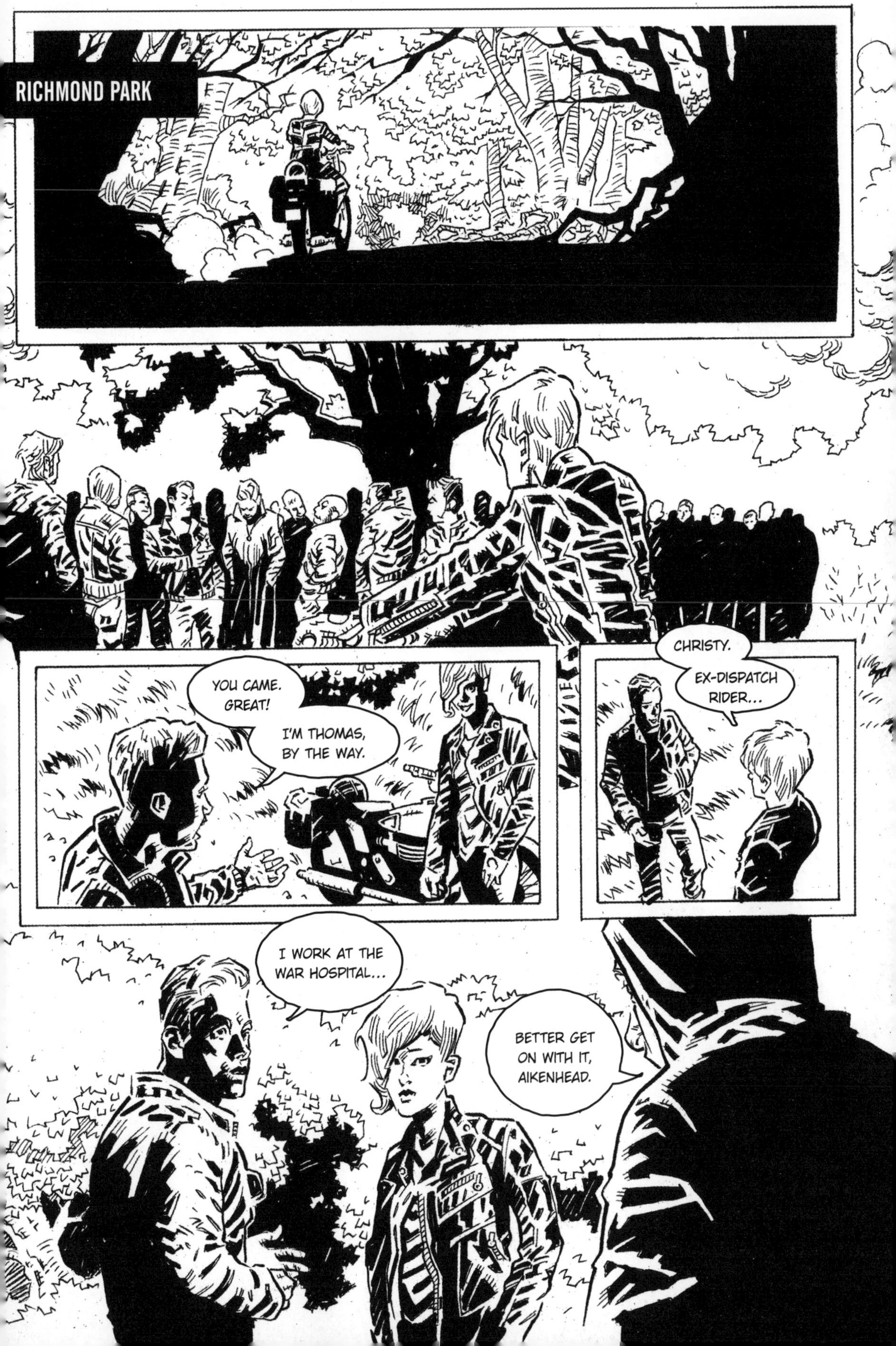
RICHMOND PARK
YOU CAME. GREAT!
I'M THOMAS, BY THE WAY.
CHRISTY.
EX-DISPATCH RIDER...
I WORK AT THE WAR HOSPITAL...
BETTER GET ON WITH IT, AIKENHEAD.

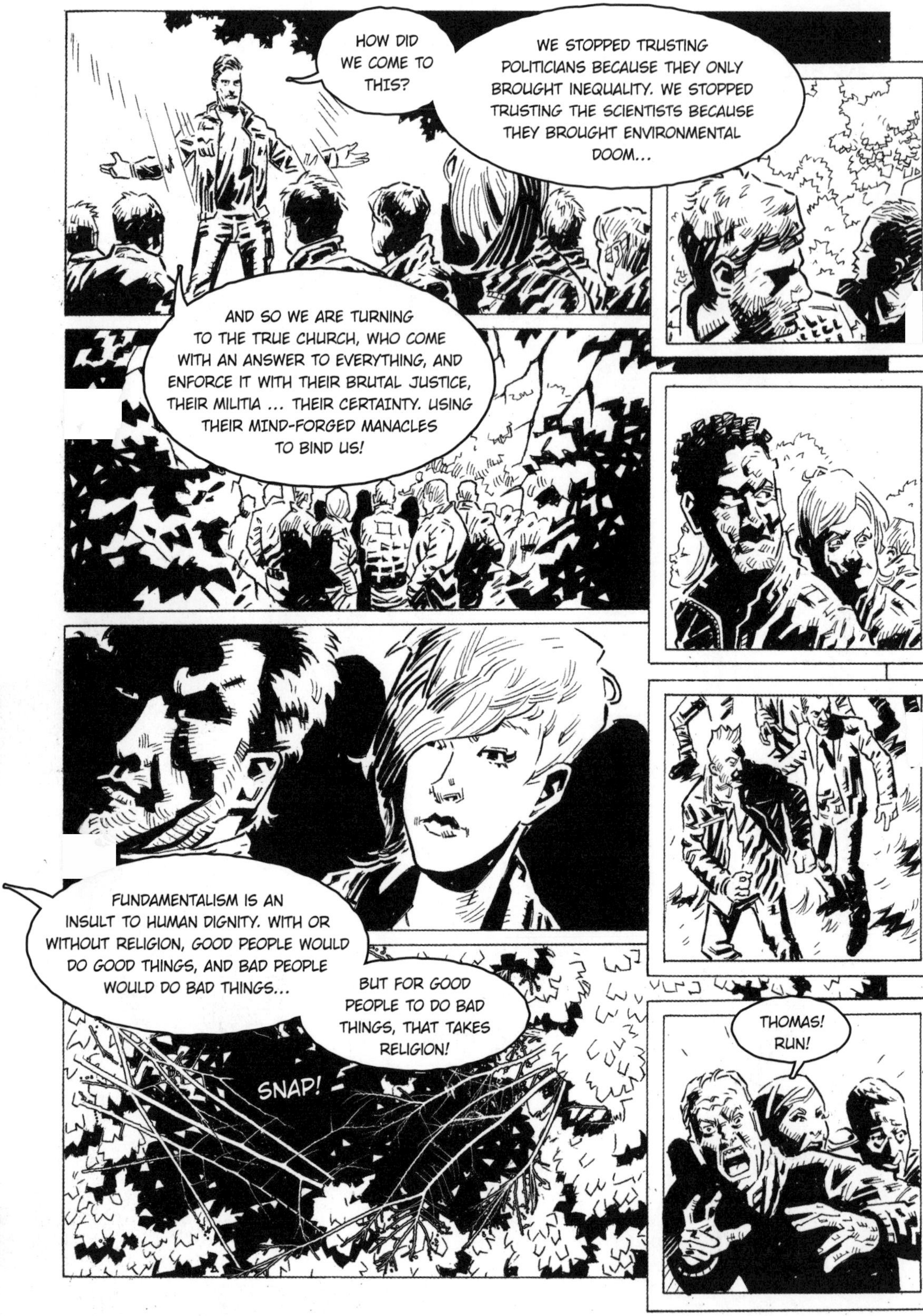

HOW DID WE COME TO THIS?
WE STOPPED TRUSTING POLITICIANS BECAUSE THEY ONLY BROUGHT INEQUALITY. WE STOPPED TRUSTING THE SCIENTISTS BECAUSE THEY BROUGHT ENVIRONMENTAL DOOM...
AND SO WE ARE TURNING TO THE TRUE CHURCH, WHO COME WITH AN ANSWER TO EVERYTHING, AND ENFORCE IT WITH THEIR BRUTAL JUSTICE, THEIR MILITIA ... THEIR CERTAINTY. USING THEIR MIND-FORGED MANACLES TO BIND US!
FUNDAMENTALISM IS AN INSULT TO HUMAN DIGNITY. WITH OR WITHOUT RELIGION, GOOD PEOPLE WOULD DO GOOD THINGS, AND BAD PEOPLE WOULD DO BAD THINGS...
BUT FOR GOOD PEOPLE TO DO BAD THINGS, THAT TAKES RELIGION!
SNAP!
THOMAS! RUN!

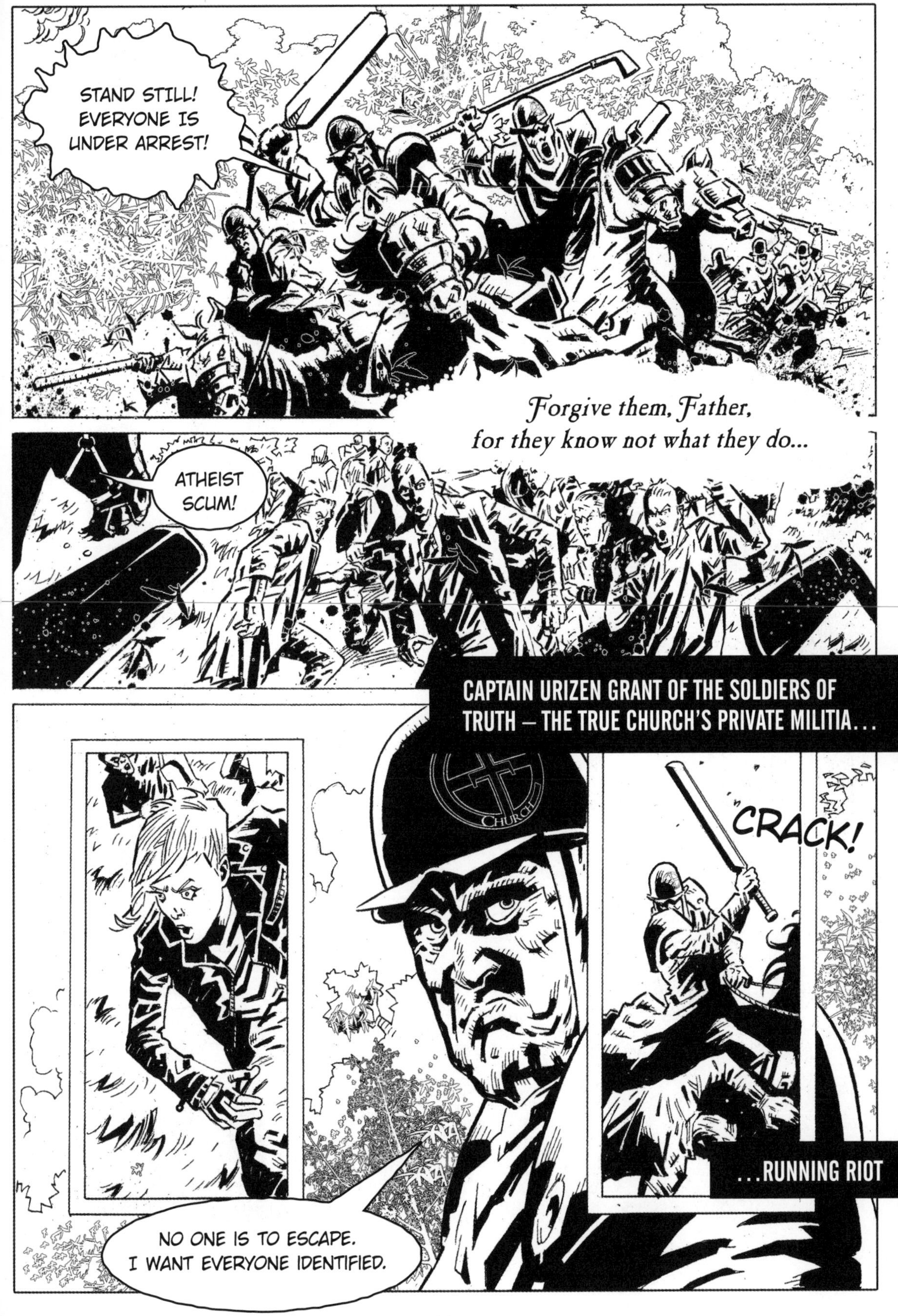
STAND STILL! EVERYONE IS UNDER ARREST!
Forgive them, Father, for they know not what they do...
ATHEIST SCUM!
CAPTAIN URIZEN GRANT OF THE SOLDIERS OF TRUTH – THE TRUE CHURCH'S PRIVATE MILITIA...
CHURCH
CRACK!
...RUNNING RIOT
NO ONE IS TO ESCAPE. I WANT EVERYONE IDENTIFIED.

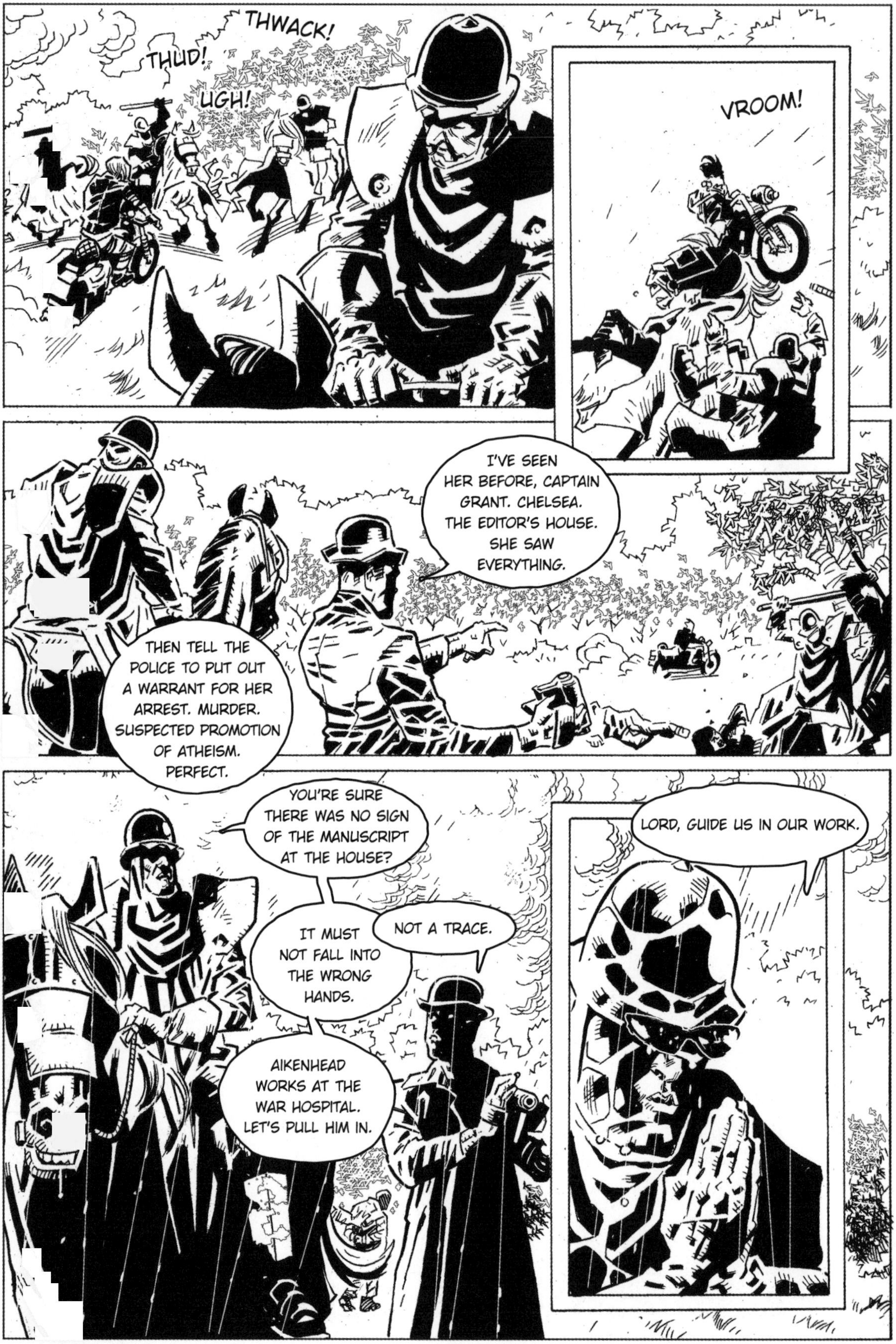
THUD!
THWACK!
UGH!
VROOM!
I'VE SEEN HER BEFORE, CAPTAIN GRANT. CHELSEA. THE EDITOR'S HOUSE. SHE SAW EVERYTHING.
THEN TELL THE POLICE TO PUT OUT A WARRANT FOR HER ARREST. MURDER. SUSPECTED PROMOTION OF ATHEISM. PERFECT.
YOU'RE SURE THERE WAS NO SIGN OF THE MANUSCRIPT AT THE HOUSE?
NOT A TRACE.
IT MUST NOT FALL INTO THE WRONG HANDS.
AIKENHEAD WORKS AT THE WAR HOSPITAL. LET'S PULL HIM IN.
LORD, GUIDE US IN OUR WORK.

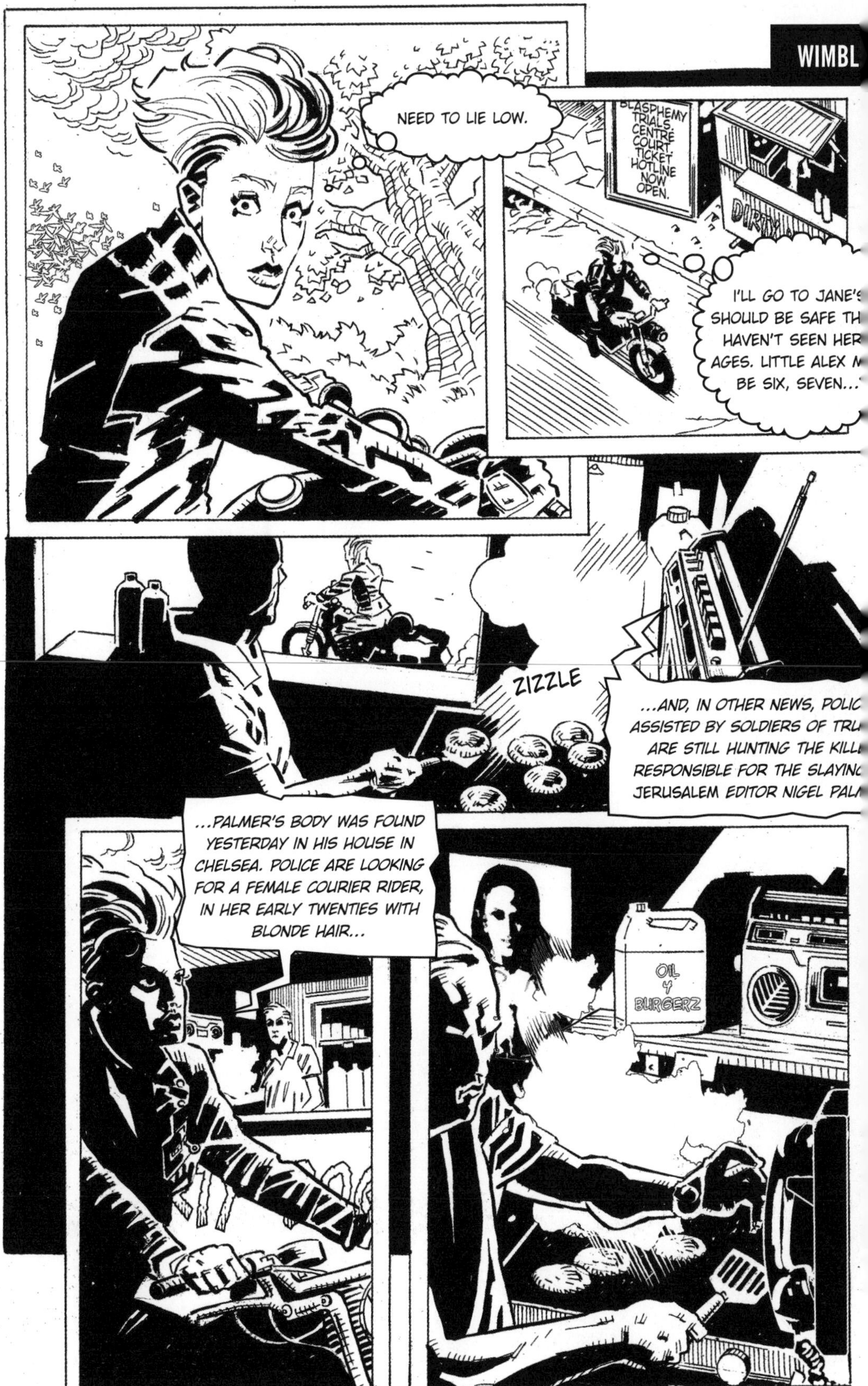
NEED TO LIE LOW.
BLASPHEMY TRIALS. CENTRE COURT. TICKET HOTLINE NOW OPEN.
DIRTY
I'LL GO TO JANE'S SHOULD BE SAFE TH HAVEN'T SEEN HER AGES. LITTLE ALEX M BE SIX, SEVEN...
ZIZZLE
...AND, IN OTHER NEWS, POLIC ASSISTED BY SOLDIERS OF TRU ARE STILL HUNTING THE KILLE RESPONSIBLE FOR THE SLAYING JERUSALEM EDITOR NIGEL PAL
...PALMER'S BODY WAS FOUND YESTERDAY IN HIS HOUSE IN CHELSEA. POLICE ARE LOOKING FOR A FEMALE COURIER RIDER, IN HER EARLY TWENTIES WITH BLONDE HAIR...
OIL 4 BURGERZ

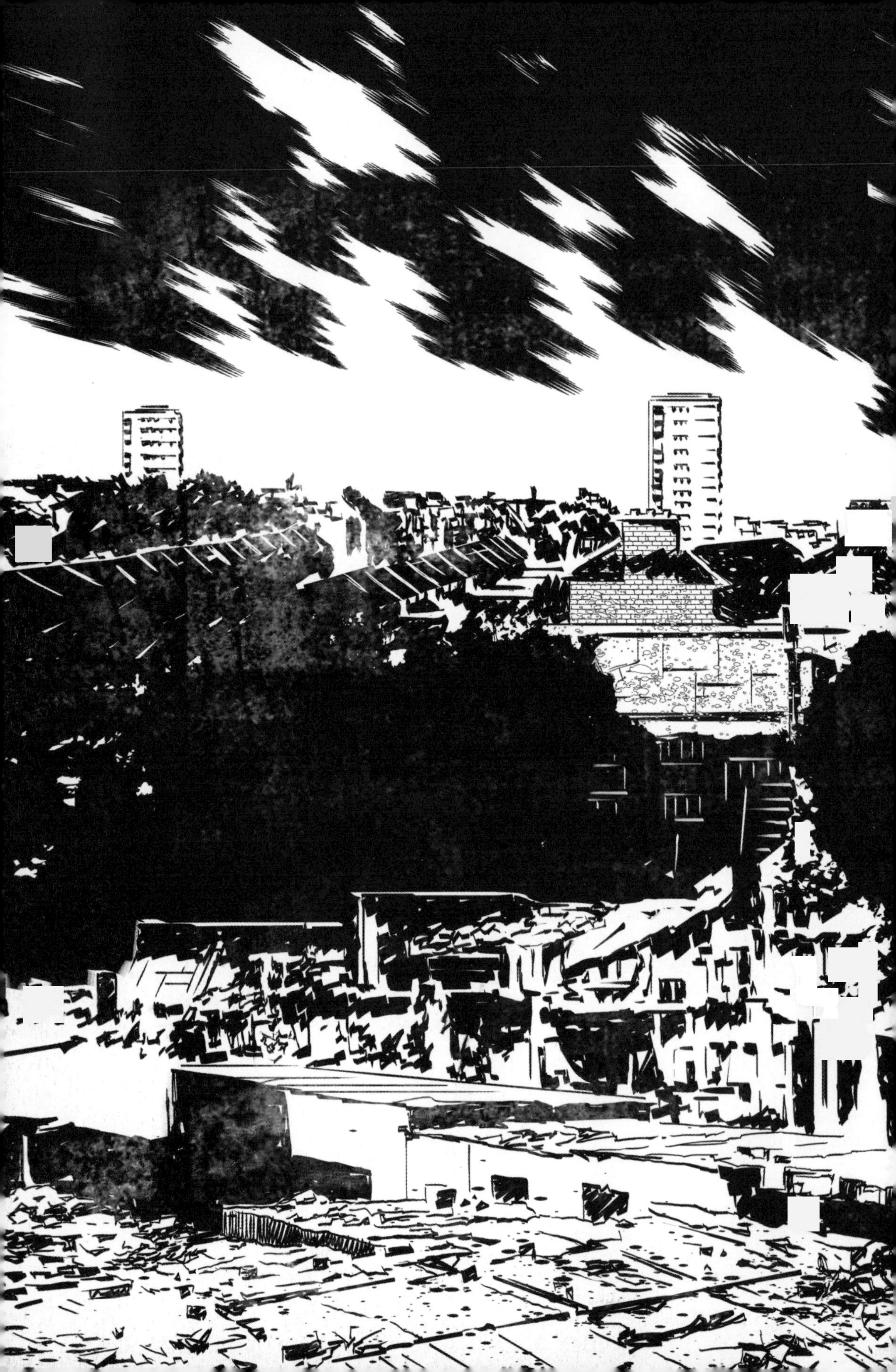

Lesson Two

This day thou shalt be with me in Paradise

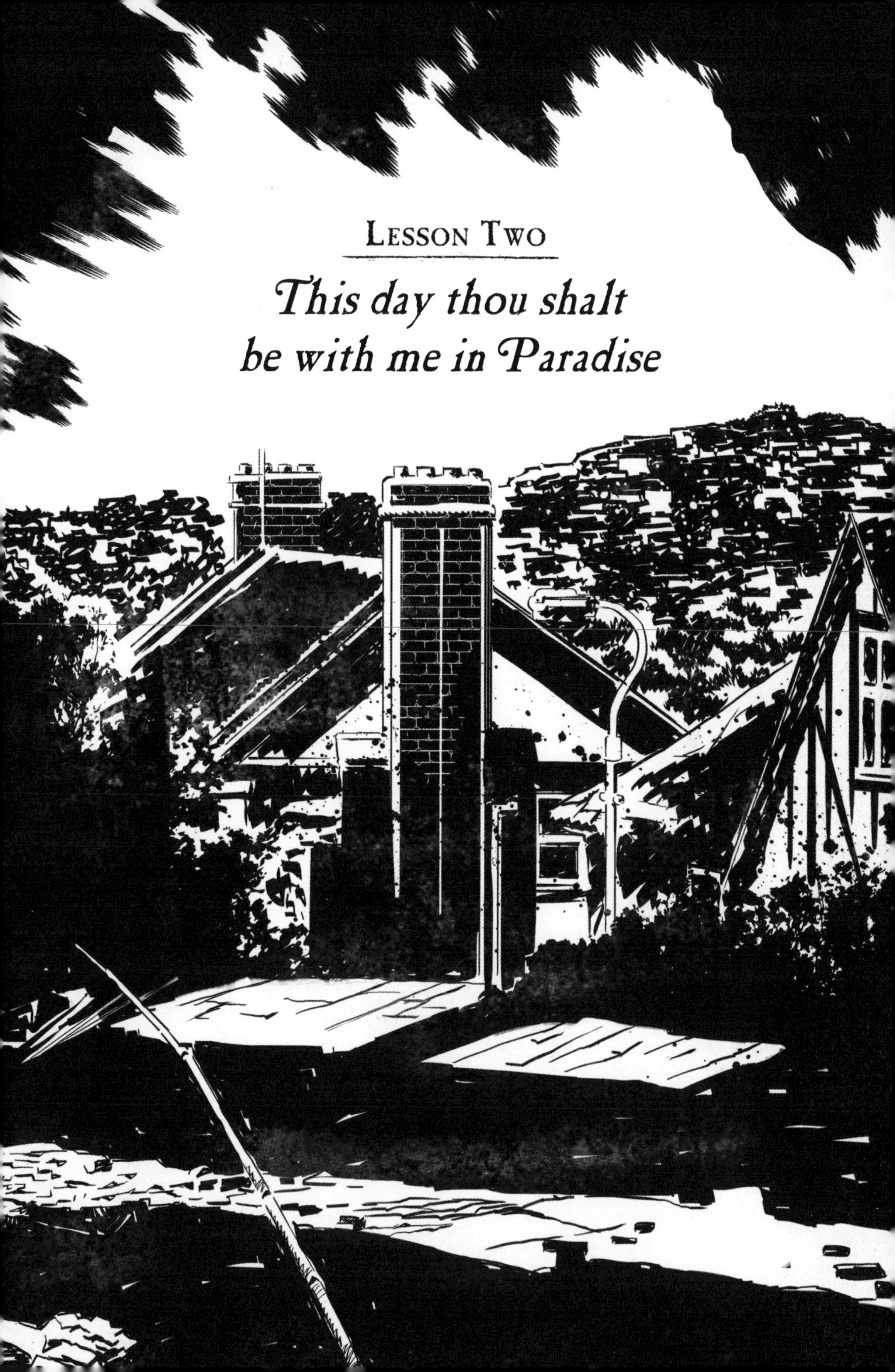

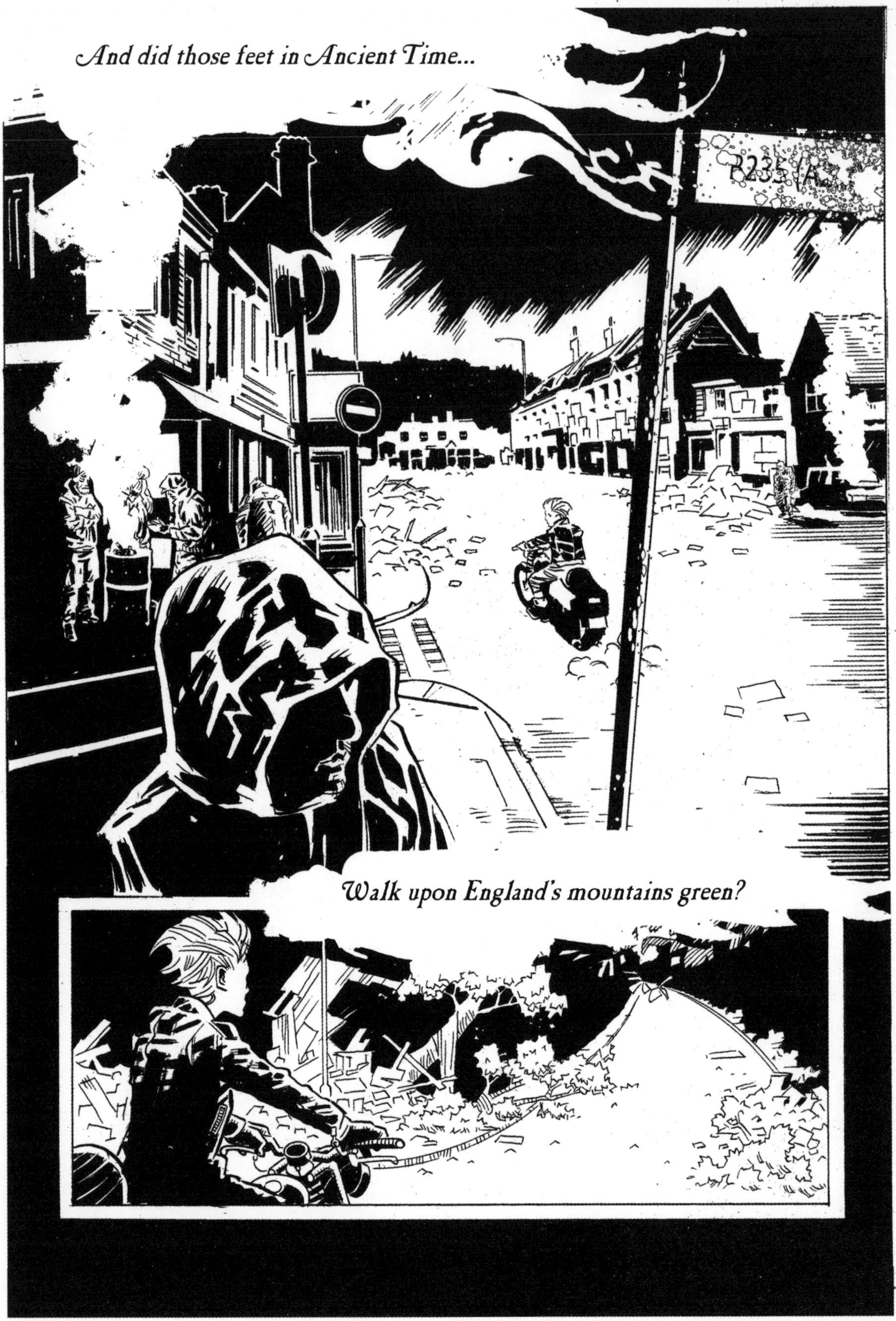
And did those feet in Ancient Time...
Walk upon England's mountains green?

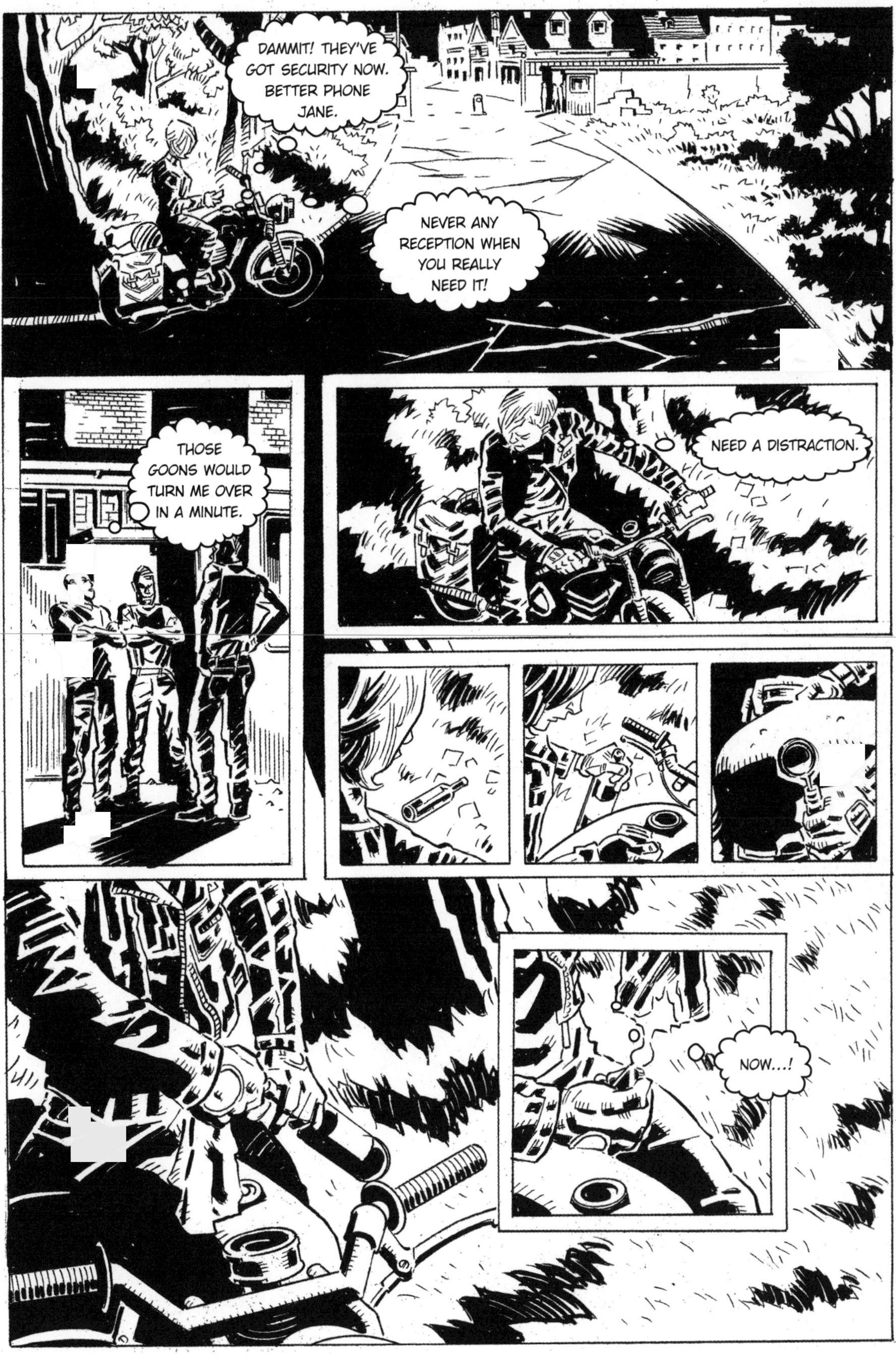
DAMMIT! THEY'VE GOT SECURITY NOW. BETTER PHONE JANE.
NEVER ANY RECEPTION WHEN YOU REALLY NEED IT!
THOSE GOONS WOULD TURN ME OVER IN A MINUTE.
NEED A DISTRACTION.
NOW...!

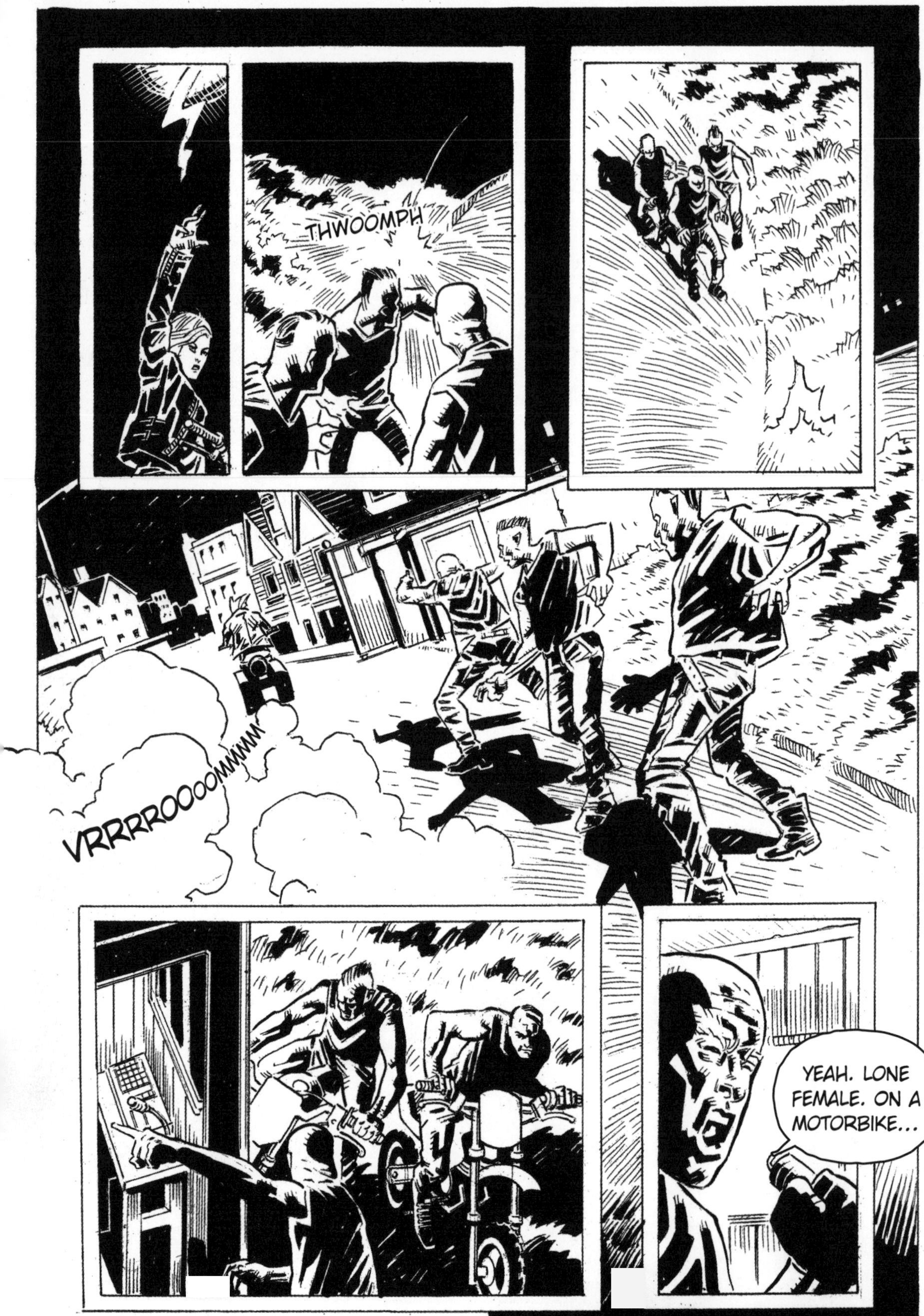
THWOOMPH
VRRRROOOOMMMM
YEAH. LONE FEMALE. ON A MOTORBIKE...

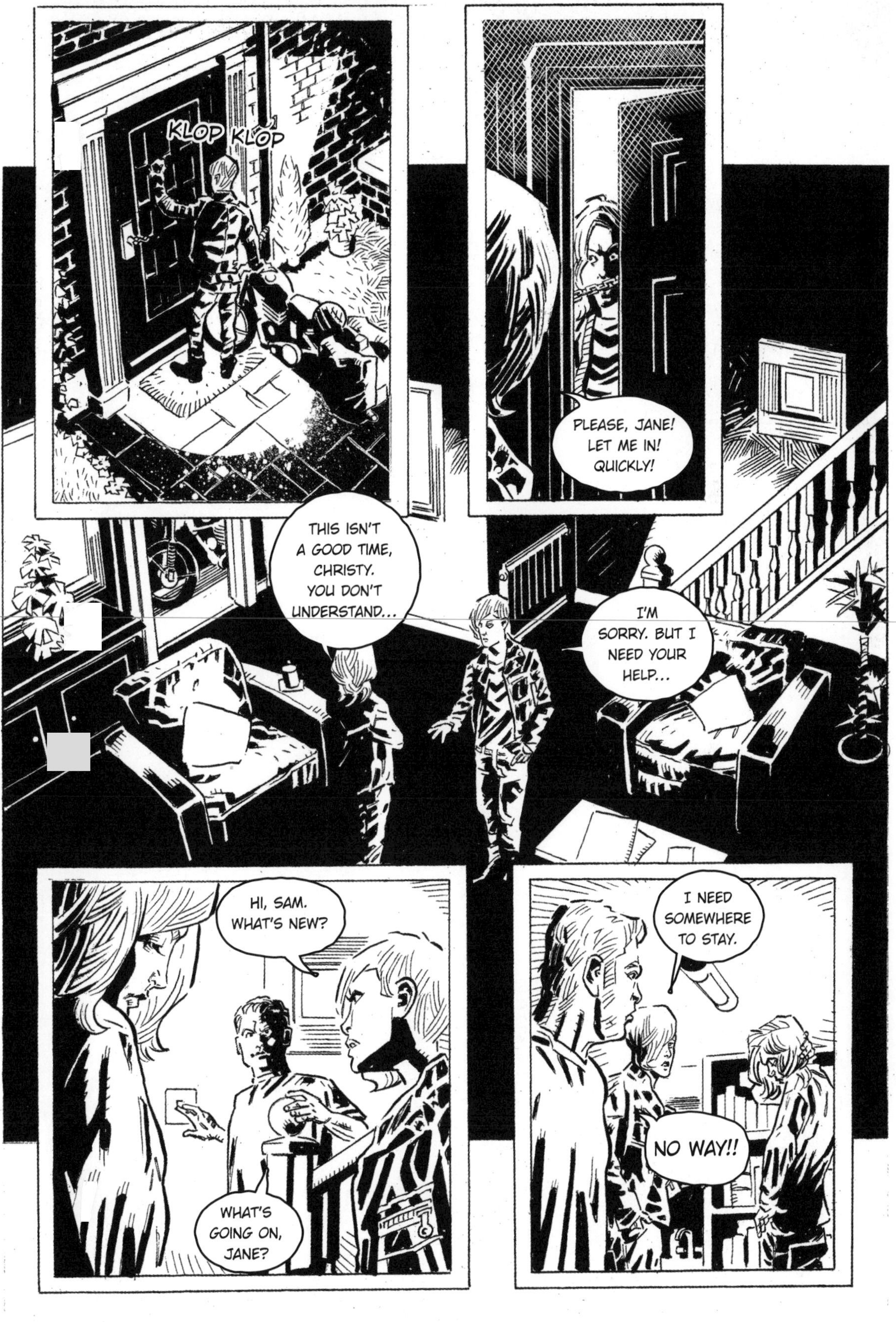
KLOP KLOP
PLEASE, JANE! LET ME IN! QUICKLY!
THIS ISN'T A GOOD TIME, CHRISTY. YOU DON'T UNDERSTAND...
I'M SORRY. BUT I NEED YOUR HELP...
HI, SAM. WHAT'S NEW?
WHAT'S GOING ON, JANE?
I NEED SOMEWHERE TO STAY.
NO WAY!!

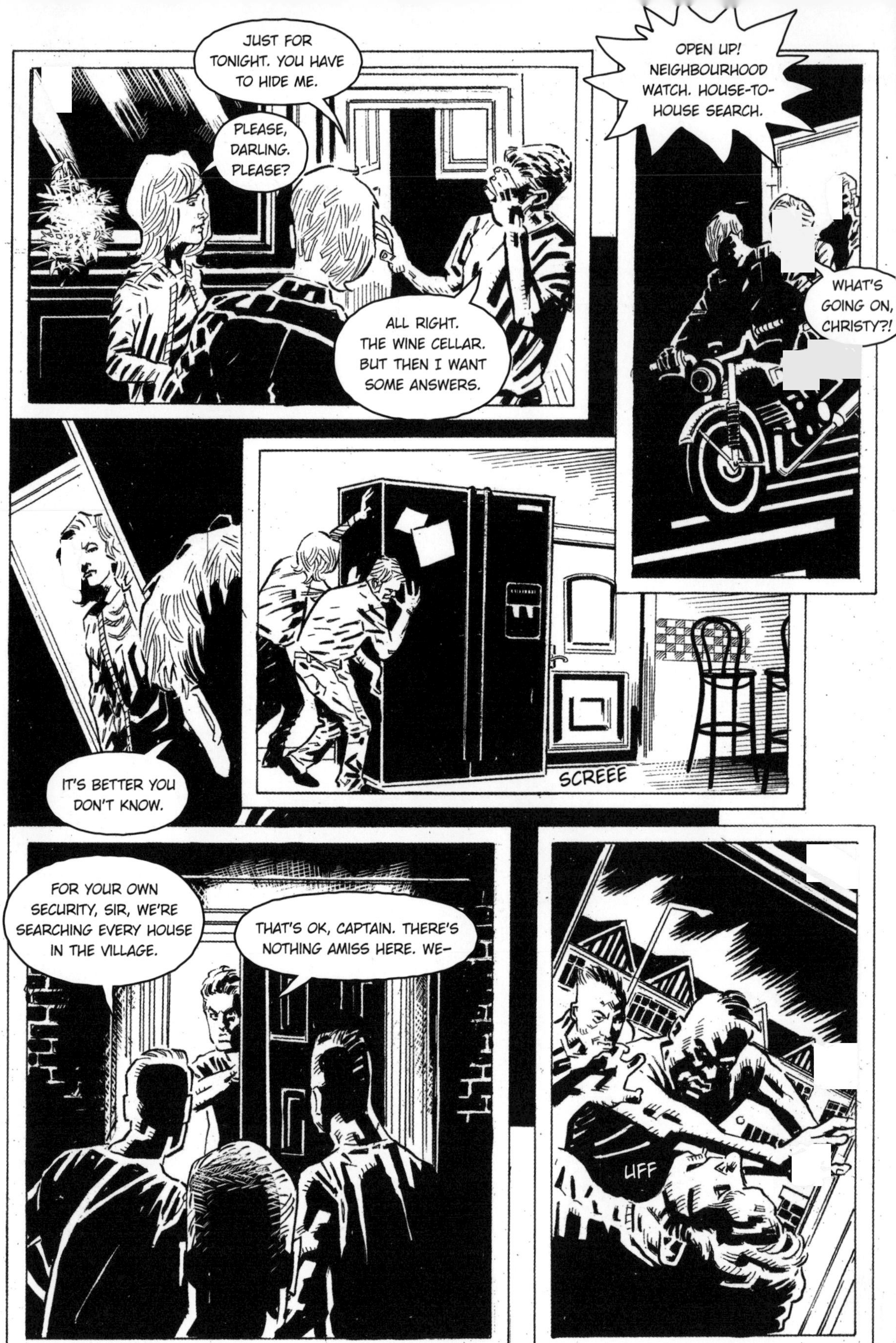
JUST FOR TONIGHT. YOU HAVE TO HIDE ME.
PLEASE, DARLING. PLEASE?
ALL RIGHT. THE WINE CELLAR. BUT THEN I WANT SOME ANSWERS.
OPEN UP! NEIGHBOURHOOD WATCH. HOUSE-TO-HOUSE SEARCH.
WHAT'S GOING ON, CHRISTY?!
IT'S BETTER YOU DON'T KNOW.
SCREEE
FOR YOUR OWN SECURITY, SIR, WE'RE SEARCHING EVERY HOUSE IN THE VILLAGE.
THAT'S OK, CAPTAIN. THERE'S NOTHING AMISS HERE. WE-
UFF

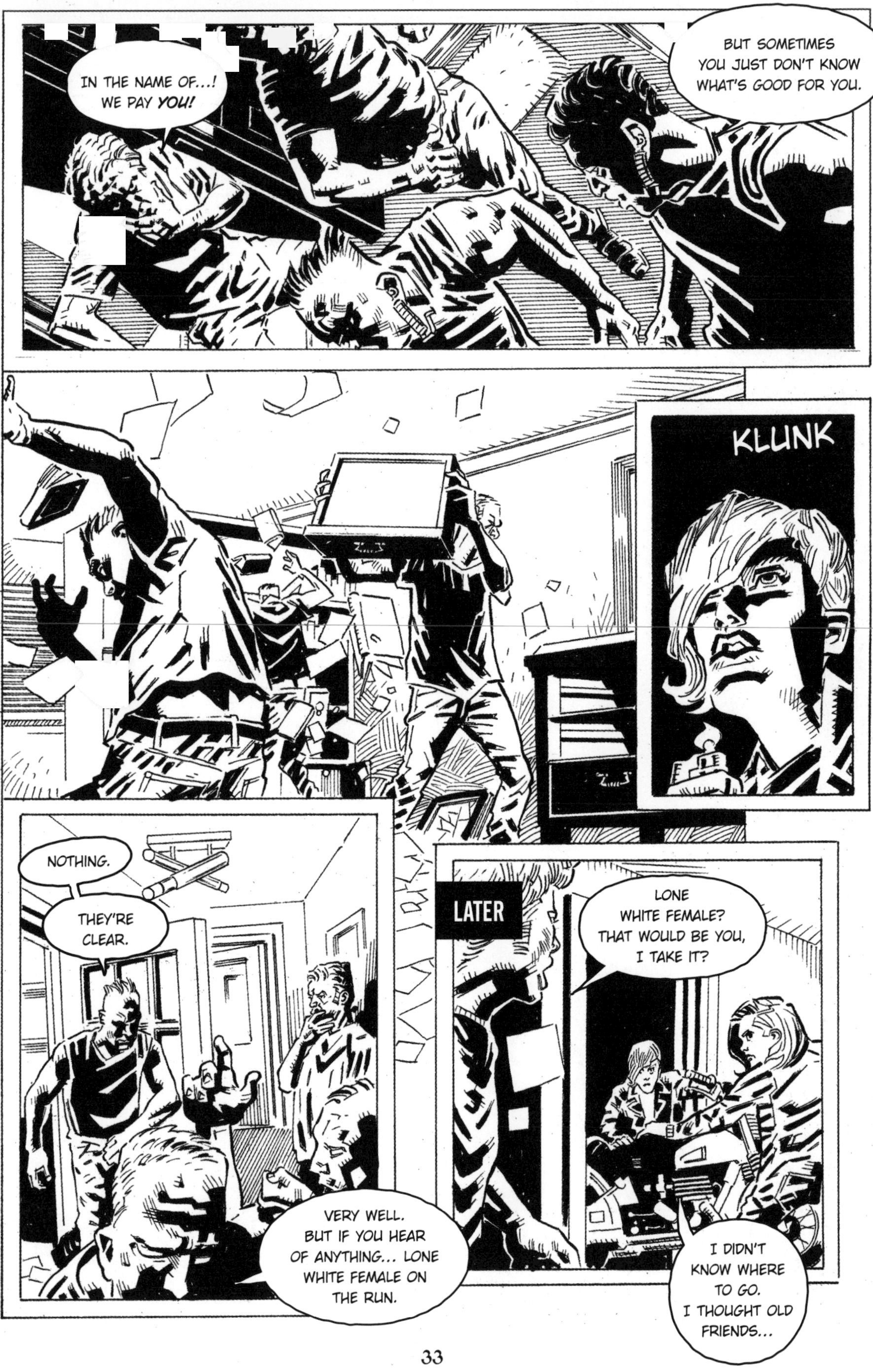
IN THE NAME OF...! WE PAY *YOU!*
BUT SOMETIMES YOU JUST DON'T KNOW WHAT'S GOOD FOR YOU.
KLUNK
NOTHING.
THEY'RE CLEAR.
VERY WELL. BUT IF YOU HEAR OF ANYTHING... LONE WHITE FEMALE ON THE RUN.
LATER
LONE WHITE FEMALE? THAT WOULD BE YOU, I TAKE IT?
I DIDN'T KNOW WHERE TO GO. I THOUGHT OLD FRIENDS...

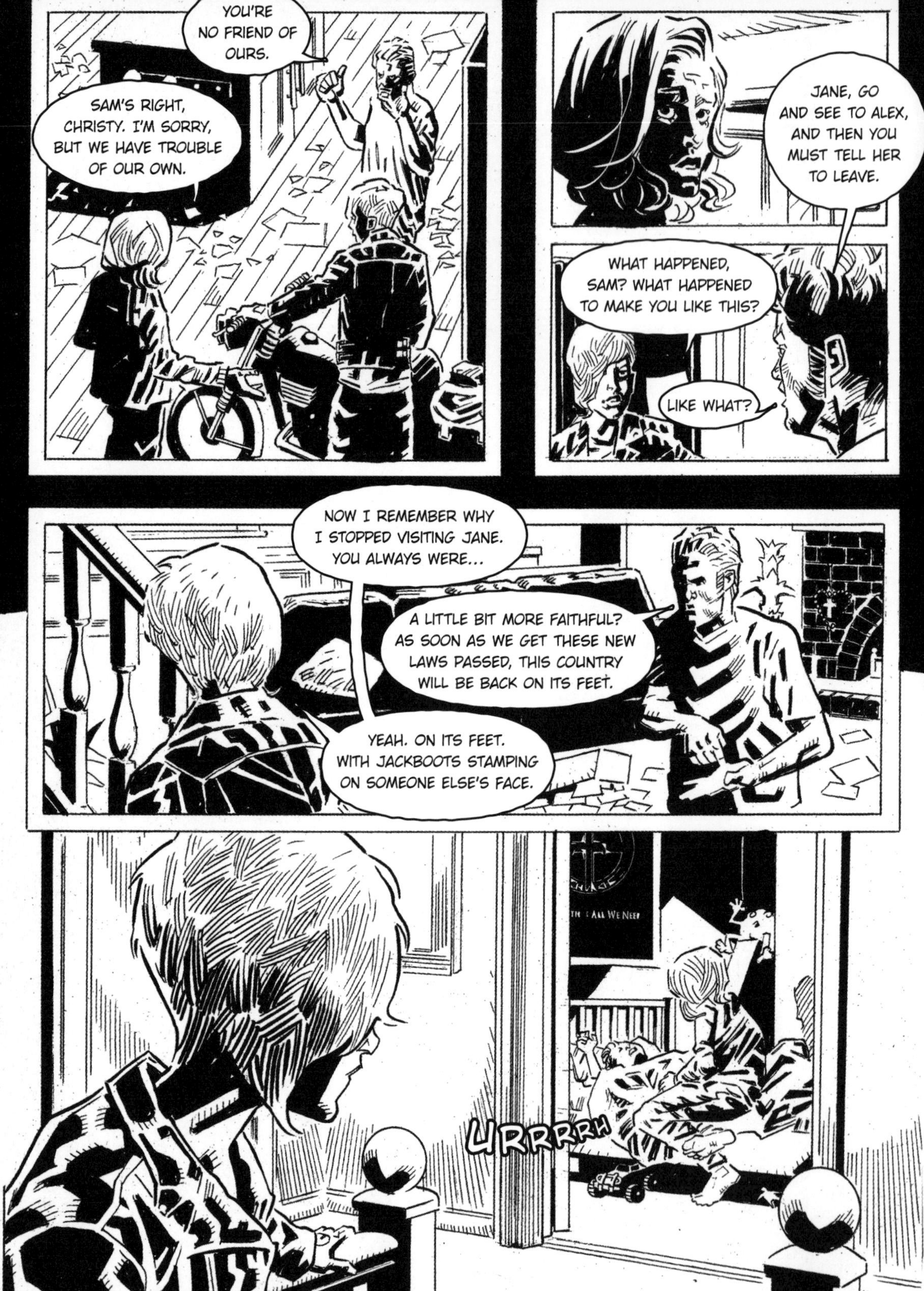
YOU'RE NO FRIEND OF OURS.
SAM'S RIGHT, CHRISTY. I'M SORRY, BUT WE HAVE TROUBLE OF OUR OWN.
JANE, GO AND SEE TO ALEX, AND THEN YOU MUST TELL HER TO LEAVE.
WHAT HAPPENED, SAM? WHAT HAPPENED TO MAKE YOU LIKE THIS?
LIKE WHAT?
NOW I REMEMBER WHY I STOPPED VISITING JANE. YOU ALWAYS WERE...
A LITTLE BIT MORE FAITHFUL? AS SOON AS WE GET THESE NEW LAWS PASSED, THIS COUNTRY WILL BE BACK ON ITS FEET.
YEAH. ON ITS FEET. WITH JACKBOOTS STAMPING ON SOMEONE ELSE'S FACE.
URRRRH

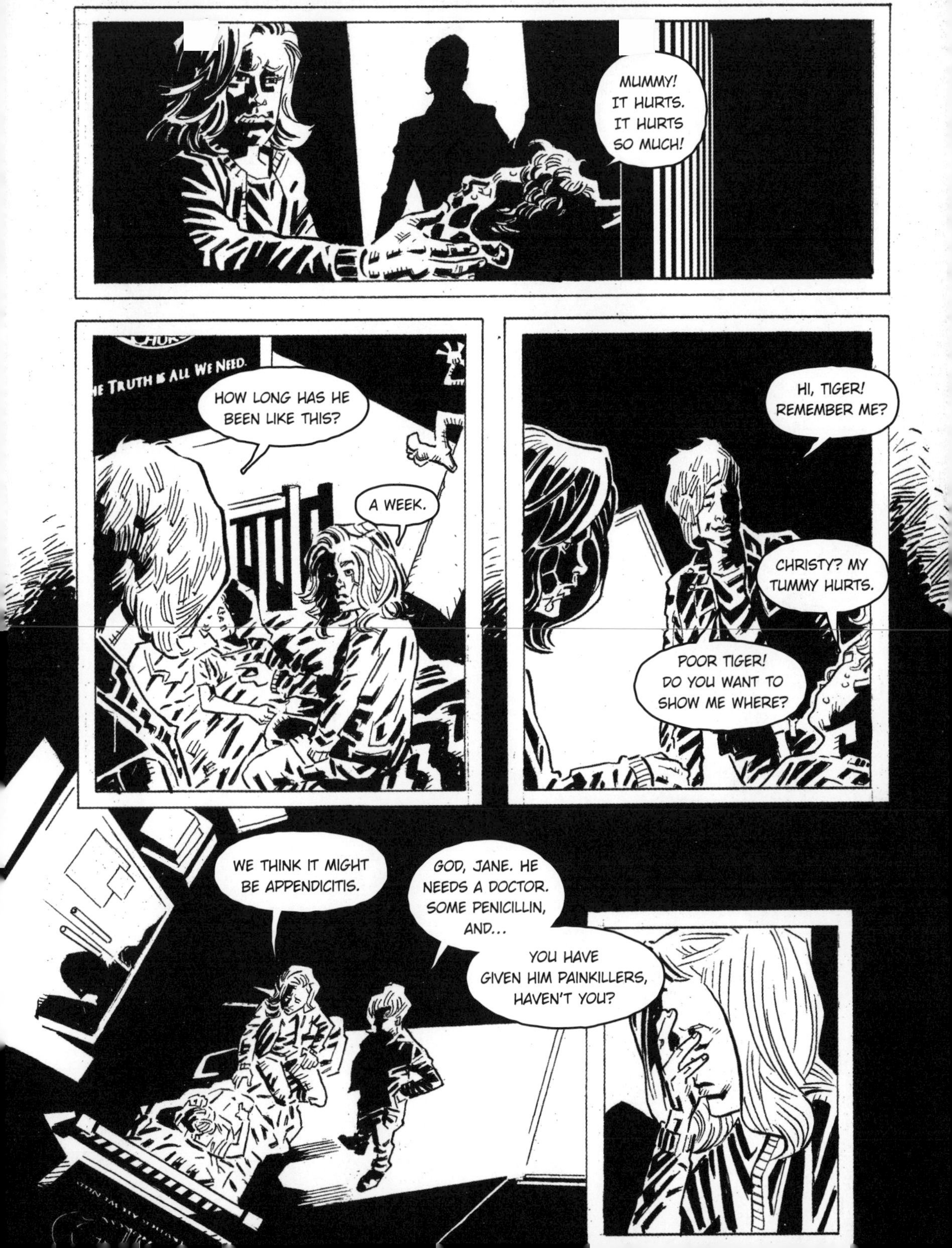
MUMMY! IT HURTS. IT HURTS SO MUCH!
HE TRUTH IS ALL WE NEED.
HOW LONG HAS HE BEEN LIKE THIS?
A WEEK.
HI, TIGER! REMEMBER ME?
CHRISTY? MY TUMMY HURTS.
POOR TIGER! DO YOU WANT TO SHOW ME WHERE?
WE THINK IT MIGHT BE APPENDICITIS.
GOD, JANE. HE NEEDS A DOCTOR. SOME PENICILLIN, AND...
YOU HAVE GIVEN HIM PAINKILLERS, HAVEN'T YOU?

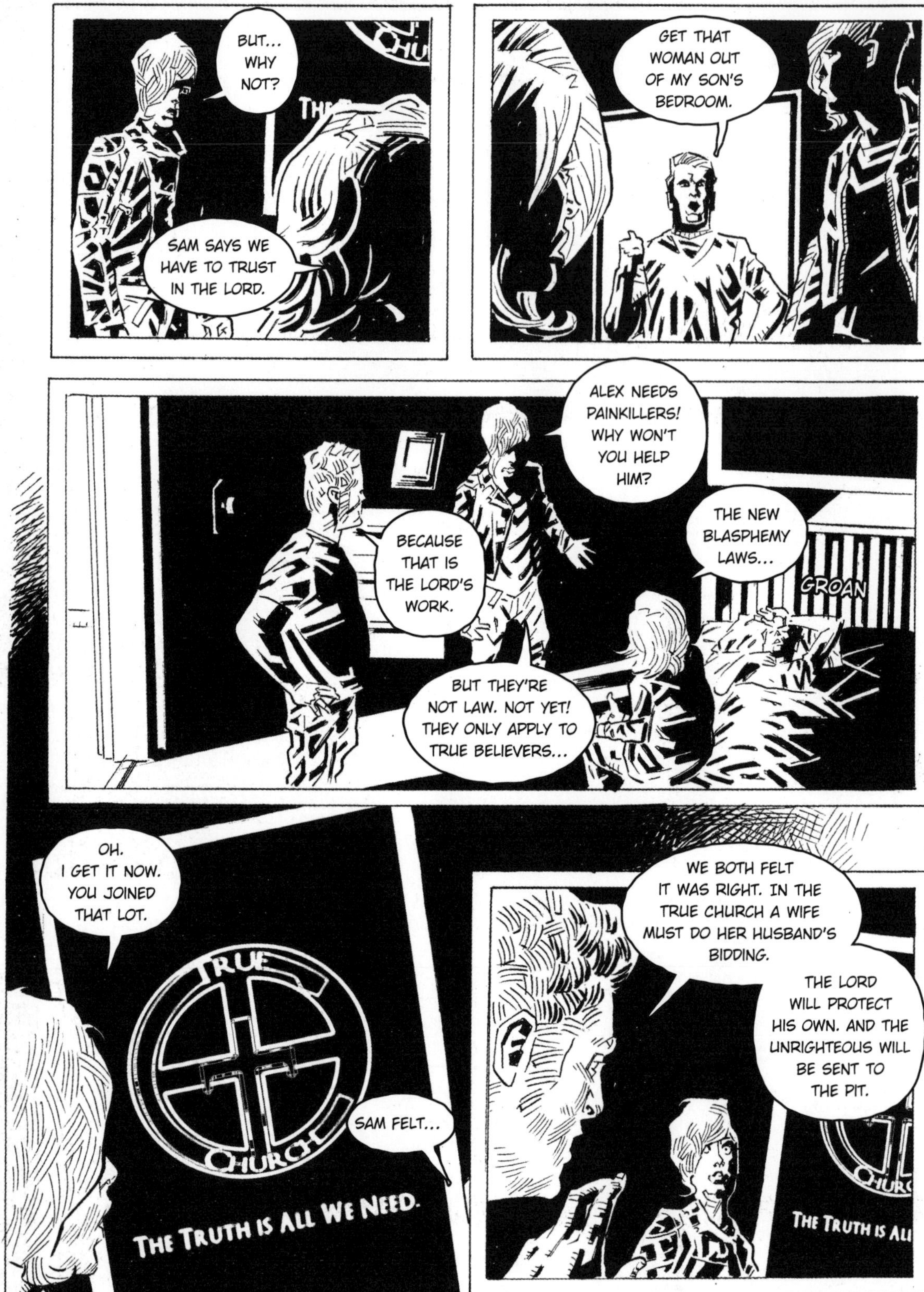
BUT... WHY NOT?
SAM SAYS WE HAVE TO TRUST IN THE LORD.
GET THAT WOMAN OUT OF MY SON'S BEDROOM.
ALEX NEEDS PAINKILLERS! WHY WON'T YOU HELP HIM?
BECAUSE THAT IS THE LORD'S WORK.
THE NEW BLASPHEMY LAWS...
GROAN
BUT THEY'RE NOT LAW. NOT YET! THEY ONLY APPLY TO TRUE BELIEVERS...
OH. I GET IT NOW. YOU JOINED THAT LOT.
TRUE CHURCH
SAM FELT...
THE TRUTH IS ALL WE NEED.
WE BOTH FELT IT WAS RIGHT. IN THE TRUE CHURCH A WIFE MUST DO HER HUSBAND'S BIDDING.
THE LORD WILL PROTECT HIS OWN. AND THE UNRIGHTEOUS WILL BE SENT TO THE PIT.

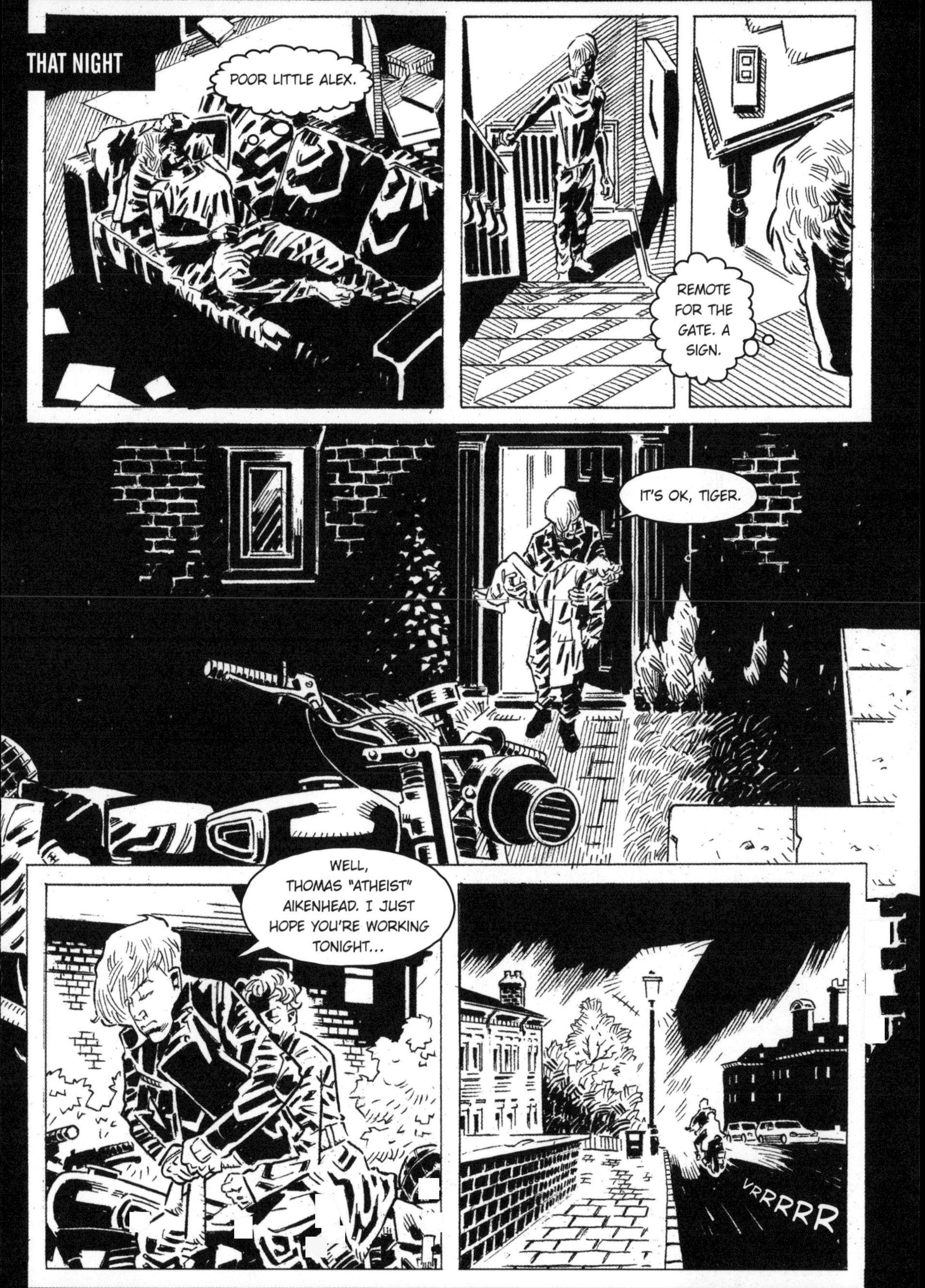
THAT NIGHT
POOR LITTLE ALEX.
REMOTE FOR THE GATE. A SIGN.
IT'S OK, TIGER.
WELL, THOMAS "ATHEIST" AIKENHEAD. I JUST HOPE YOU'RE WORKING TONIGHT...
VRRRRR

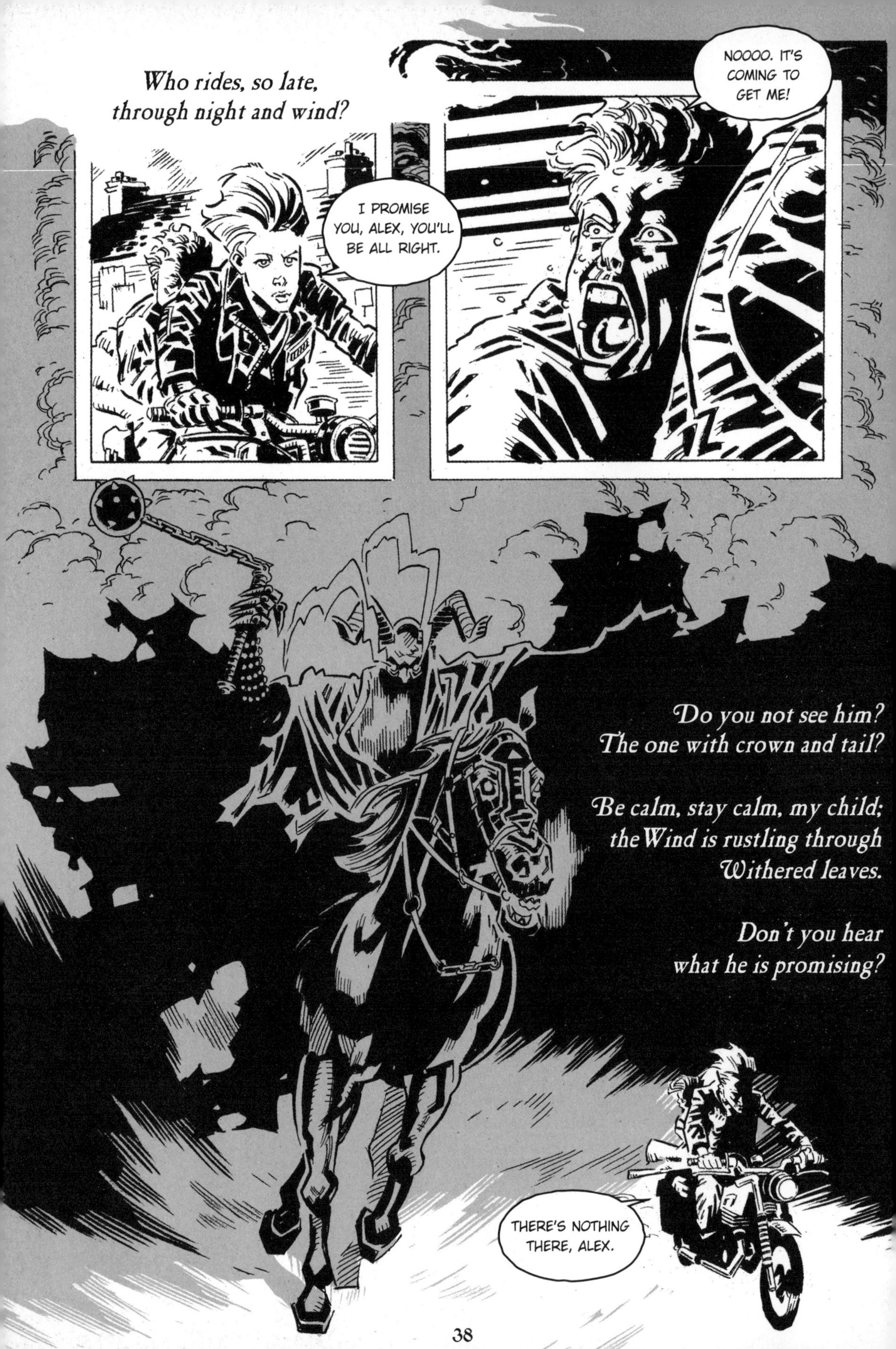
Who rides, so late, through night and wind?
I PROMISE YOU, ALEX, YOU'LL BE ALL RIGHT.
NOOOO. IT'S COMING TO GET ME!
Do you not see him? The one with crown and tail?
Be calm, stay calm, my child; the Wind is rustling through Withered leaves.
Don't you hear what he is promising?
THERE'S NOTHING THERE, ALEX.

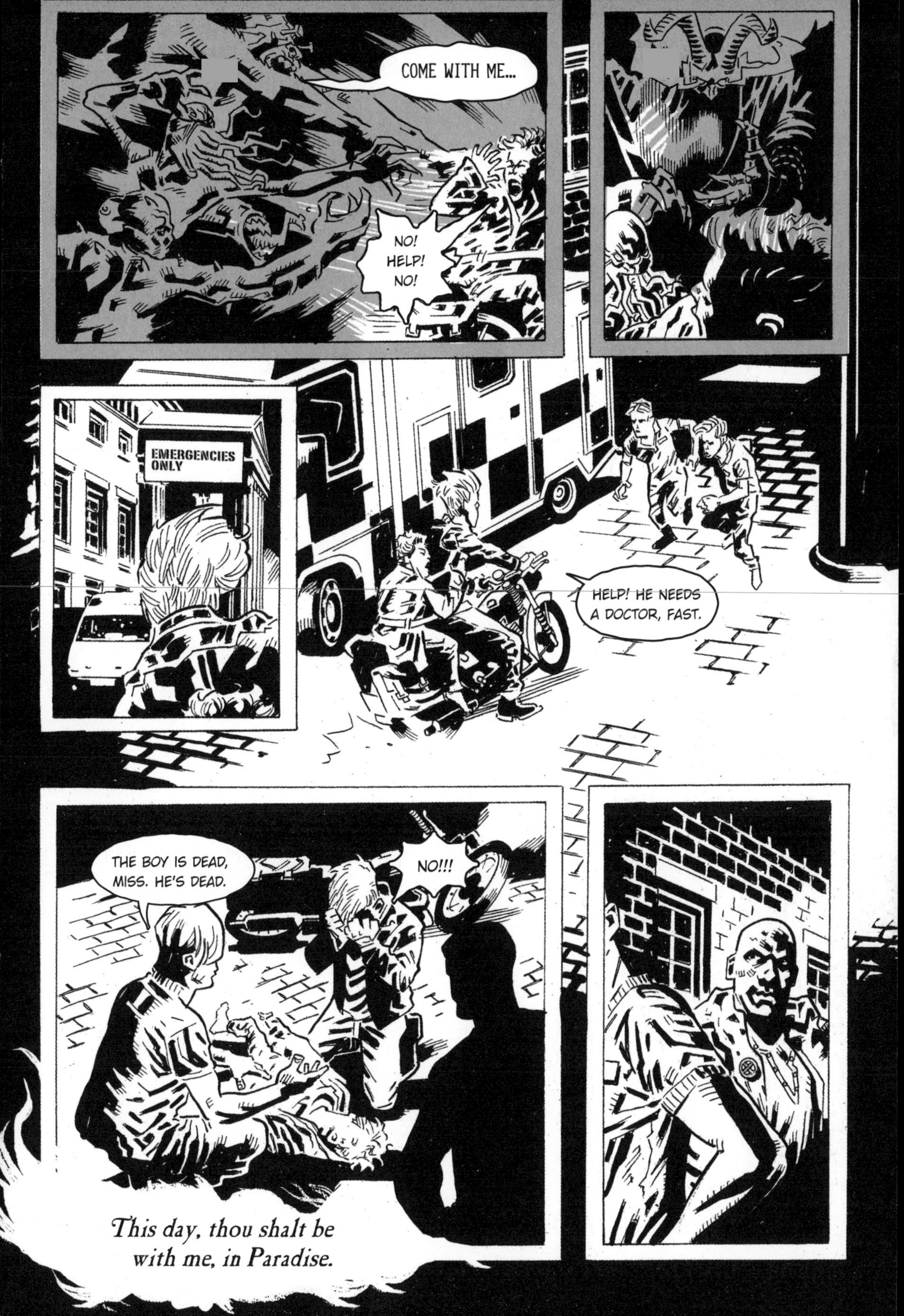
COME WITH ME...
NO! HELP! NO!
EMERGENCIES ONLY
HELP! HE NEEDS A DOCTOR, FAST.
THE BOY IS DEAD, MISS. HE'S DEAD.
NO!!!
This day, thou shalt be with me, in Paradise.

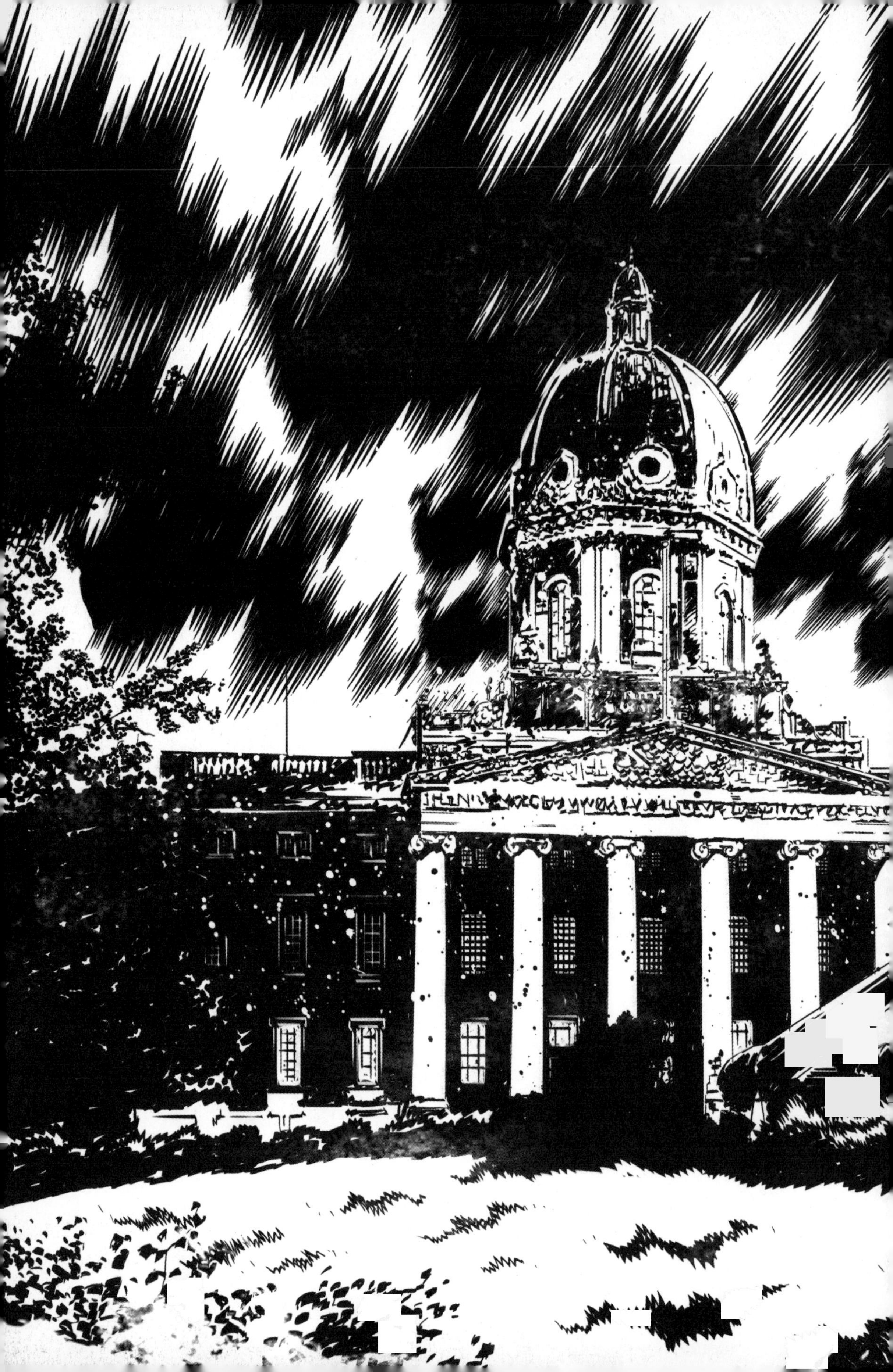

Lesson Three

Woman, Behold thy Son

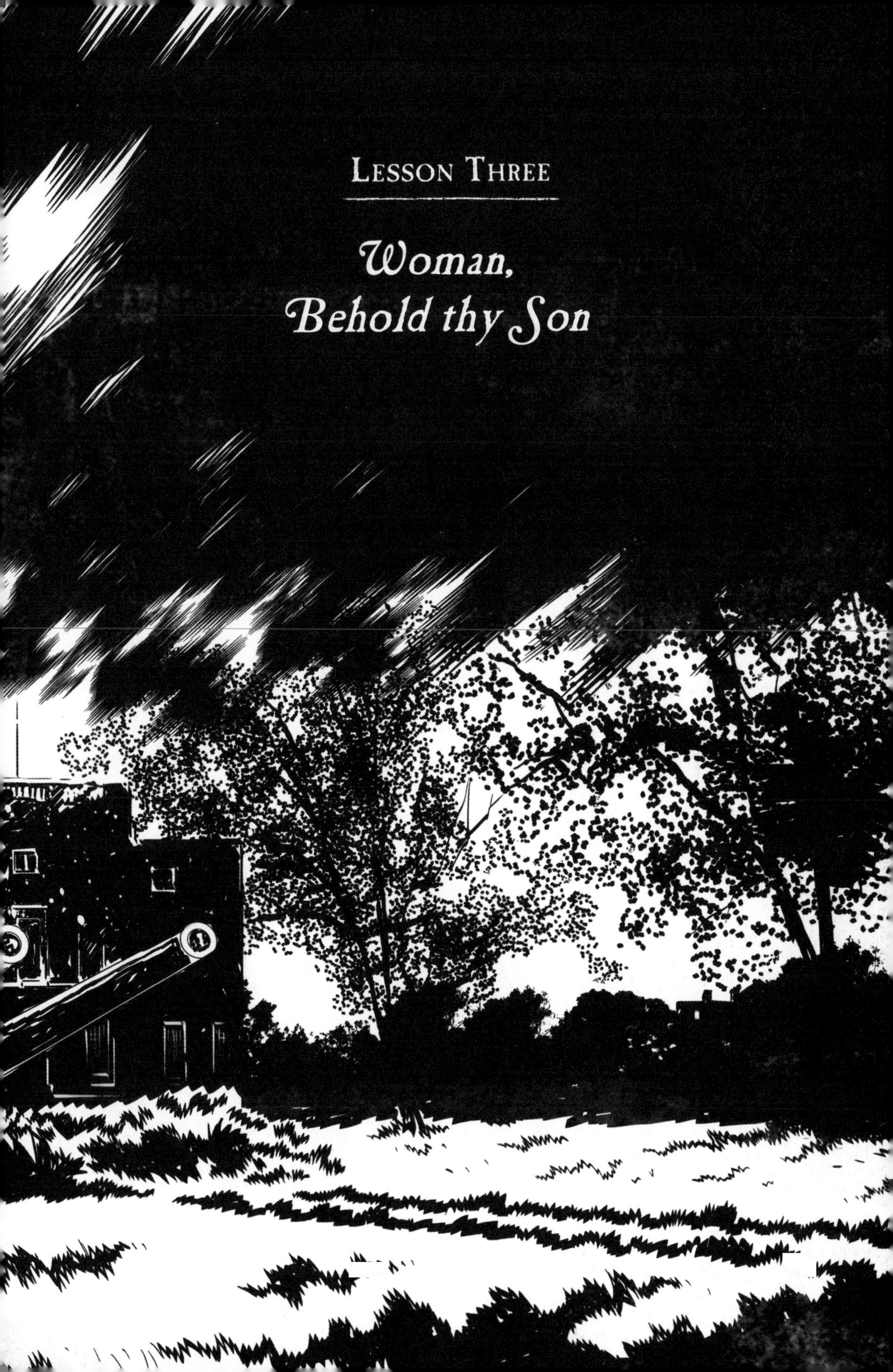

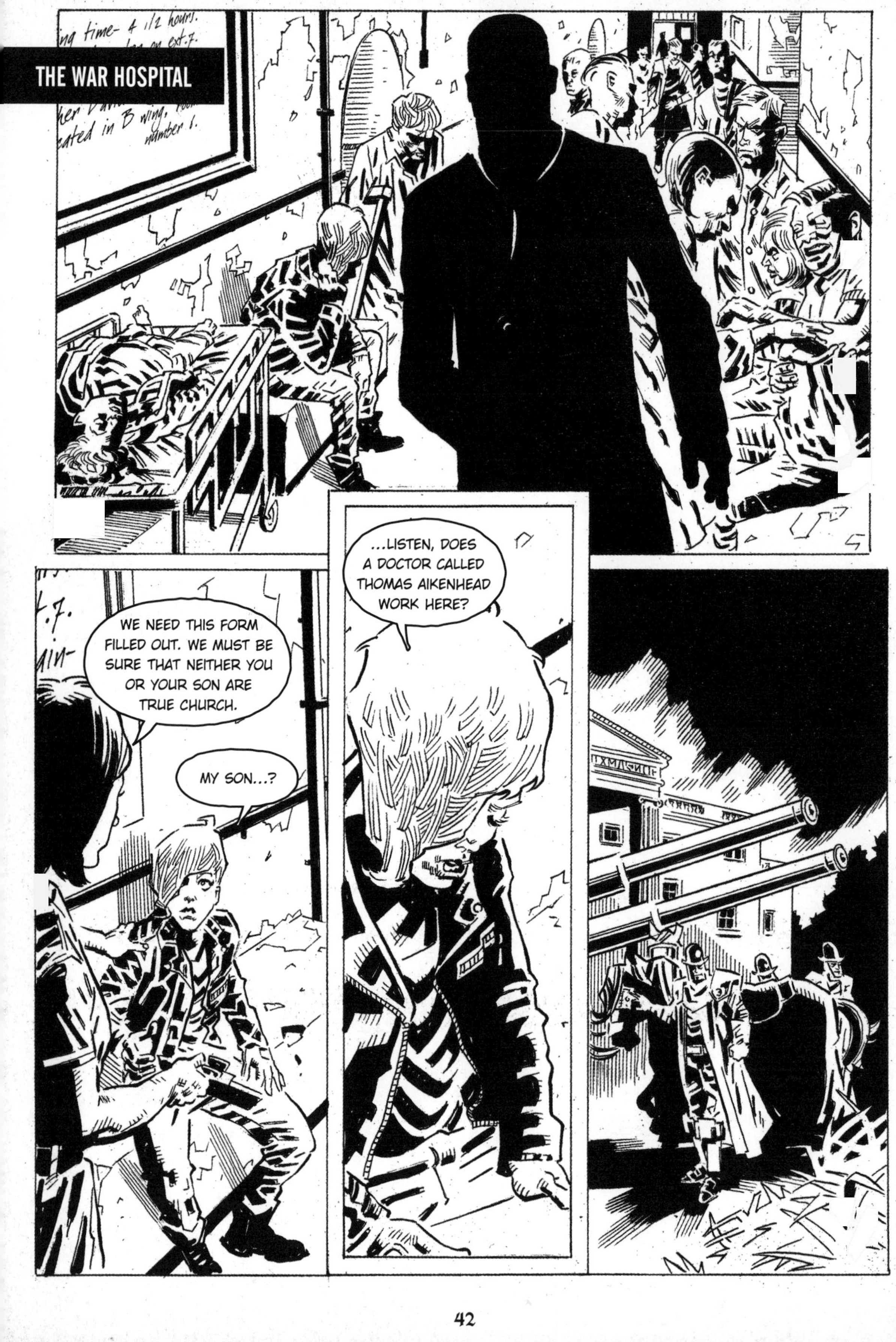
THE WAR HOSPITAL
WE NEED THIS FORM FILLED OUT. WE MUST BE SURE THAT NEITHER YOU OR YOUR SON ARE TRUE CHURCH.
MY SON...?
...LISTEN, DOES A DOCTOR CALLED THOMAS AIKENHEAD WORK HERE?

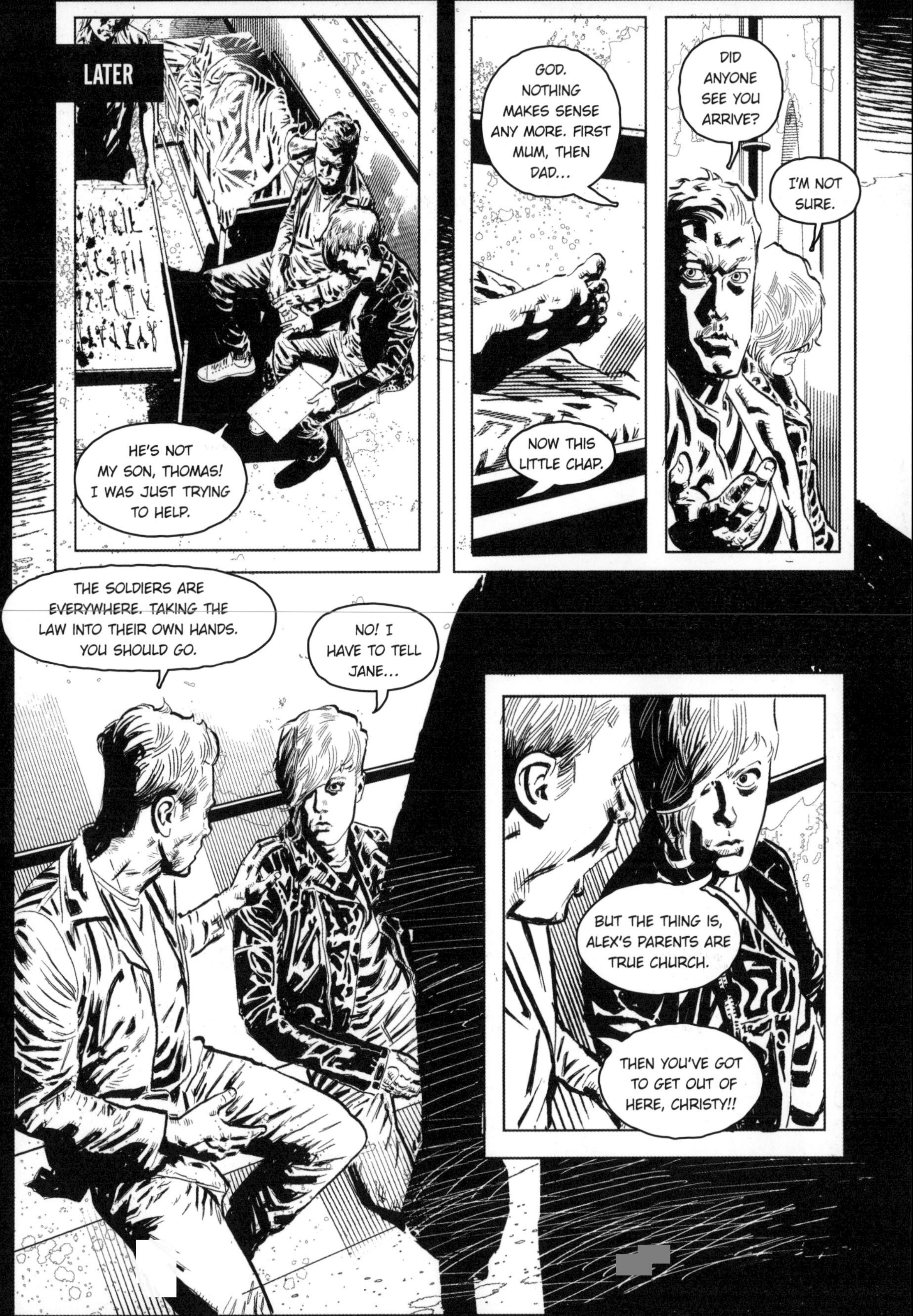
LATER
HE'S NOT MY SON, THOMAS! I WAS JUST TRYING TO HELP.
GOD. NOTHING MAKES SENSE ANY MORE. FIRST MUM, THEN DAD...
NOW THIS LITTLE CHAP.
DID ANYONE SEE YOU ARRIVE?
I'M NOT SURE.
THE SOLDIERS ARE EVERYWHERE. TAKING THE LAW INTO THEIR OWN HANDS. YOU SHOULD GO.
NO! I HAVE TO TELL JANE...
BUT THE THING IS, ALEX'S PARENTS ARE TRUE CHURCH.
THEN YOU'VE GOT TO GET OUT OF HERE, CHRISTY!!

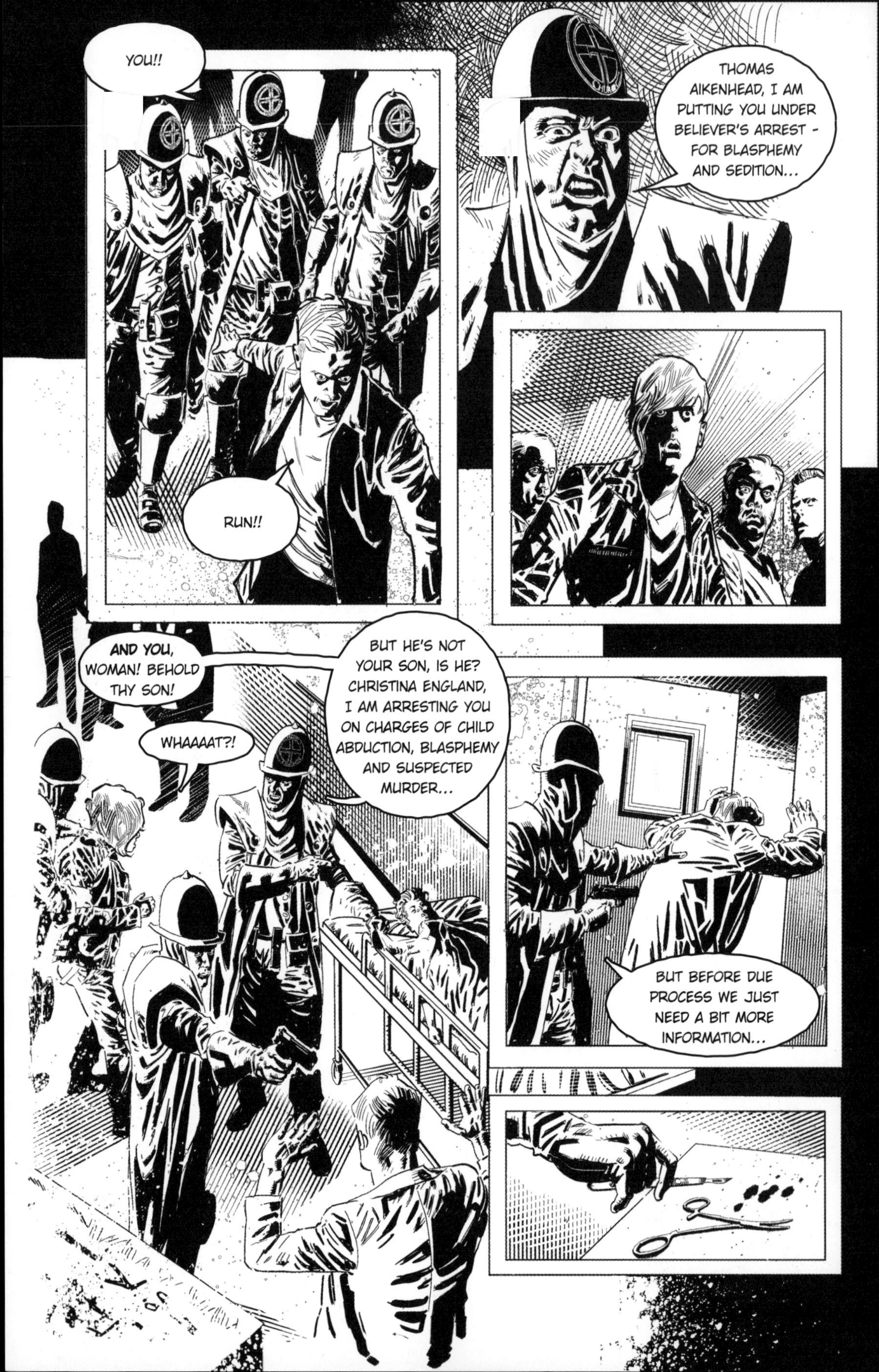
YOU!!
THOMAS AIKENHEAD, I AM PUTTING YOU UNDER BELIEVER'S ARREST - FOR BLASPHEMY AND SEDITION...
RUN!!
AND YOU, WOMAN! BEHOLD THY SON!
WHAAAAT?!
BUT HE'S NOT YOUR SON, IS HE? CHRISTINA ENGLAND, I AM ARRESTING YOU ON CHARGES OF CHILD ABDUCTION, BLASPHEMY AND SUSPECTED MURDER...
BUT BEFORE DUE PROCESS WE JUST NEED A BIT MORE INFORMATION...

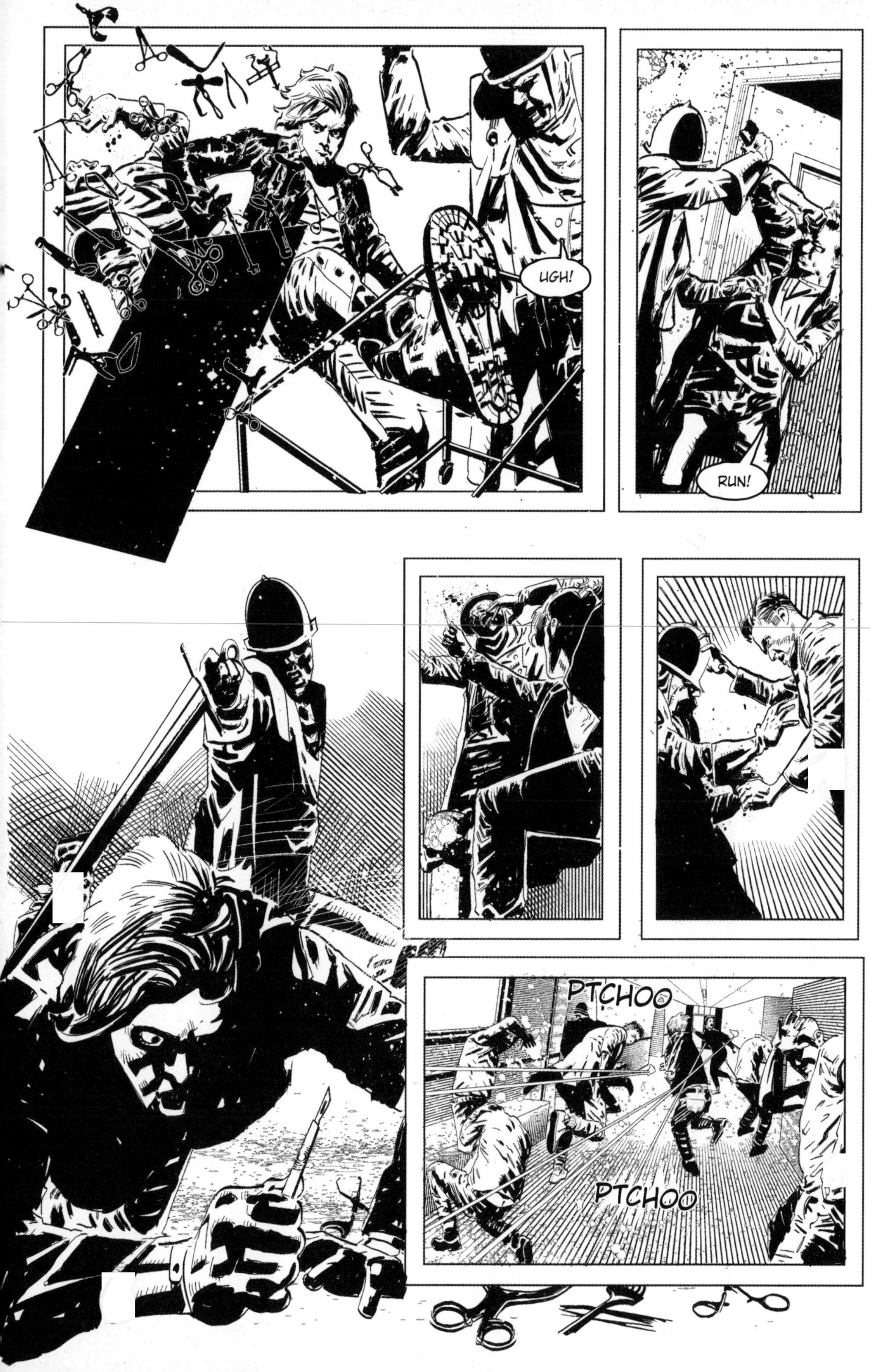
UGH!
RUN!
PTCHOO
PTCHOO

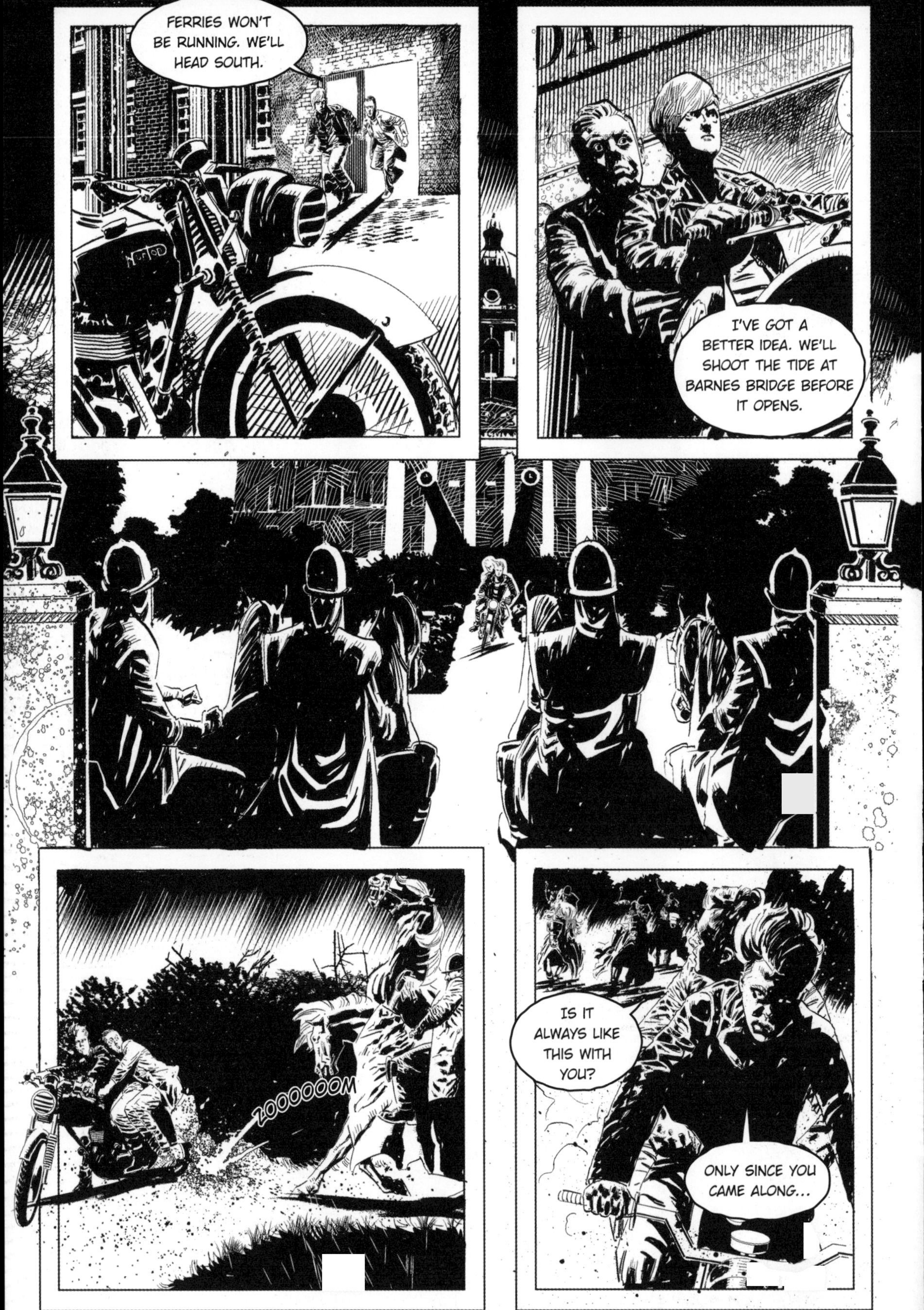
FERRIES WON'T BE RUNNING. WE'LL HEAD SOUTH.
I'VE GOT A BETTER IDEA. WE'LL SHOOT THE TIDE AT BARNES BRIDGE BEFORE IT OPENS.
ZOOOOOOM
IS IT ALWAYS LIKE THIS WITH YOU?
ONLY SINCE YOU CAME ALONG...

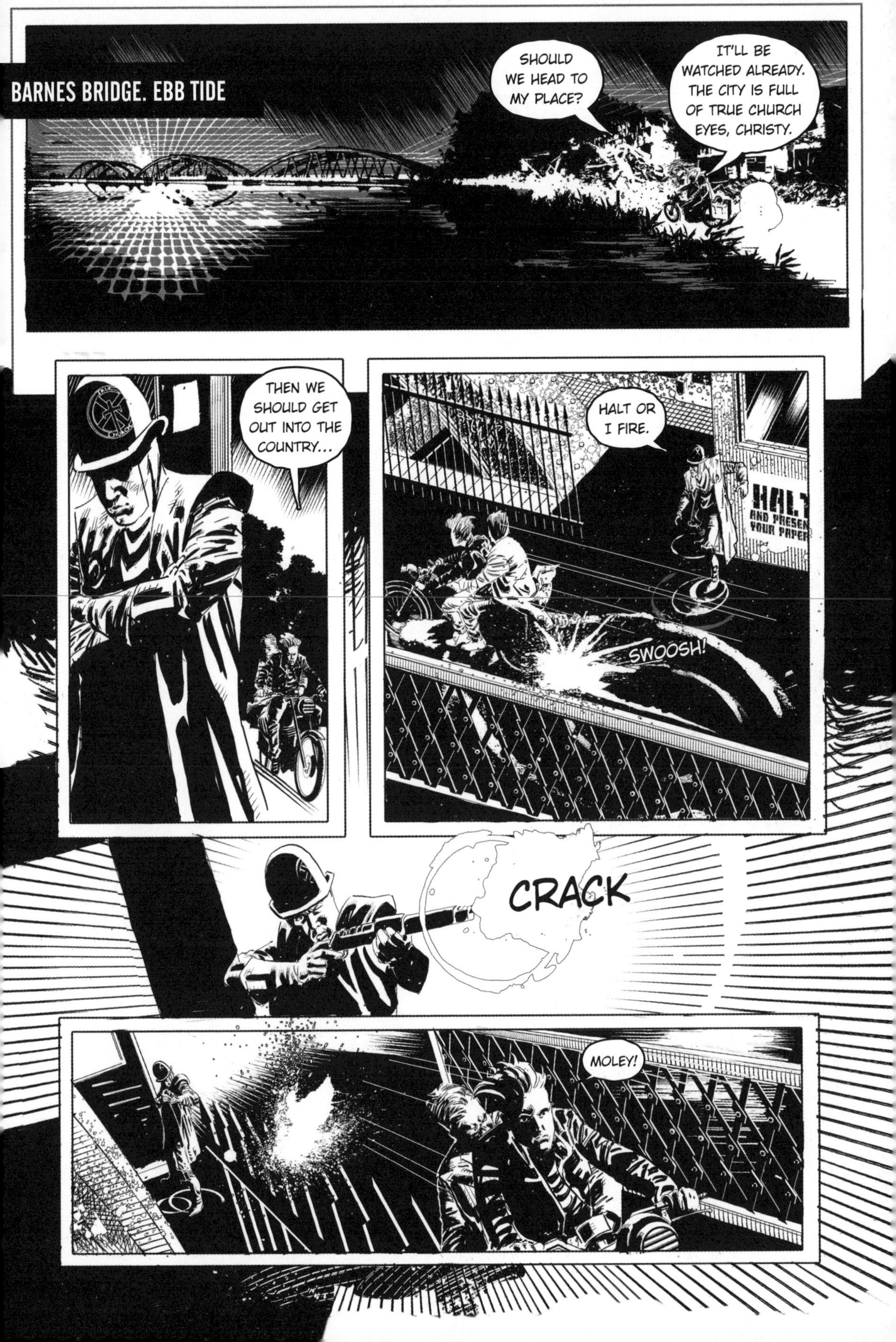
BARNES BRIDGE. EBB TIDE
SHOULD WE HEAD TO MY PLACE?
IT'LL BE WATCHED ALREADY. THE CITY IS FULL OF TRUE CHURCH EYES, CHRISTY.
THEN WE SHOULD GET OUT INTO THE COUNTRY...
HALT OR I FIRE.
SWOOSH!
CRACK
MOLEY!

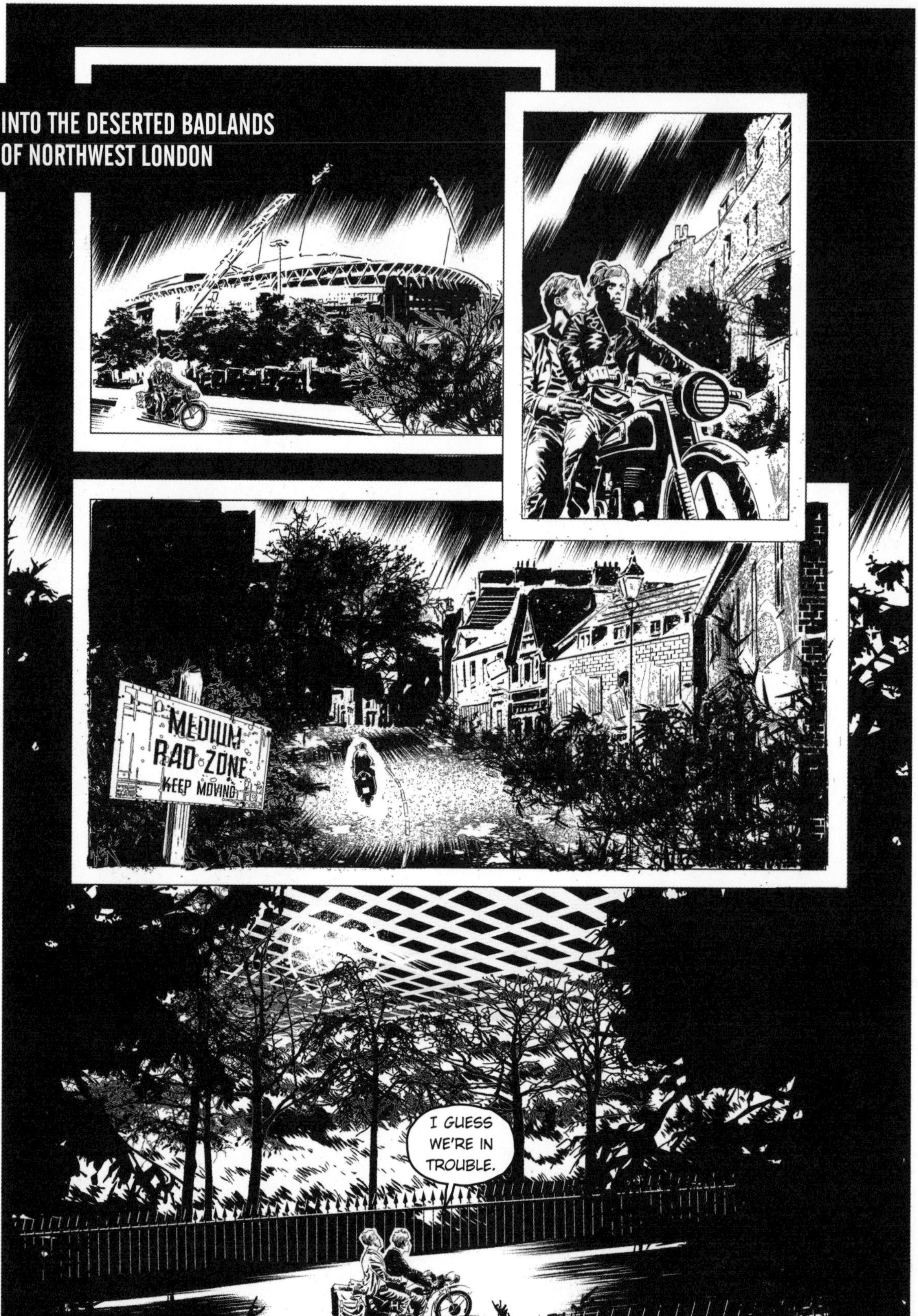
INTO THE DESERTED BADLANDS OF NORTHWEST LONDON
MEDIUM RAD ZONE KEEP MOVING
I GUESS WE'RE IN TROUBLE.

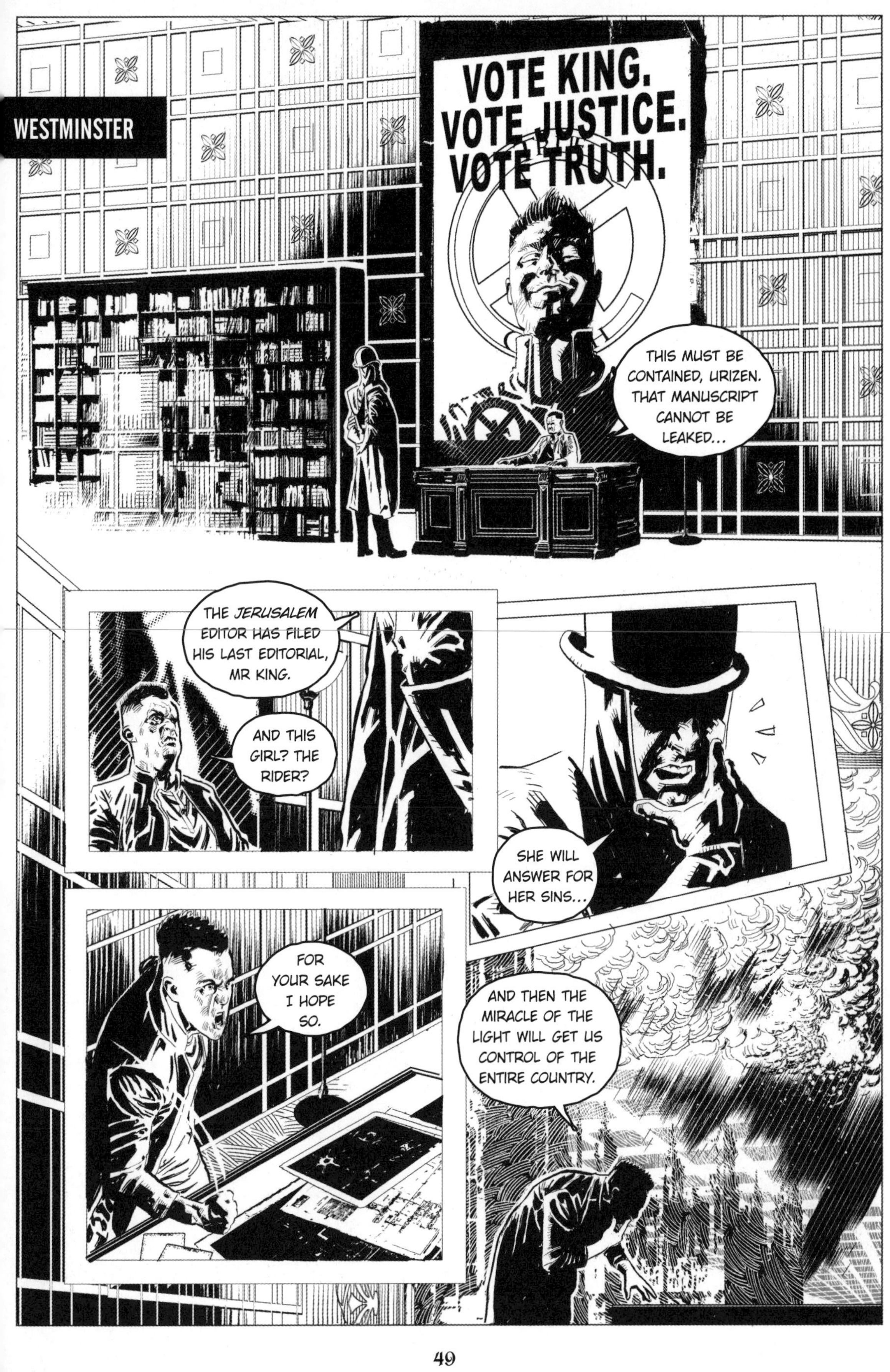
WESTMINSTER
VOTE KING.
VOTE JUSTICE.
VOTE TRUTH.
THIS MUST BE CONTAINED, URIZEN. THAT MANUSCRIPT CANNOT BE LEAKED...
THE *JERUSALEM* EDITOR HAS FILED HIS LAST EDITORIAL, MR KING.
AND THIS GIRL? THE RIDER?
SHE WILL ANSWER FOR HER SINS...
FOR YOUR SAKE I HOPE SO.
AND THEN THE MIRACLE OF THE LIGHT WILL GET US CONTROL OF THE ENTIRE COUNTRY.

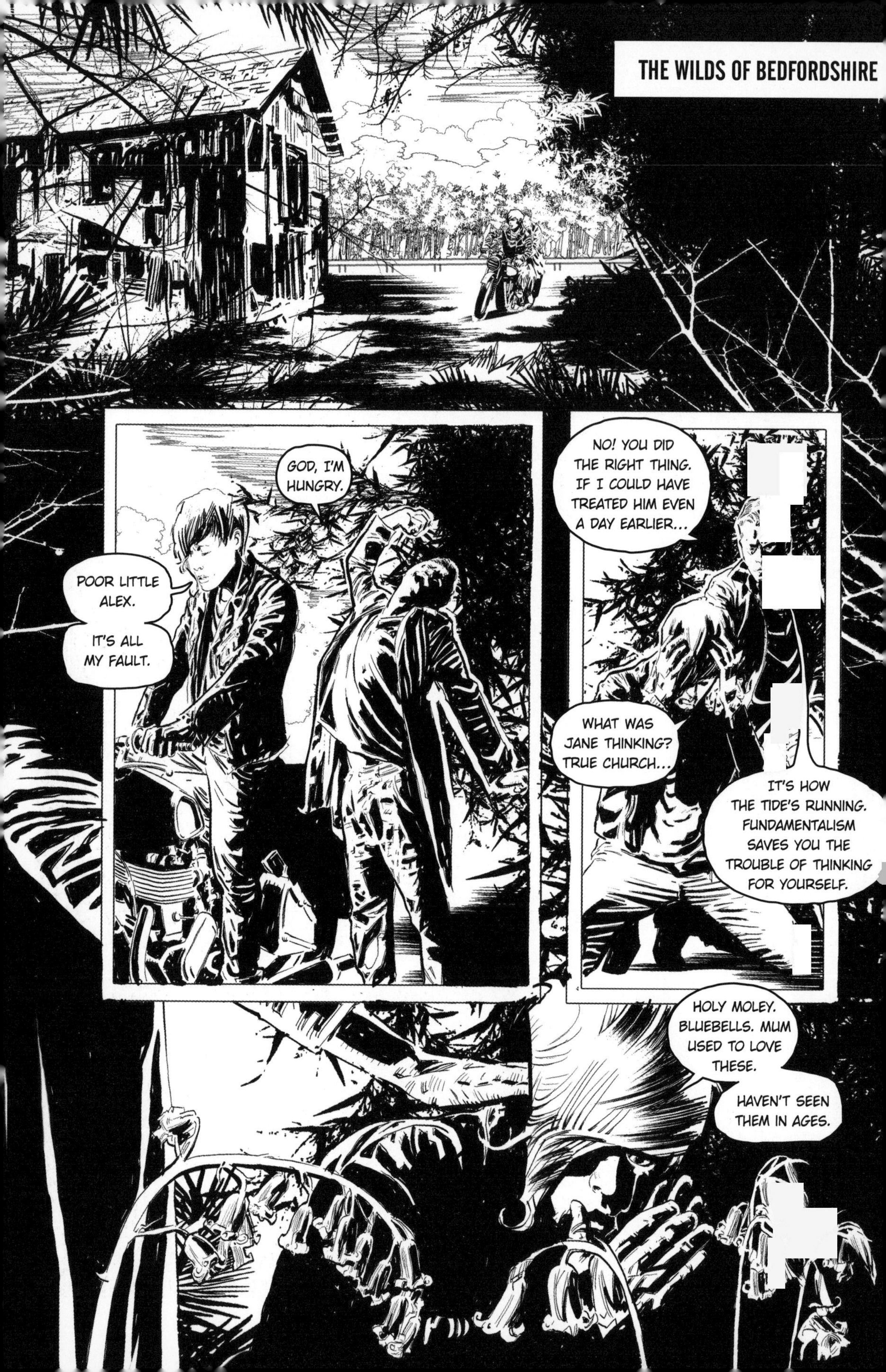
THE WILDS OF BEDFORDSHIRE
GOD, I'M HUNGRY.
POOR LITTLE ALEX.
IT'S ALL MY FAULT.
NO! YOU DID THE RIGHT THING. IF I COULD HAVE TREATED HIM EVEN A DAY EARLIER...
WHAT WAS JANE THINKING? TRUE CHURCH...
IT'S HOW THE TIDE'S RUNNING. FUNDAMENTALISM SAVES YOU THE TROUBLE OF THINKING FOR YOURSELF.
HOLY MOLEY. BLUEBELLS. MUM USED TO LOVE THESE.
HAVEN'T SEEN THEM IN AGES.

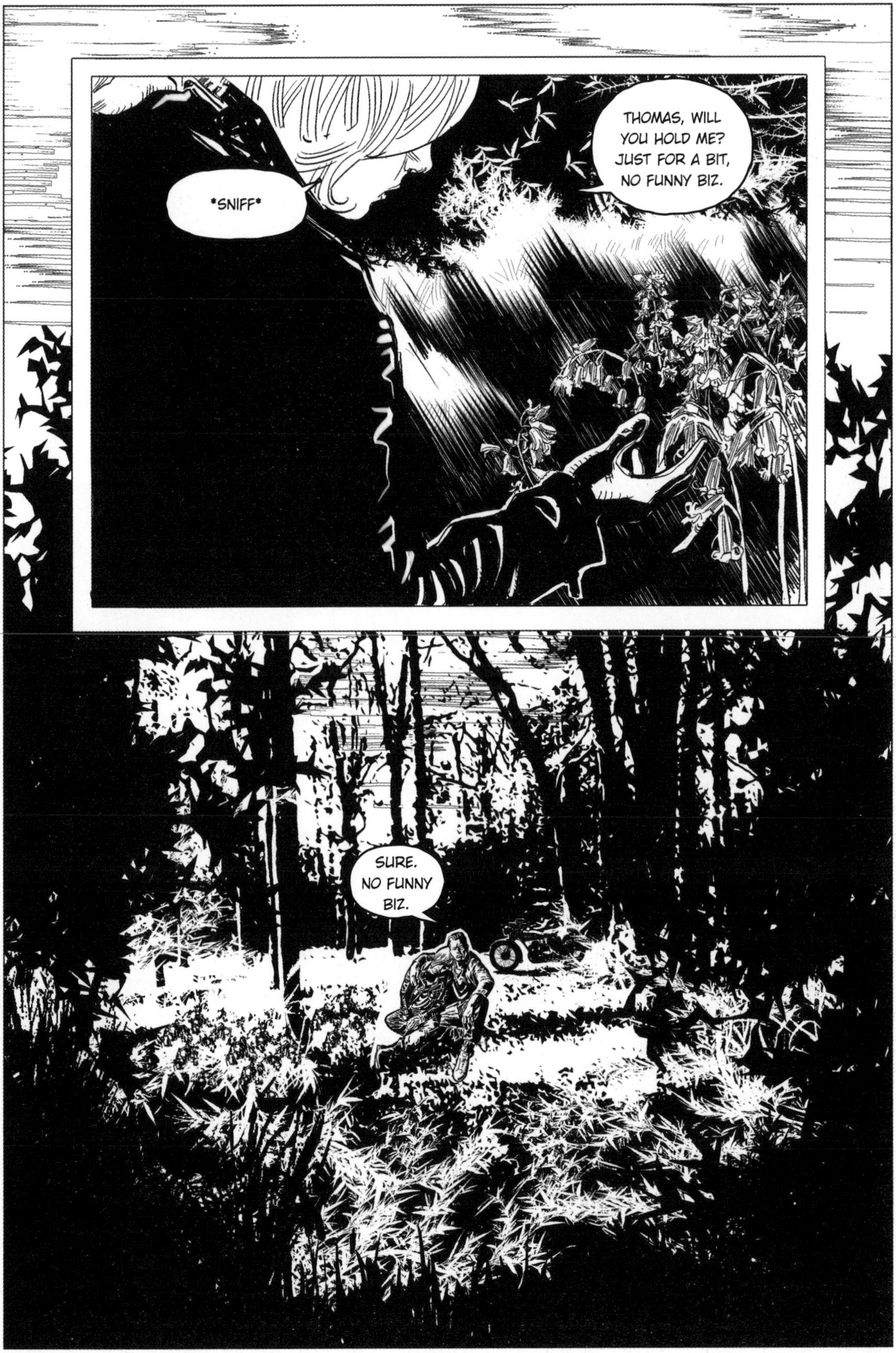
THOMAS, WILL YOU HOLD ME? JUST FOR A BIT, NO FUNNY BIZ.
SNIFF
SURE. NO FUNNY BIZ.

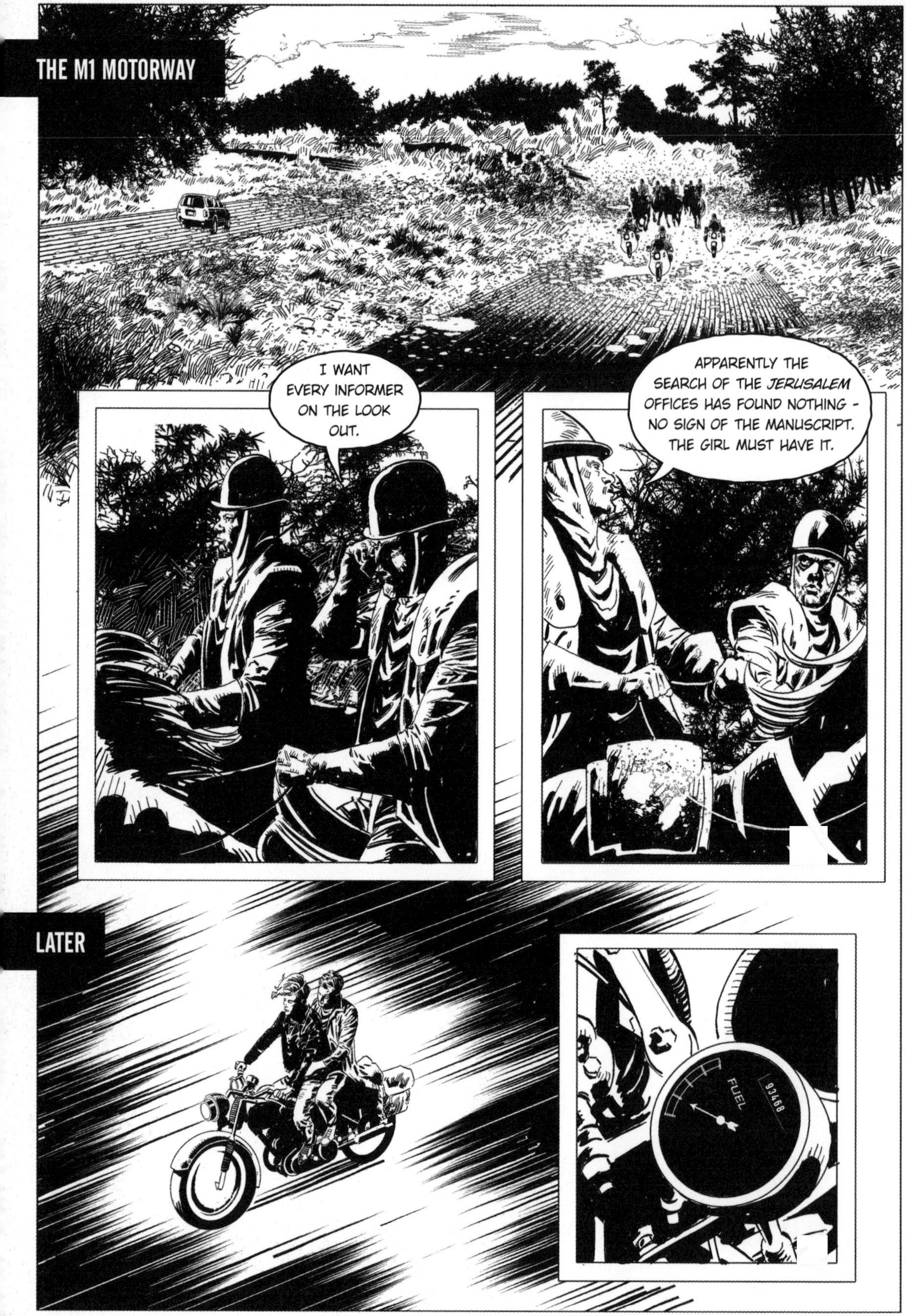
THE M1 MOTORWAY
I WANT EVERY INFORMER ON THE LOOK OUT.
APPARENTLY THE SEARCH OF THE *JERUSALEM* OFFICES HAS FOUND NOTHING - NO SIGN OF THE MANUSCRIPT. THE GIRL MUST HAVE IT.
LATER
FUEL
93468

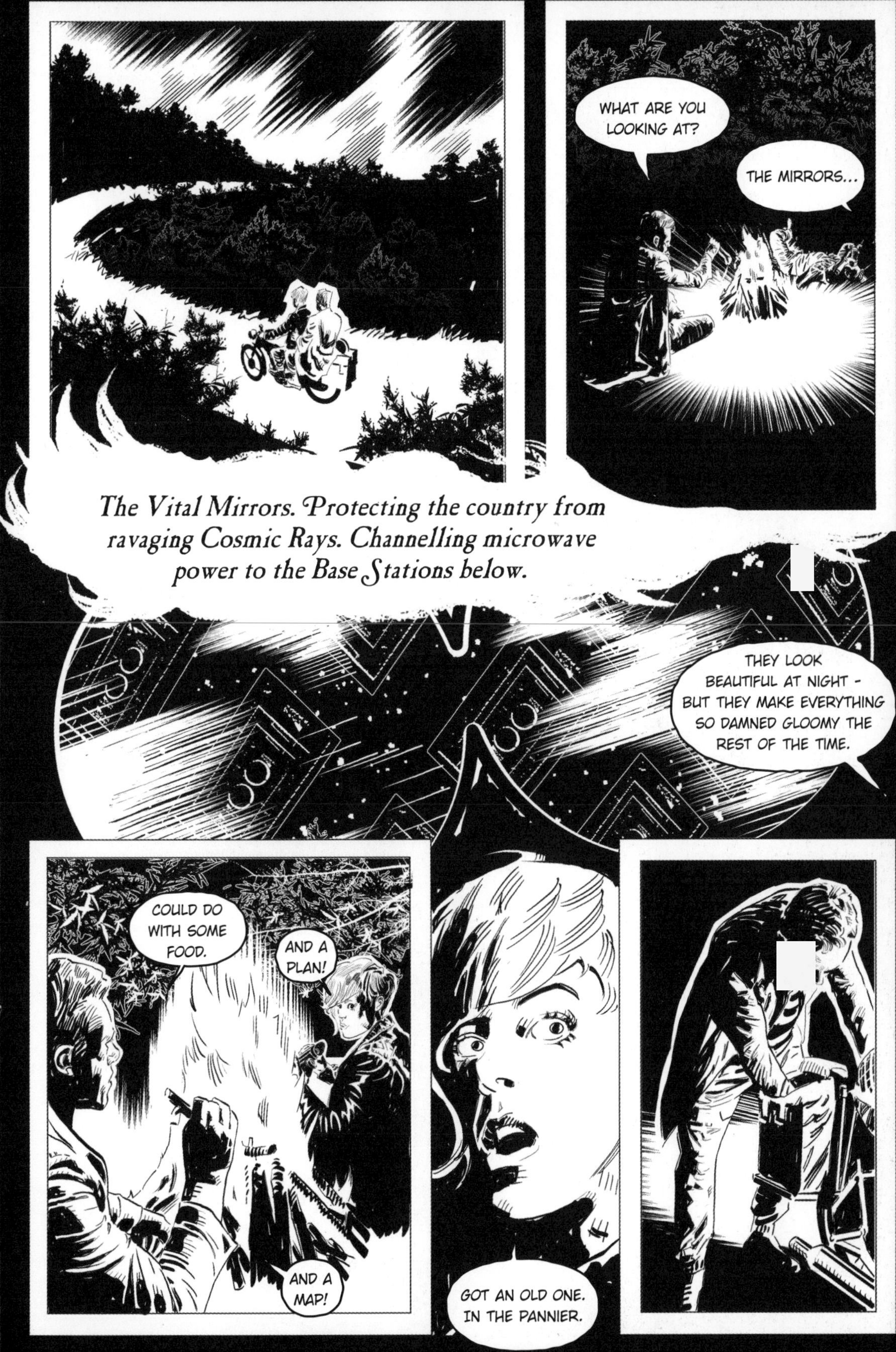
WHAT ARE YOU LOOKING AT?
THE MIRRORS...
The Vital Mirrors. Protecting the country from ravaging Cosmic Rays. Channelling microwave power to the Base Stations below.
THEY LOOK BEAUTIFUL AT NIGHT - BUT THEY MAKE EVERYTHING SO DAMNED GLOOMY THE REST OF THE TIME.
COULD DO WITH SOME FOOD.
AND A PLAN!
AND A MAP!
GOT AN OLD ONE. IN THE PANNIER.

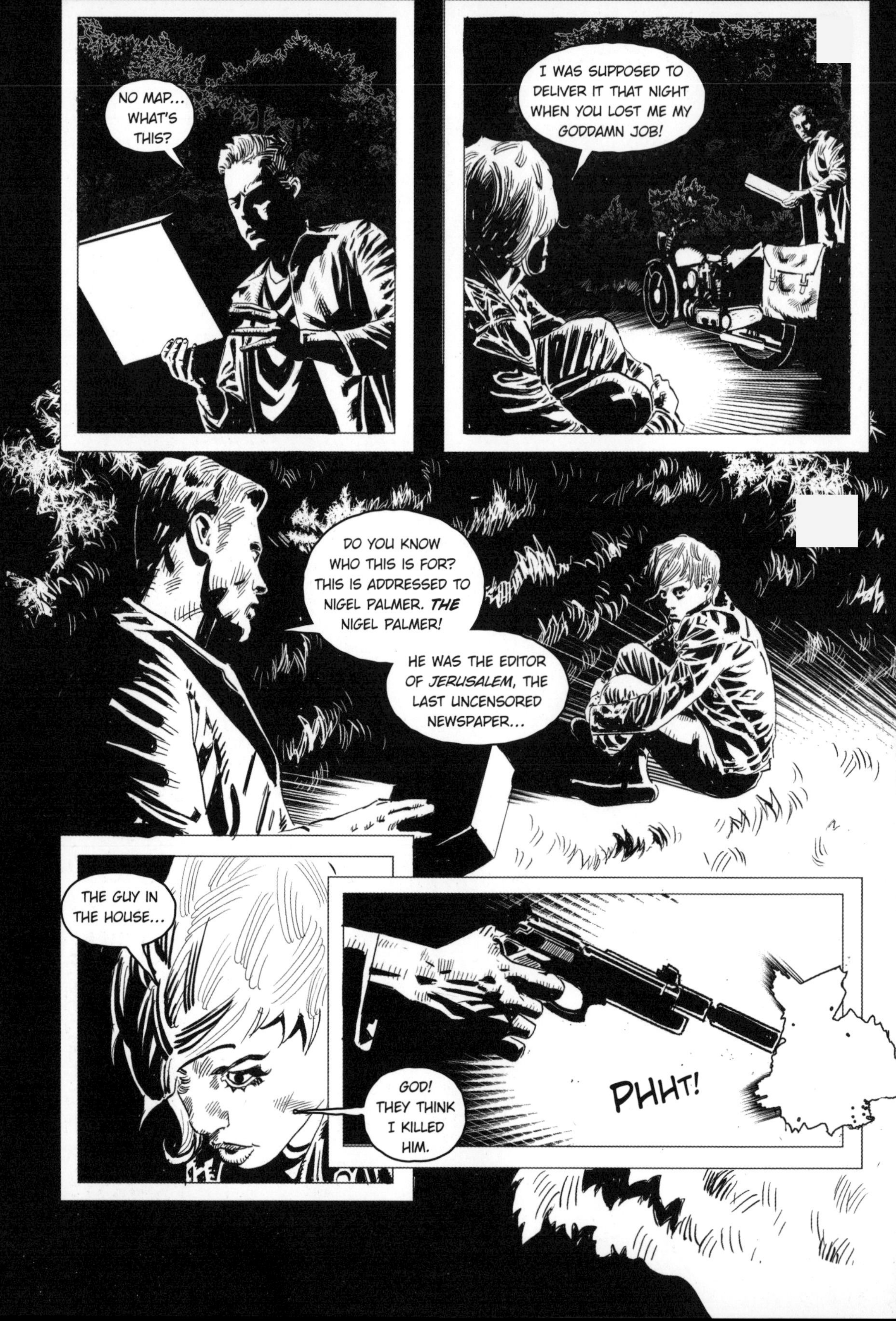
NO MAP... WHAT'S THIS?
I WAS SUPPOSED TO DELIVER IT THAT NIGHT WHEN YOU LOST ME MY GODDAMN JOB!
DO YOU KNOW WHO THIS IS FOR? THIS IS ADDRESSED TO NIGEL PALMER. *THE* NIGEL PALMER!
HE WAS THE EDITOR OF *JERUSALEM*, THE LAST UNCENSORED NEWSPAPER...
THE GUY IN THE HOUSE...
GOD! THEY THINK I KILLED HIM.
PHHT!

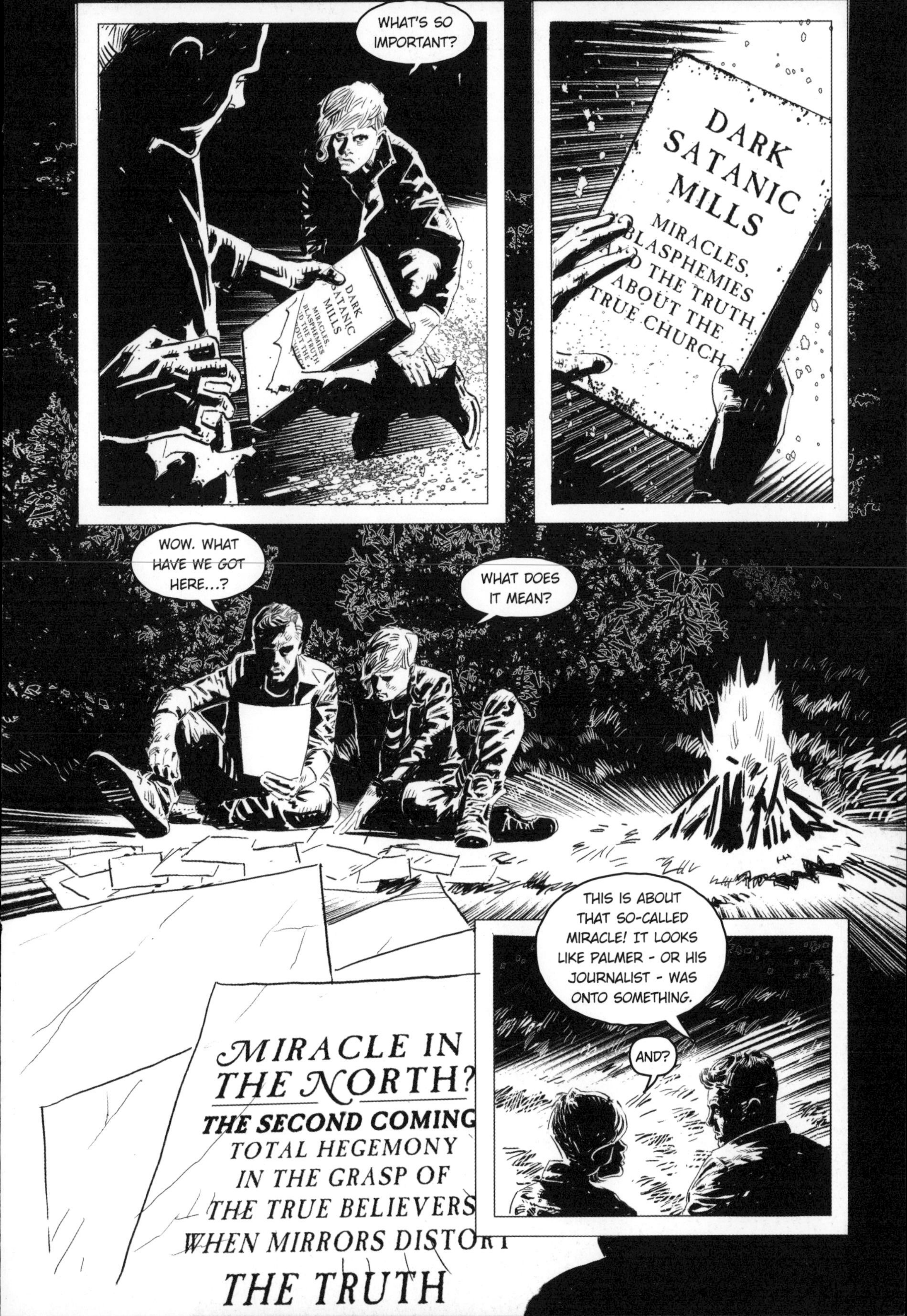
WHAT'S SO IMPORTANT?
DARK SATANIC MILLS
MIRACLES, BLASPHEMIES AND THE TRUTH ABOUT THE TRUE CHURCH
WOW. WHAT HAVE WE GOT HERE...?
WHAT DOES IT MEAN?
MIRACLE IN THE NORTH?
THE SECOND COMING
TOTAL HEGEMONY IN THE GRASP OF THE TRUE BELIEVERS
WHEN MIRRORS DISTORT
THE TRUTH
THIS IS ABOUT THAT SO-CALLED MIRACLE! IT LOOKS LIKE PALMER - OR HIS JOURNALIST - WAS ONTO SOMETHING.
AND?

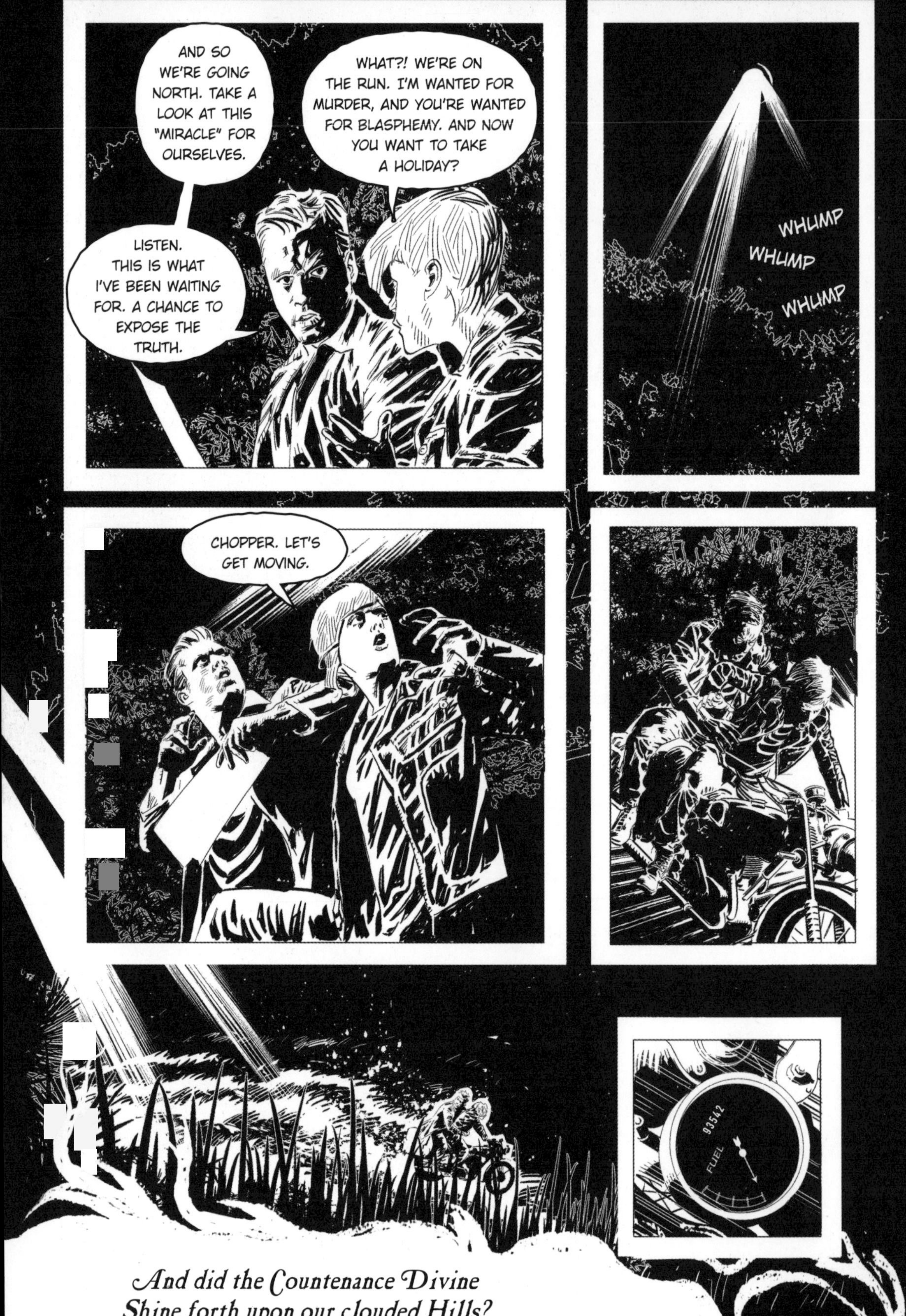
AND SO WE'RE GOING NORTH. TAKE A LOOK AT THIS "MIRACLE" FOR OURSELVES.
WHAT?! WE'RE ON THE RUN. I'M WANTED FOR MURDER, AND YOU'RE WANTED FOR BLASPHEMY. AND NOW YOU WANT TO TAKE A HOLIDAY?
LISTEN. THIS IS WHAT I'VE BEEN WAITING FOR. A CHANCE TO EXPOSE THE TRUTH.
WHUMP
WHUMP
WHUMP
CHOPPER. LET'S GET MOVING.
93542
FUEL

And did the Countenance Divine
Shine forth upon our clouded Hills?

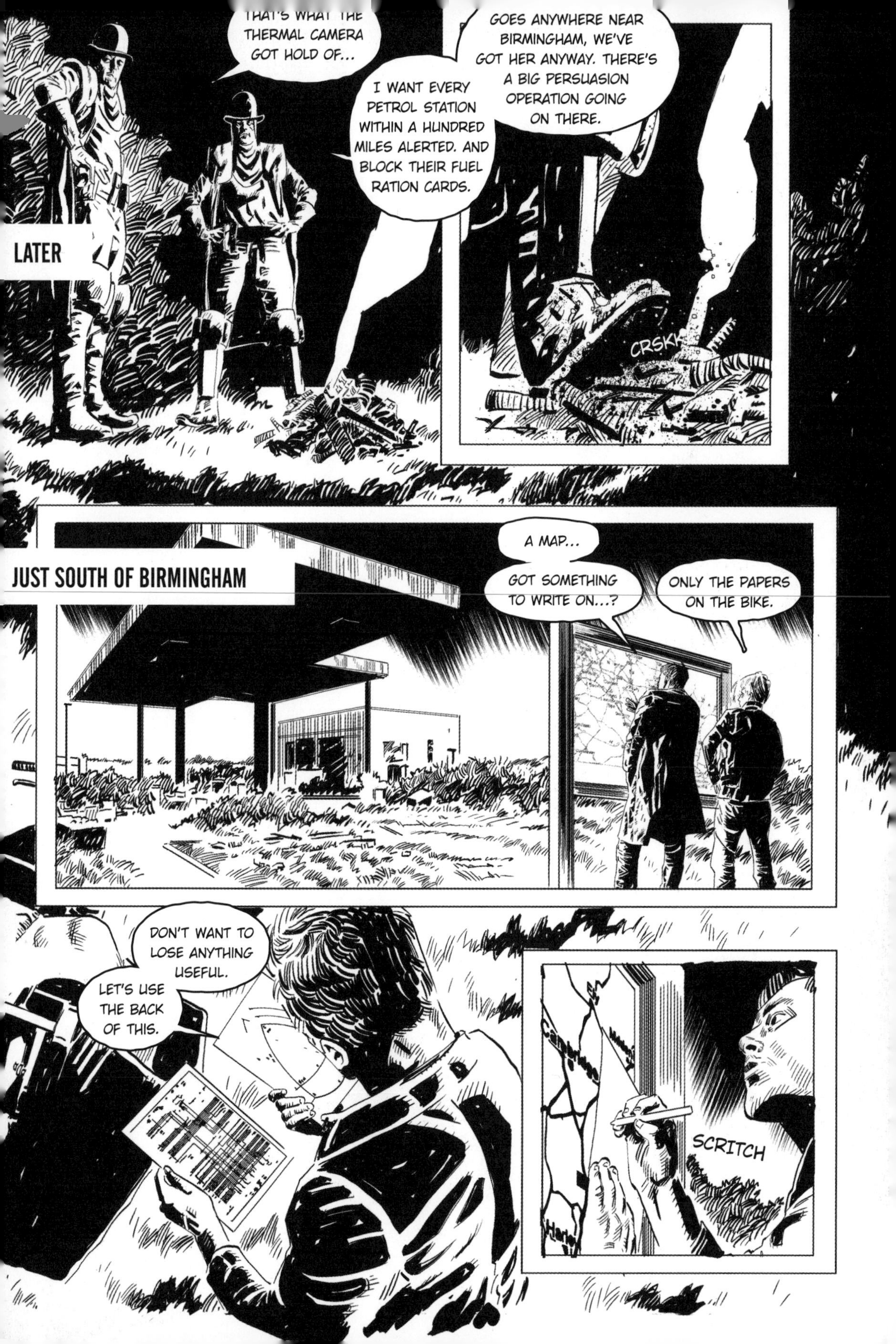
THAT'S WHAT THE THERMAL CAMERA GOT HOLD OF...
I WANT EVERY PETROL STATION WITHIN A HUNDRED MILES ALERTED. AND BLOCK THEIR FUEL RATION CARDS.
GOES ANYWHERE NEAR BIRMINGHAM, WE'VE GOT HER ANYWAY. THERE'S A BIG PERSUASION OPERATION GOING ON THERE.
LATER
CRSKK
JUST SOUTH OF BIRMINGHAM
A MAP...
GOT SOMETHING TO WRITE ON...?
ONLY THE PAPERS ON THE BIKE.
DON'T WANT TO LOSE ANYTHING USEFUL.
LET'S USE THE BACK OF THIS.
SCRITCH

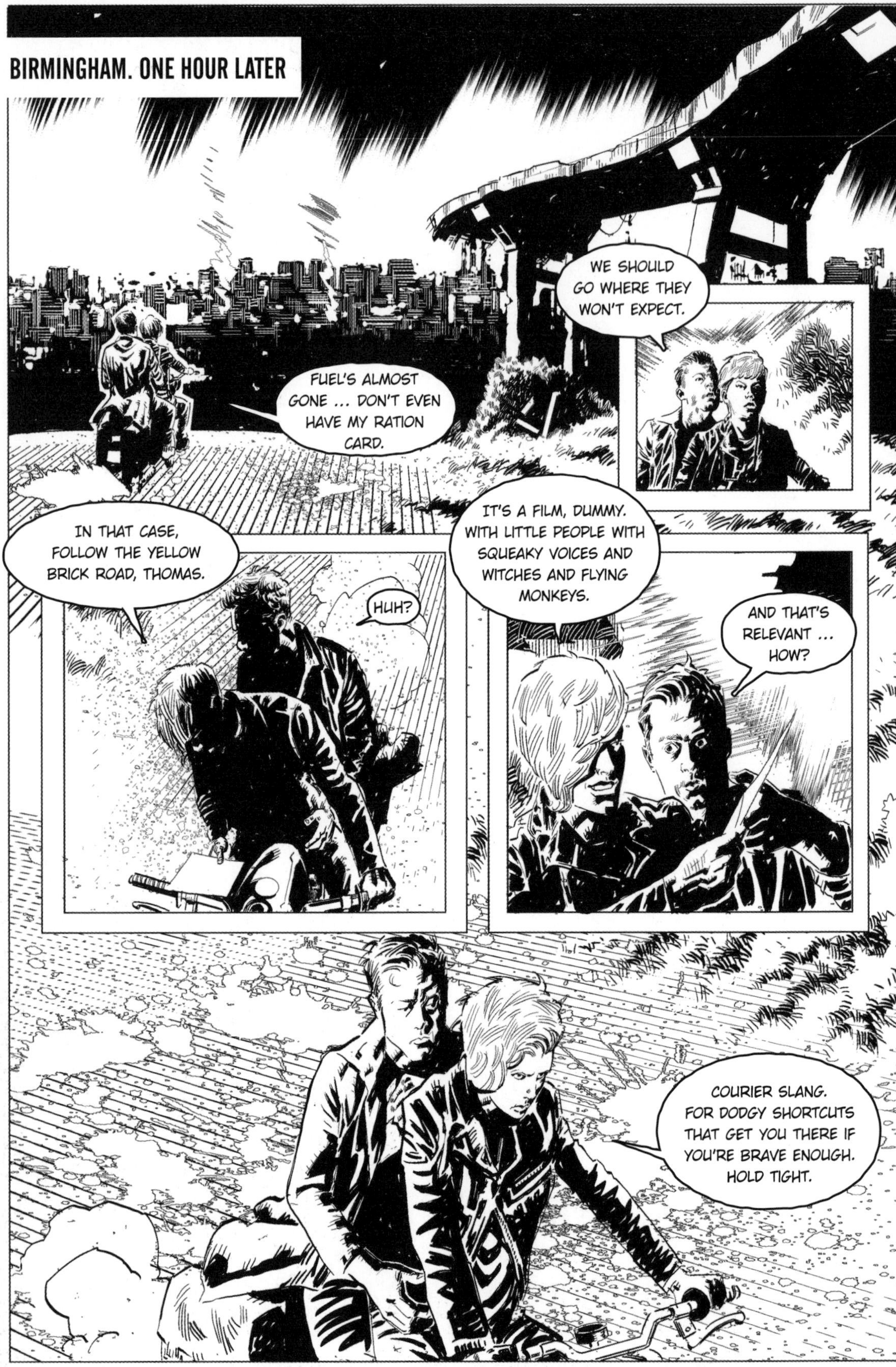
BIRMINGHAM. ONE HOUR LATER
FUEL'S ALMOST GONE ... DON'T EVEN HAVE MY RATION CARD.
WE SHOULD GO WHERE THEY WON'T EXPECT.
IN THAT CASE, FOLLOW THE YELLOW BRICK ROAD, THOMAS.
HUH?
IT'S A FILM, DUMMY. WITH LITTLE PEOPLE WITH SQUEAKY VOICES AND WITCHES AND FLYING MONKEYS.
AND THAT'S RELEVANT ... HOW?
COURIER SLANG. FOR DODGY SHORTCUTS THAT GET YOU THERE IF YOU'RE BRAVE ENOUGH. HOLD TIGHT.

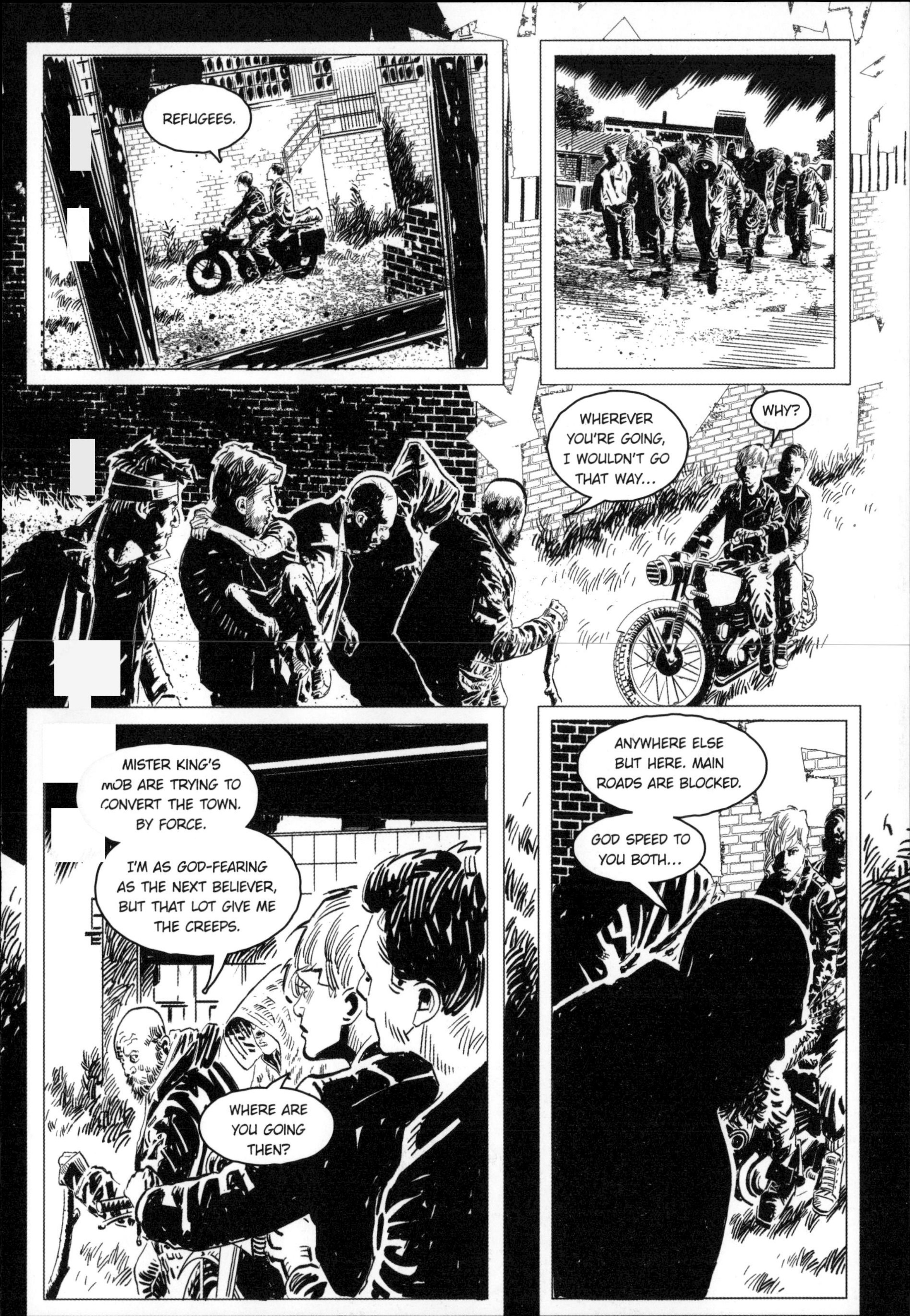
REFUGEES.
WHEREVER YOU'RE GOING, I WOULDN'T GO THAT WAY...
WHY?
MISTER KING'S MOB ARE TRYING TO CONVERT THE TOWN. BY FORCE.
I'M AS GOD-FEARING AS THE NEXT BELIEVER, BUT THAT LOT GIVE ME THE CREEPS.
WHERE ARE YOU GOING THEN?
ANYWHERE ELSE BUT HERE. MAIN ROADS ARE BLOCKED.
GOD SPEED TO YOU BOTH...

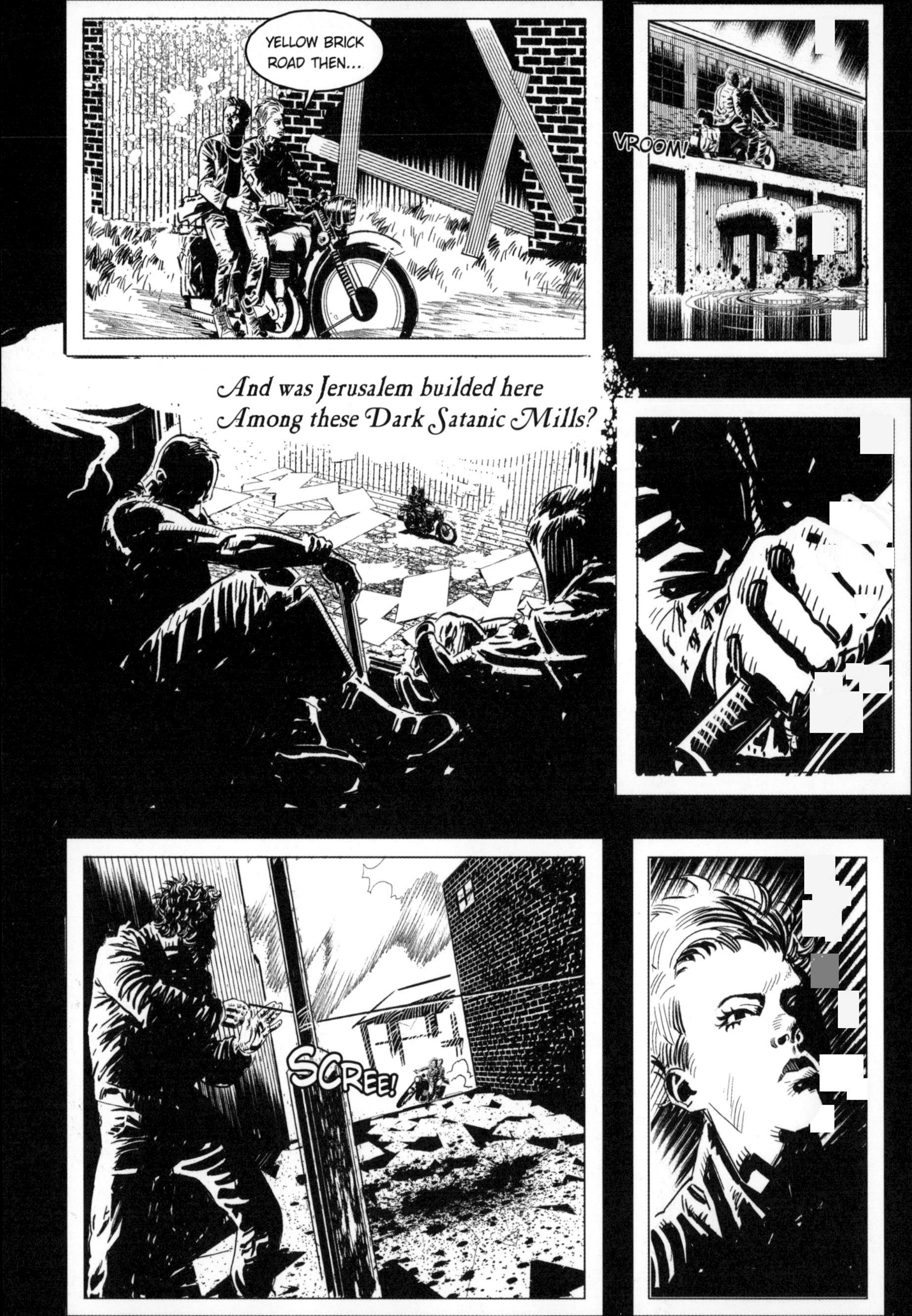
YELLOW BRICK ROAD THEN...
VROOM!
And was Jerusalem builded here
Among these Dark Satanic Mills?
SCREE!

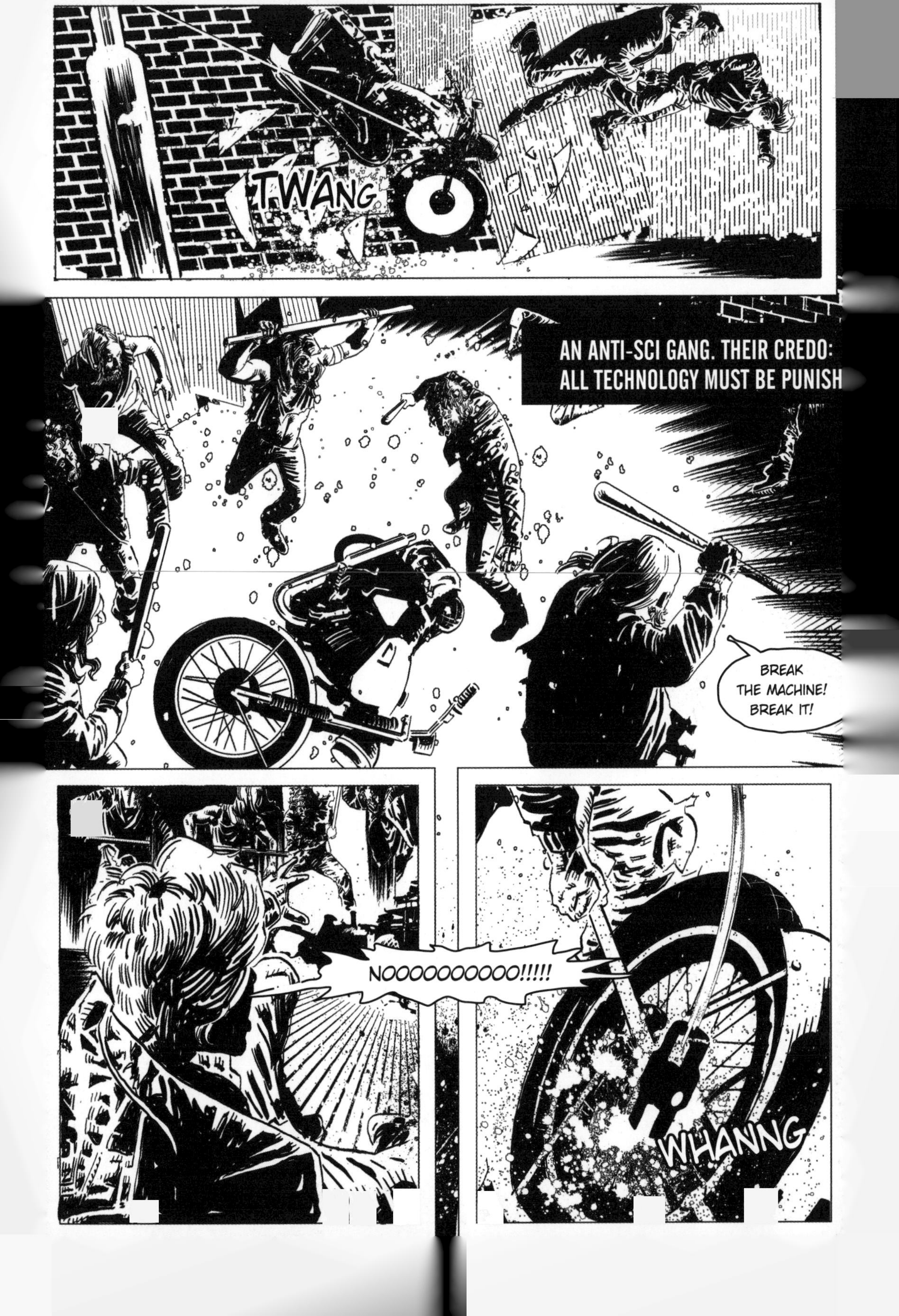
TWANG
AN ANTI-SCI GANG. THEIR CREDO:
ALL TECHNOLOGY MUST BE PUNISH
BREAK THE MACHINE! BREAK IT!
NOOOOOOOOOO!!!!!
WHANNG

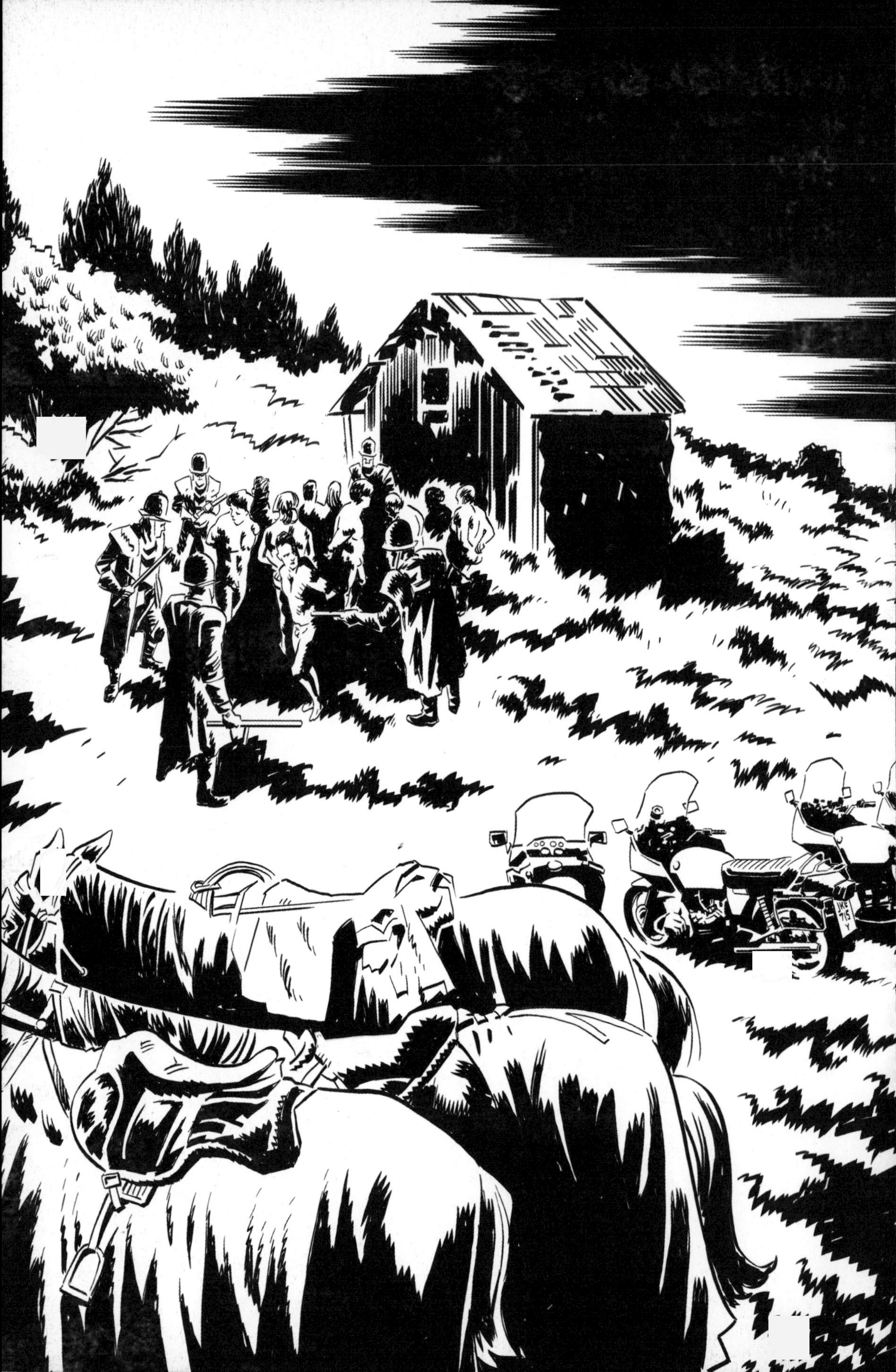

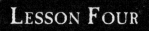

Lesson Four

My God, my God, why hast Thou forsaken me?

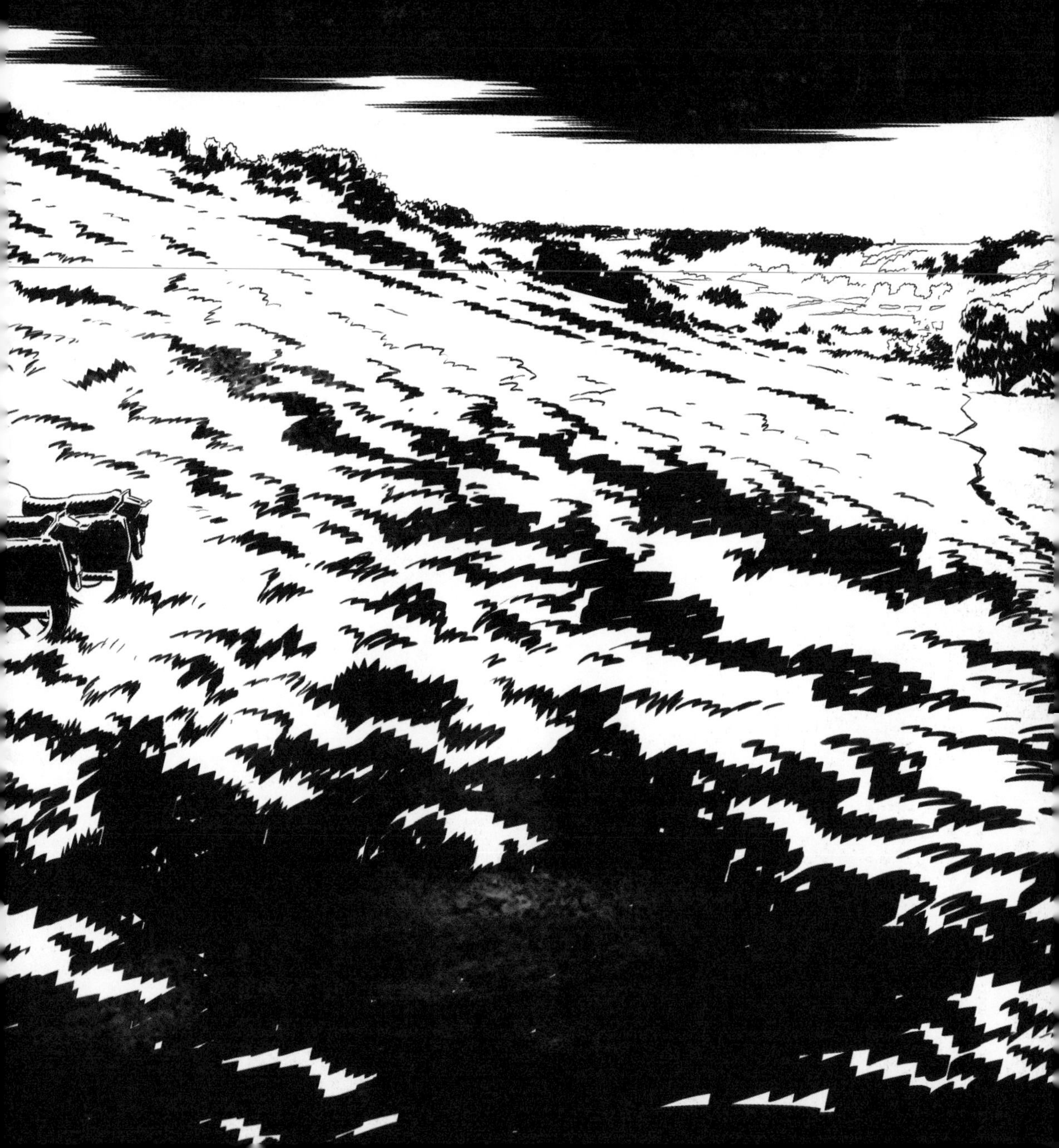

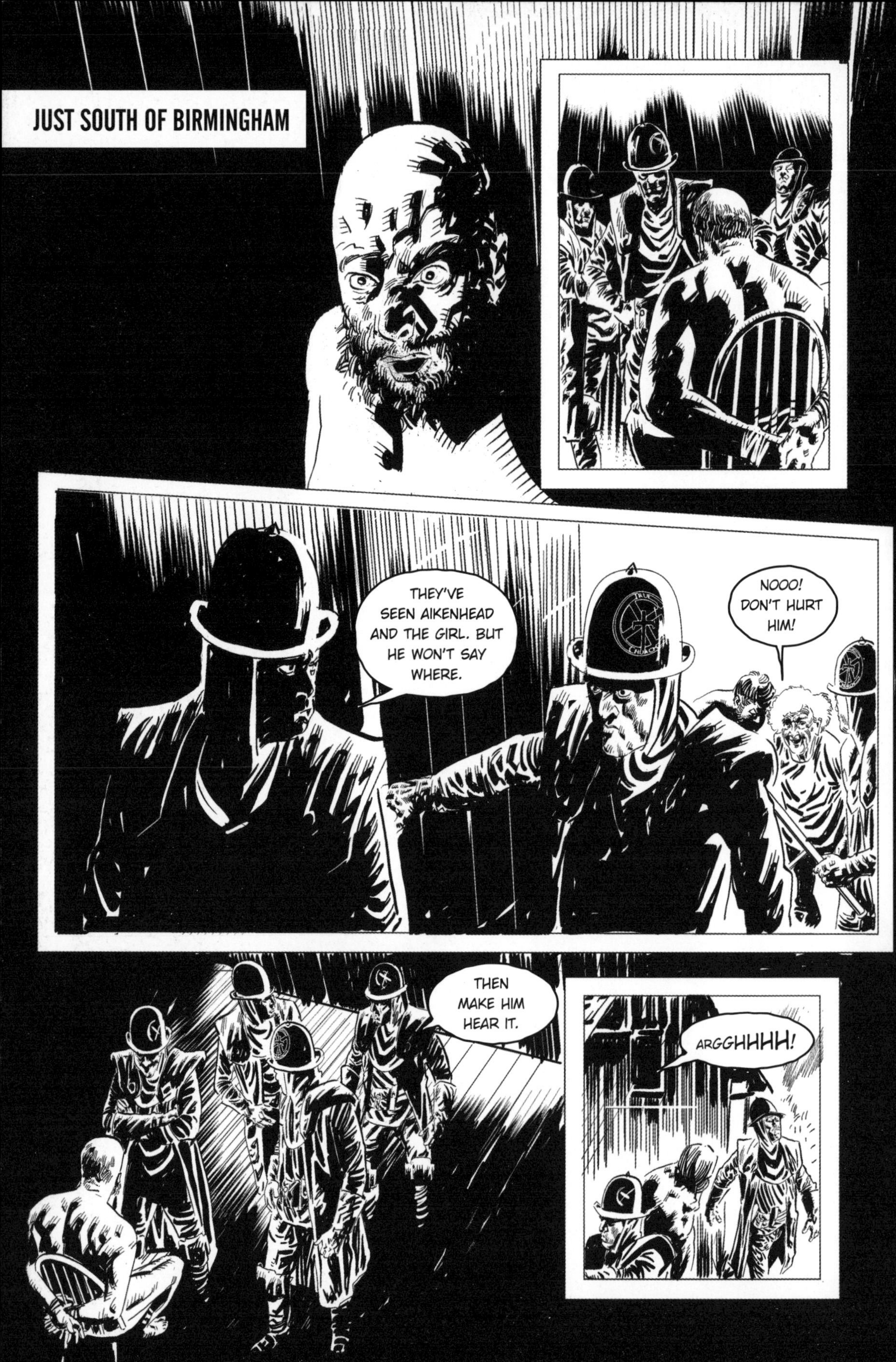
JUST SOUTH OF BIRMINGHAM
THEY'VE SEEN AIKENHEAD AND THE GIRL. BUT HE WON'T SAY WHERE.
NOOO! DON'T HURT HIM!
THEN MAKE HIM HEAR IT.
ARGGHHHH!

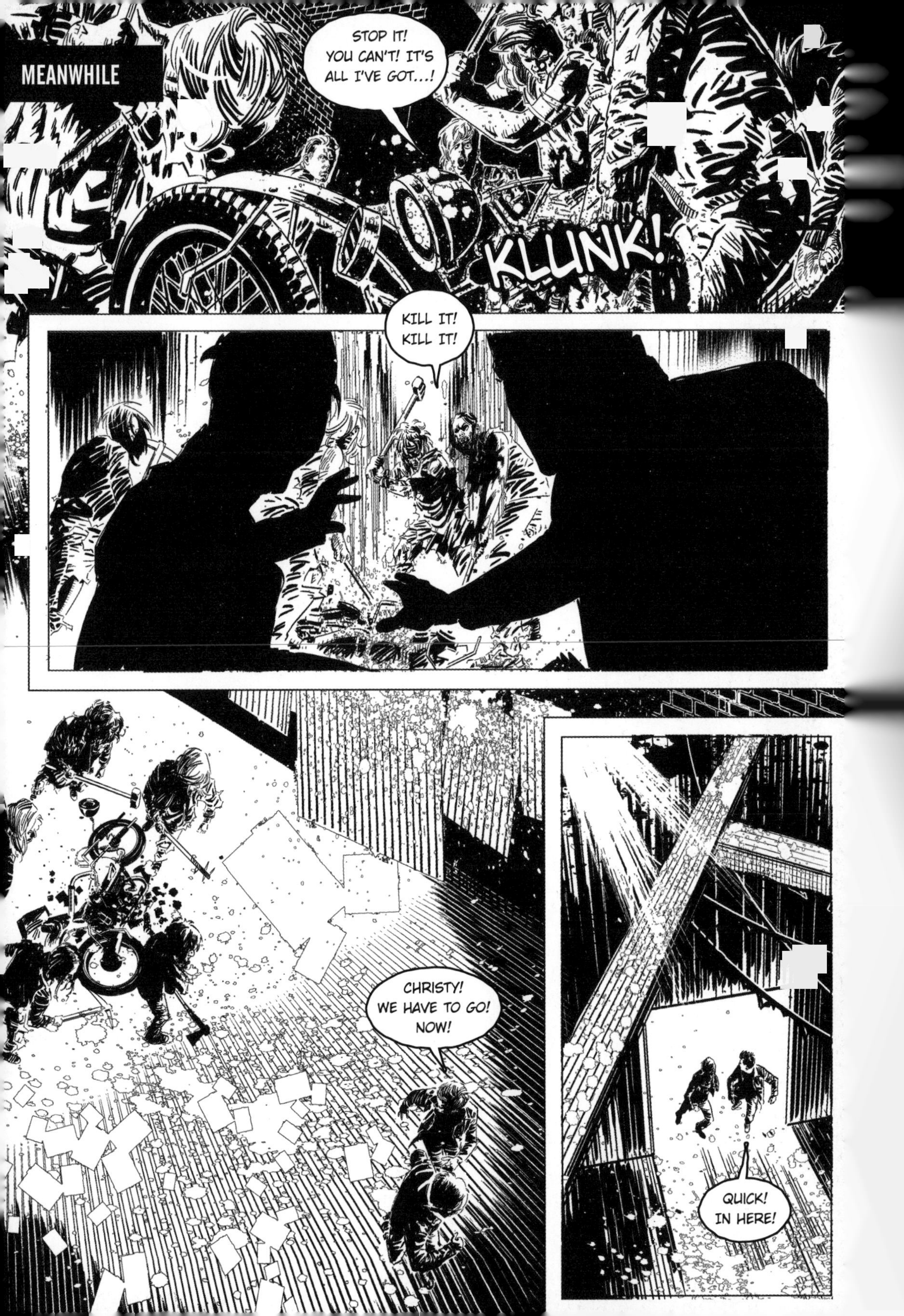
MEANWHILE
STOP IT! YOU CAN'T! IT'S ALL I'VE GOT...!
KLUNK!
KILL IT! KILL IT!
CHRISTY! WE HAVE TO GO! NOW!
QUICK! IN HERE!

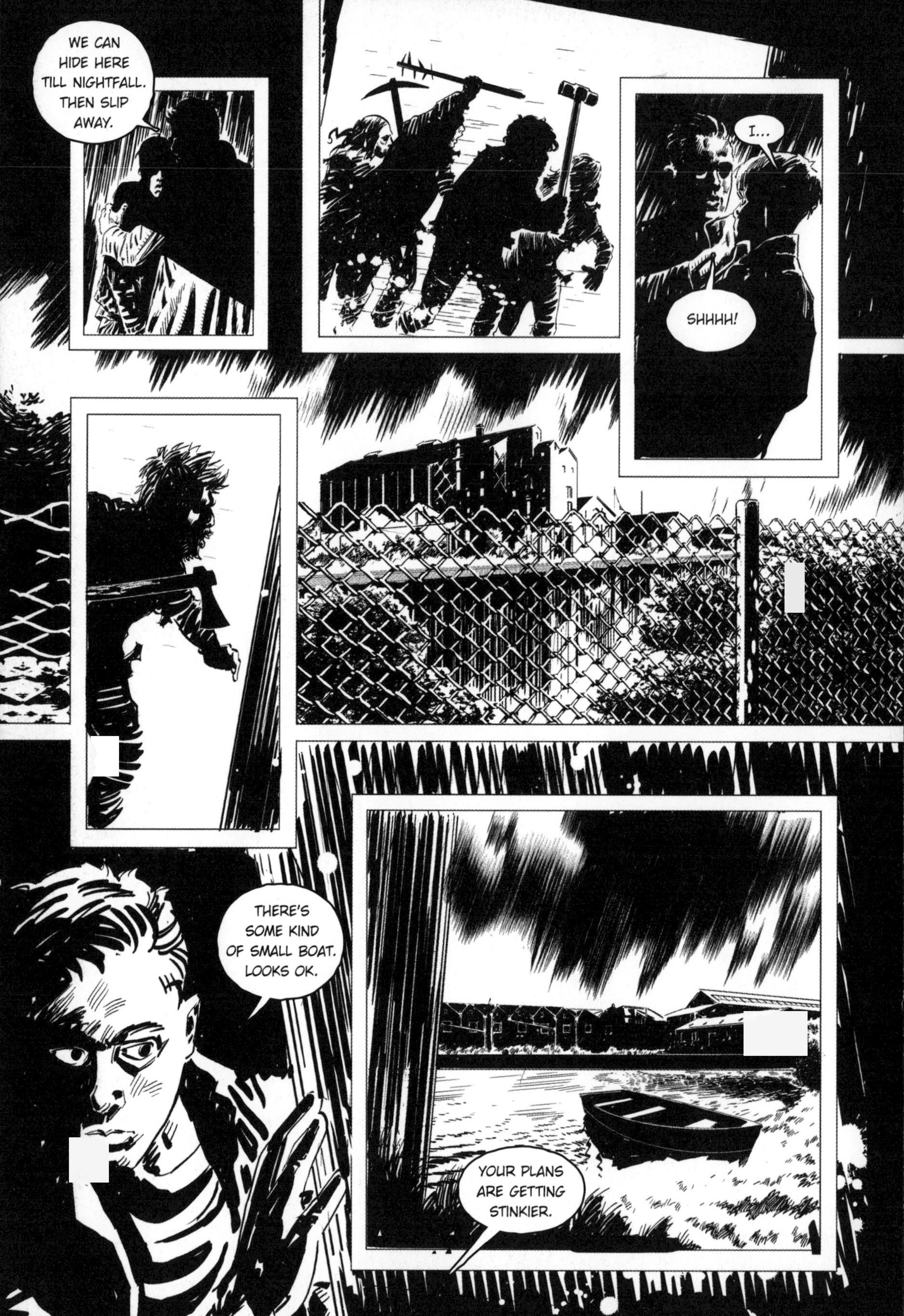
WE CAN HIDE HERE TILL NIGHTFALL. THEN SLIP AWAY.
I...
SHHHH!
THERE'S SOME KIND OF SMALL BOAT. LOOKS OK.
YOUR PLANS ARE GETTING STINKIER.

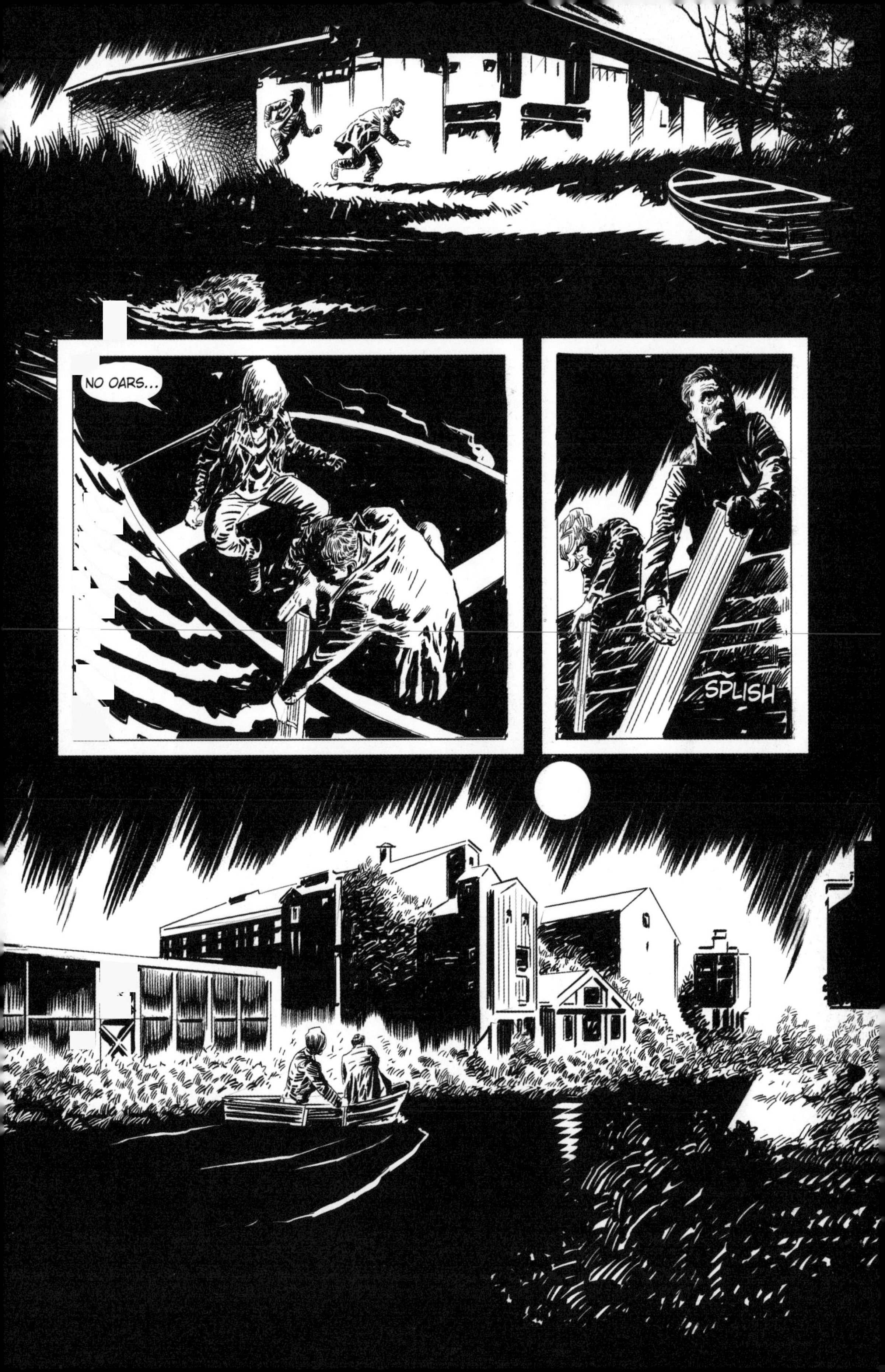
NO OARS...
SPLISH

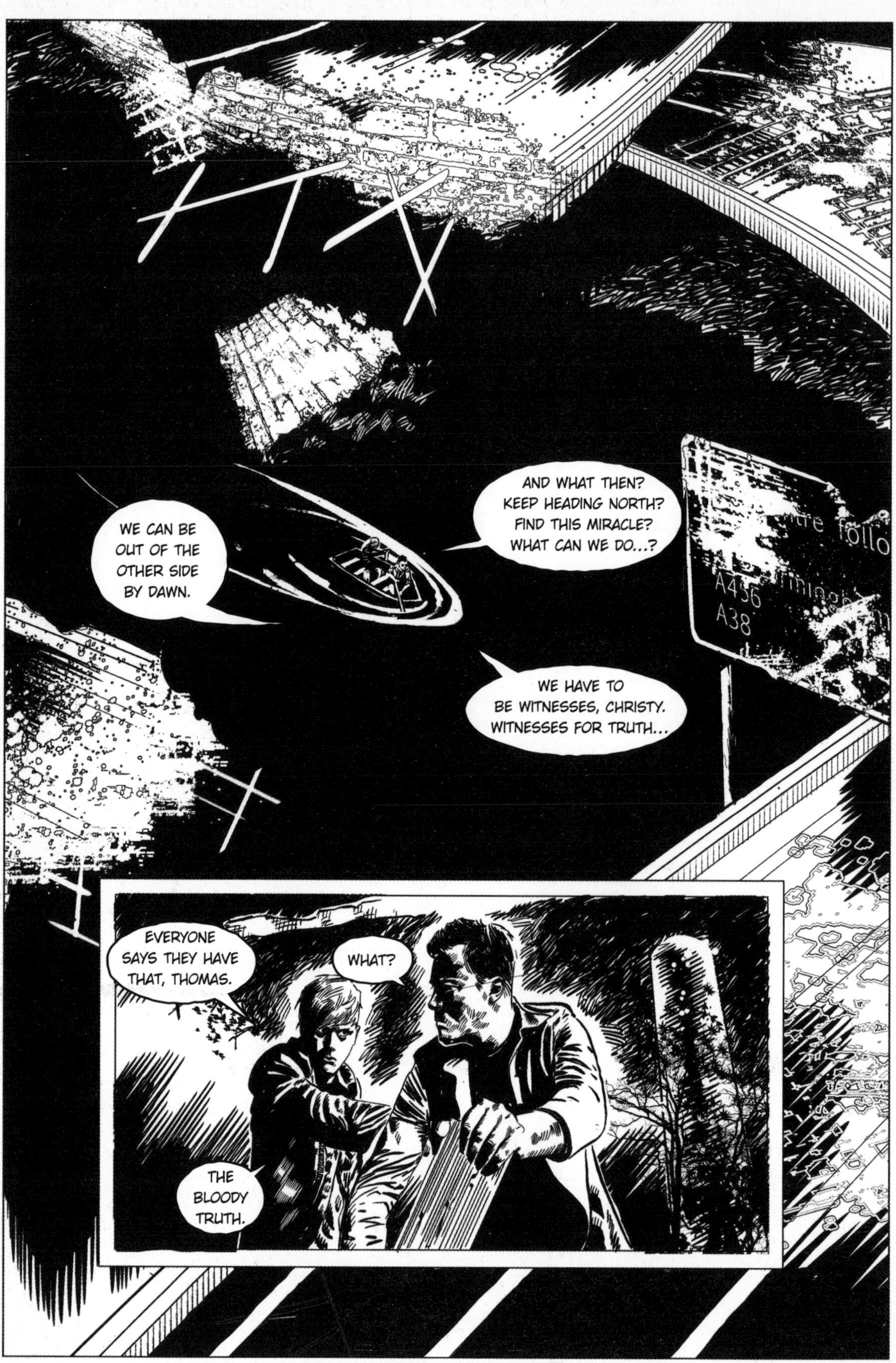
WE CAN BE OUT OF THE OTHER SIDE BY DAWN.
AND WHAT THEN? KEEP HEADING NORTH? FIND THIS MIRACLE? WHAT CAN WE DO...?
A456
A38
WE HAVE TO BE WITNESSES, CHRISTY. WITNESSES FOR TRUTH...
EVERYONE SAYS THEY HAVE THAT, THOMAS.
WHAT?
THE BLOODY TRUTH.

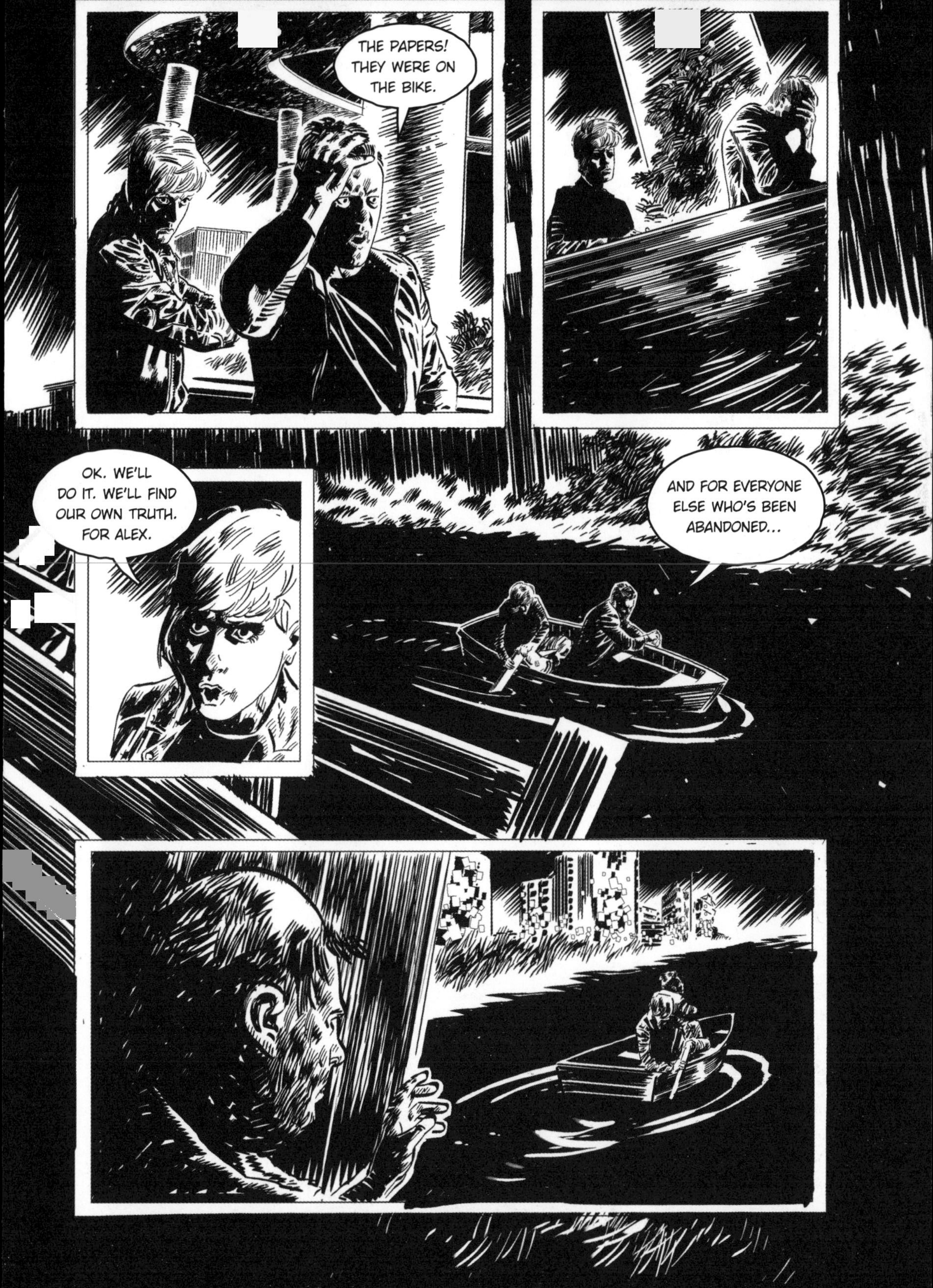
THE PAPERS! THEY WERE ON THE BIKE.
OK. WE'LL DO IT. WE'LL FIND OUR OWN TRUTH. FOR ALEX.
AND FOR EVERYONE ELSE WHO'S BEEN ABANDONED...

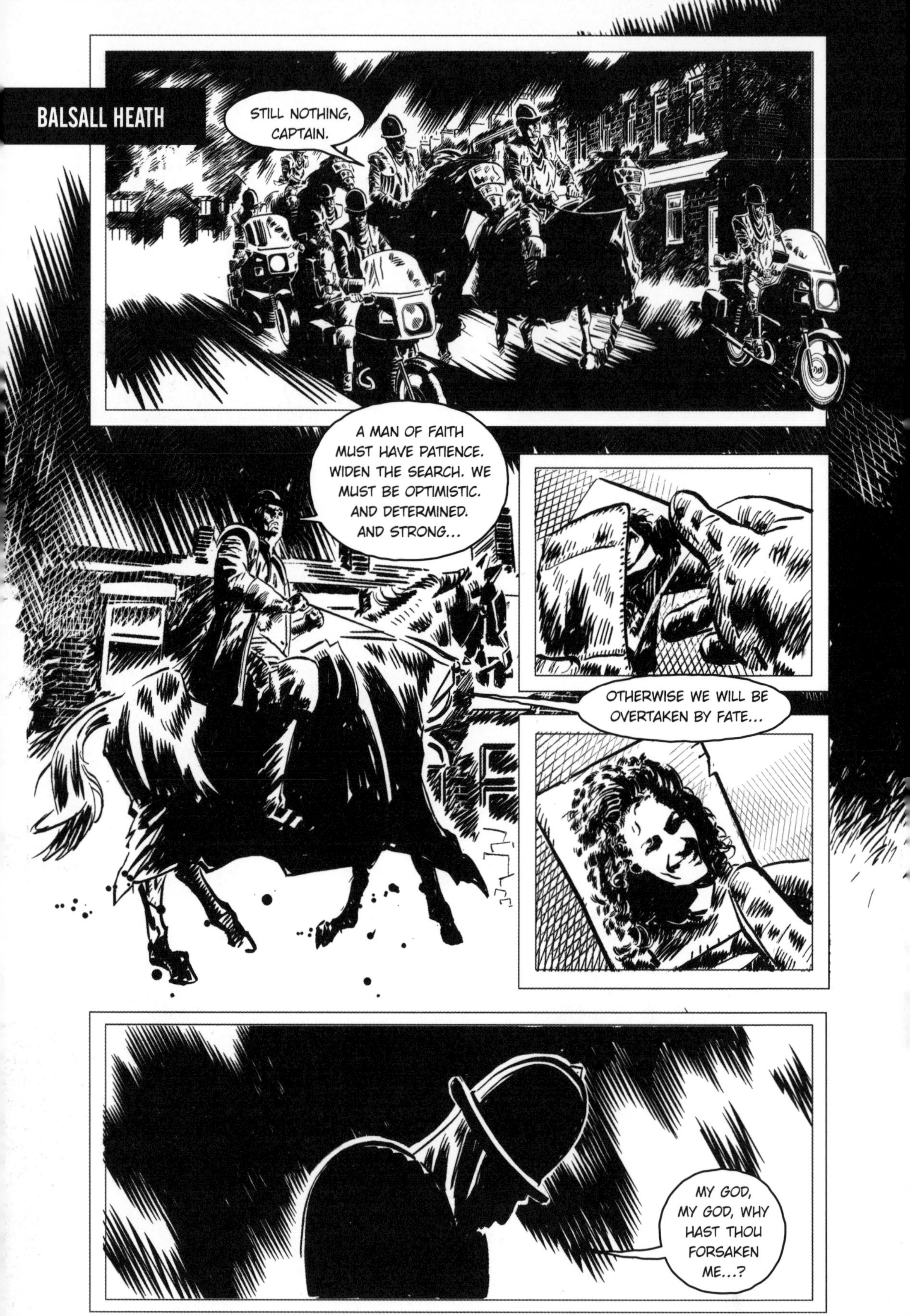
BALSALL HEATH
STILL NOTHING, CAPTAIN.
A MAN OF FAITH MUST HAVE PATIENCE. WIDEN THE SEARCH. WE MUST BE OPTIMISTIC. AND DETERMINED. AND STRONG...
OTHERWISE WE WILL BE OVERTAKEN BY FATE...
MY GOD, MY GOD, WHY HAST THOU FORSAKEN ME...?

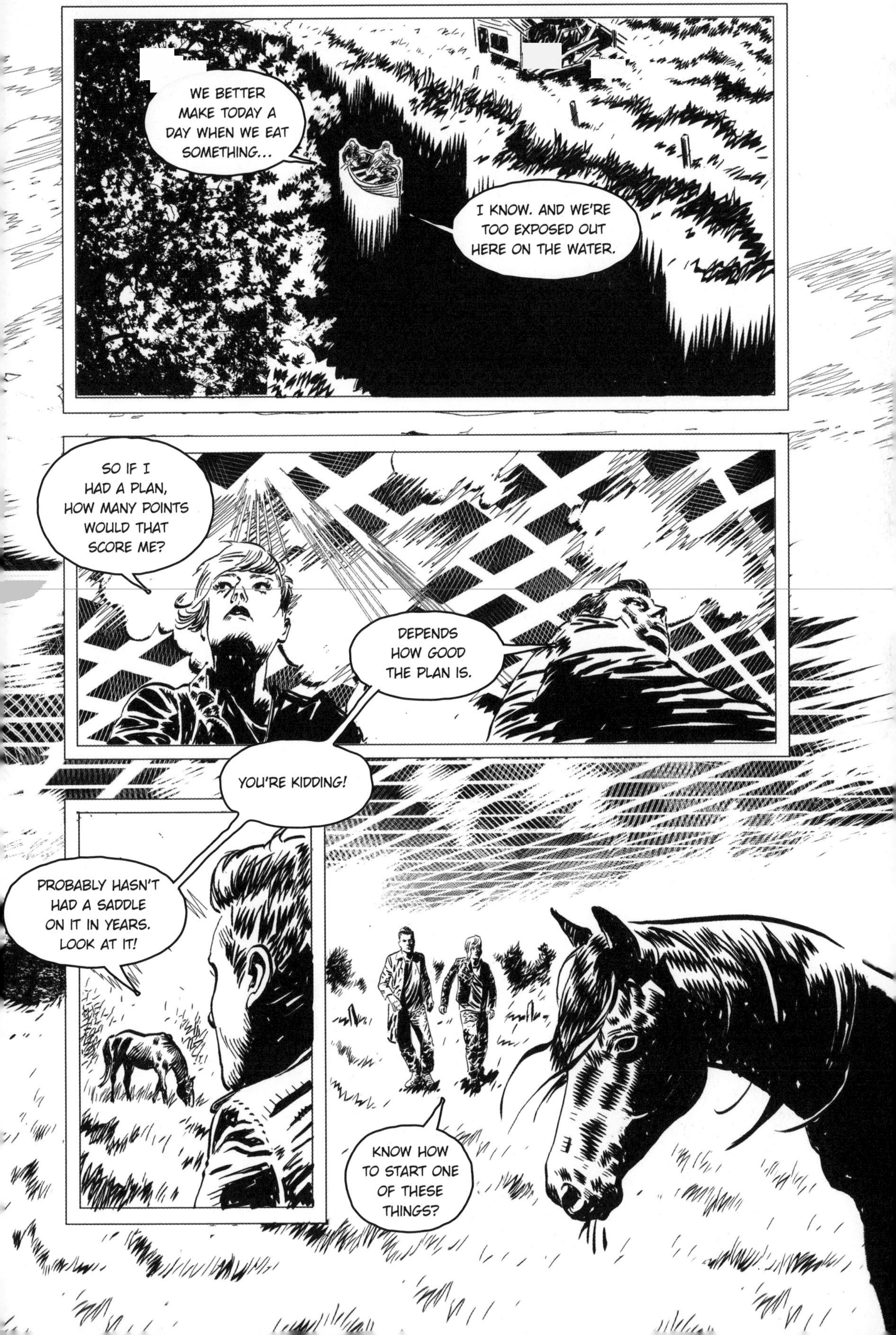
WE BETTER MAKE TODAY A DAY WHEN WE EAT SOMETHING...
I KNOW. AND WE'RE TOO EXPOSED OUT HERE ON THE WATER.
SO IF I HAD A PLAN, HOW MANY POINTS WOULD THAT SCORE ME?
DEPENDS HOW GOOD THE PLAN IS.
YOU'RE KIDDING!
PROBABLY HASN'T HAD A SADDLE ON IT IN YEARS. LOOK AT IT!
KNOW HOW TO START ONE OF THESE THINGS?

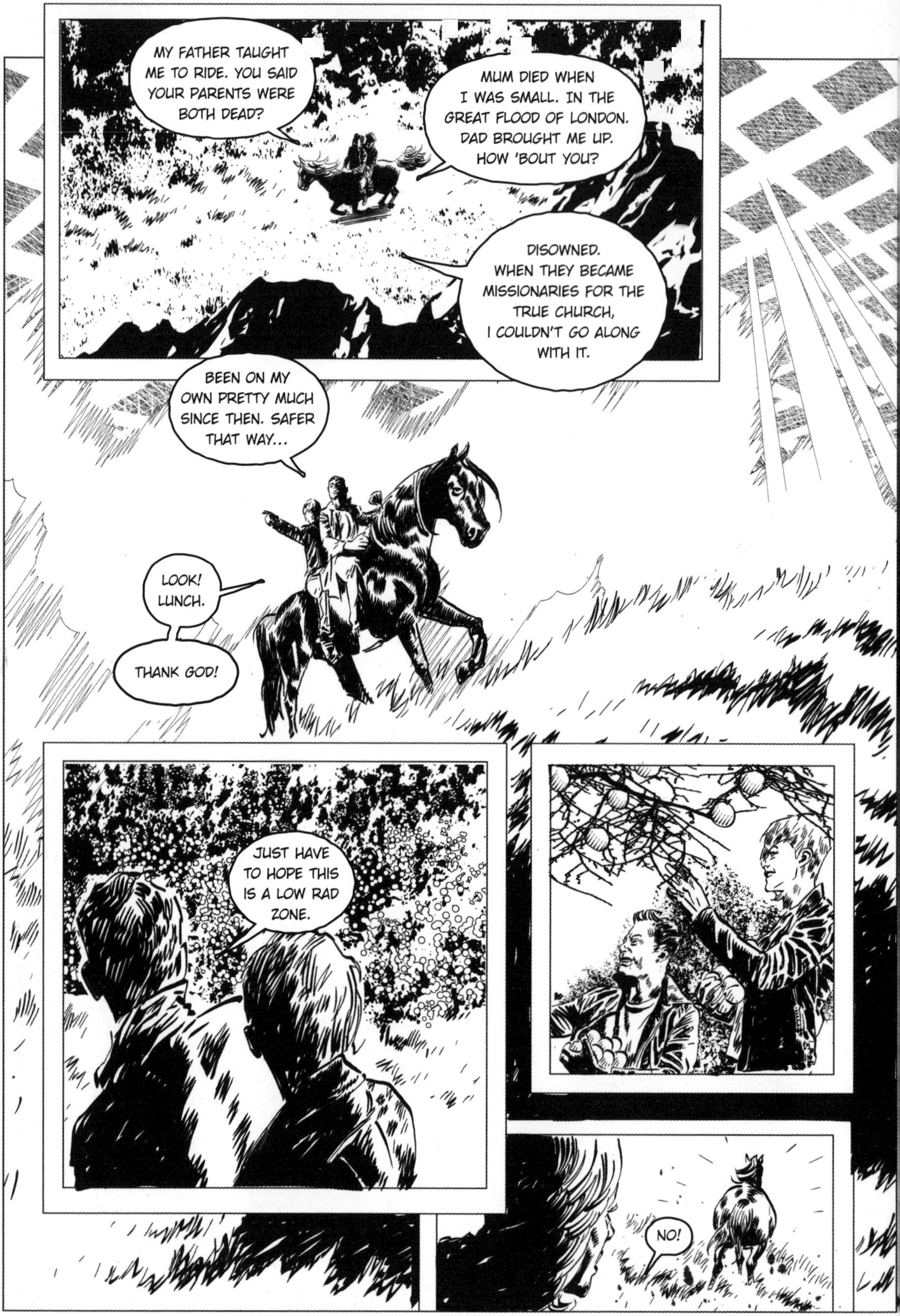
MY FATHER TAUGHT ME TO RIDE. YOU SAID YOUR PARENTS WERE BOTH DEAD?
MUM DIED WHEN I WAS SMALL. IN THE GREAT FLOOD OF LONDON. DAD BROUGHT ME UP. HOW 'BOUT YOU?
DISOWNED. WHEN THEY BECAME MISSIONARIES FOR THE TRUE CHURCH, I COULDN'T GO ALONG WITH IT.
BEEN ON MY OWN PRETTY MUCH SINCE THEN. SAFER THAT WAY...
LOOK! LUNCH.
THANK GOD!
JUST HAVE TO HOPE THIS IS A LOW RAD ZONE.
NO!

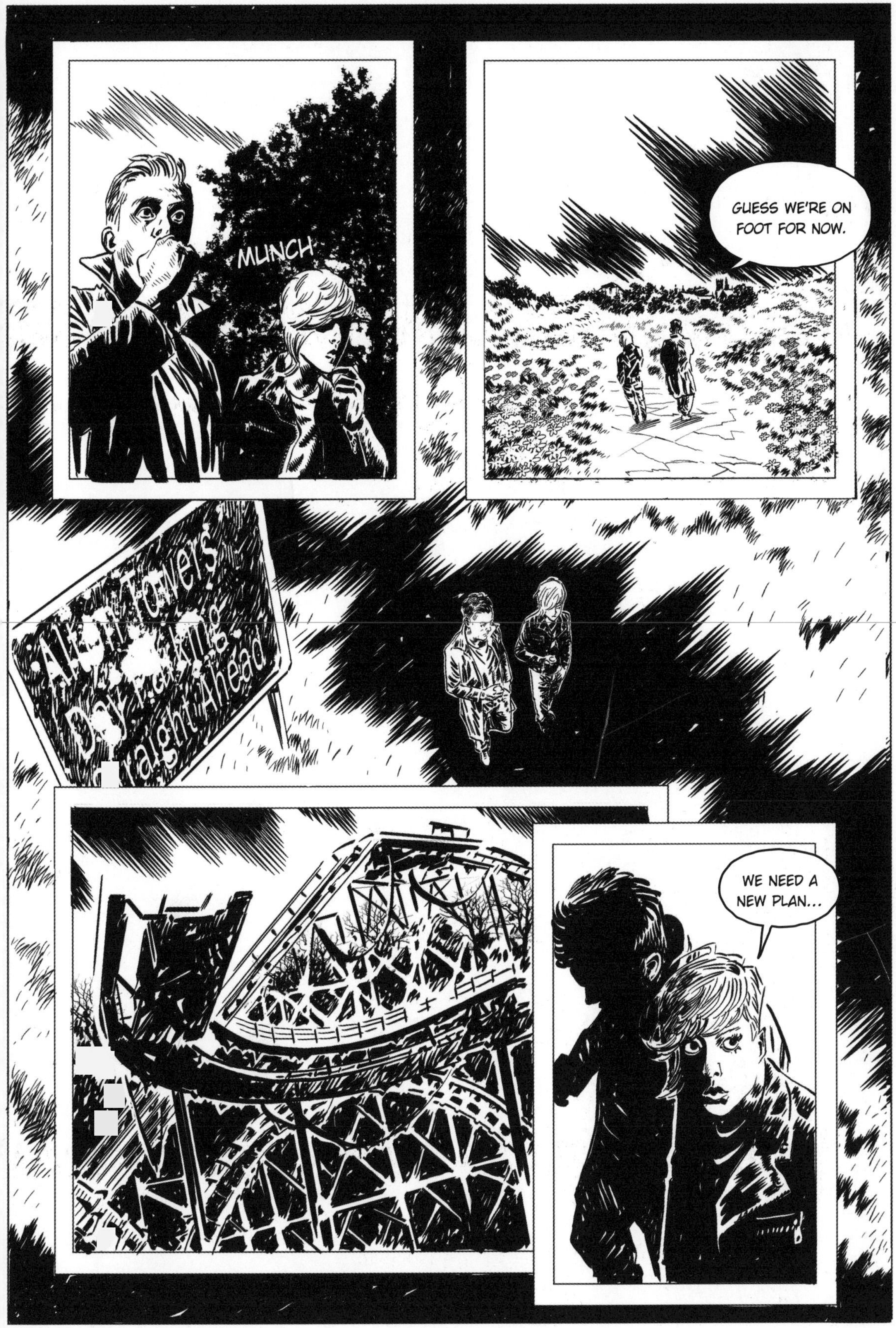
MUNCH
GUESS WE'RE ON FOOT FOR NOW.
WE NEED A NEW PLAN...

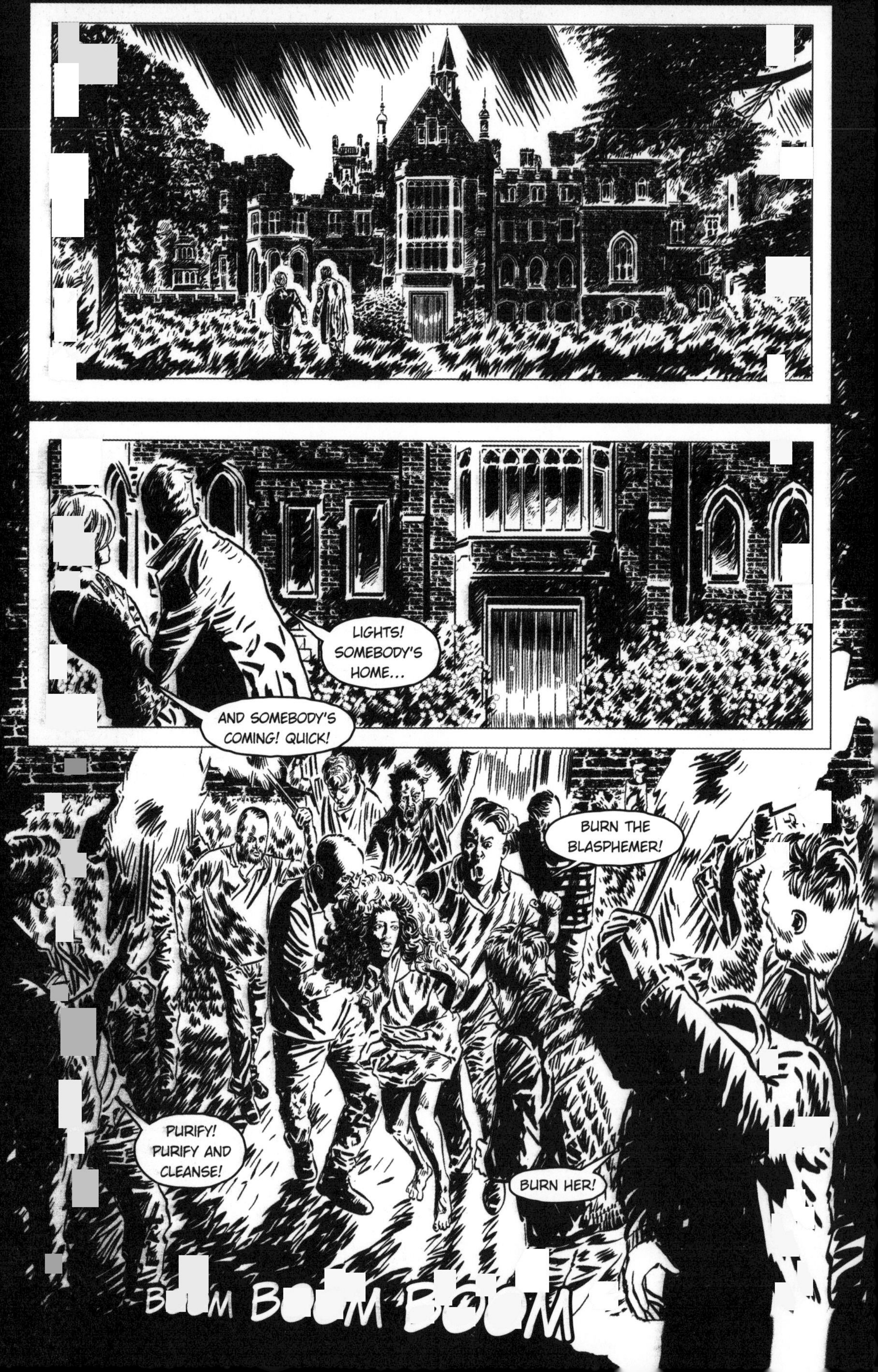
LIGHTS! SOMEBODY'S HOME...
AND SOMEBODY'S COMING! QUICK!
BURN THE BLASPHEMER!
PURIFY! PURIFY AND CLEANSE!
BURN HER!

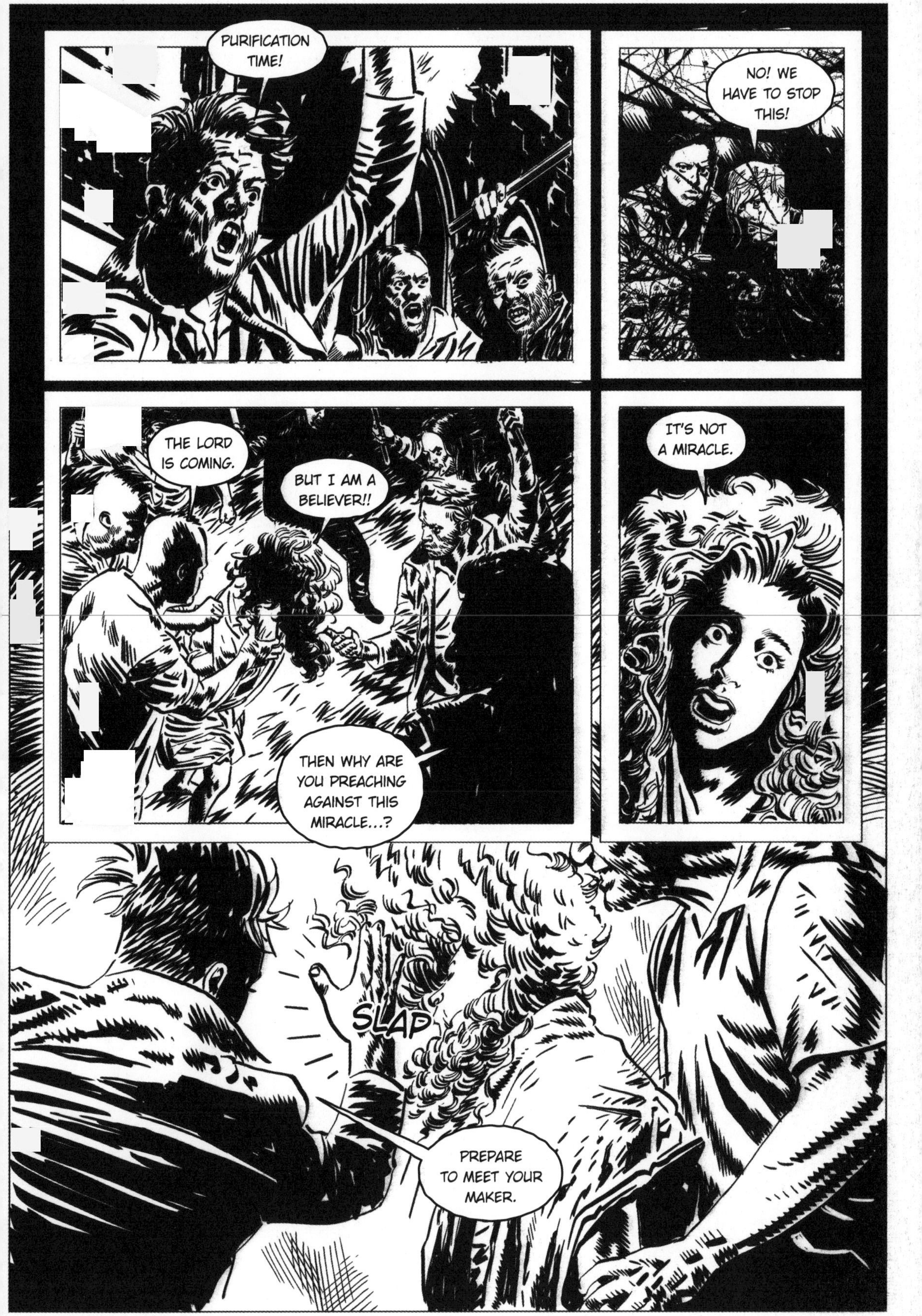
PURIFICATION TIME!
NO! WE HAVE TO STOP THIS!
THE LORD IS COMING.
BUT I AM A BELIEVER!!
THEN WHY ARE YOU PREACHING AGAINST THIS MIRACLE...?
IT'S NOT A MIRACLE.
SLAP
PREPARE TO MEET YOUR MAKER.

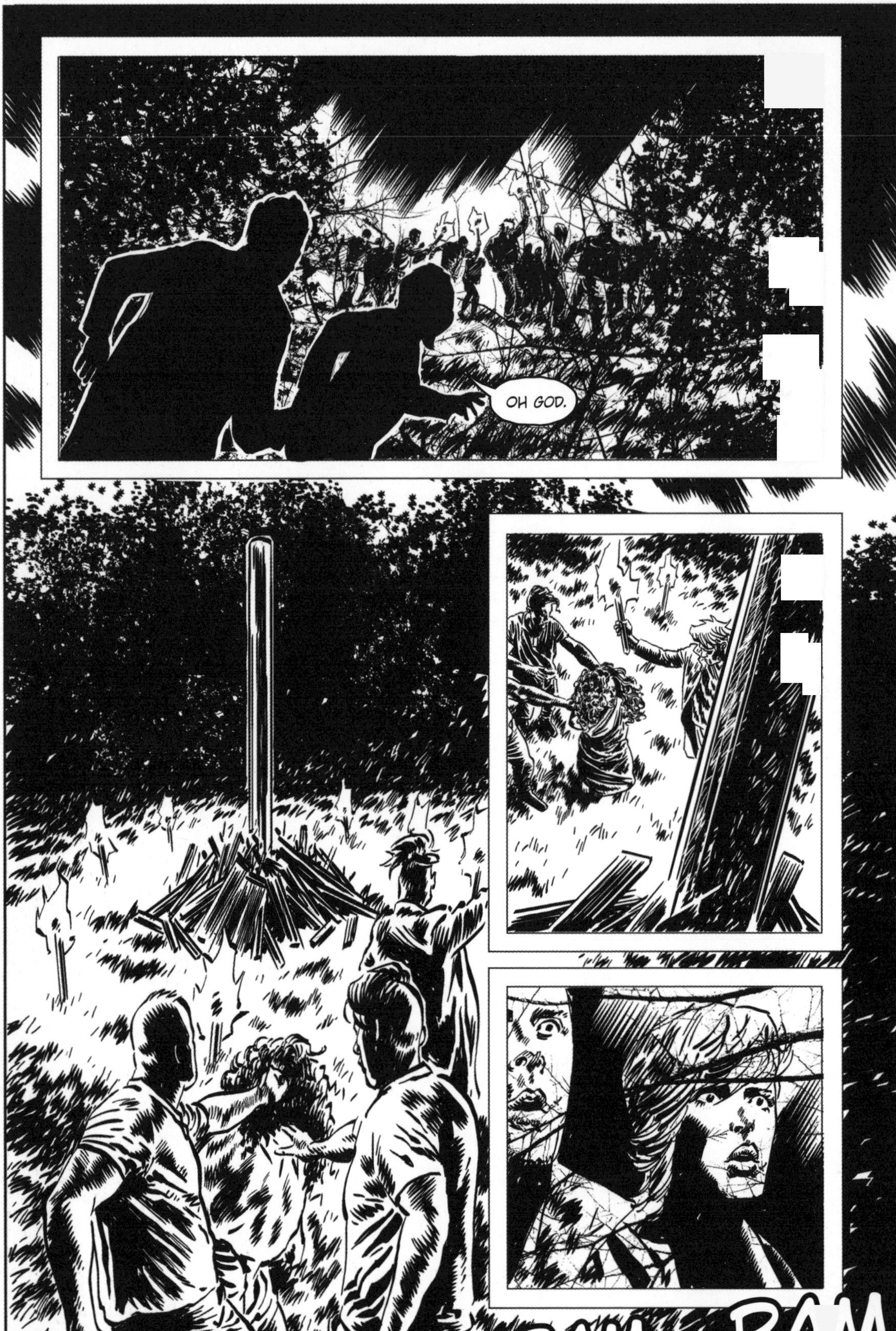
OH GOD.
BAM BAM

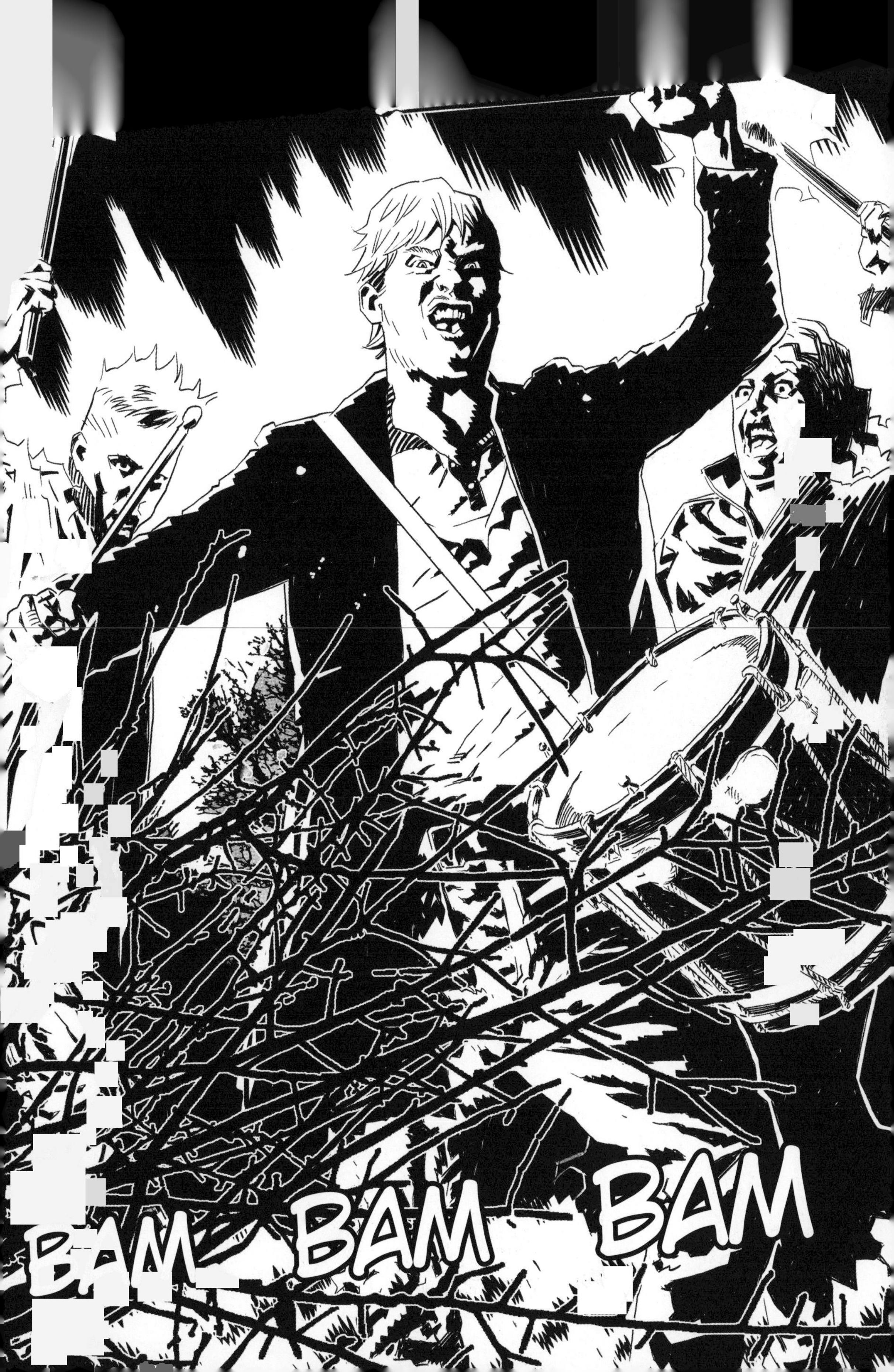
BAM BAM BAM

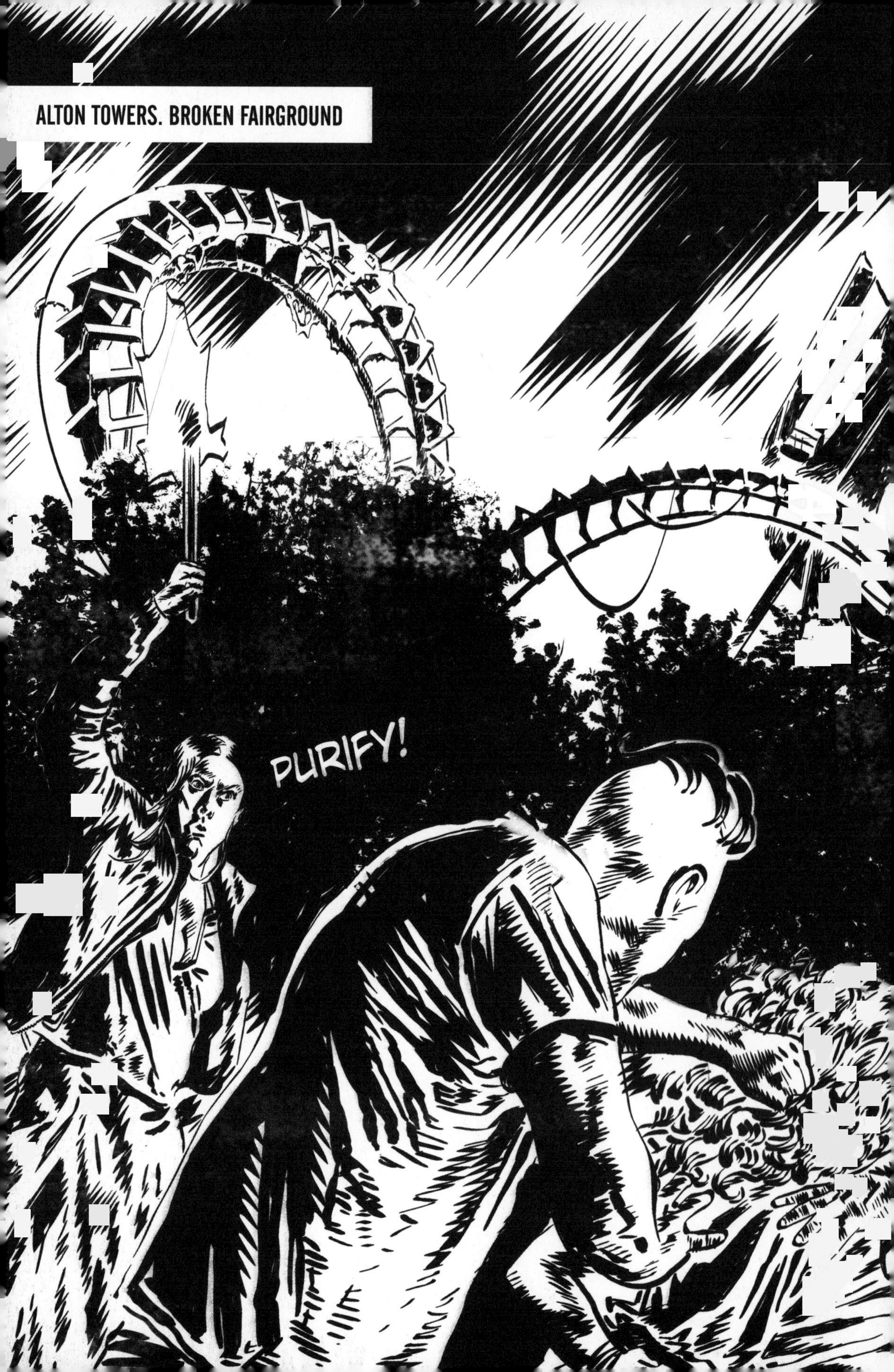
ALTON TOWERS. BROKEN FAIRGROUND
PURIFY!

Lesson Five

I thirst!

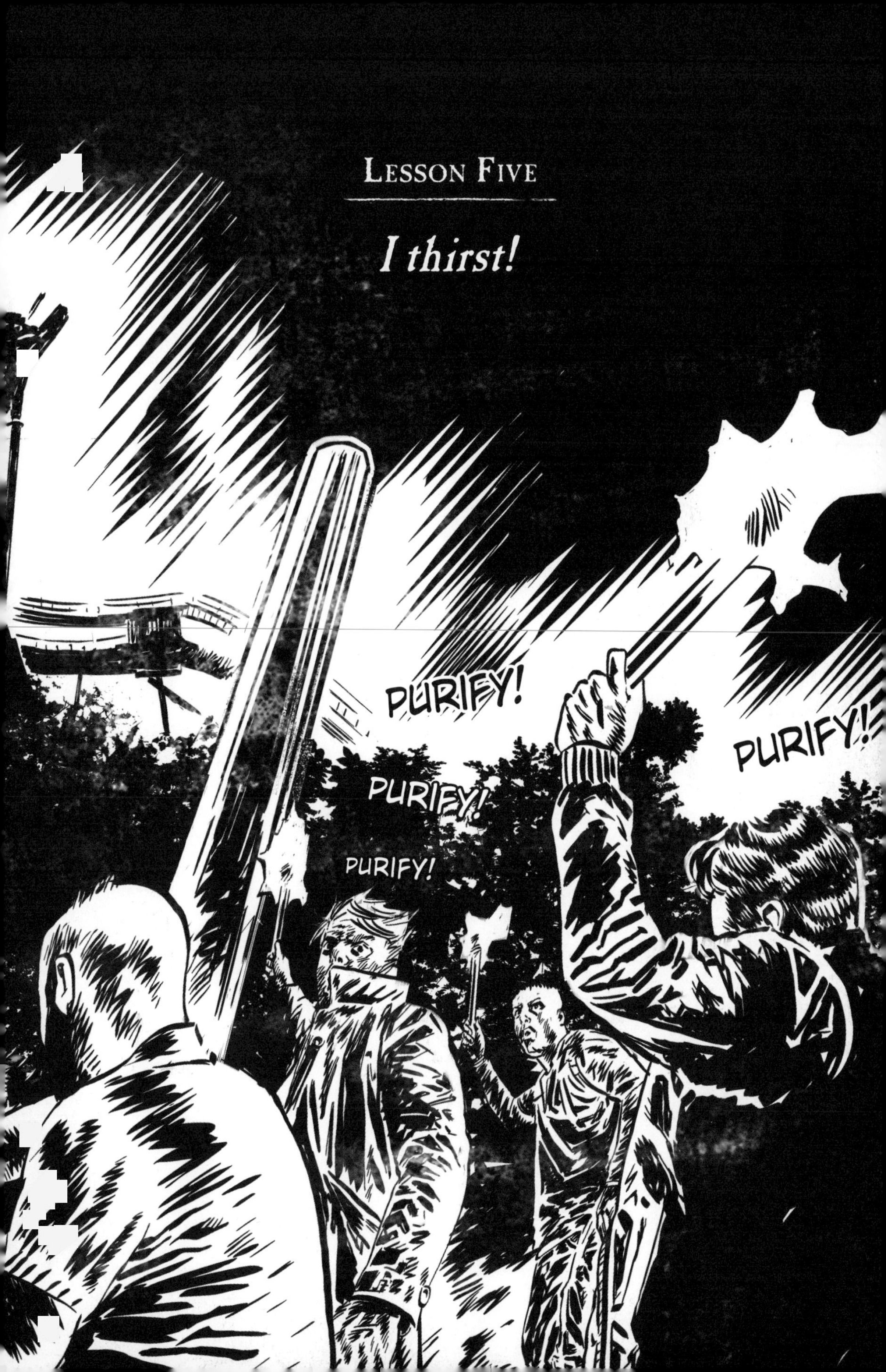
PURIFY!
PURIFY!
PURIFY!
PURIFY!

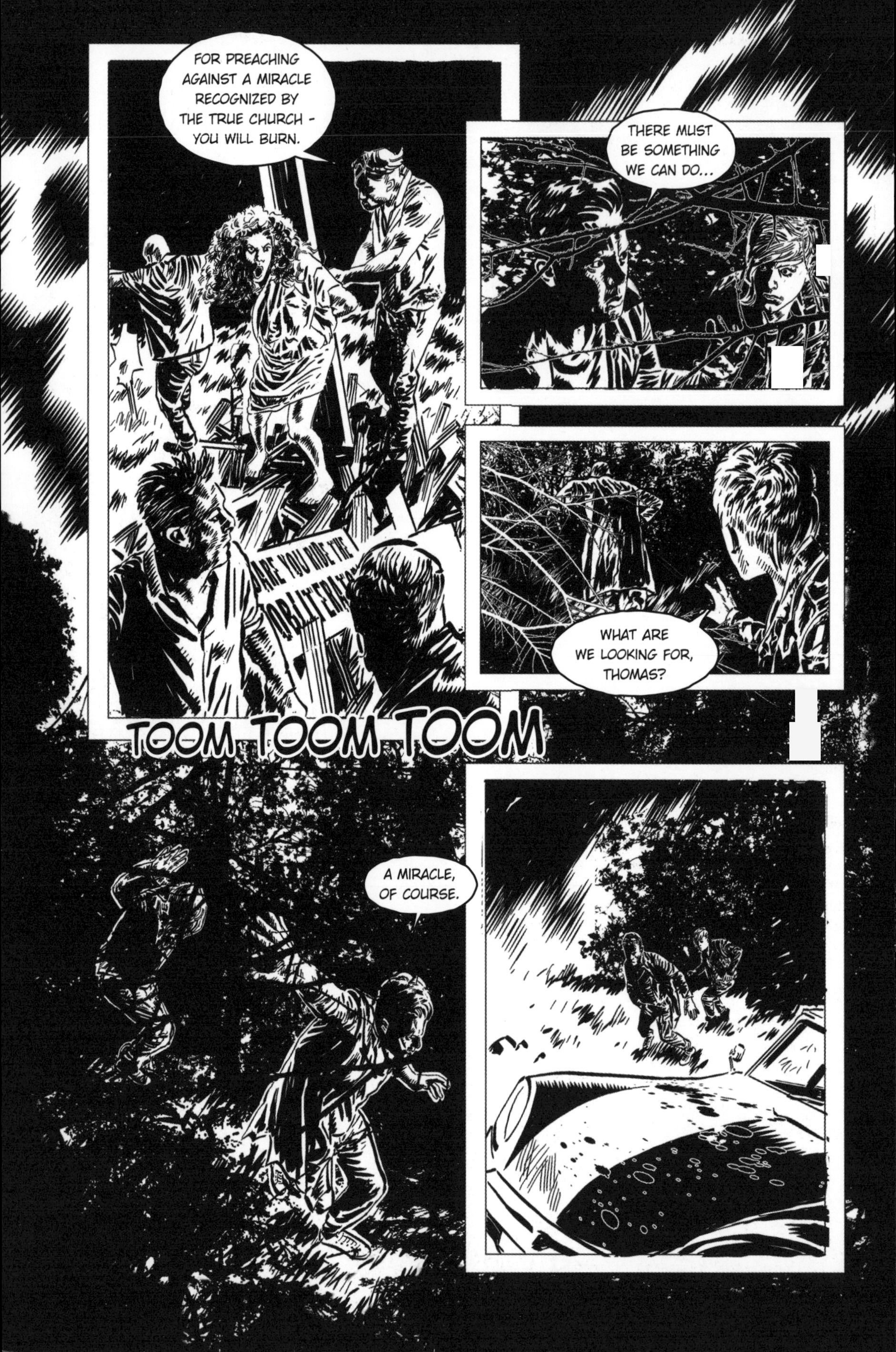
FOR PREACHING AGAINST A MIRACLE RECOGNIZED BY THE TRUE CHURCH - YOU WILL BURN.
THERE MUST BE SOMETHING WE CAN DO...
WHAT ARE WE LOOKING FOR, THOMAS?
TOOM TOOM TOOM
A MIRACLE, OF COURSE.

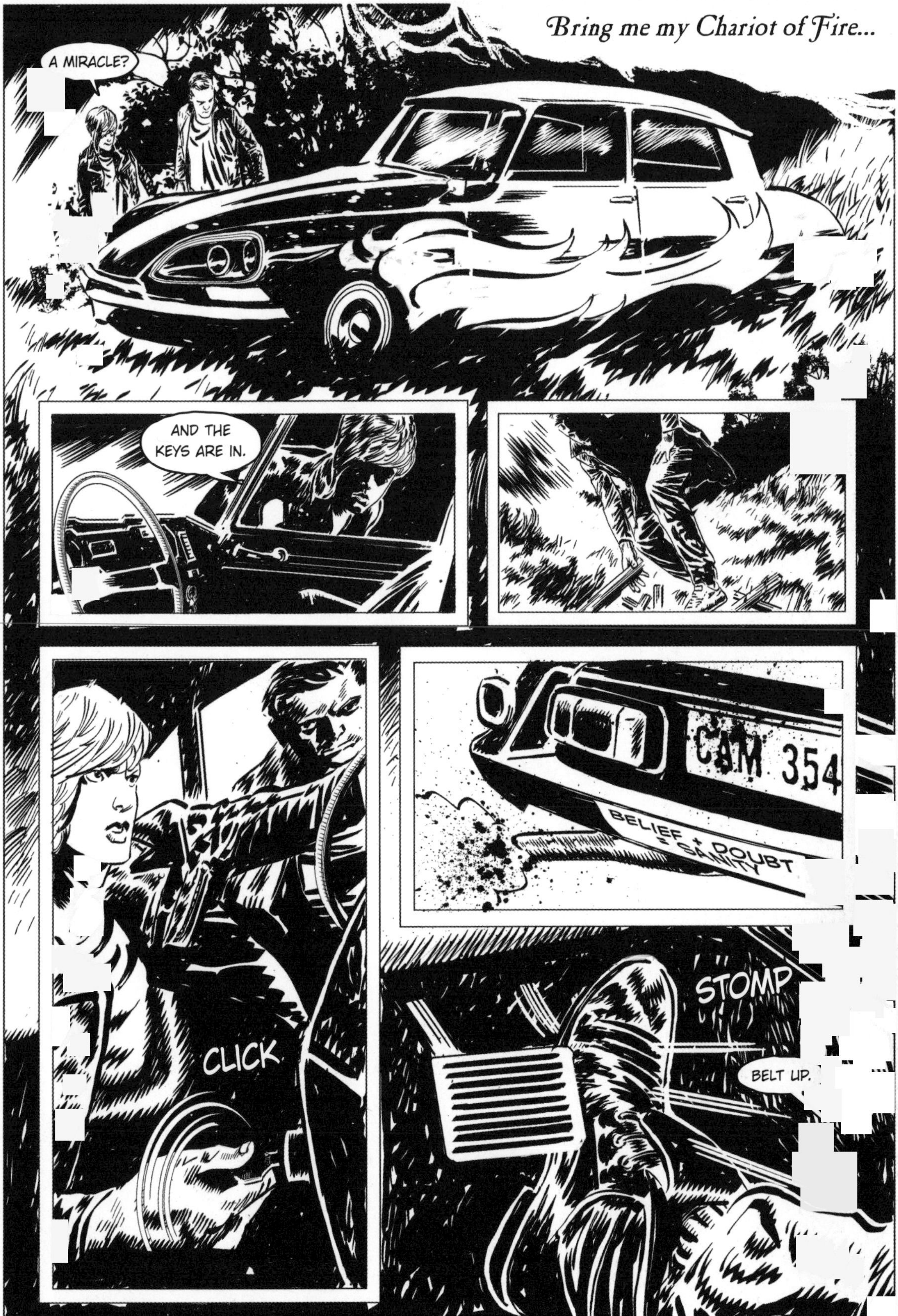
Bring me my Chariot of Fire...
A MIRACLE?
AND THE KEYS ARE IN.
CAM 354
BELIEF + DOUBT = SANITY
CLICK
STOMP
BELT UP.

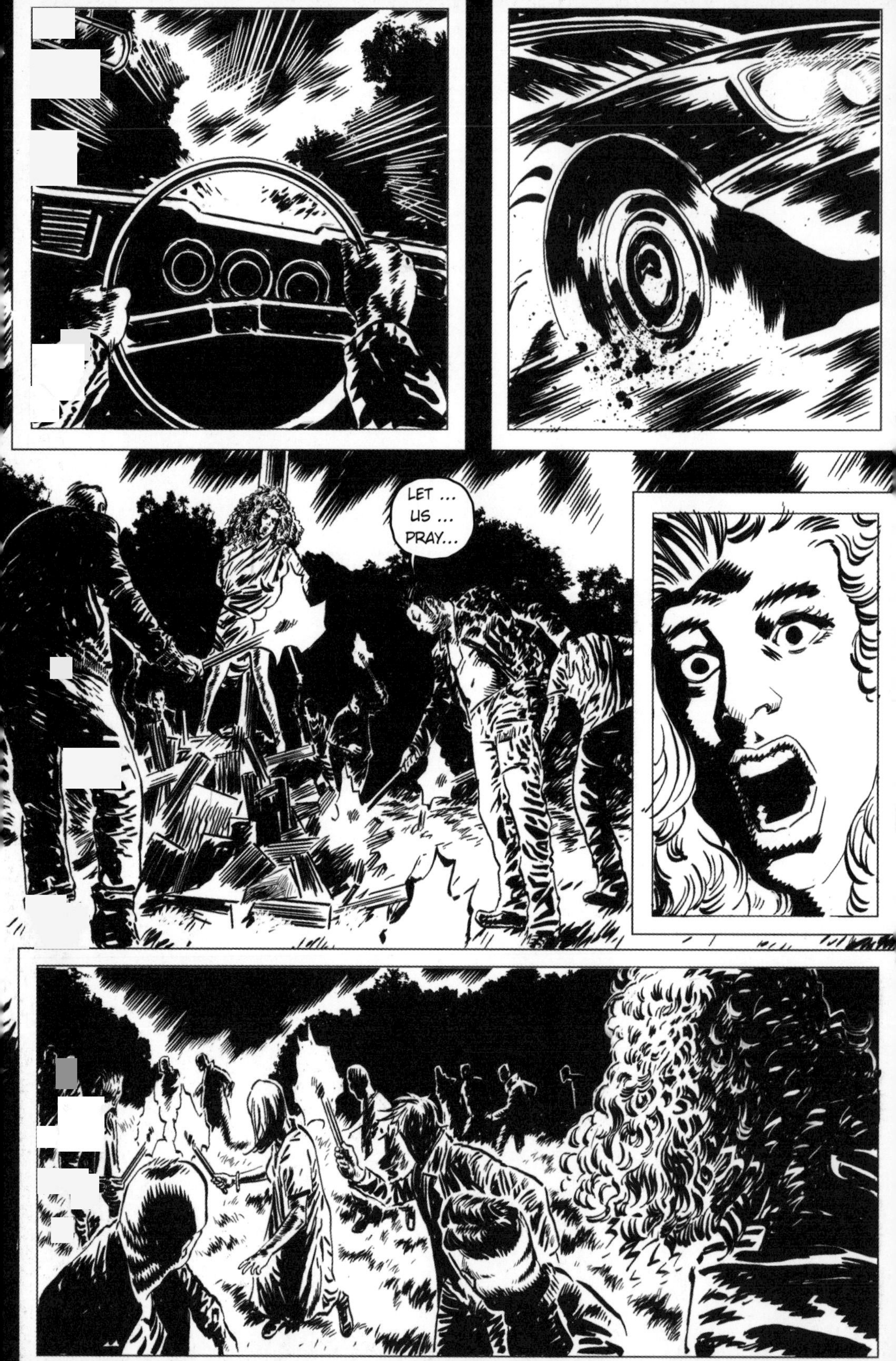
LET ... US ... PRAY...

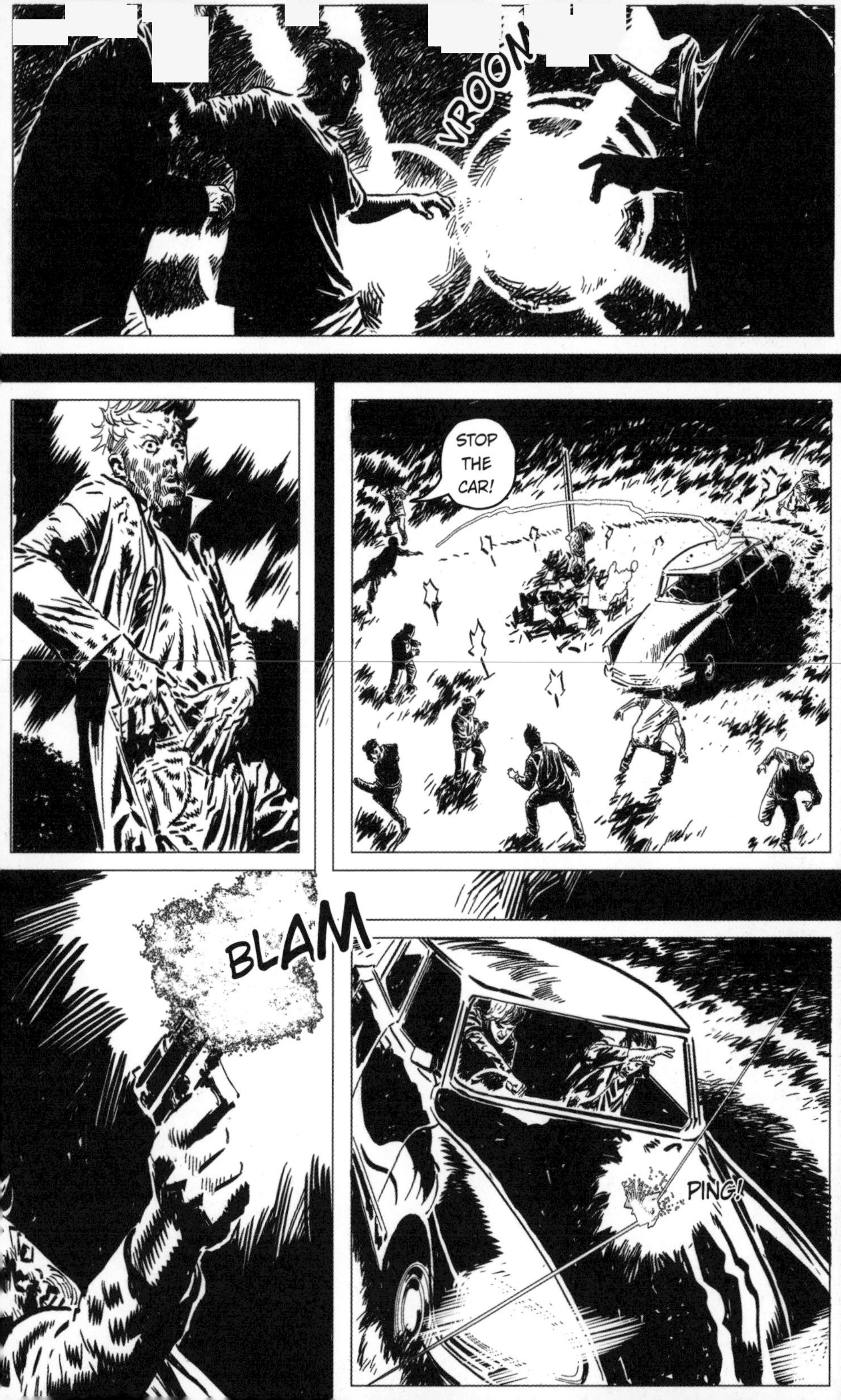
STOP THE CAR!
BLAM
PING!

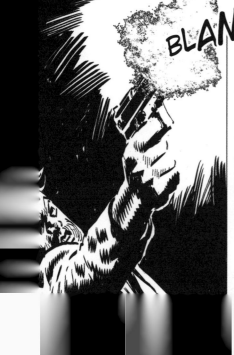

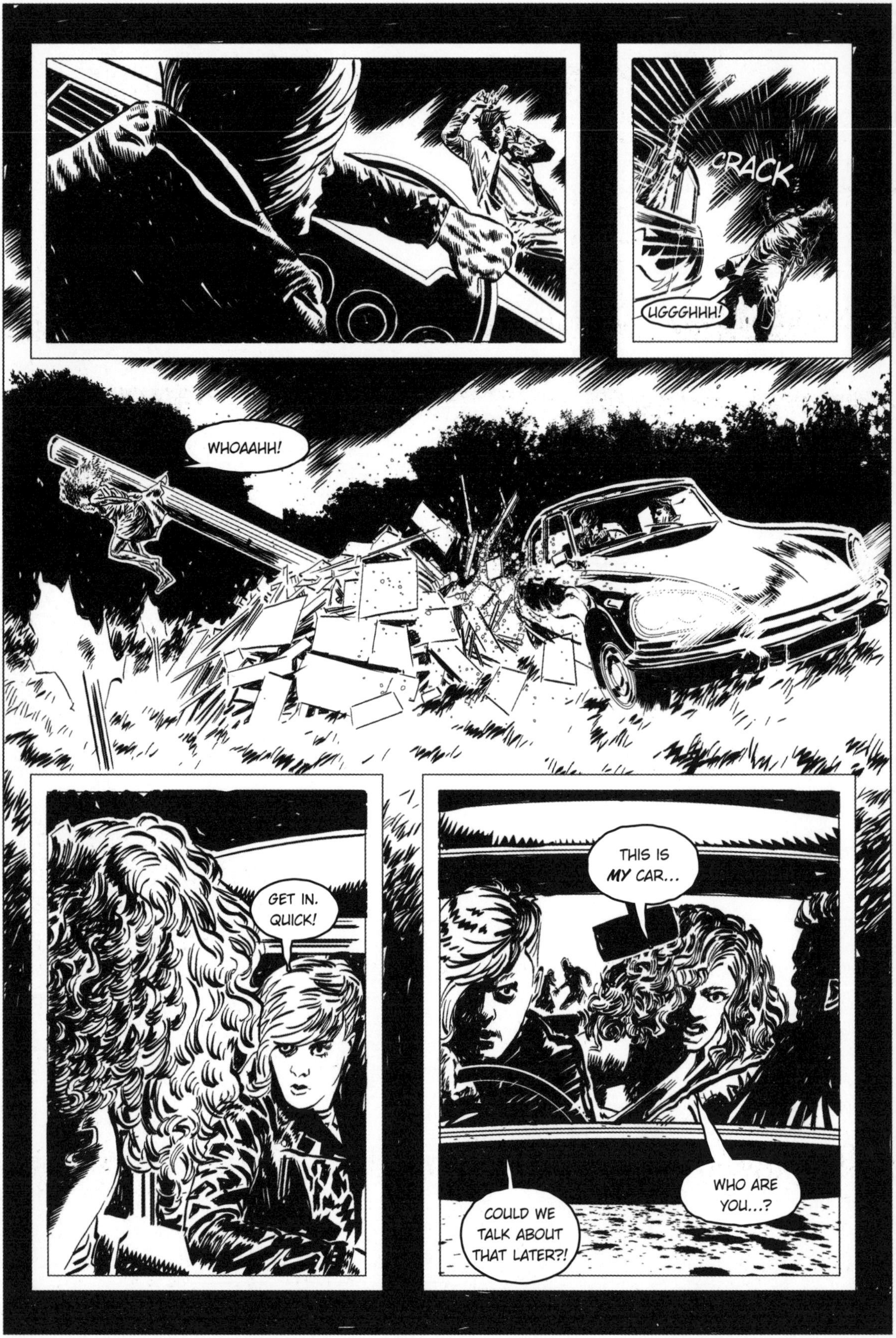
CRACK
UGGGHHH!
WHOAAHH!
GET IN. QUICK!
THIS IS MY CAR...
WHO ARE YOU...?
COULD WE TALK ABOUT THAT LATER?!

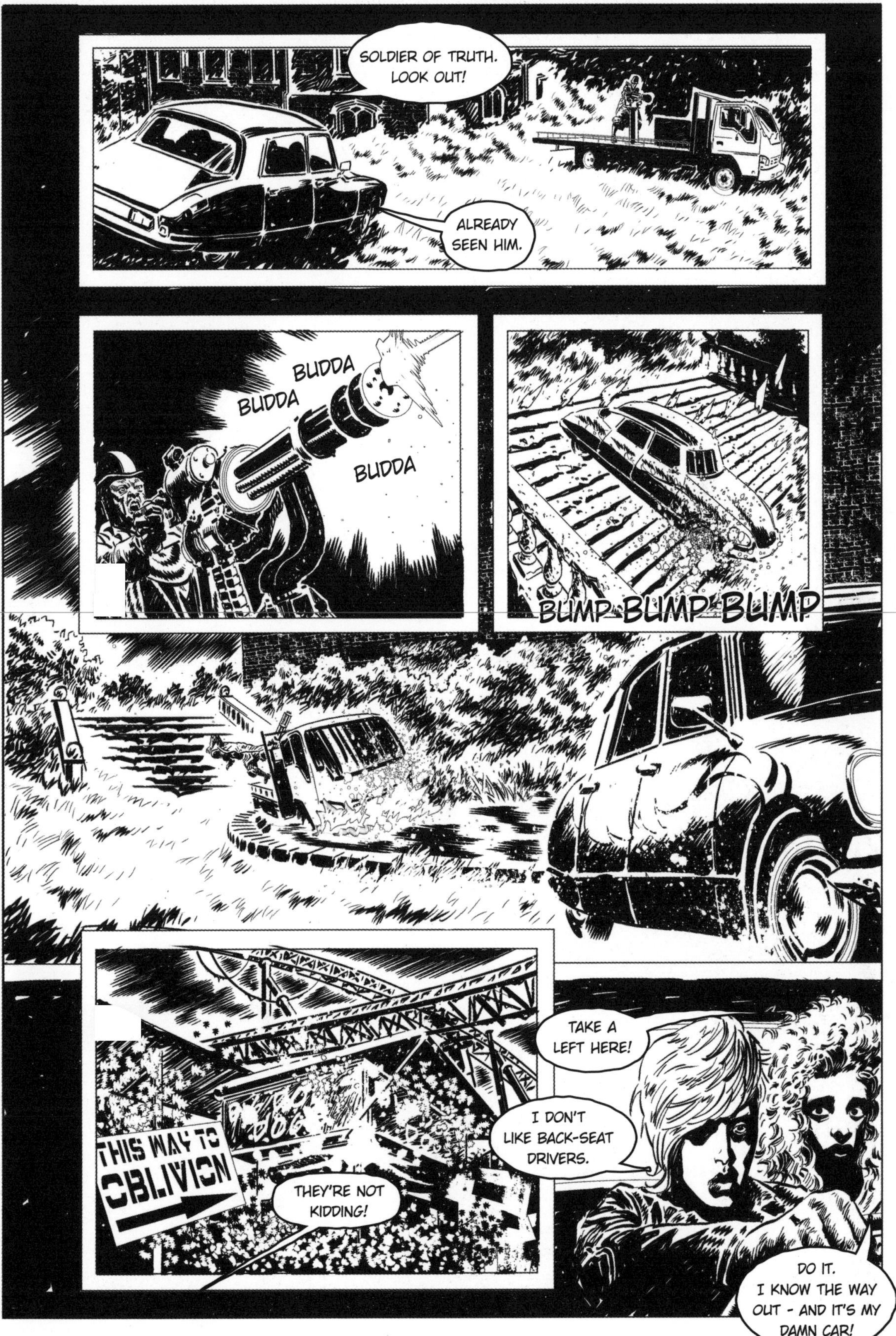
SOLDIER OF TRUTH. LOOK OUT!
ALREADY SEEN HIM.
BUDDA
BUDDA
BUDDA
BUMP BUMP BUMP
THIS WAY TO OBLIVION
THEY'RE NOT KIDDING!
TAKE A LEFT HERE!
I DON'T LIKE BACK-SEAT DRIVERS.
DO IT. I KNOW THE WAY OUT - AND IT'S MY DAMN CAR!

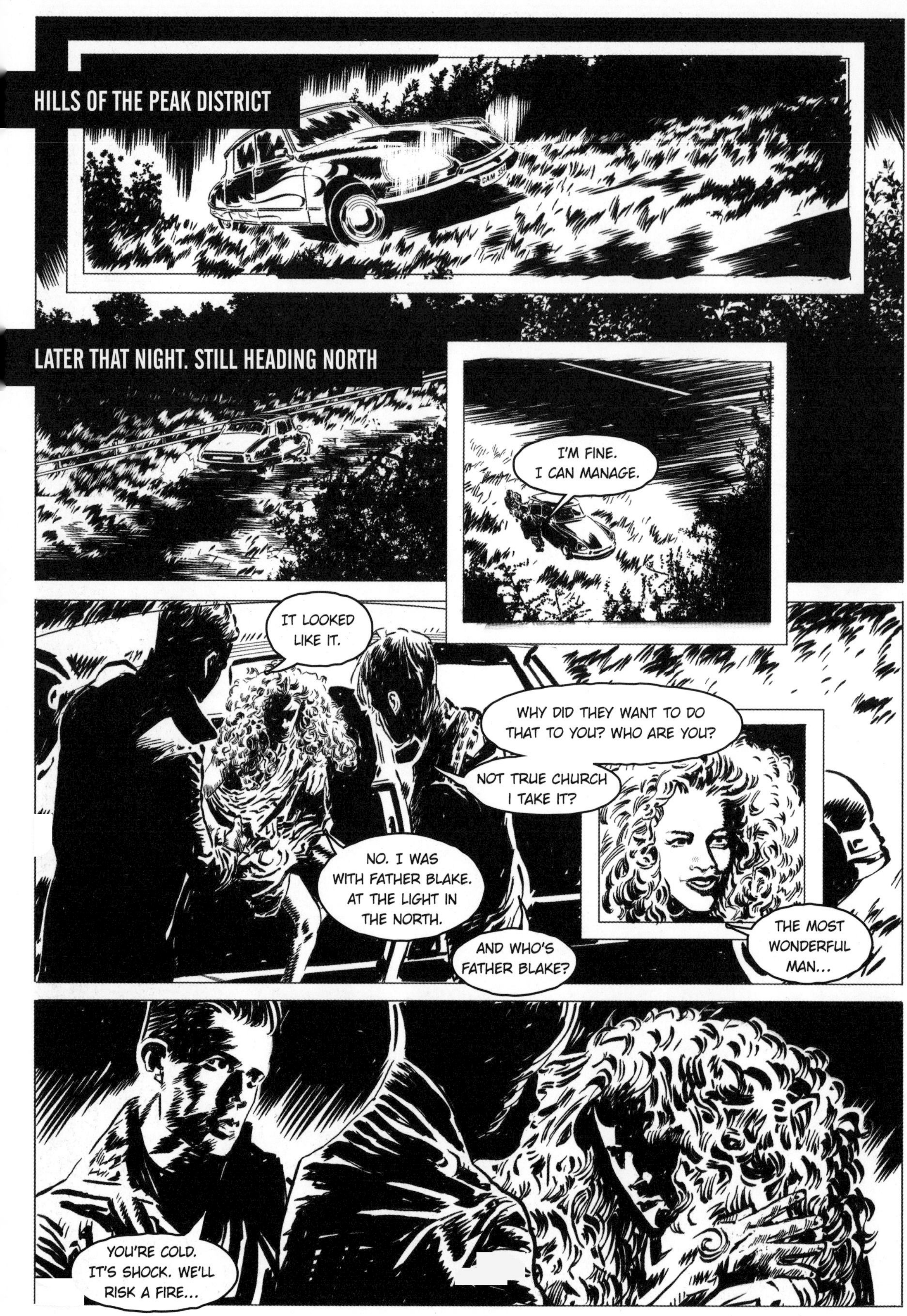
HILLS OF THE PEAK DISTRICT
CAM 354
LATER THAT NIGHT. STILL HEADING NORTH
I'M FINE. I CAN MANAGE.
IT LOOKED LIKE IT.
WHY DID THEY WANT TO DO THAT TO YOU? WHO ARE YOU?
NOT TRUE CHURCH I TAKE IT?
NO. I WAS WITH FATHER BLAKE. AT THE LIGHT IN THE NORTH.
AND WHO'S FATHER BLAKE?
THE MOST WONDERFUL MAN...
YOU'RE COLD. IT'S SHOCK. WE'LL RISK A FIRE...

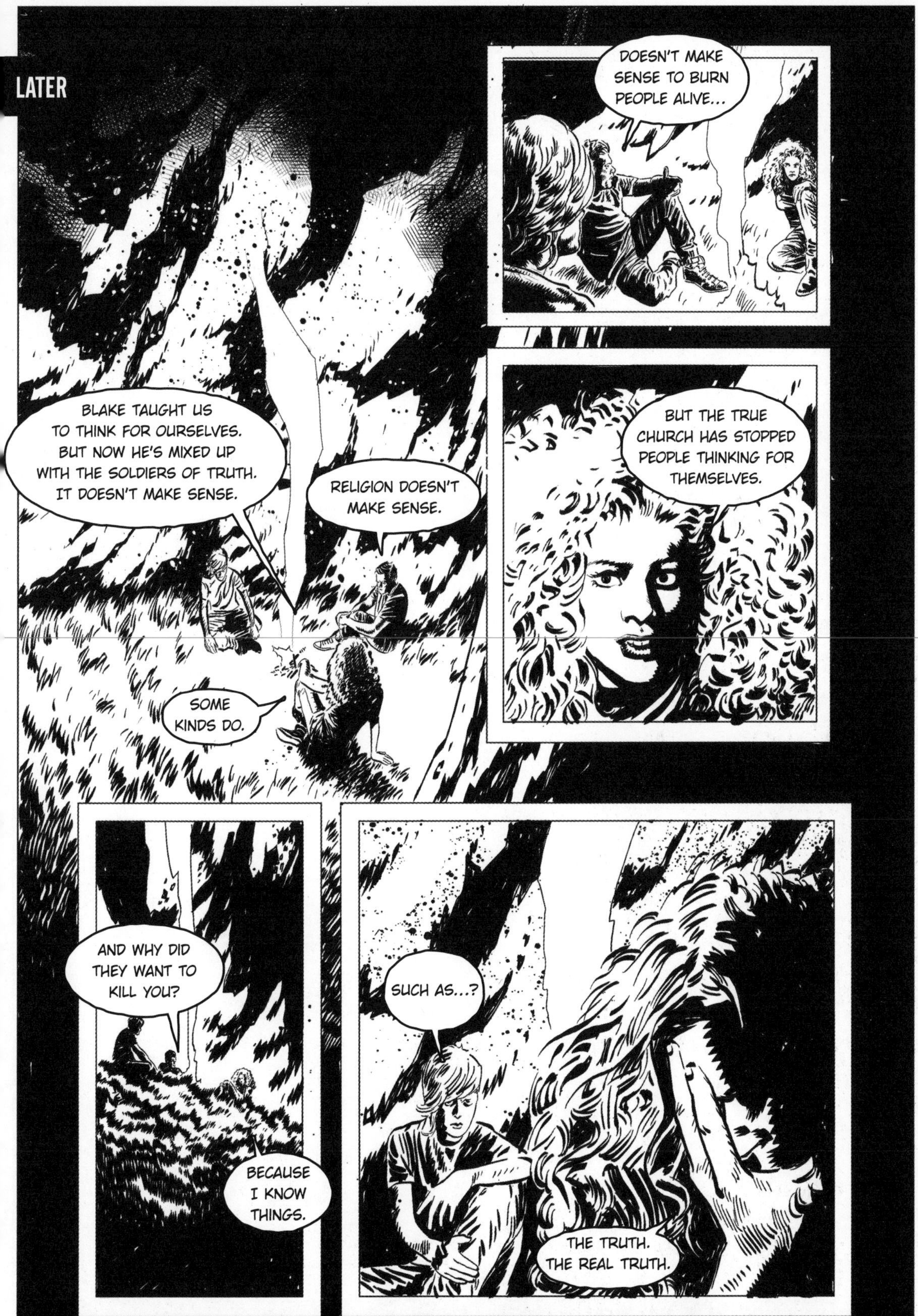
LATER
DOESN'T MAKE SENSE TO BURN PEOPLE ALIVE...
BLAKE TAUGHT US TO THINK FOR OURSELVES. BUT NOW HE'S MIXED UP WITH THE SOLDIERS OF TRUTH. IT DOESN'T MAKE SENSE.
RELIGION DOESN'T MAKE SENSE.
SOME KINDS DO.
BUT THE TRUE CHURCH HAS STOPPED PEOPLE THINKING FOR THEMSELVES.
AND WHY DID THEY WANT TO KILL YOU?
BECAUSE I KNOW THINGS.
SUCH AS...?
THE TRUTH. THE REAL TRUTH.

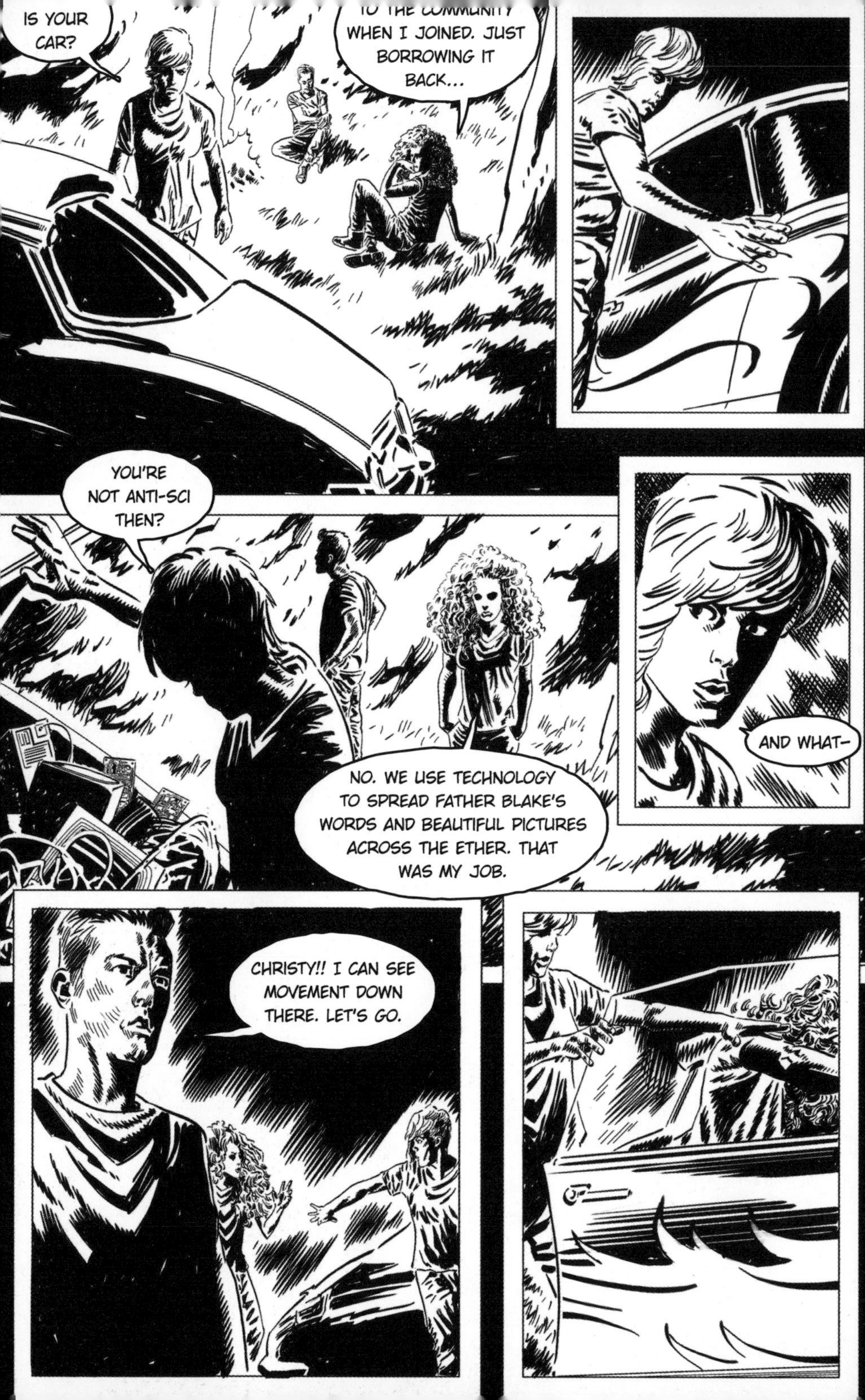
IS YOUR CAR?
TO THE COMMUNITY WHEN I JOINED. JUST BORROWING IT BACK...
YOU'RE NOT ANTI-SCI THEN?
AND WHAT-
NO. WE USE TECHNOLOGY TO SPREAD FATHER BLAKE'S WORDS AND BEAUTIFUL PICTURES ACROSS THE ETHER. THAT WAS MY JOB.
CHRISTY!! I CAN SEE MOVEMENT DOWN THERE. LET'S GO.

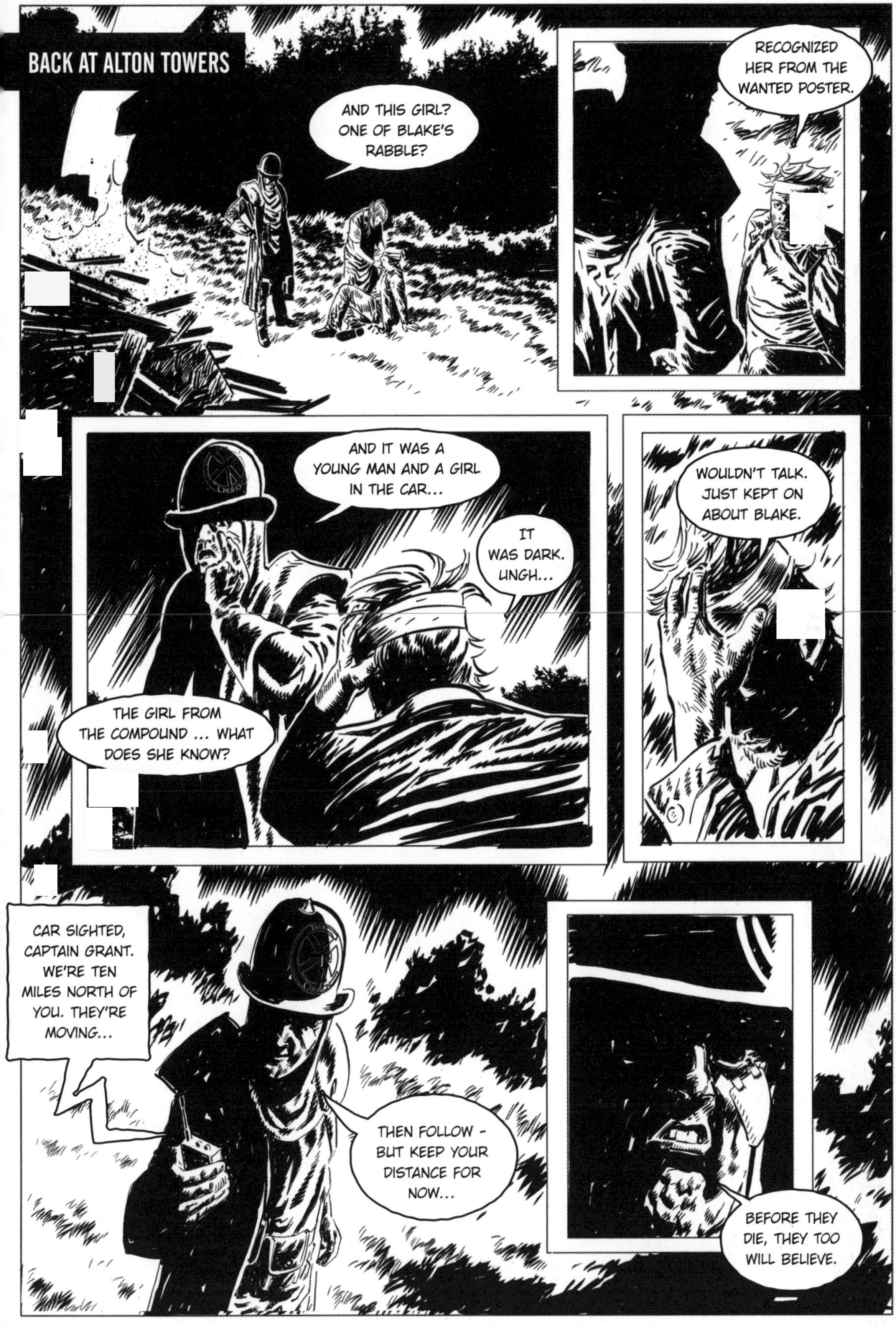
BACK AT ALTON TOWERS
AND THIS GIRL? ONE OF BLAKE'S RABBLE?
RECOGNIZED HER FROM THE WANTED POSTER.
AND IT WAS A YOUNG MAN AND A GIRL IN THE CAR...
IT WAS DARK. UNGH...
THE GIRL FROM THE COMPOUND ... WHAT DOES SHE KNOW?
WOULDN'T TALK. JUST KEPT ON ABOUT BLAKE.
CAR SIGHTED, CAPTAIN GRANT. WE'RE TEN MILES NORTH OF YOU. THEY'RE MOVING...
THEN FOLLOW - BUT KEEP YOUR DISTANCE FOR NOW...
BEFORE THEY DIE, THEY TOO WILL BELIEVE.

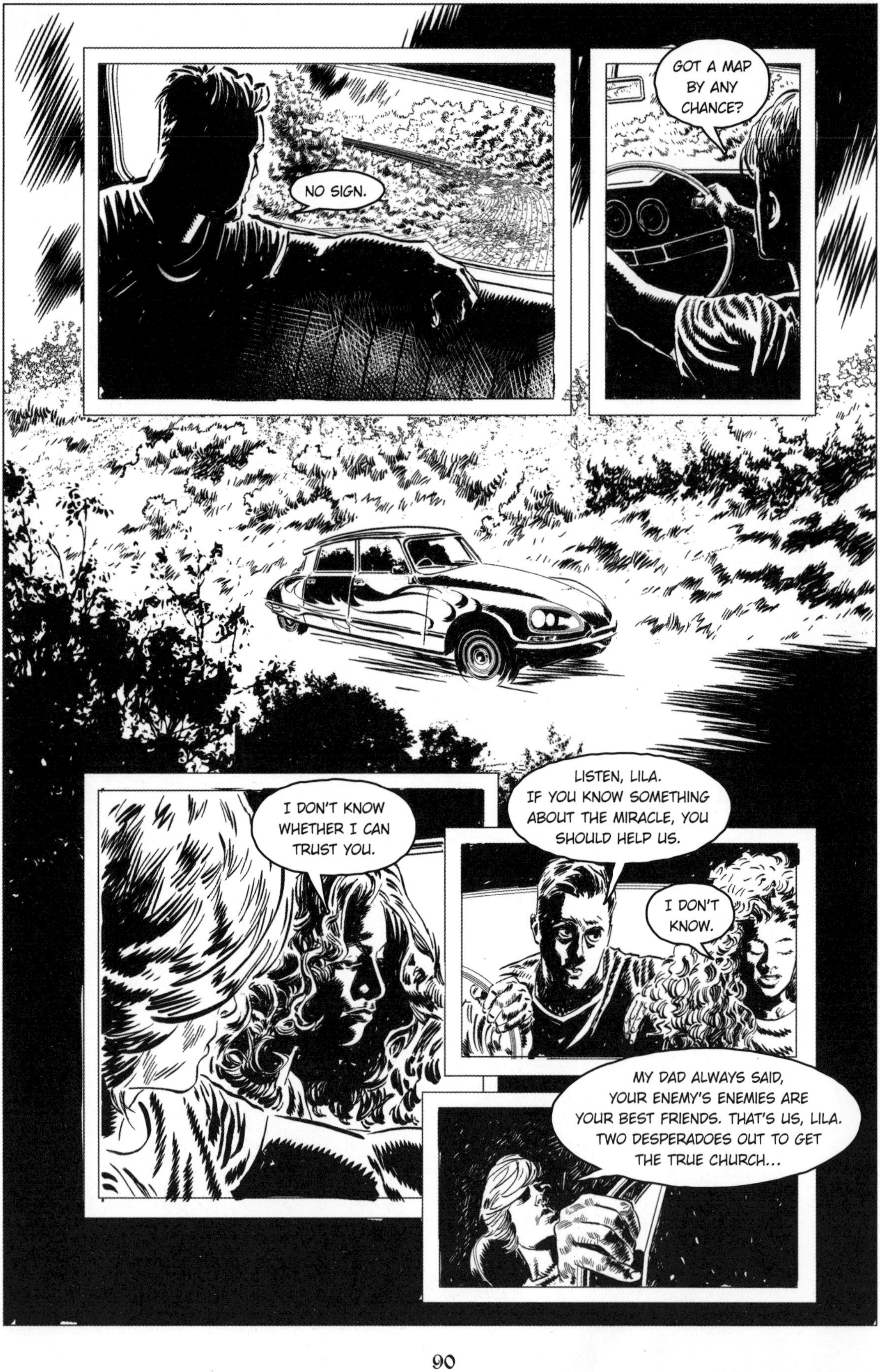
NO SIGN.
GOT A MAP BY ANY CHANCE?
I DON'T KNOW WHETHER I CAN TRUST YOU.
LISTEN, LILA. IF YOU KNOW SOMETHING ABOUT THE MIRACLE, YOU SHOULD HELP US.
I DON'T KNOW.
MY DAD ALWAYS SAID, YOUR ENEMY'S ENEMIES ARE YOUR BEST FRIENDS. THAT'S US, LILA. TWO DESPERADOES OUT TO GET THE TRUE CHURCH...

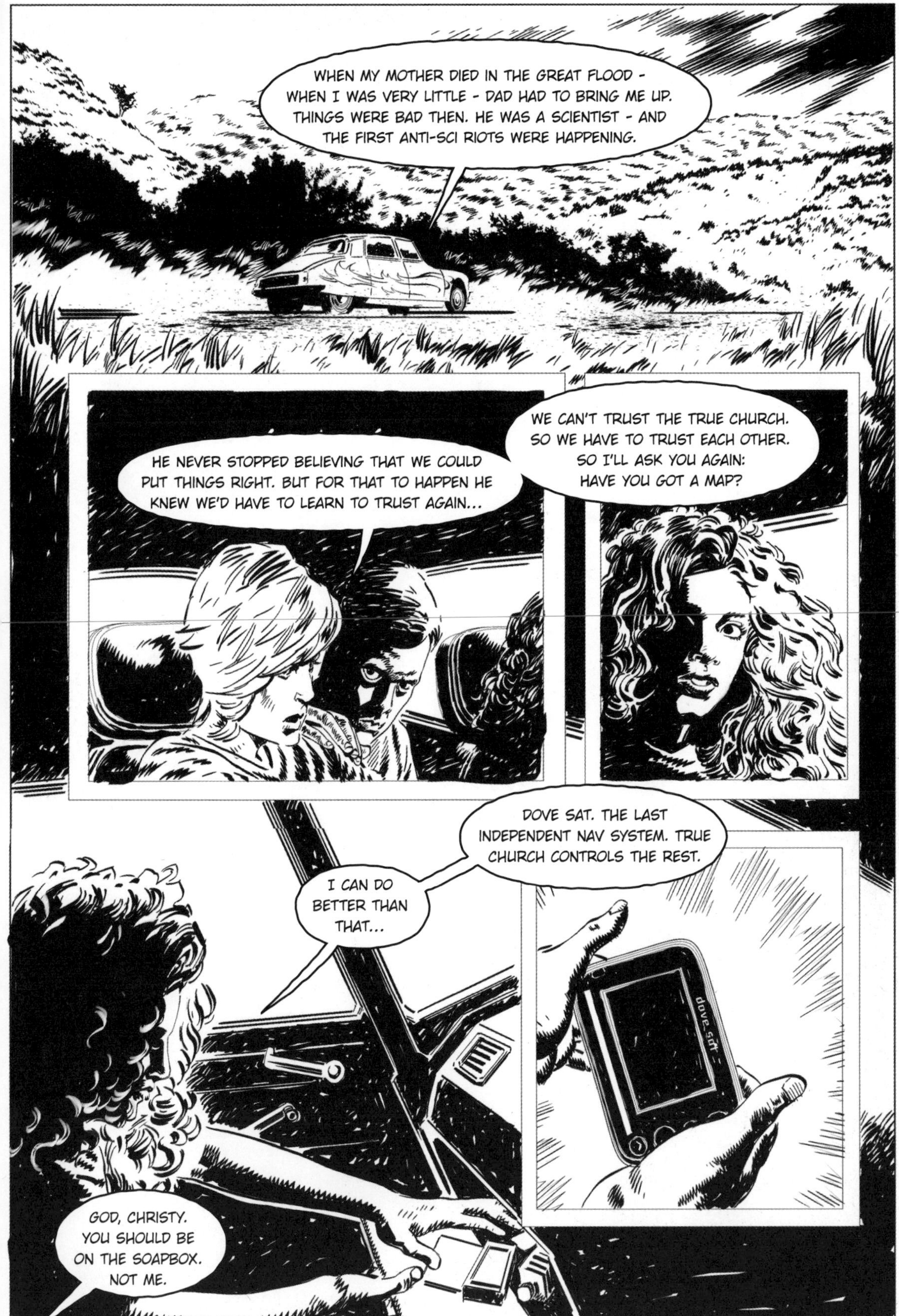
WHEN MY MOTHER DIED IN THE GREAT FLOOD - WHEN I WAS VERY LITTLE - DAD HAD TO BRING ME UP. THINGS WERE BAD THEN. HE WAS A SCIENTIST - AND THE FIRST ANTI-SCI RIOTS WERE HAPPENING.
HE NEVER STOPPED BELIEVING THAT WE COULD PUT THINGS RIGHT. BUT FOR THAT TO HAPPEN HE KNEW WE'D HAVE TO LEARN TO TRUST AGAIN...
WE CAN'T TRUST THE TRUE CHURCH. SO WE HAVE TO TRUST EACH OTHER. SO I'LL ASK YOU AGAIN: HAVE YOU GOT A MAP?
I CAN DO BETTER THAN THAT...
DOVE SAT. THE LAST INDEPENDENT NAV SYSTEM. TRUE CHURCH CONTROLS THE REST.
dove_sat
GOD, CHRISTY. YOU SHOULD BE ON THE SOAPBOX. NOT ME.

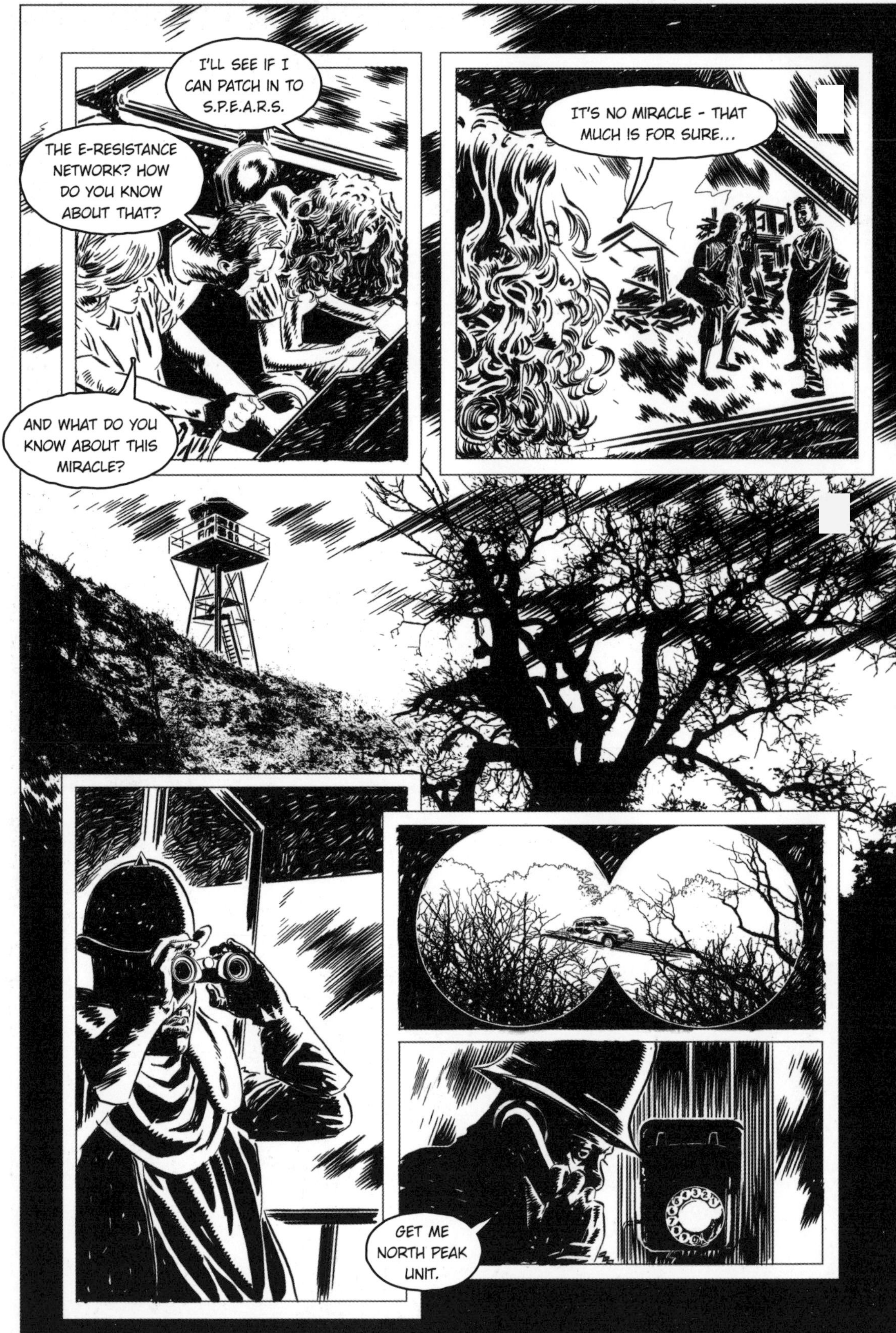
I'LL SEE IF I CAN PATCH IN TO S.P.E.A.R.S.
THE E-RESISTANCE NETWORK? HOW DO YOU KNOW ABOUT THAT?
AND WHAT DO YOU KNOW ABOUT THIS MIRACLE?
IT'S NO MIRACLE - THAT MUCH IS FOR SURE...
GET ME NORTH PEAK UNIT.

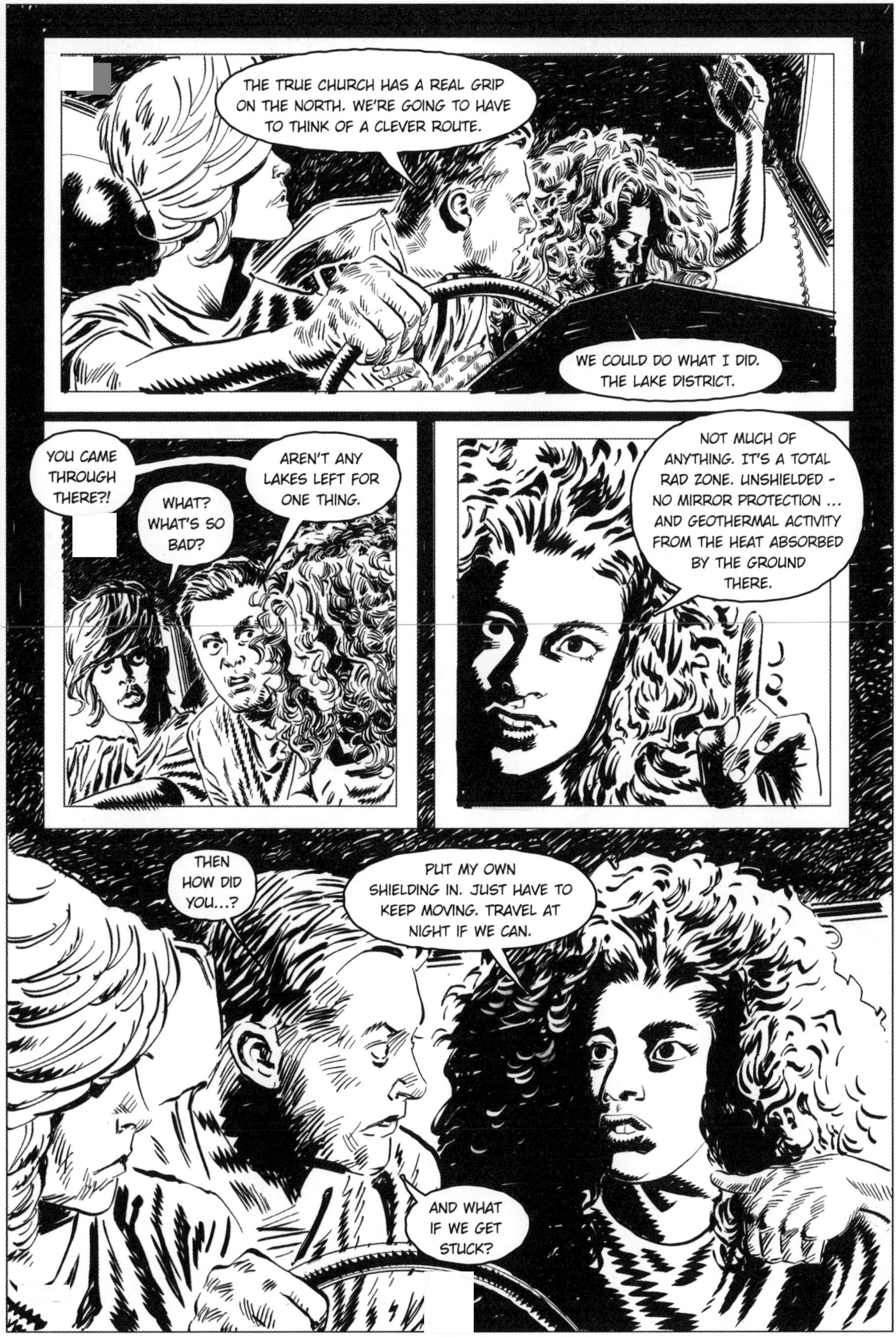
THE TRUE CHURCH HAS A REAL GRIP ON THE NORTH. WE'RE GOING TO HAVE TO THINK OF A CLEVER ROUTE.
WE COULD DO WHAT I DID. THE LAKE DISTRICT.
YOU CAME THROUGH THERE?!
AREN'T ANY LAKES LEFT FOR ONE THING.
WHAT? WHAT'S SO BAD?
NOT MUCH OF ANYTHING. IT'S A TOTAL RAD ZONE. UNSHIELDED - NO MIRROR PROTECTION ... AND GEOTHERMAL ACTIVITY FROM THE HEAT ABSORBED BY THE GROUND THERE.
THEN HOW DID YOU...?
PUT MY OWN SHIELDING IN. JUST HAVE TO KEEP MOVING. TRAVEL AT NIGHT IF WE CAN.
AND WHAT IF WE GET STUCK?

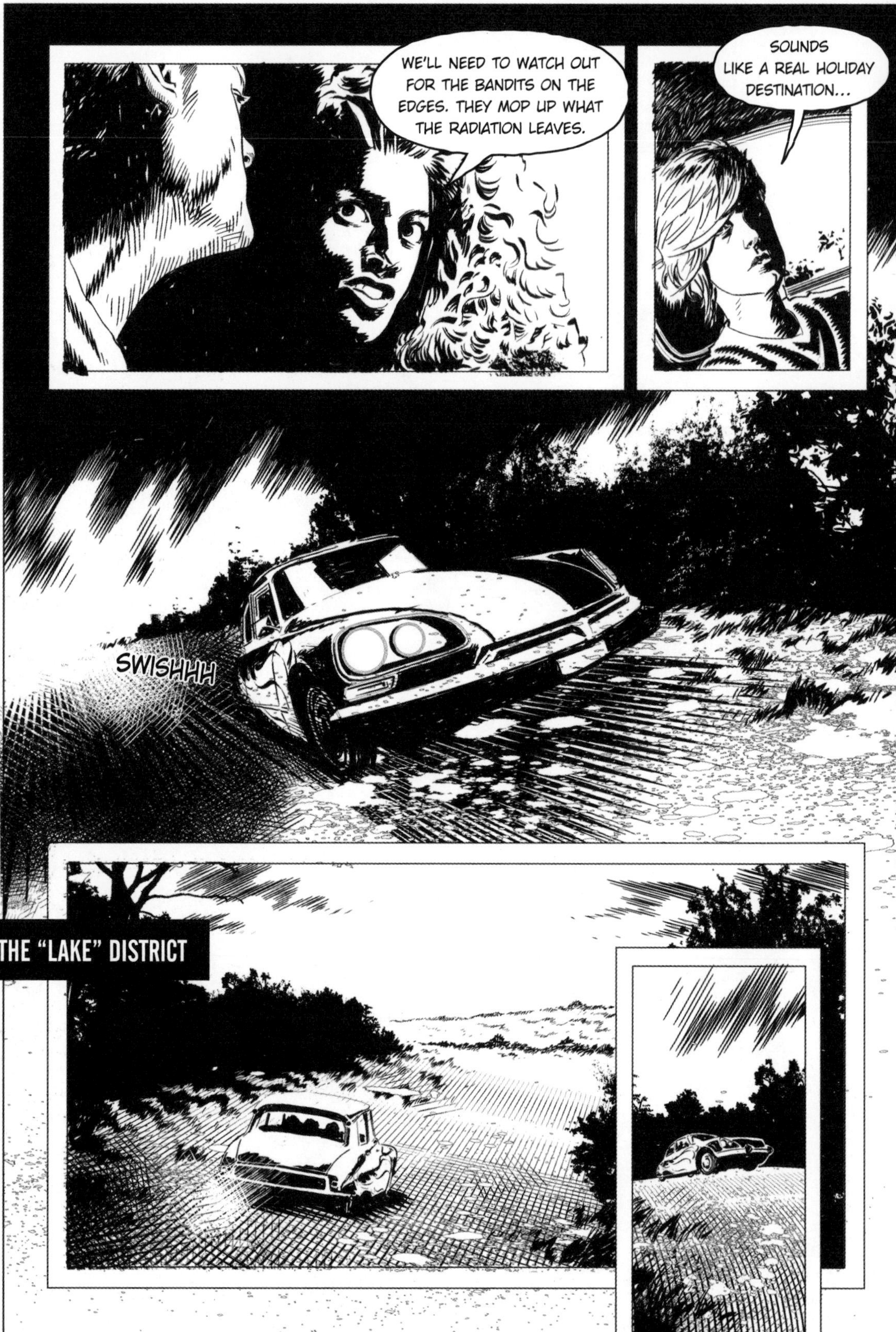
WE'LL NEED TO WATCH OUT FOR THE BANDITS ON THE EDGES. THEY MOP UP WHAT THE RADIATION LEAVES.
SOUNDS LIKE A REAL HOLIDAY DESTINATION...
SWISHHH
THE "LAKE" DISTRICT

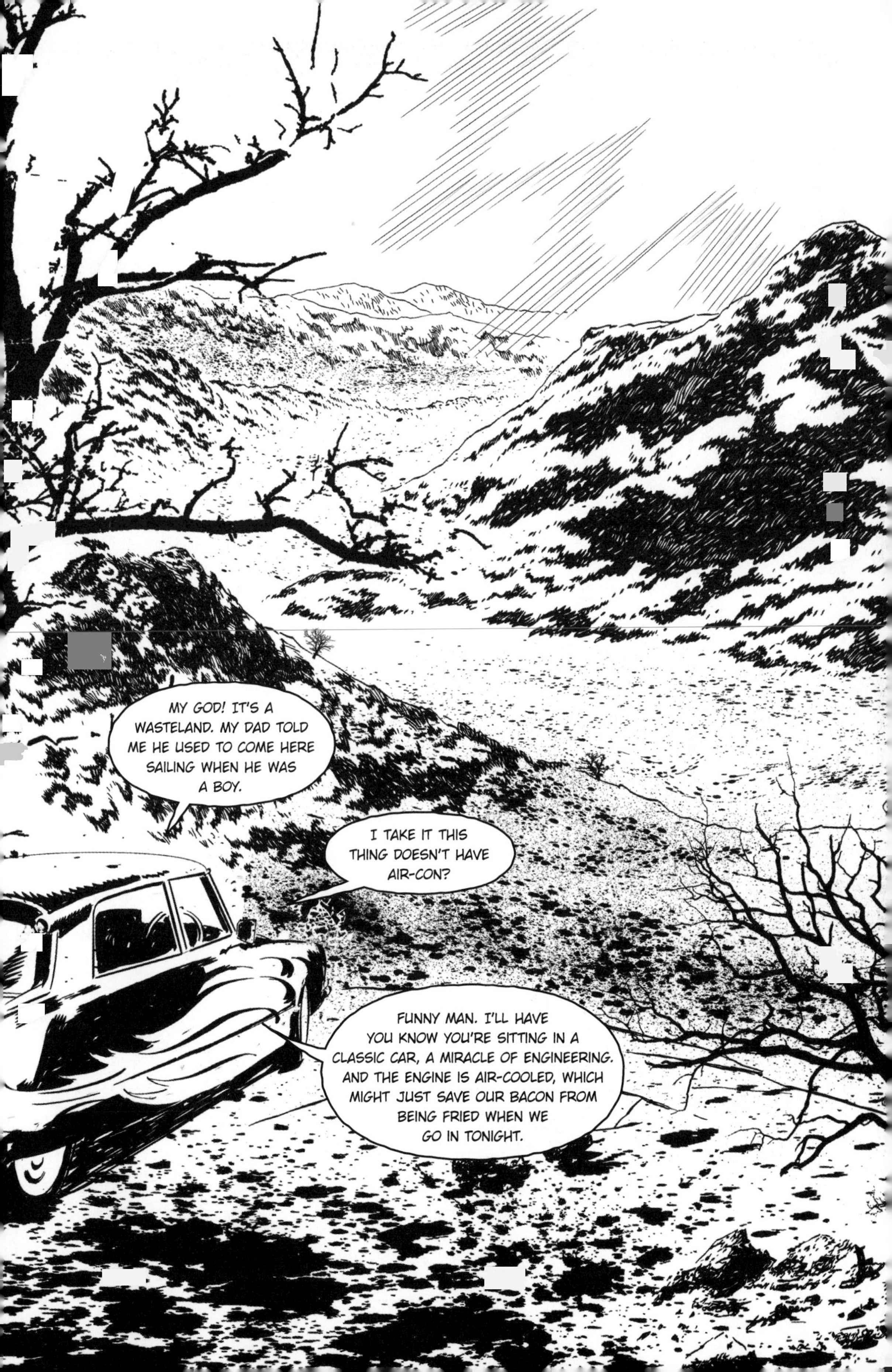
MY GOD! IT'S A WASTELAND. MY DAD TOLD ME HE USED TO COME HERE SAILING WHEN HE WAS A BOY.
I TAKE IT THIS THING DOESN'T HAVE AIR-CON?
FUNNY MAN. I'LL HAVE YOU KNOW YOU'RE SITTING IN A CLASSIC CAR, A MIRACLE OF ENGINEERING. AND THE ENGINE IS AIR-COOLED, WHICH MIGHT JUST SAVE OUR BACON FROM BEING FRIED WHEN WE GO IN TONIGHT.

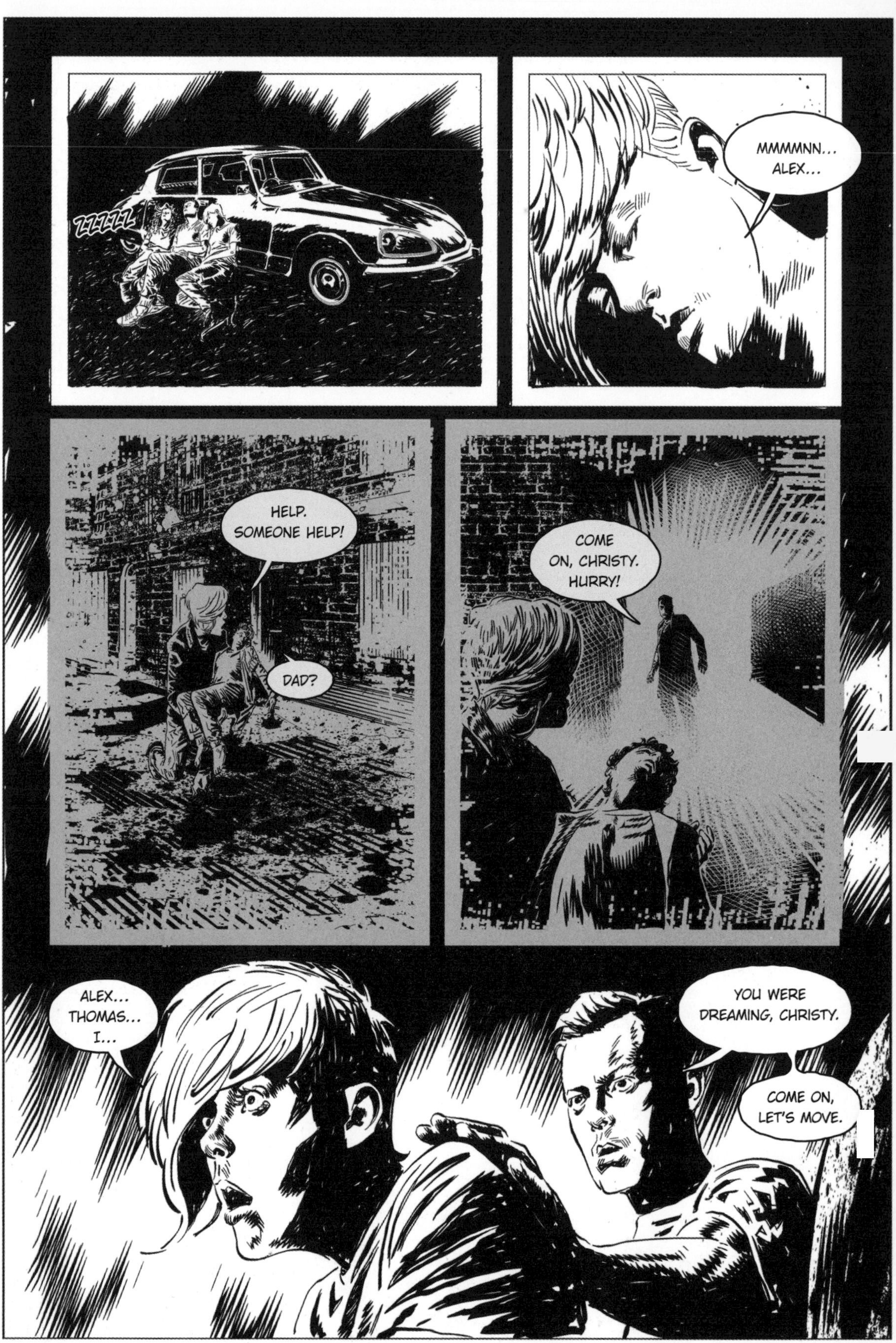
ZZZZZ
MMMMNN... ALEX...
HELP. SOMEONE HELP!
DAD?
COME ON, CHRISTY. HURRY!
ALEX... THOMAS... I...
YOU WERE DREAMING, CHRISTY.
COME ON, LET'S MOVE.

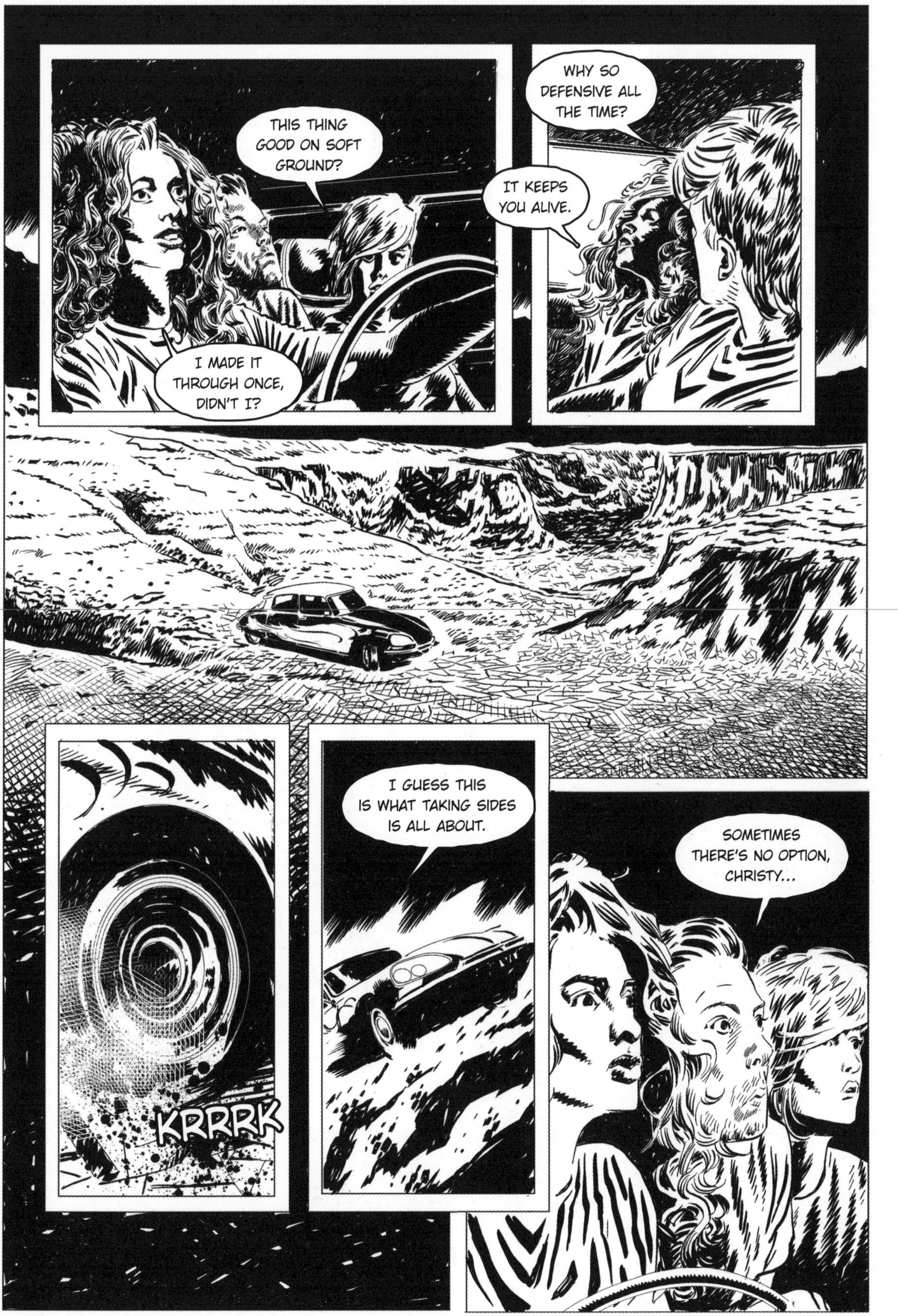
THIS THING GOOD ON SOFT GROUND?
I MADE IT THROUGH ONCE, DIDN'T I?
WHY SO DEFENSIVE ALL THE TIME?
IT KEEPS YOU ALIVE.
KRRRK
I GUESS THIS IS WHAT TAKING SIDES IS ALL ABOUT.
SOMETIMES THERE'S NO OPTION, CHRISTY...

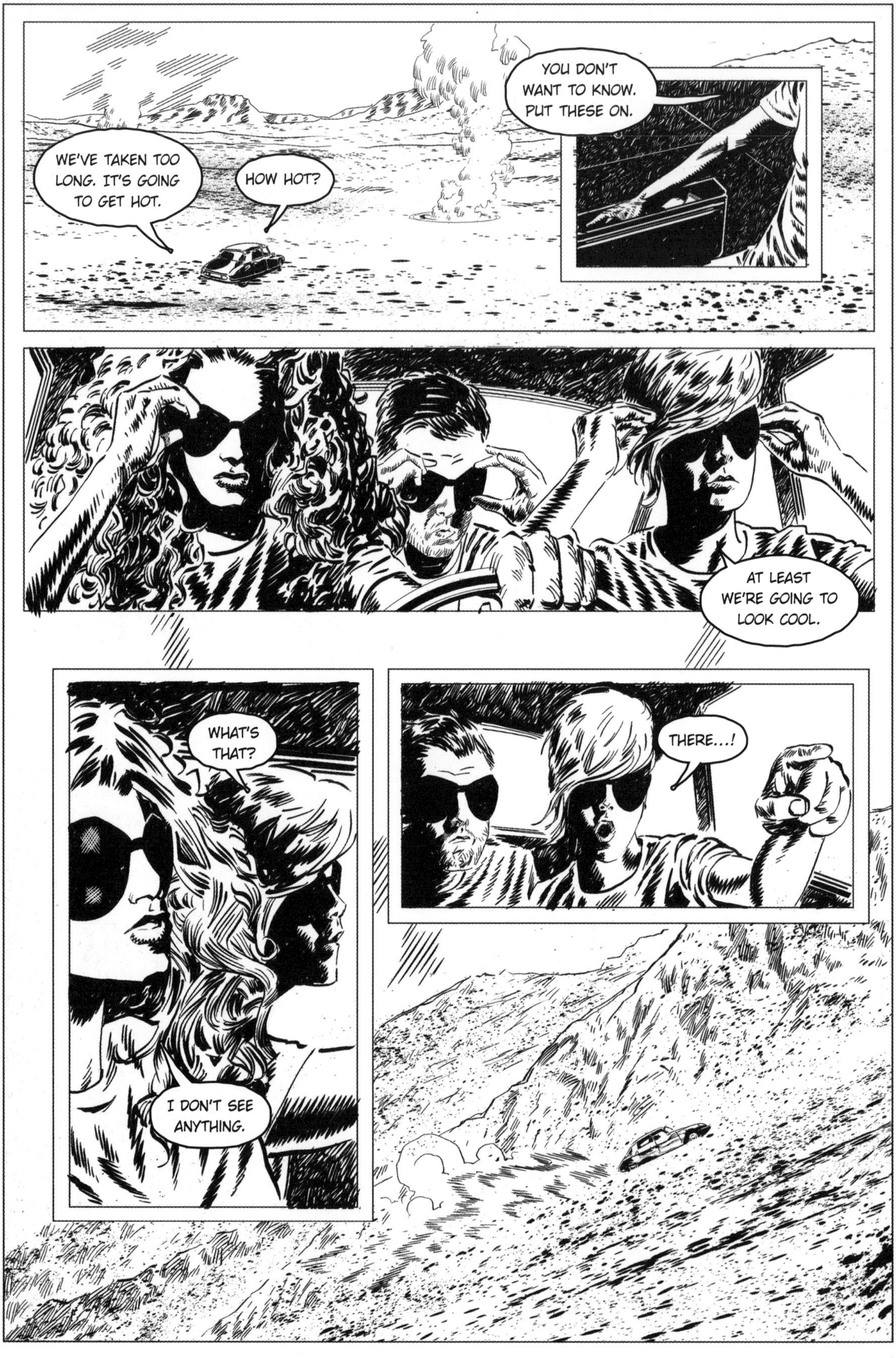
WE'VE TAKEN TOO LONG. IT'S GOING TO GET HOT.
HOW HOT?
YOU DON'T WANT TO KNOW. PUT THESE ON.
AT LEAST WE'RE GOING TO LOOK COOL.
WHAT'S THAT?
I DON'T SEE ANYTHING.
THERE...!

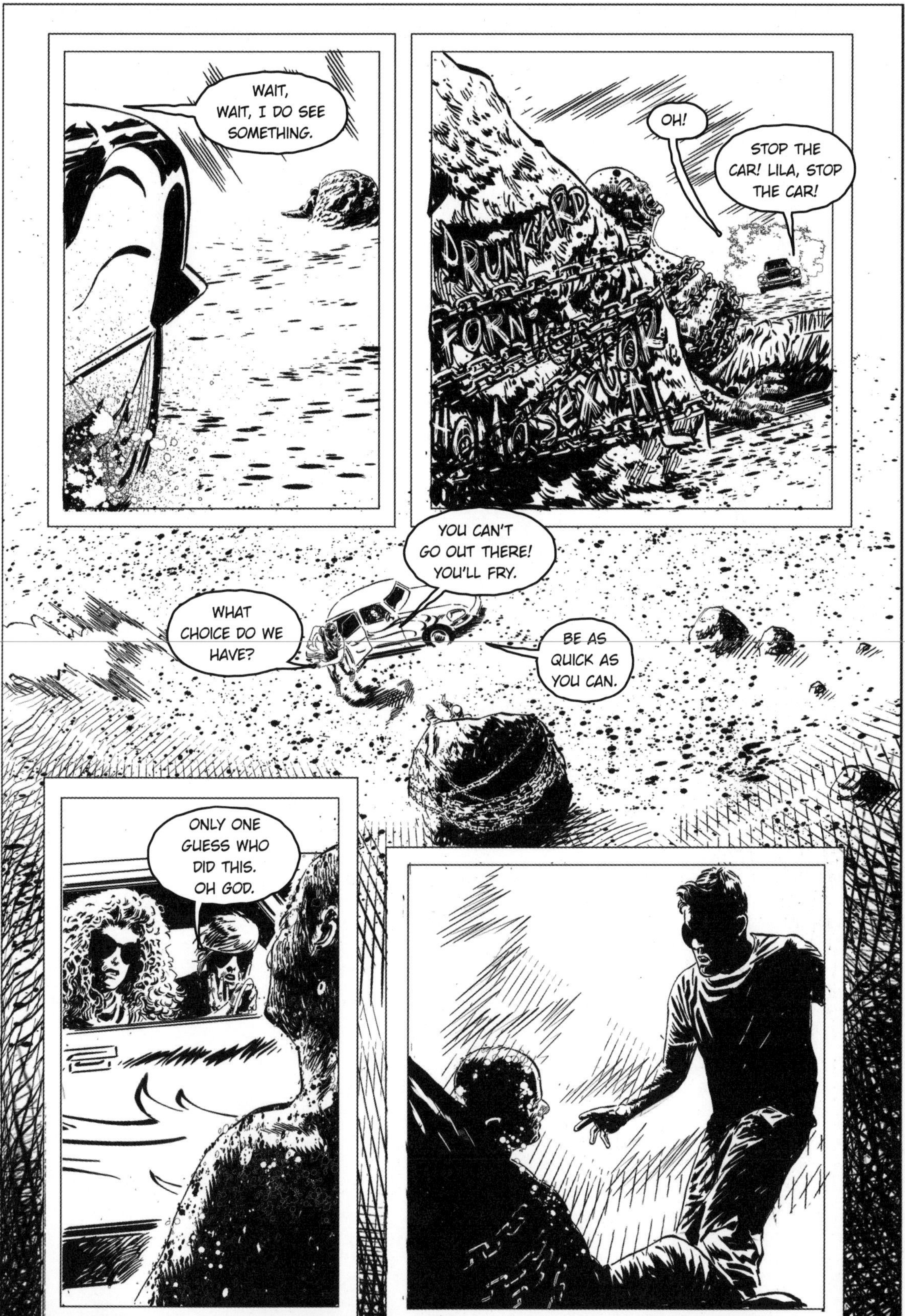
WAIT, WAIT, I DO SEE SOMETHING.
OH!
STOP THE CAR! LILA, STOP THE CAR!
YOU CAN'T GO OUT THERE! YOU'LL FRY.
WHAT CHOICE DO WE HAVE?
BE AS QUICK AS YOU CAN.
ONLY ONE GUESS WHO DID THIS. OH GOD.

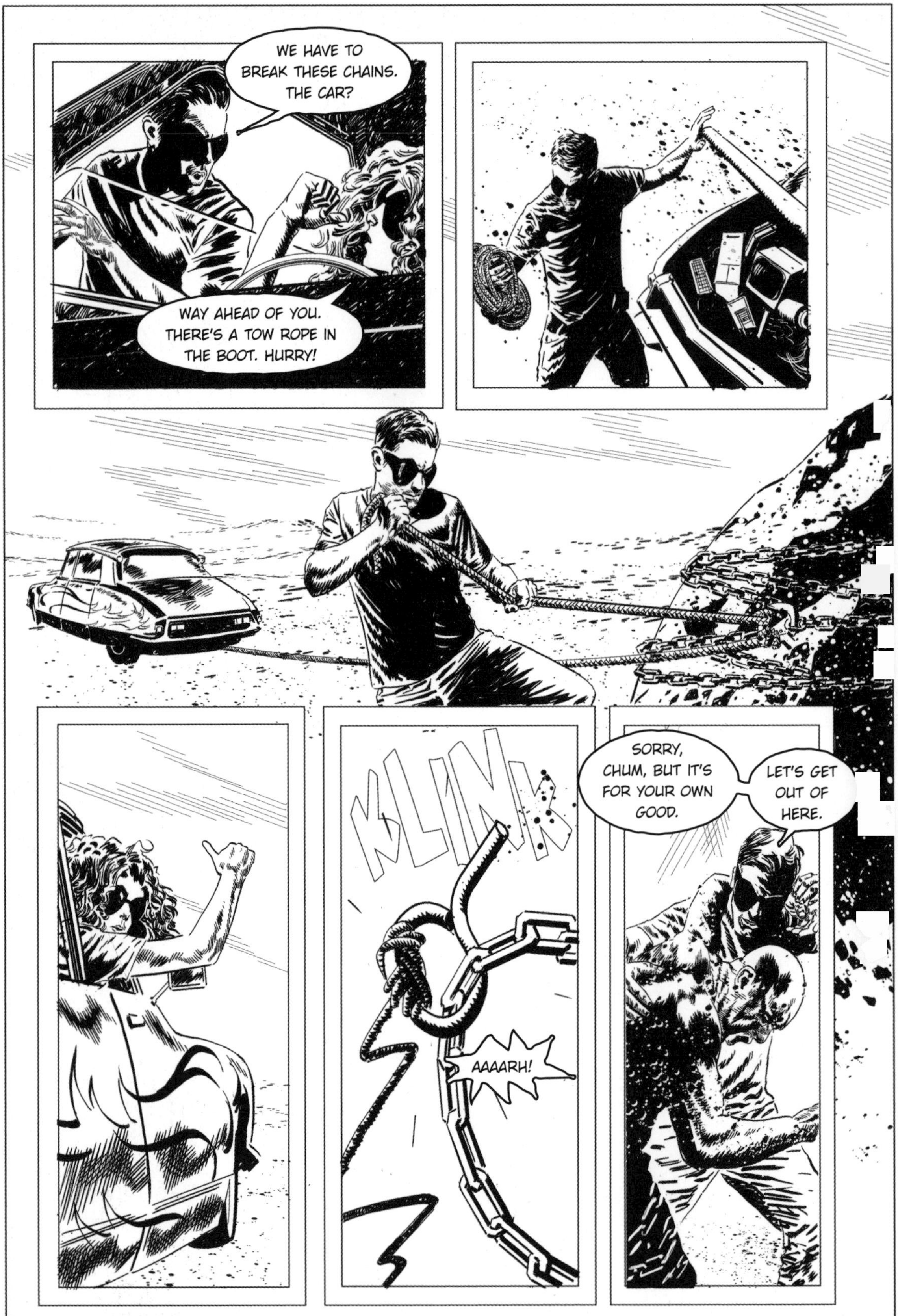
WE HAVE TO BREAK THESE CHAINS. THE CAR?
WAY AHEAD OF YOU. THERE'S A TOW ROPE IN THE BOOT. HURRY!
KLINK
AAAARH!
SORRY, CHUM, BUT IT'S FOR YOUR OWN GOOD.
LET'S GET OUT OF HERE.

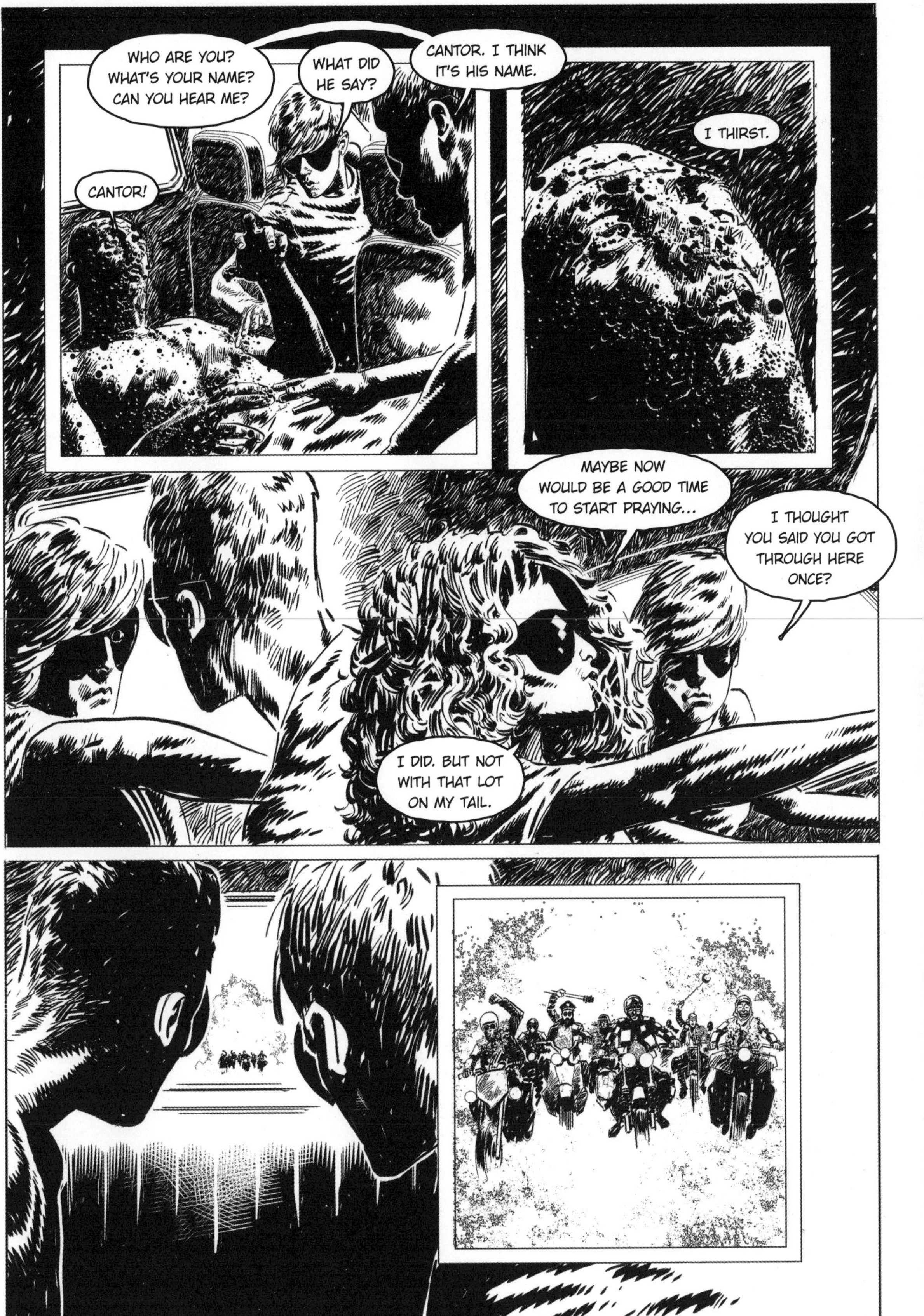
WHO ARE YOU? WHAT'S YOUR NAME? CAN YOU HEAR ME?
WHAT DID HE SAY?
CANTOR. I THINK IT'S HIS NAME.
CANTOR!
I THIRST.
MAYBE NOW WOULD BE A GOOD TIME TO START PRAYING...
I THOUGHT YOU SAID YOU GOT THROUGH HERE ONCE?
I DID. BUT NOT WITH THAT LOT ON MY TAIL.

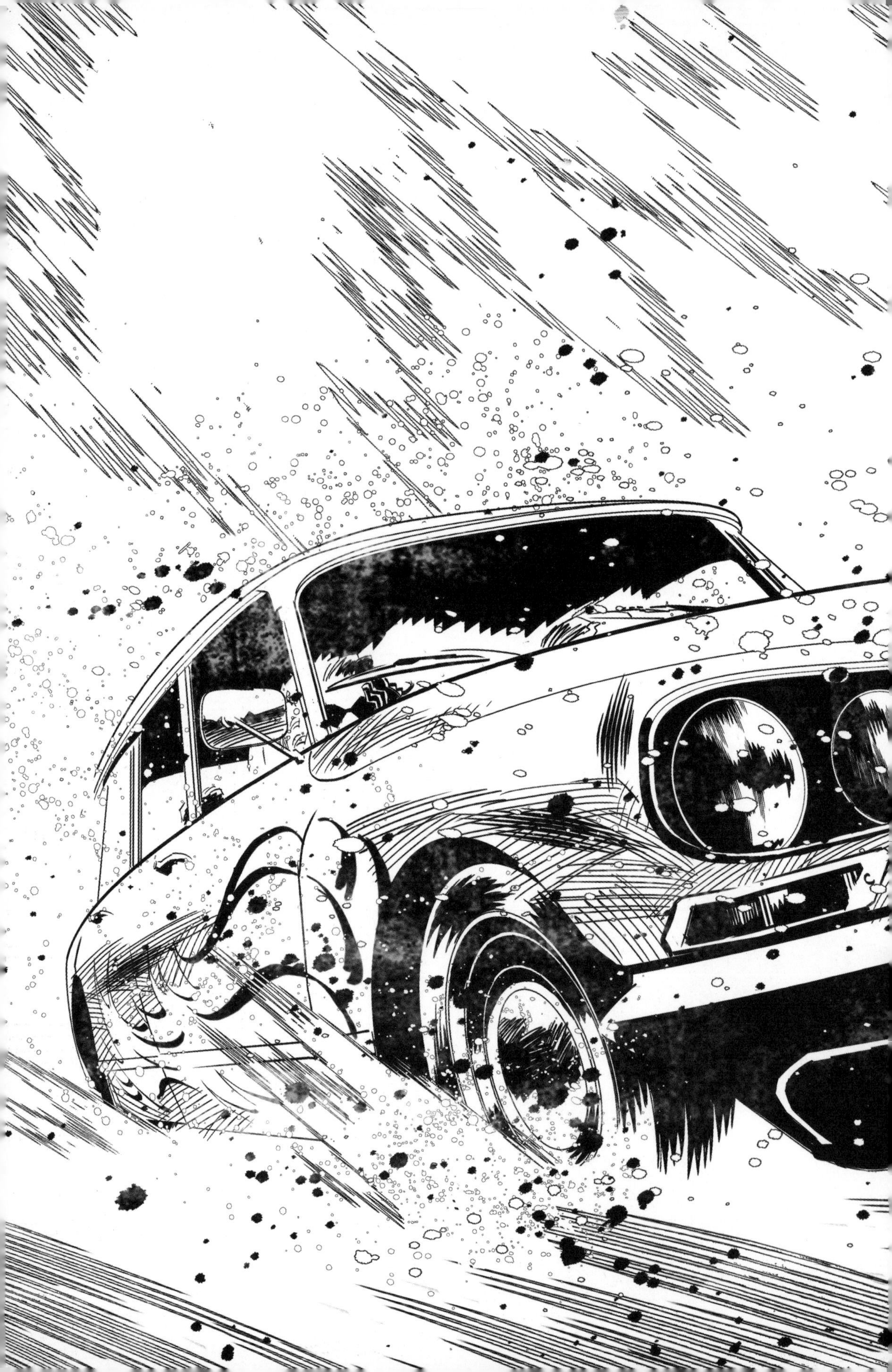

Lesson Six

It is finished

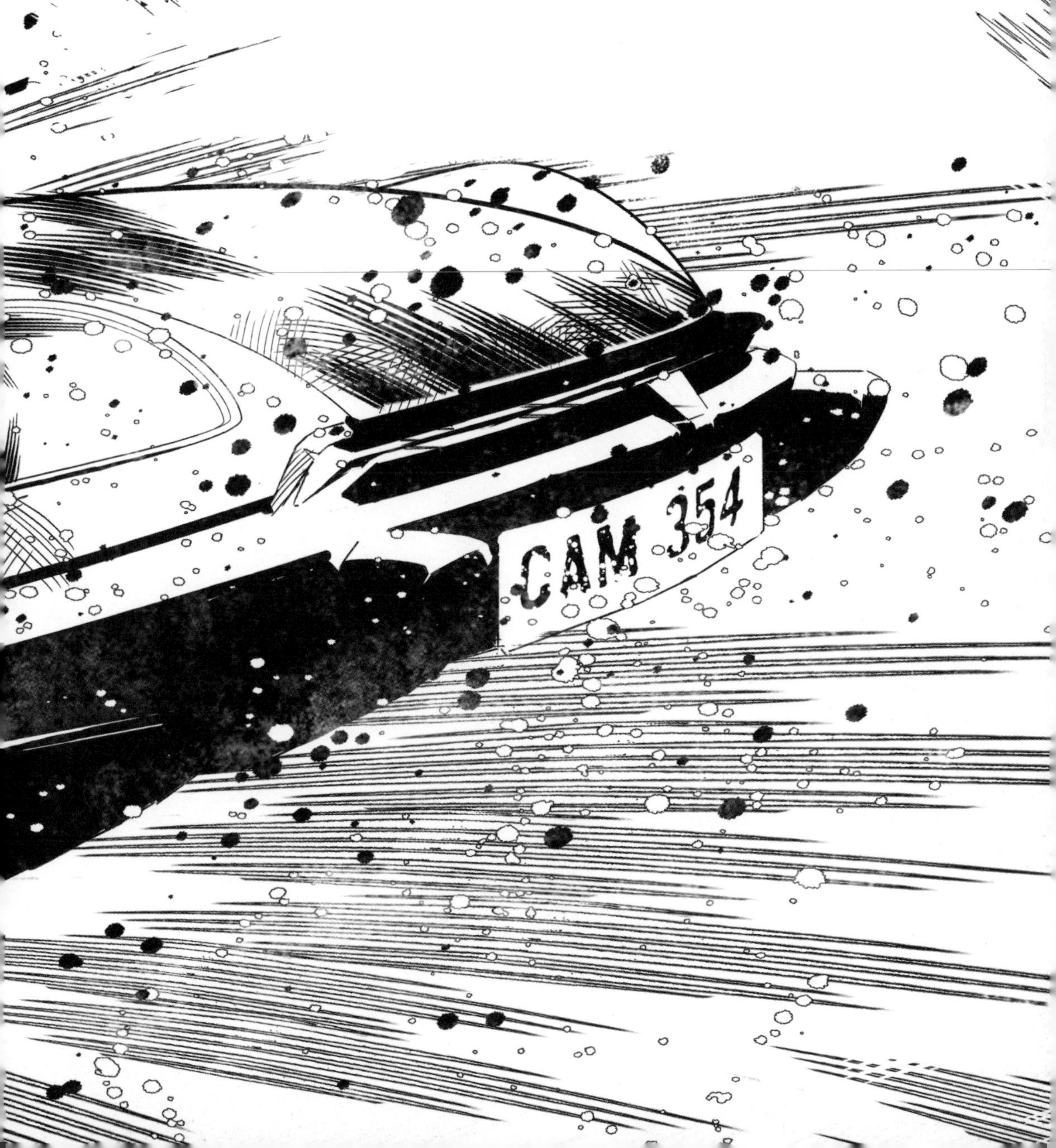
CAM 354

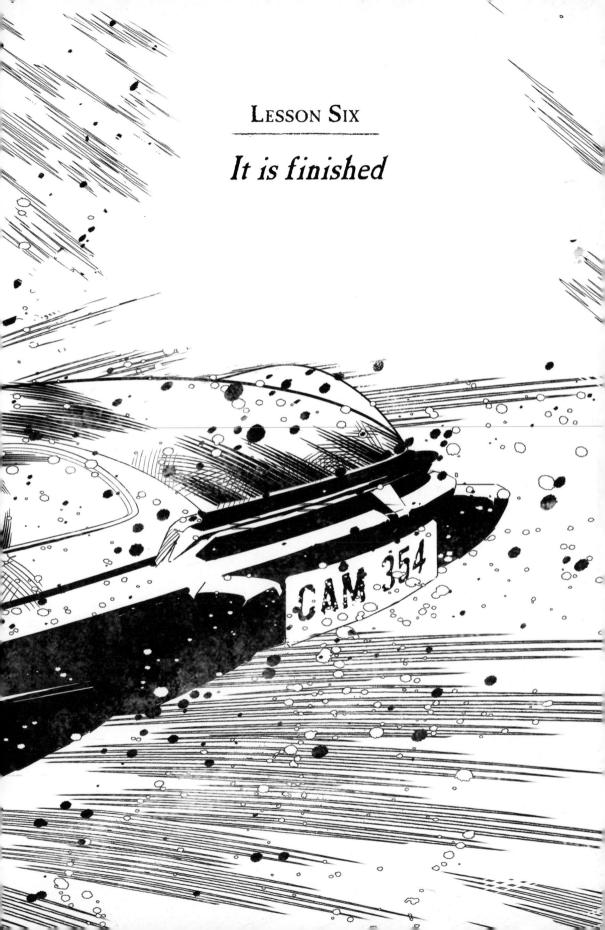

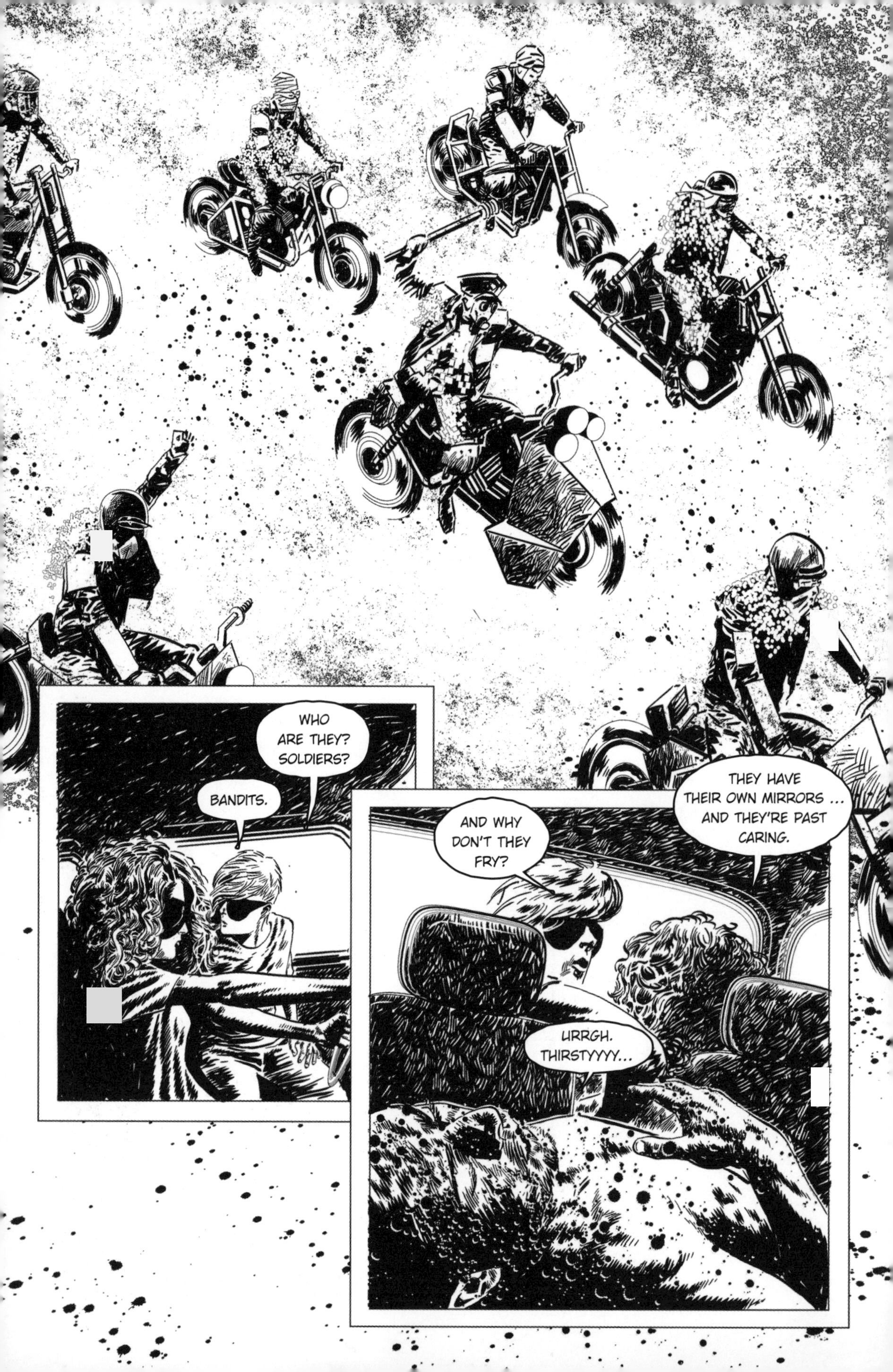
WHO ARE THEY? SOLDIERS?
BANDITS.
AND WHY DON'T THEY FRY?
THEY HAVE THEIR OWN MIRRORS ... AND THEY'RE PAST CARING.
URRGH. THIRSTYYYY...

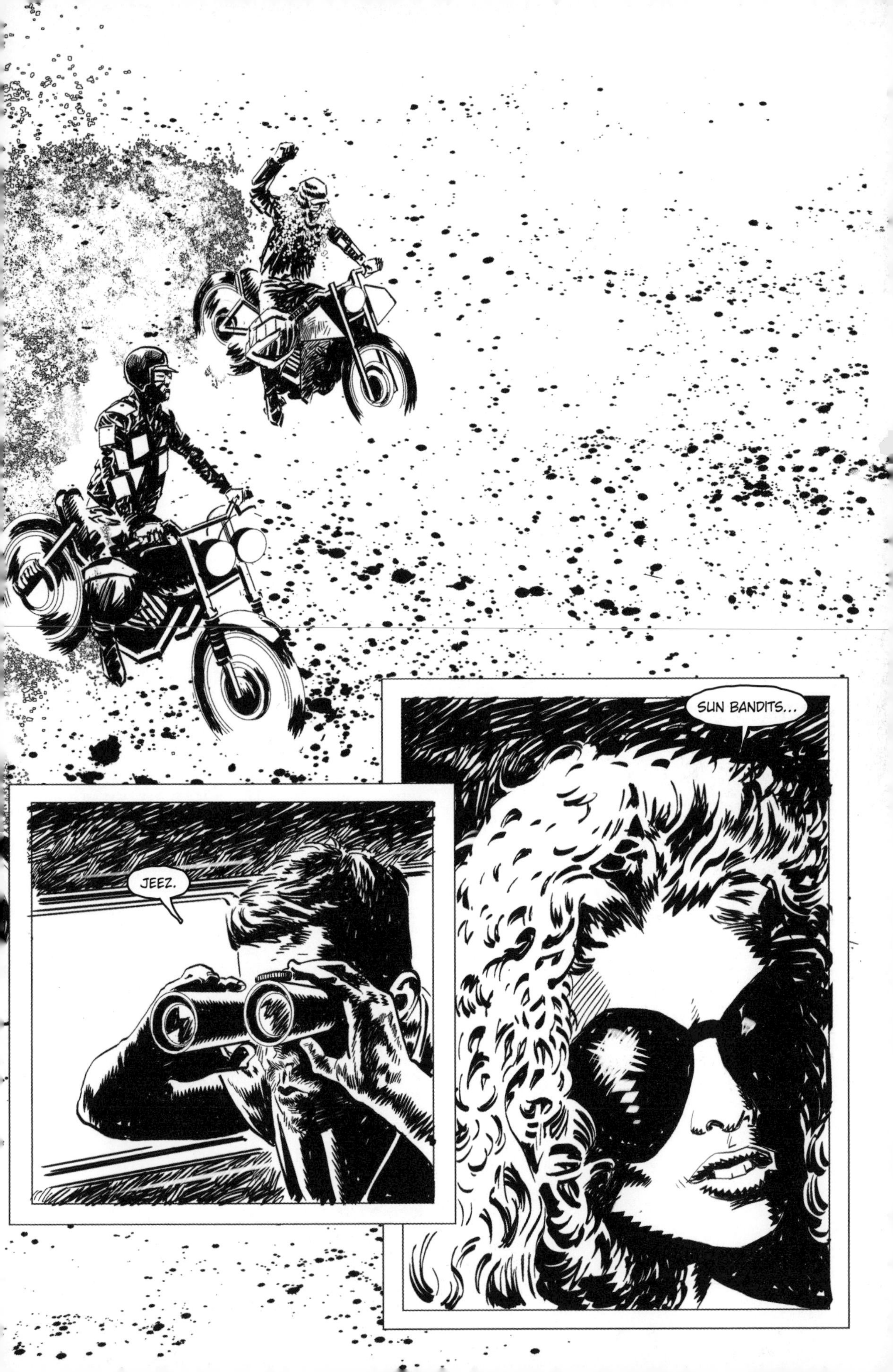
JEEZ.
SUN BANDITS...

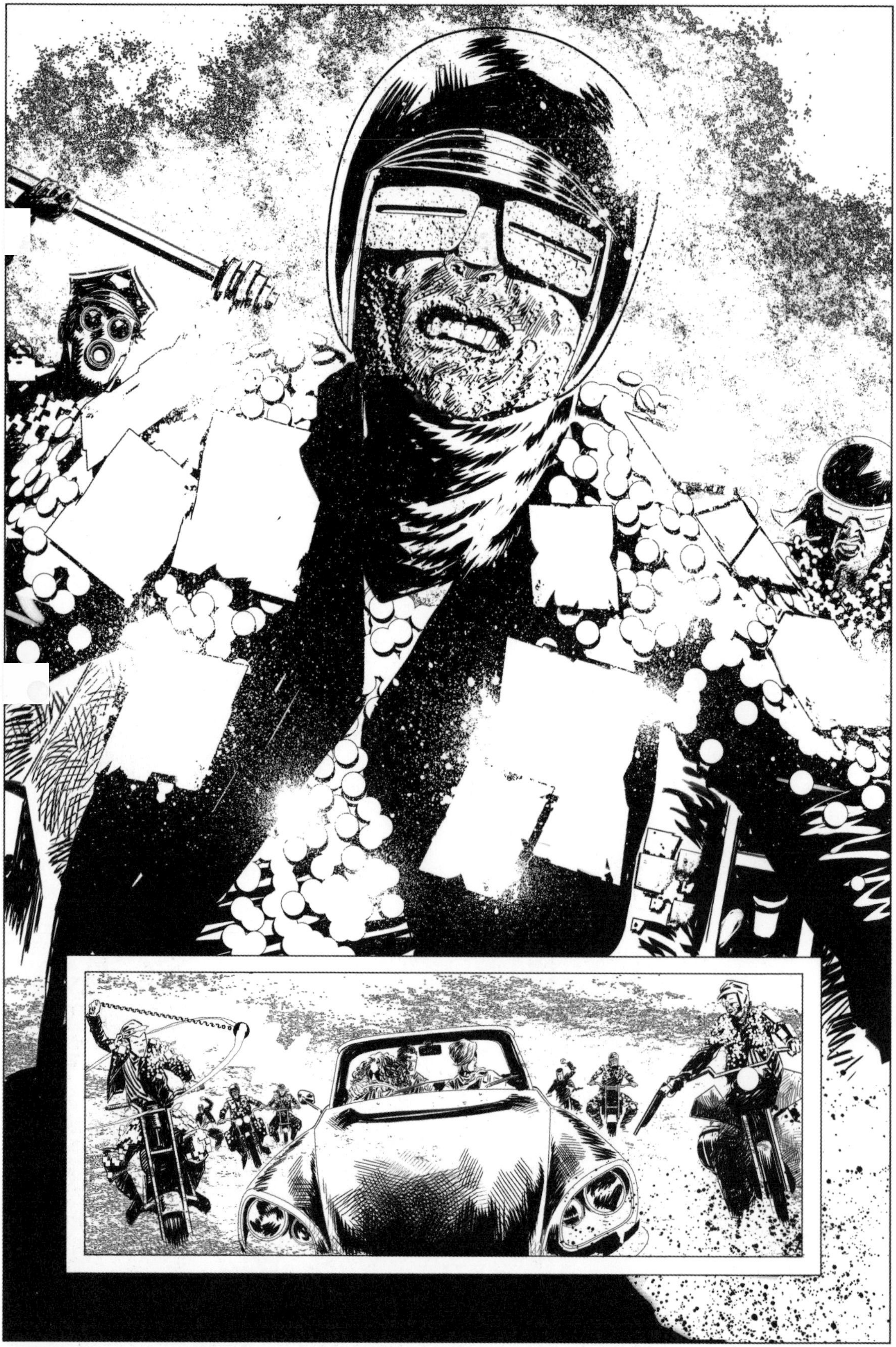

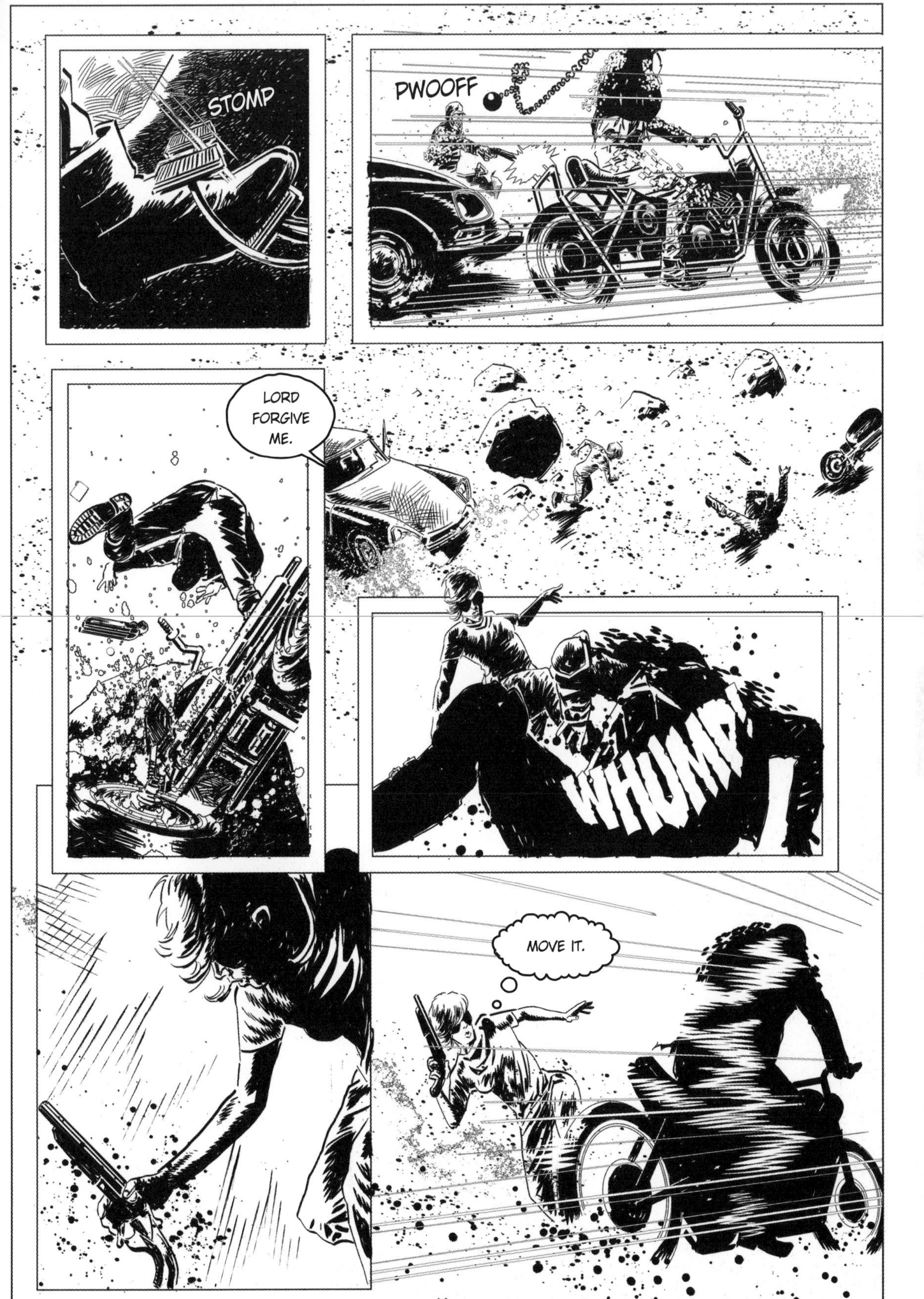
STOMP
PWOOFF
LORD FORGIVE ME.
WHUMP!
MOVE IT.

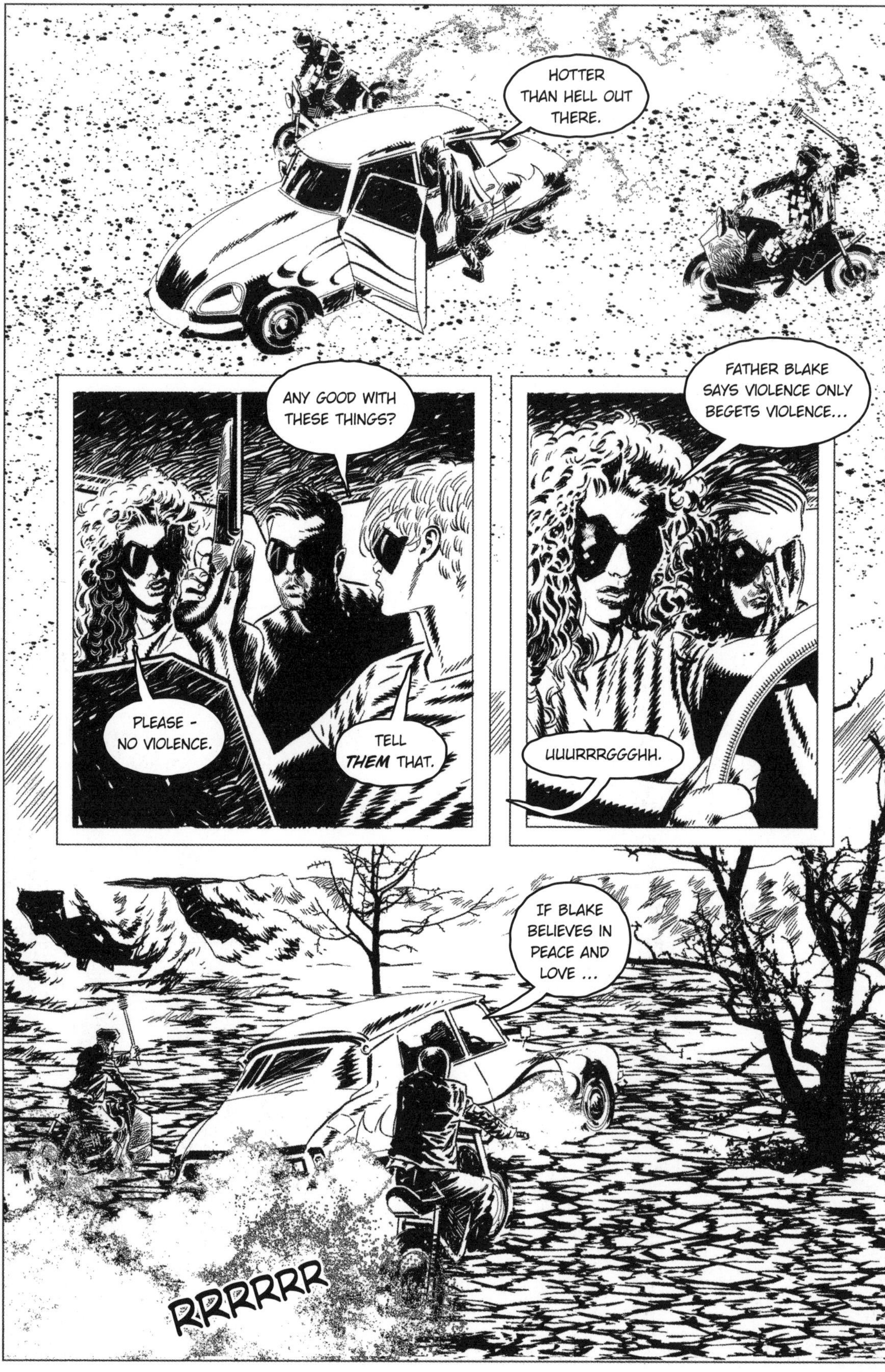
HOTTER THAN HELL OUT THERE.
ANY GOOD WITH THESE THINGS?
PLEASE - NO VIOLENCE.
TELL *THEM* THAT.
FATHER BLAKE SAYS VIOLENCE ONLY BEGETS VIOLENCE...
UUURRRGGGHH.
IF BLAKE BELIEVES IN PEACE AND LOVE ...
RRRRRR

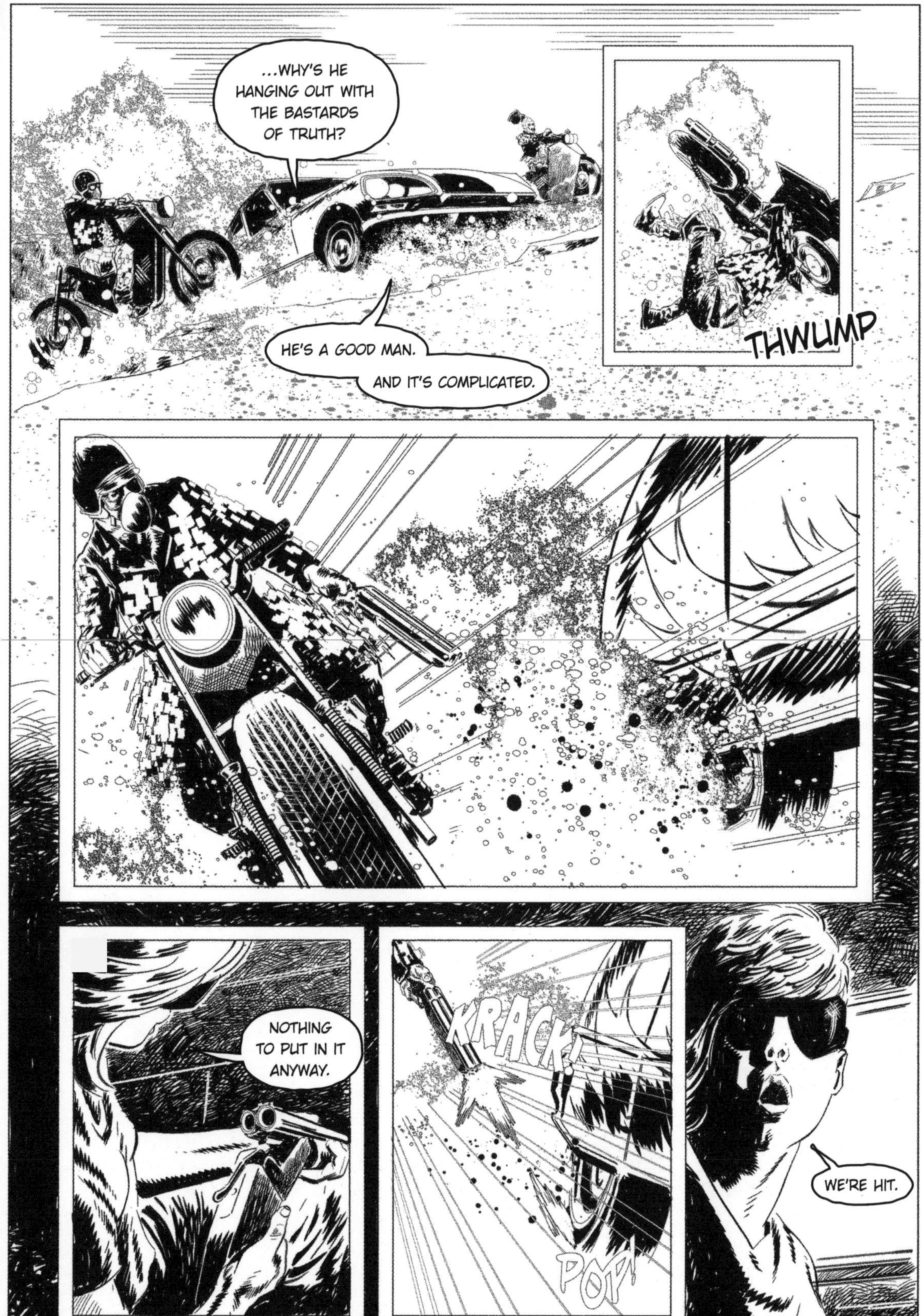
...WHY'S HE HANGING OUT WITH THE BASTARDS OF TRUTH?
HE'S A GOOD MAN.
AND IT'S COMPLICATED.
THWUMP
NOTHING TO PUT IN IT ANYWAY.
KRACK!
POP!
WE'RE HIT.

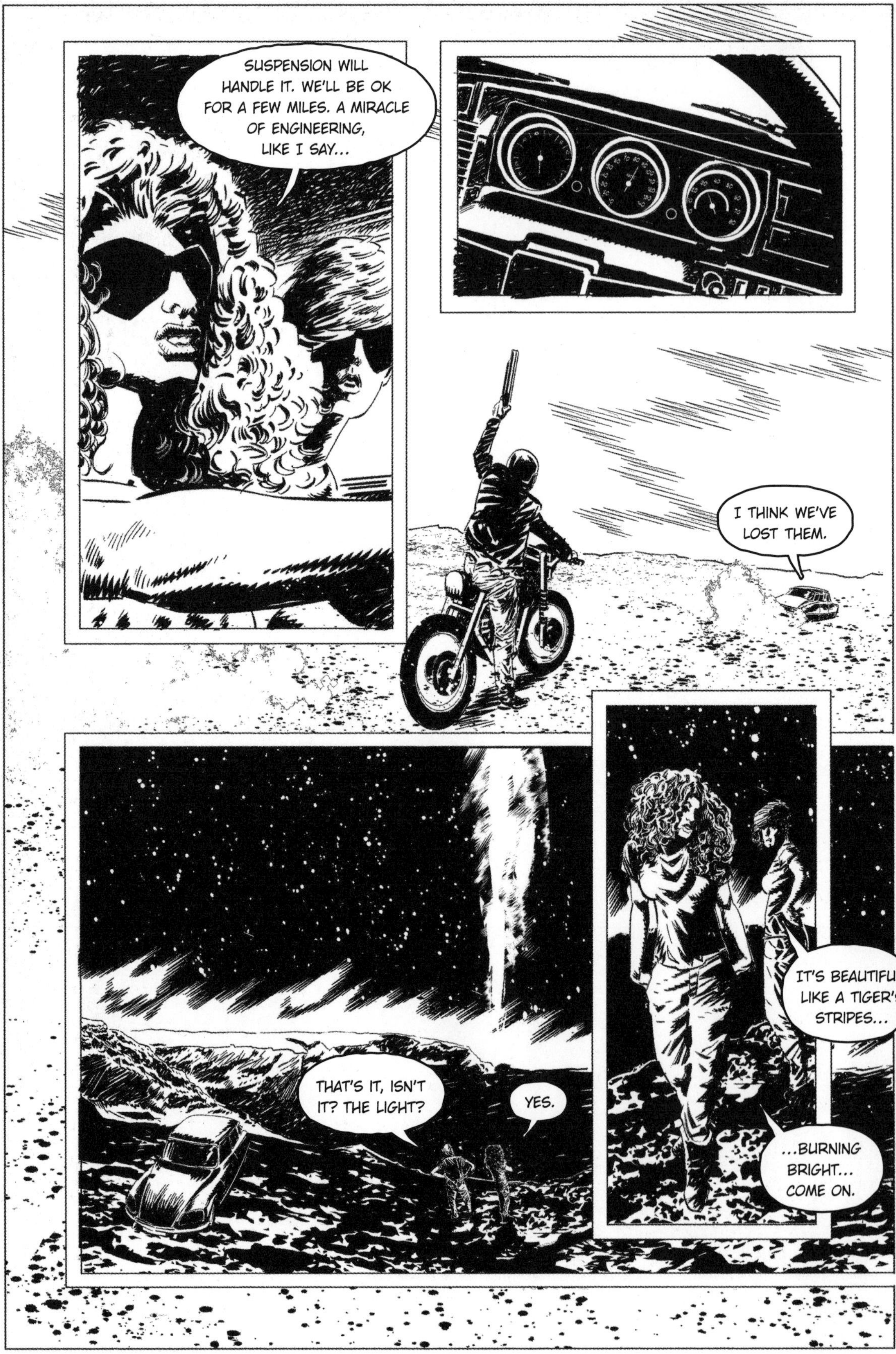
SUSPENSION WILL HANDLE IT. WE'LL BE OK FOR A FEW MILES. A MIRACLE OF ENGINEERING, LIKE I SAY...
I THINK WE'VE LOST THEM.
THAT'S IT, ISN'T IT? THE LIGHT?
YES.
IT'S BEAUTIFUL LIKE A TIGER'S STRIPES...
...BURNING BRIGHT... COME ON.

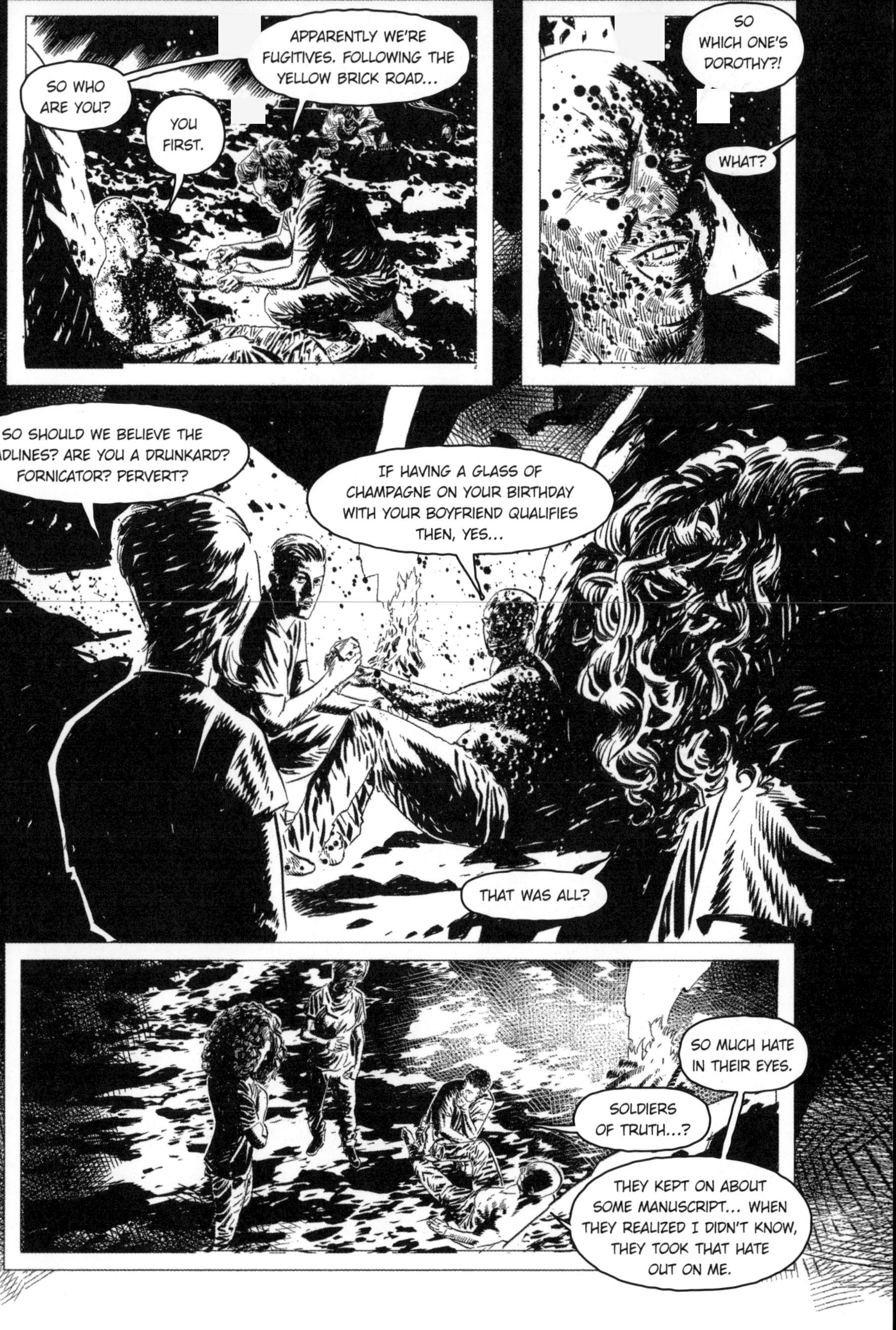
SO WHO ARE YOU?
YOU FIRST.
APPARENTLY WE'RE FUGITIVES. FOLLOWING THE YELLOW BRICK ROAD...
SO WHICH ONE'S DOROTHY?!
WHAT?
SO SHOULD WE BELIEVE THE HEADLINES? ARE YOU A DRUNKARD? FORNICATOR? PERVERT?
IF HAVING A GLASS OF CHAMPAGNE ON YOUR BIRTHDAY WITH YOUR BOYFRIEND QUALIFIES THEN, YES...
THAT WAS ALL?
SO MUCH HATE IN THEIR EYES.
SOLDIERS OF TRUTH...?
THEY KEPT ON ABOUT SOME MANUSCRIPT... WHEN THEY REALIZED I DIDN'T KNOW, THEY TOOK THAT HATE OUT ON ME.

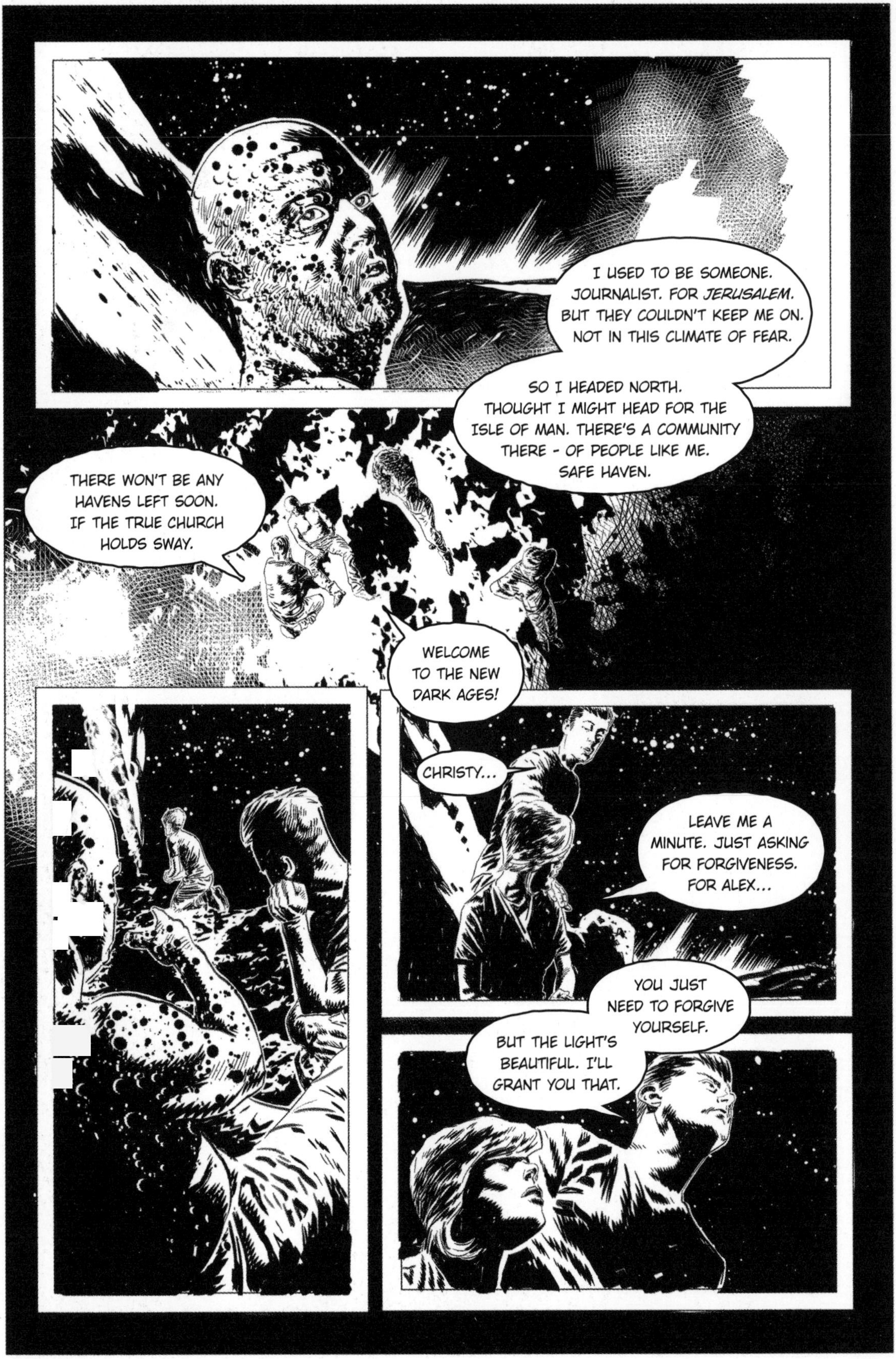
I USED TO BE SOMEONE. JOURNALIST. FOR *JERUSALEM*. BUT THEY COULDN'T KEEP ME ON. NOT IN THIS CLIMATE OF FEAR.
SO I HEADED NORTH. THOUGHT I MIGHT HEAD FOR THE ISLE OF MAN. THERE'S A COMMUNITY THERE - OF PEOPLE LIKE ME. SAFE HAVEN.
THERE WON'T BE ANY HAVENS LEFT SOON. IF THE TRUE CHURCH HOLDS SWAY.
WELCOME TO THE NEW DARK AGES!
CHRISTY...
LEAVE ME A MINUTE. JUST ASKING FOR FORGIVENESS. FOR ALEX...
YOU JUST NEED TO FORGIVE YOURSELF.
BUT THE LIGHT'S BEAUTIFUL. I'LL GRANT YOU THAT.

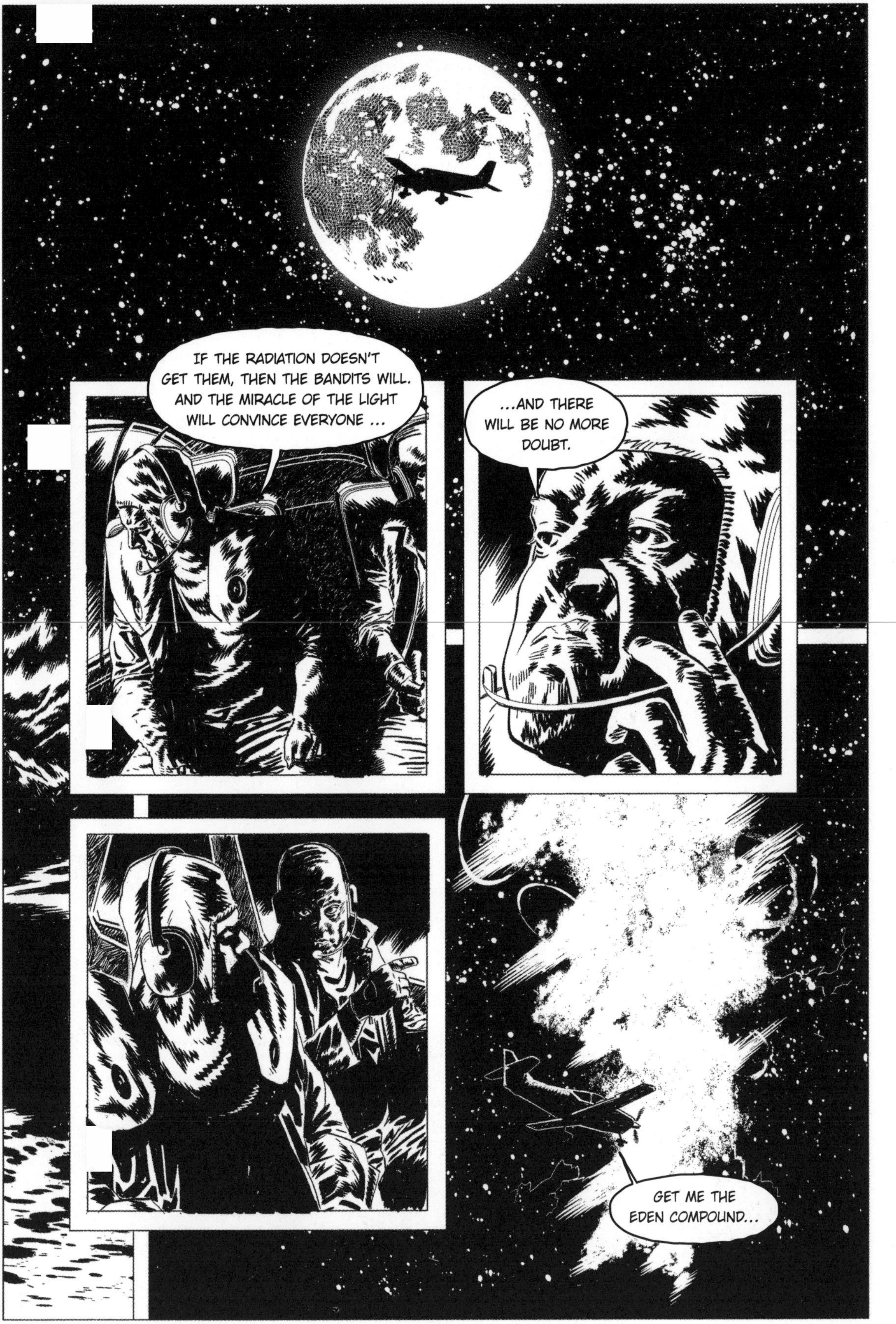
IF THE RADIATION DOESN'T GET THEM, THEN THE BANDITS WILL. AND THE MIRACLE OF THE LIGHT WILL CONVINCE EVERYONE ...
...AND THERE WILL BE NO MORE DOUBT.
GET ME THE EDEN COMPOUND...

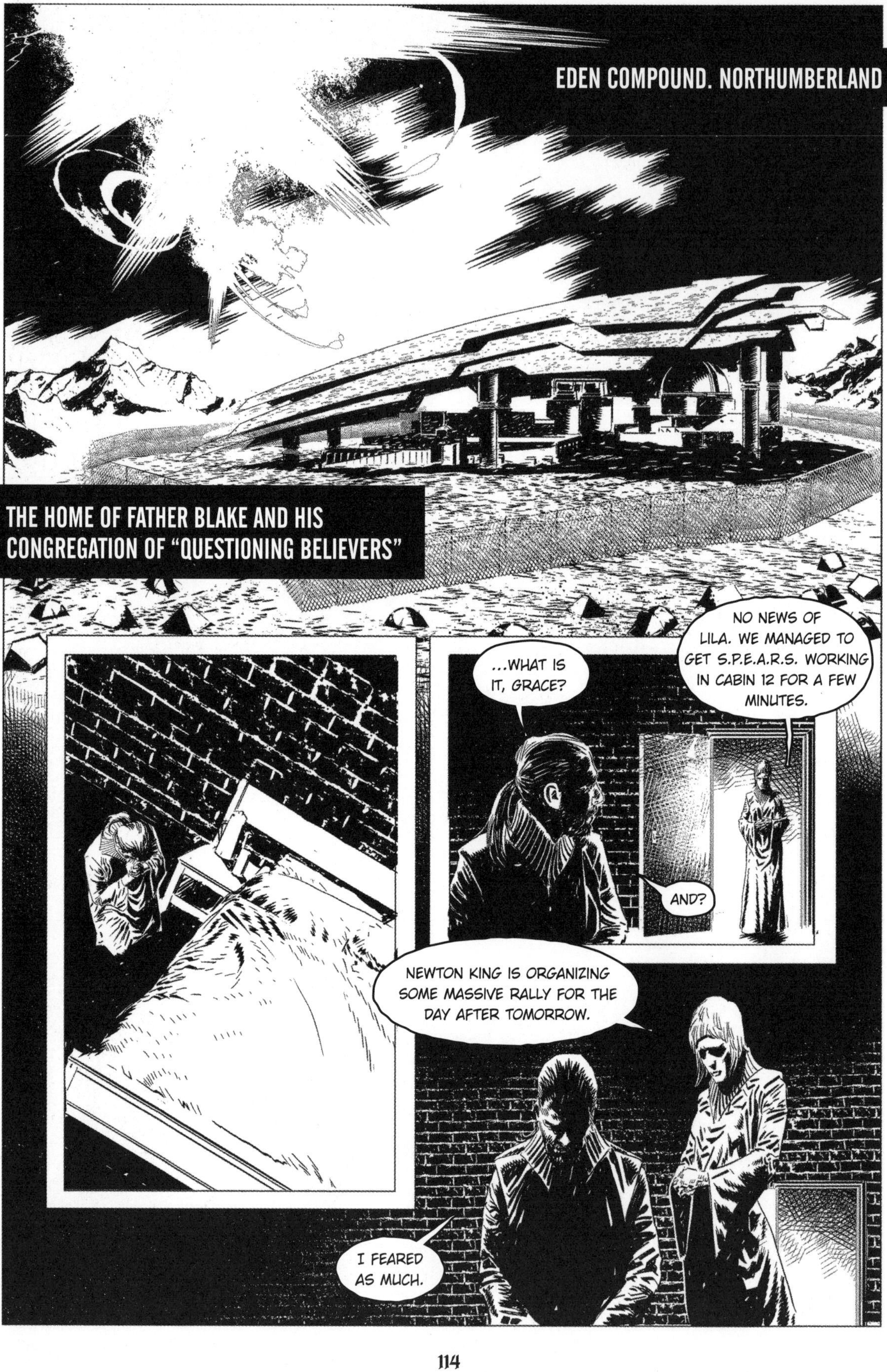
EDEN COMPOUND. NORTHUMBERLAND
THE HOME OF FATHER BLAKE AND HIS CONGREGATION OF "QUESTIONING BELIEVERS"
...WHAT IS IT, GRACE?
NO NEWS OF LILA. WE MANAGED TO GET S.P.E.A.R.S. WORKING IN CABIN 12 FOR A FEW MINUTES.
AND?
NEWTON KING IS ORGANIZING SOME MASSIVE RALLY FOR THE DAY AFTER TOMORROW.
I FEARED AS MUCH.

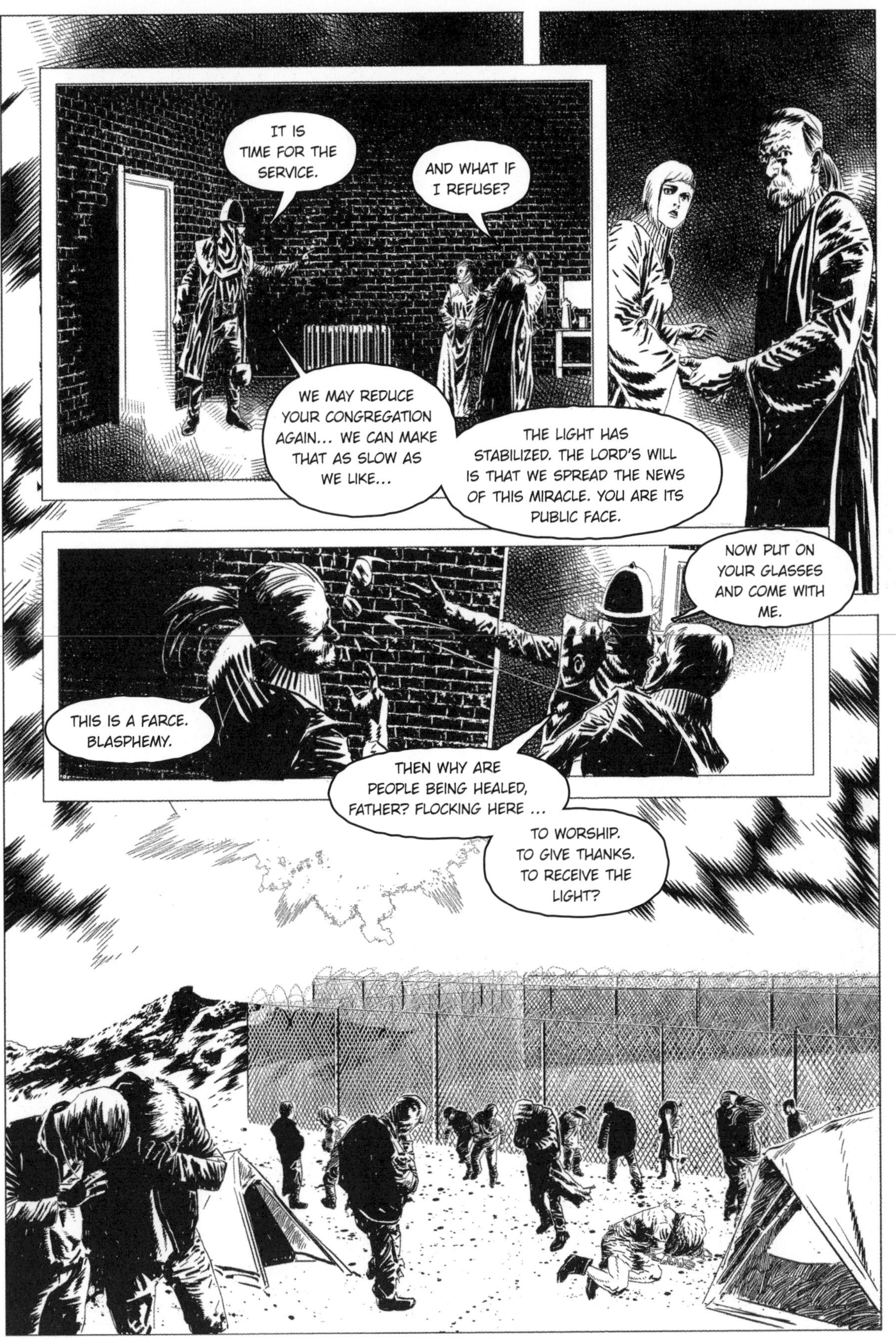
IT IS TIME FOR THE SERVICE.
AND WHAT IF I REFUSE?
WE MAY REDUCE YOUR CONGREGATION AGAIN... WE CAN MAKE THAT AS SLOW AS WE LIKE...
THE LIGHT HAS STABILIZED. THE LORD'S WILL IS THAT WE SPREAD THE NEWS OF THIS MIRACLE. YOU ARE ITS PUBLIC FACE.
NOW PUT ON YOUR GLASSES AND COME WITH ME.
THIS IS A FARCE. BLASPHEMY.
THEN WHY ARE PEOPLE BEING HEALED, FATHER? FLOCKING HERE ...
TO WORSHIP. TO GIVE THANKS. TO RECEIVE THE LIGHT?

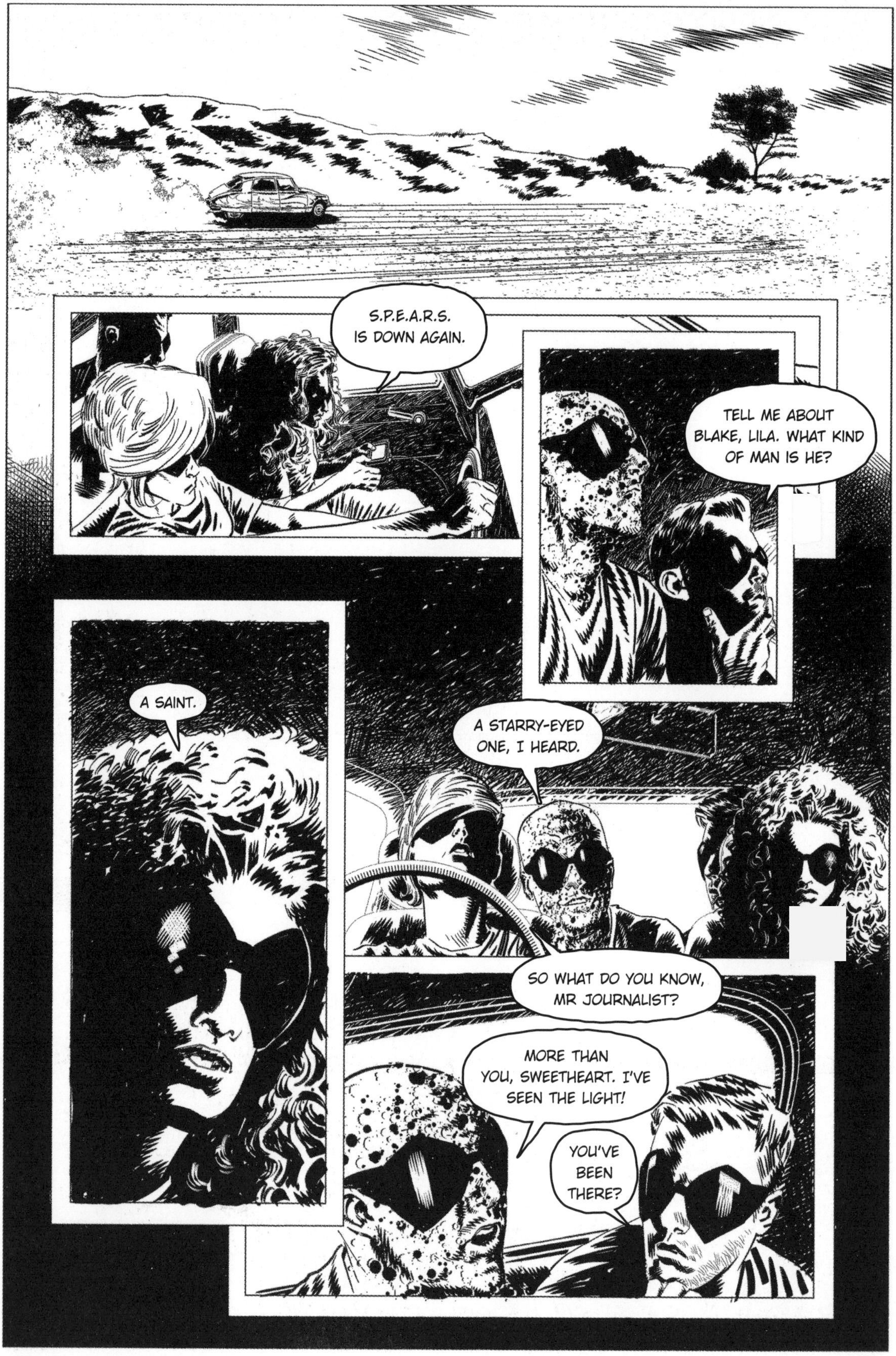
S.P.E.A.R.S. IS DOWN AGAIN.
TELL ME ABOUT BLAKE, LILA. WHAT KIND OF MAN IS HE?
A SAINT.
A STARRY-EYED ONE, I HEARD.
SO WHAT DO YOU KNOW, MR JOURNALIST?
MORE THAN YOU, SWEETHEART. I'VE SEEN THE LIGHT!
YOU'VE BEEN THERE?

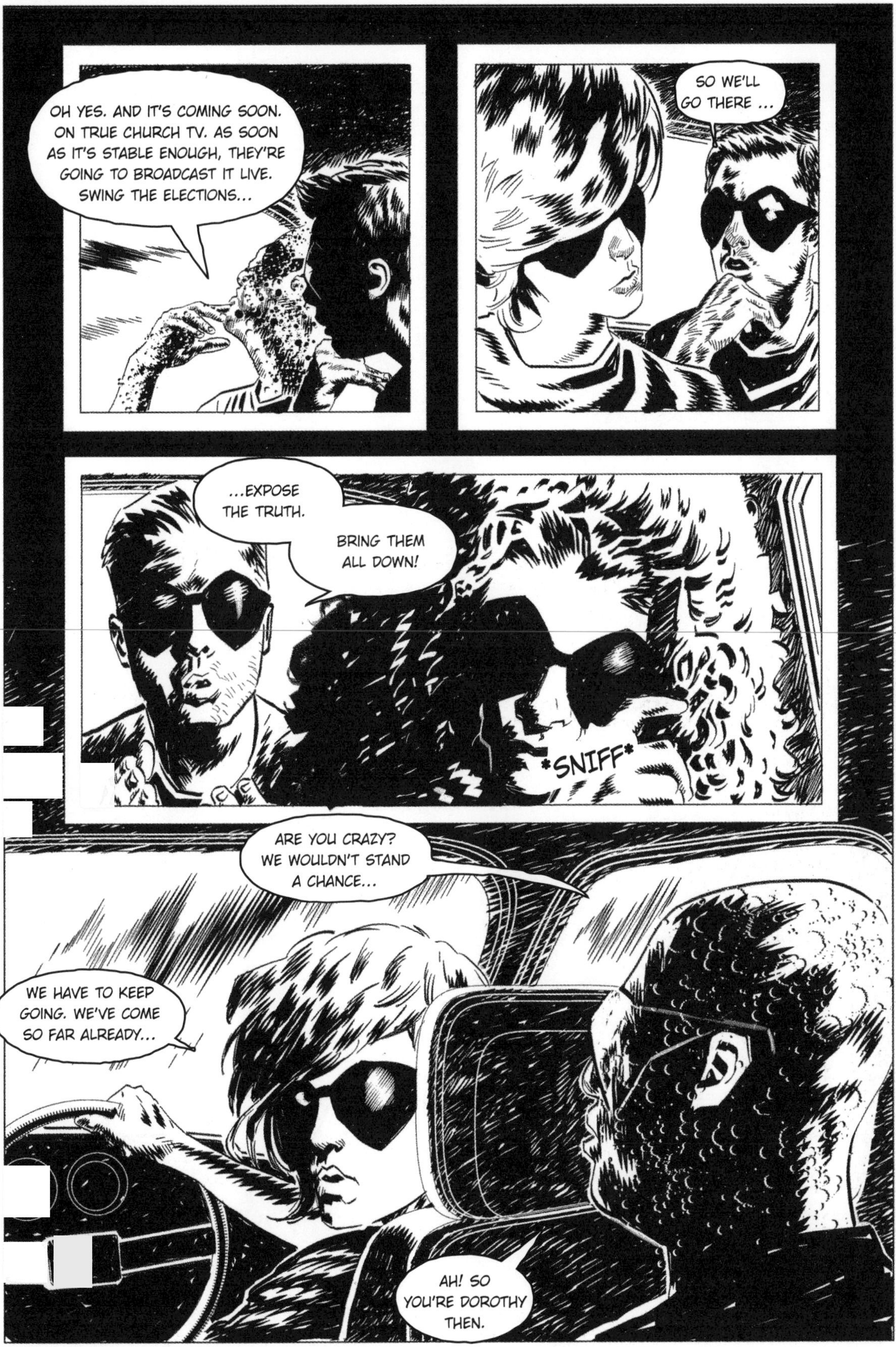
OH YES. AND IT'S COMING SOON. ON TRUE CHURCH TV. AS SOON AS IT'S STABLE ENOUGH, THEY'RE GOING TO BROADCAST IT LIVE. SWING THE ELECTIONS...
SO WE'LL GO THERE ...
...EXPOSE THE TRUTH.
BRING THEM ALL DOWN!
SNIFF
ARE YOU CRAZY? WE WOULDN'T STAND A CHANCE...
WE HAVE TO KEEP GOING. WE'VE COME SO FAR ALREADY...
AH! SO YOU'RE DOROTHY THEN.

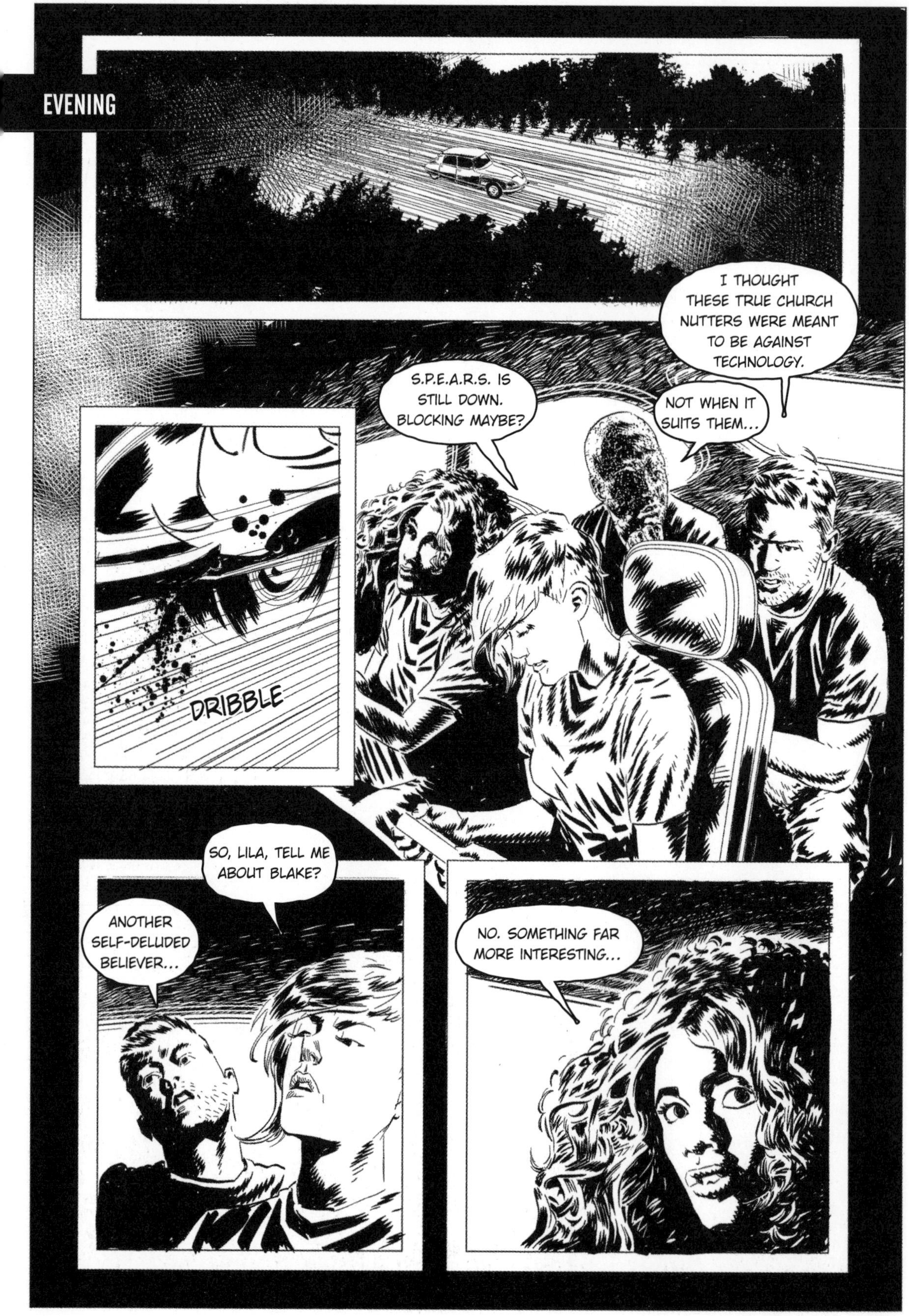
EVENING
I THOUGHT THESE TRUE CHURCH NUTTERS WERE MEANT TO BE AGAINST TECHNOLOGY.
S.P.E.A.R.S. IS STILL DOWN. BLOCKING MAYBE?
NOT WHEN IT SUITS THEM...
DRIBBLE
SO, LILA, TELL ME ABOUT BLAKE?
ANOTHER SELF-DELUDED BELIEVER...
NO. SOMETHING FAR MORE INTERESTING...

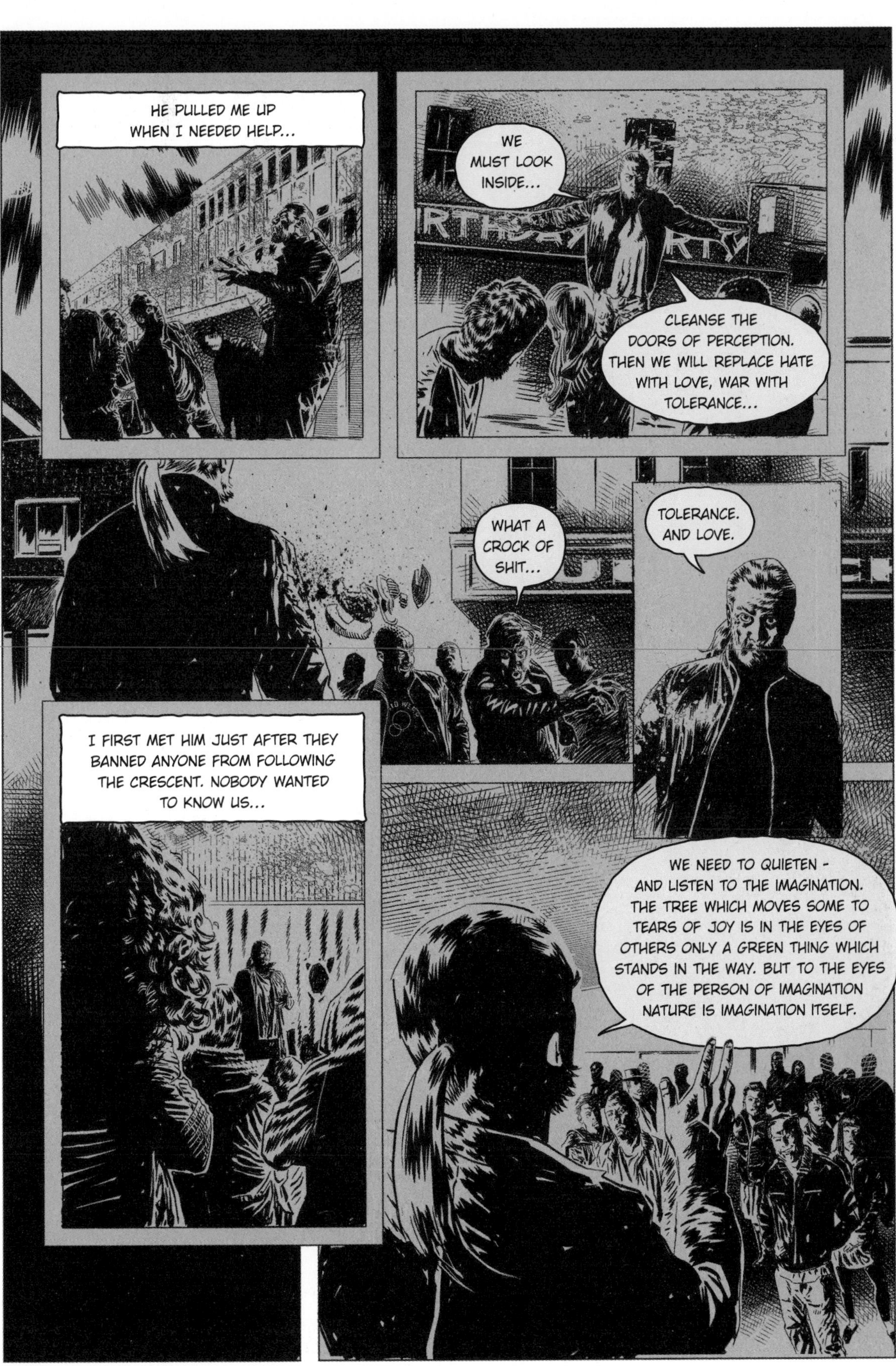
HE PULLED ME UP WHEN I NEEDED HELP...
WE MUST LOOK INSIDE...
CLEANSE THE DOORS OF PERCEPTION. THEN WE WILL REPLACE HATE WITH LOVE, WAR WITH TOLERANCE...
WHAT A CROCK OF SHIT...
TOLERANCE. AND LOVE.
I FIRST MET HIM JUST AFTER THEY BANNED ANYONE FROM FOLLOWING THE CRESCENT. NOBODY WANTED TO KNOW US...
WE NEED TO QUIETEN - AND LISTEN TO THE IMAGINATION. THE TREE WHICH MOVES SOME TO TEARS OF JOY IS IN THE EYES OF OTHERS ONLY A GREEN THING WHICH STANDS IN THE WAY. BUT TO THE EYES OF THE PERSON OF IMAGINATION NATURE IS IMAGINATION ITSELF.

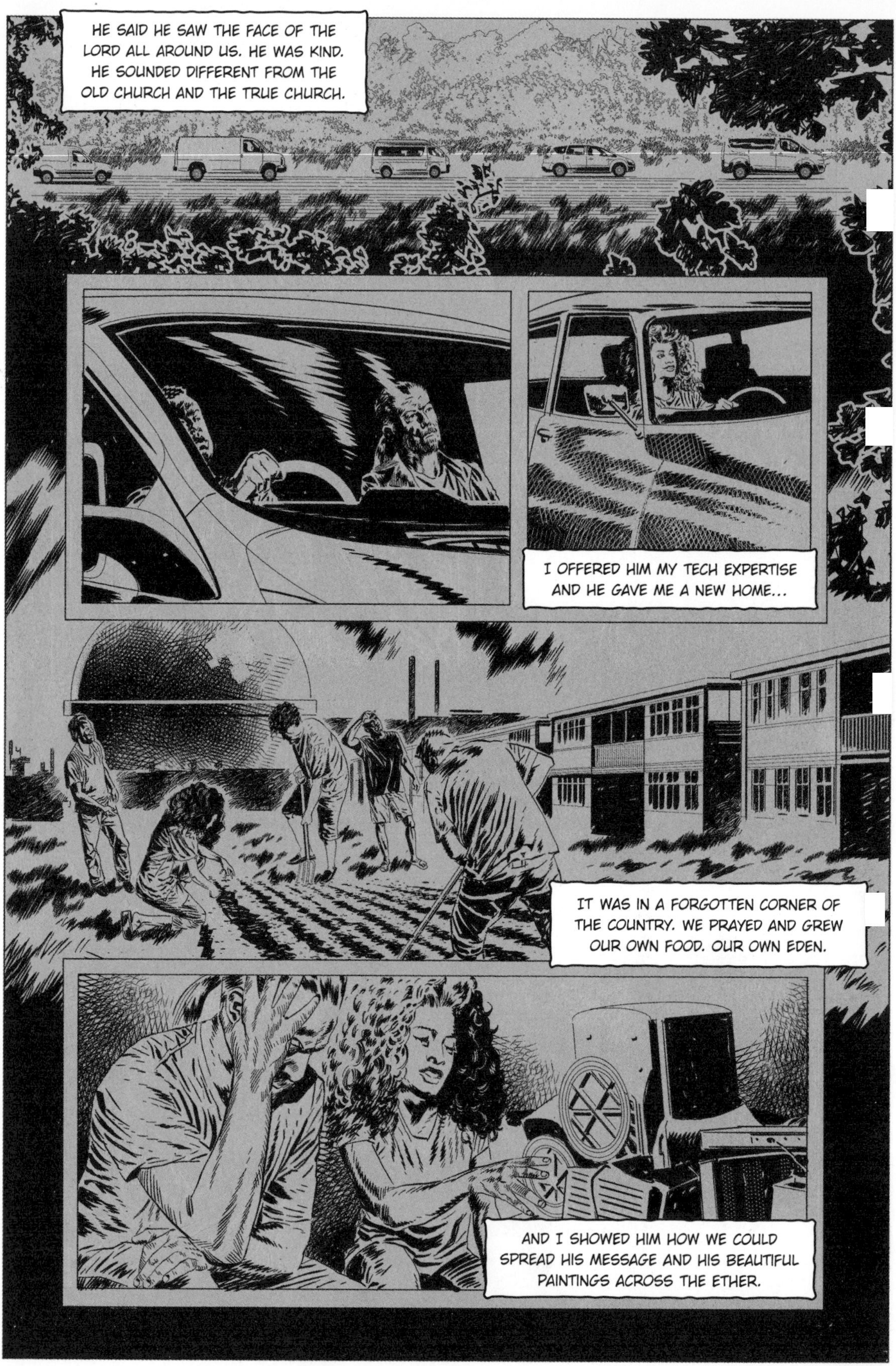
HE SAID HE SAW THE FACE OF THE LORD ALL AROUND US. HE WAS KIND. HE SOUNDED DIFFERENT FROM THE OLD CHURCH AND THE TRUE CHURCH.
I OFFERED HIM MY TECH EXPERTISE AND HE GAVE ME A NEW HOME...
IT WAS IN A FORGOTTEN CORNER OF THE COUNTRY. WE PRAYED AND GREW OUR OWN FOOD. OUR OWN EDEN.
AND I SHOWED HIM HOW WE COULD SPREAD HIS MESSAGE AND HIS BEAUTIFUL PAINTINGS ACROSS THE ETHER.

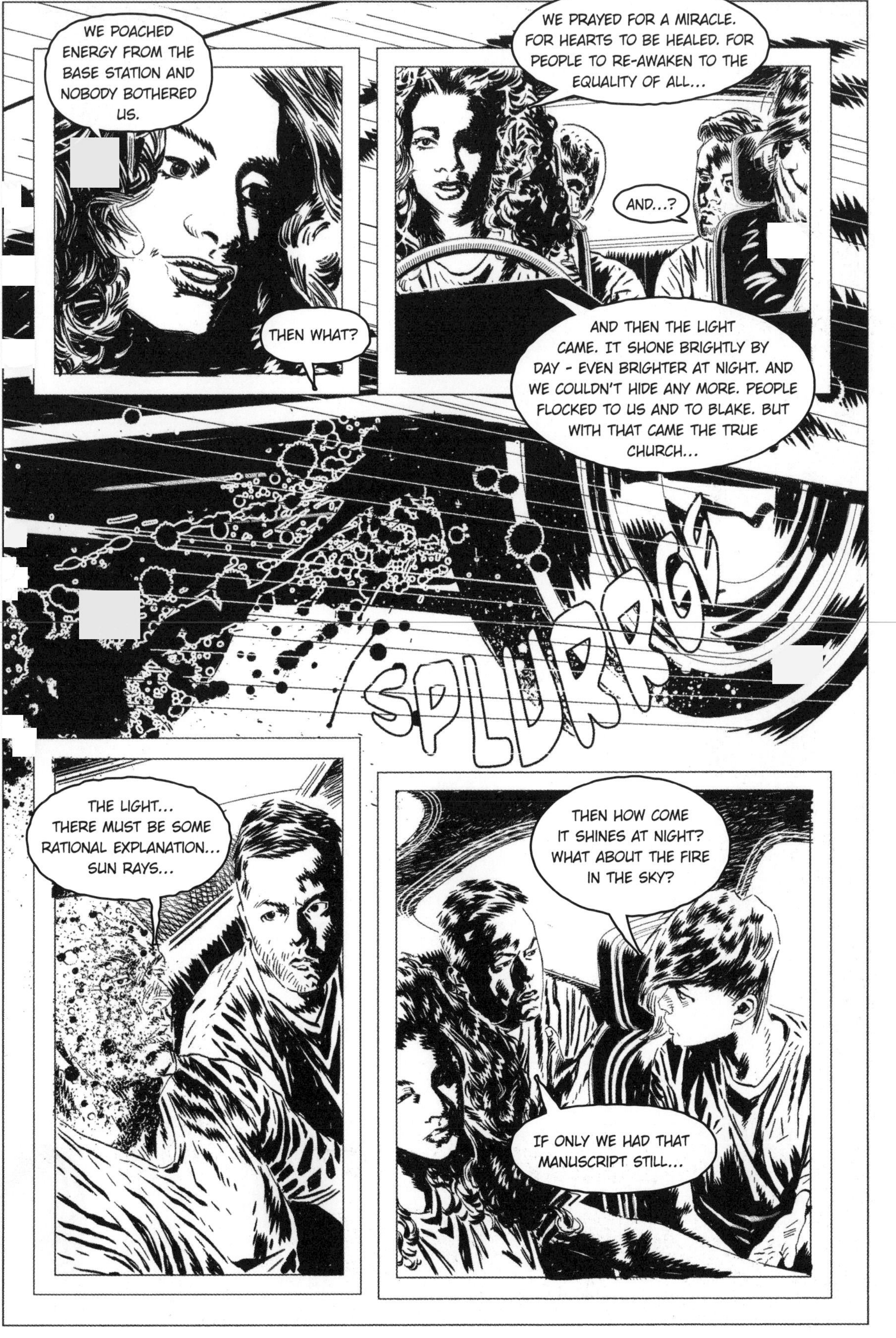
WE POACHED ENERGY FROM THE BASE STATION AND NOBODY BOTHERED US.
THEN WHAT?
WE PRAYED FOR A MIRACLE. FOR HEARTS TO BE HEALED. FOR PEOPLE TO RE-AWAKEN TO THE EQUALITY OF ALL...
AND...?
AND THEN THE LIGHT CAME. IT SHONE BRIGHTLY BY DAY - EVEN BRIGHTER AT NIGHT. AND WE COULDN'T HIDE ANY MORE. PEOPLE FLOCKED TO US AND TO BLAKE. BUT WITH THAT CAME THE TRUE CHURCH...
SPLURRG!
THE LIGHT... THERE MUST BE SOME RATIONAL EXPLANATION... SUN RAYS...
THEN HOW COME IT SHINES AT NIGHT? WHAT ABOUT THE FIRE IN THE SKY?
IF ONLY WE HAD THAT MANUSCRIPT STILL...

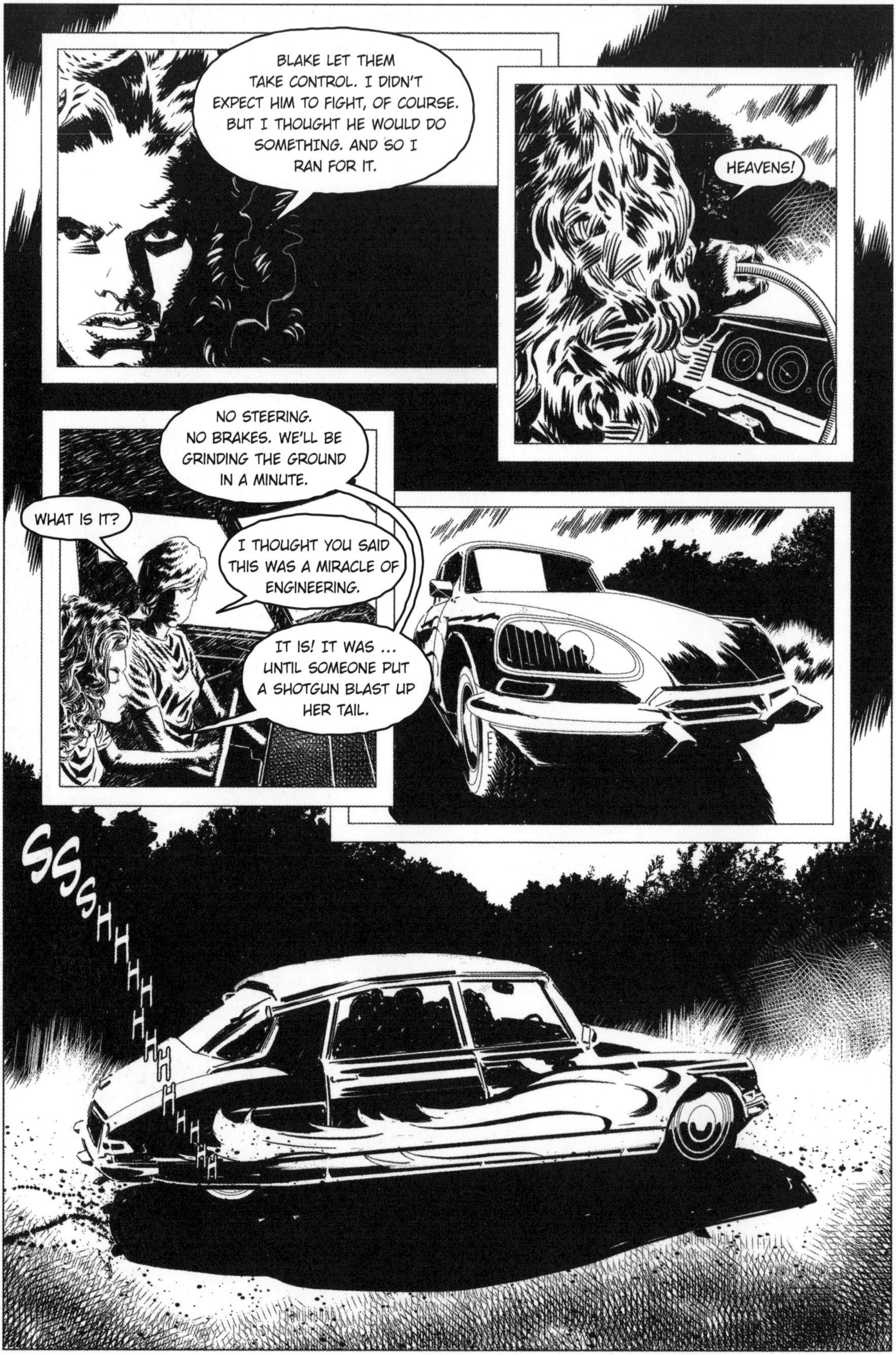
BLAKE LET THEM TAKE CONTROL. I DIDN'T EXPECT HIM TO FIGHT, OF COURSE. BUT I THOUGHT HE WOULD DO SOMETHING. AND SO I RAN FOR IT.
HEAVENS!
NO STEERING. NO BRAKES. WE'LL BE GRINDING THE GROUND IN A MINUTE.
WHAT IS IT?
I THOUGHT YOU SAID THIS WAS A MIRACLE OF ENGINEERING.
IT IS! IT WAS ... UNTIL SOMEONE PUT A SHOTGUN BLAST UP HER TAIL.
SSSHHHHHHHHHHHH

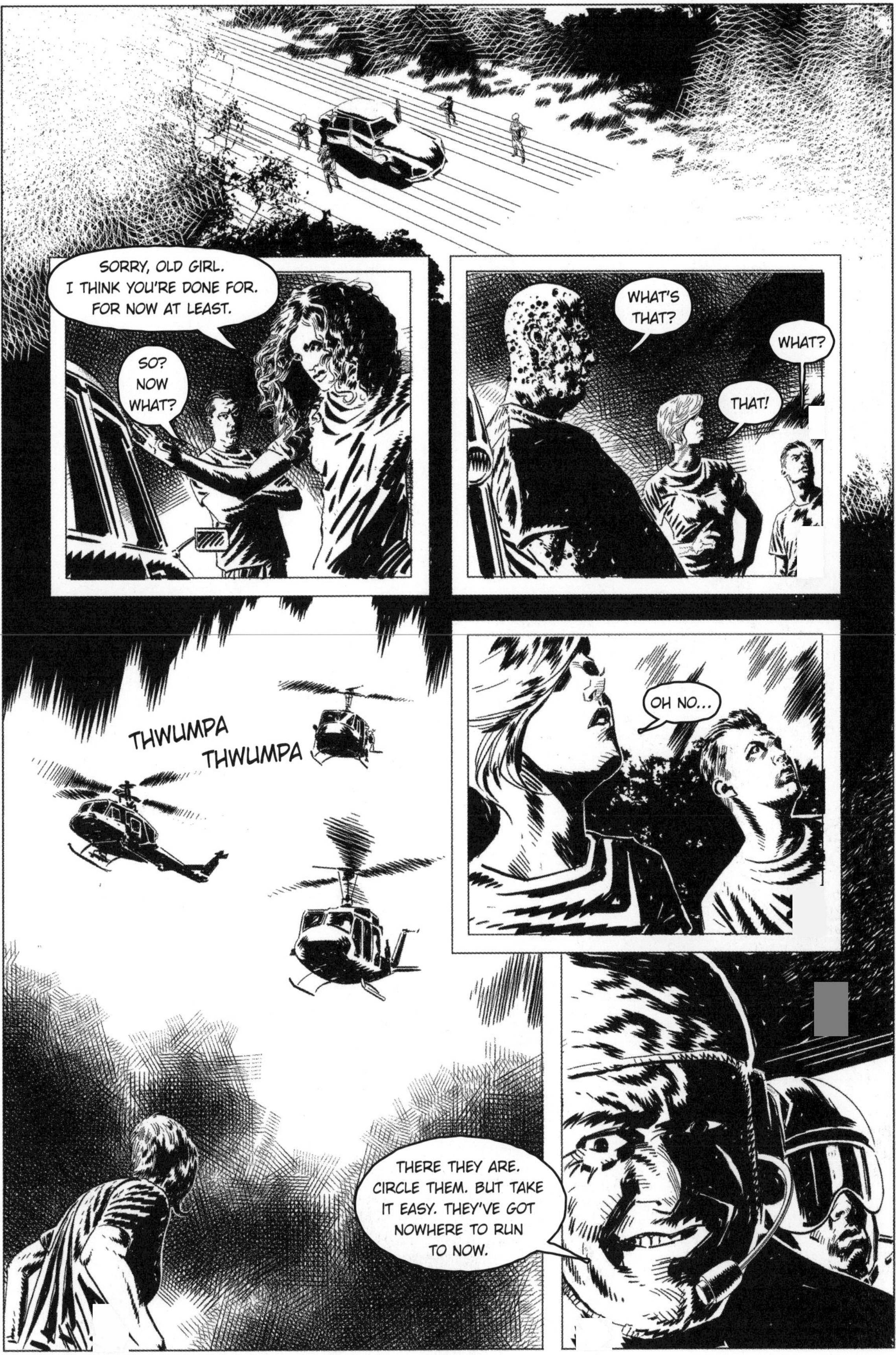
SORRY, OLD GIRL. I THINK YOU'RE DONE FOR. FOR NOW AT LEAST.
SO? NOW WHAT?
WHAT'S THAT?
WHAT?
THAT!
THWUMPA THWUMPA
OH NO...
THERE THEY ARE. CIRCLE THEM. BUT TAKE IT EASY. THEY'VE GOT NOWHERE TO RUN TO NOW.

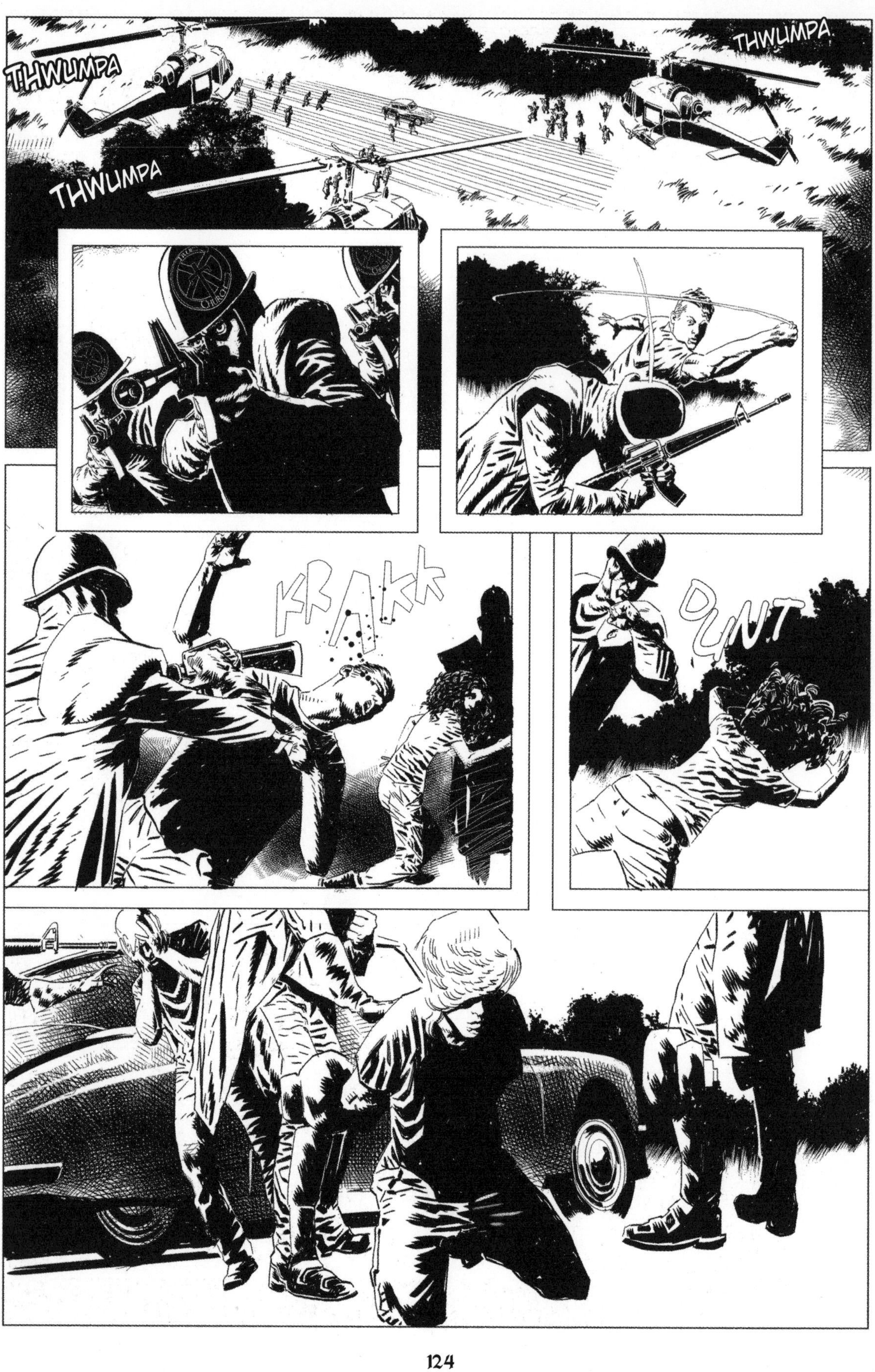
THWUMPA
THWUMPA
THWUMPA
KRAKK
DUNT

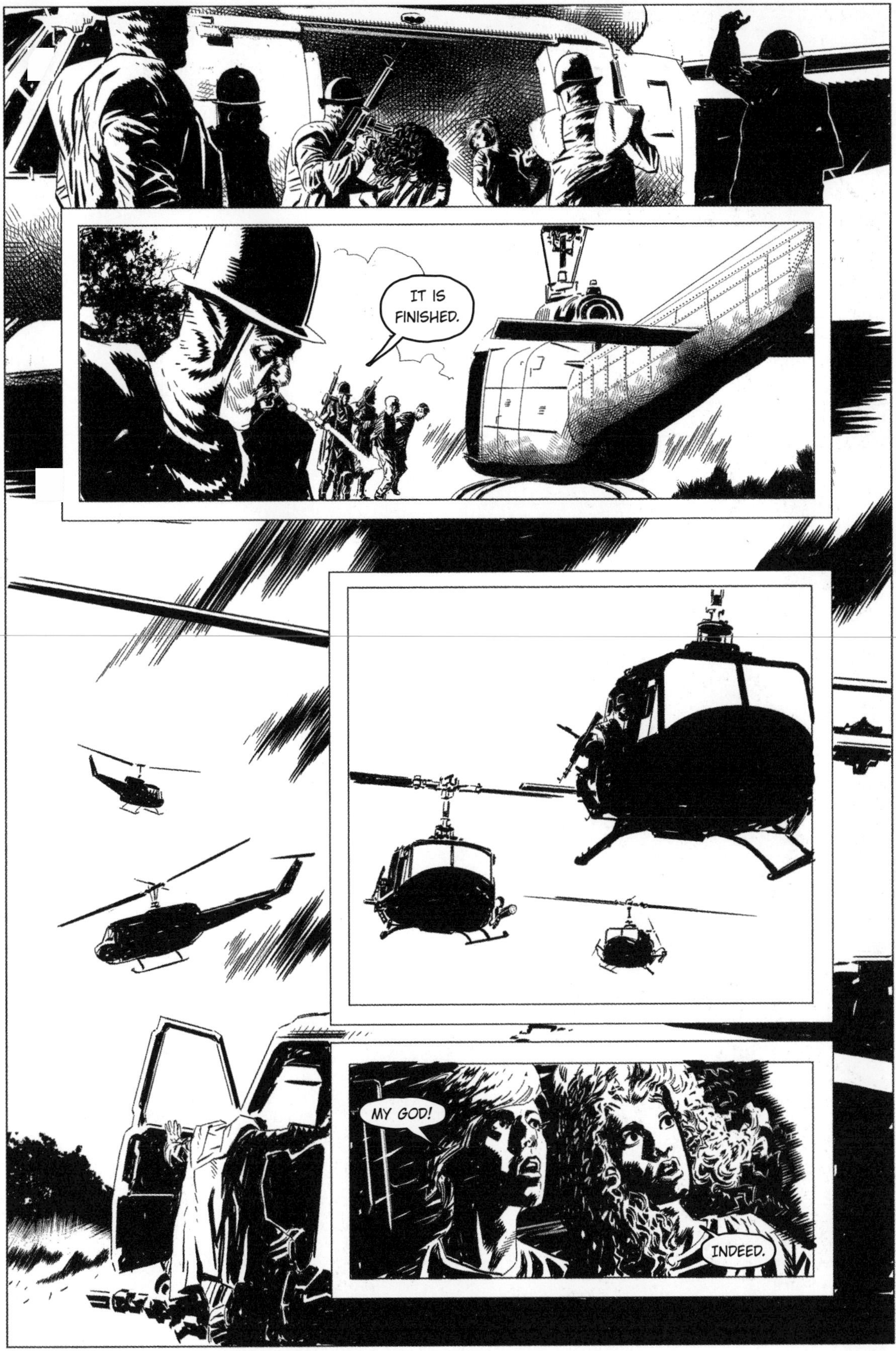
IT IS FINISHED.
MY GOD!
INDEED.

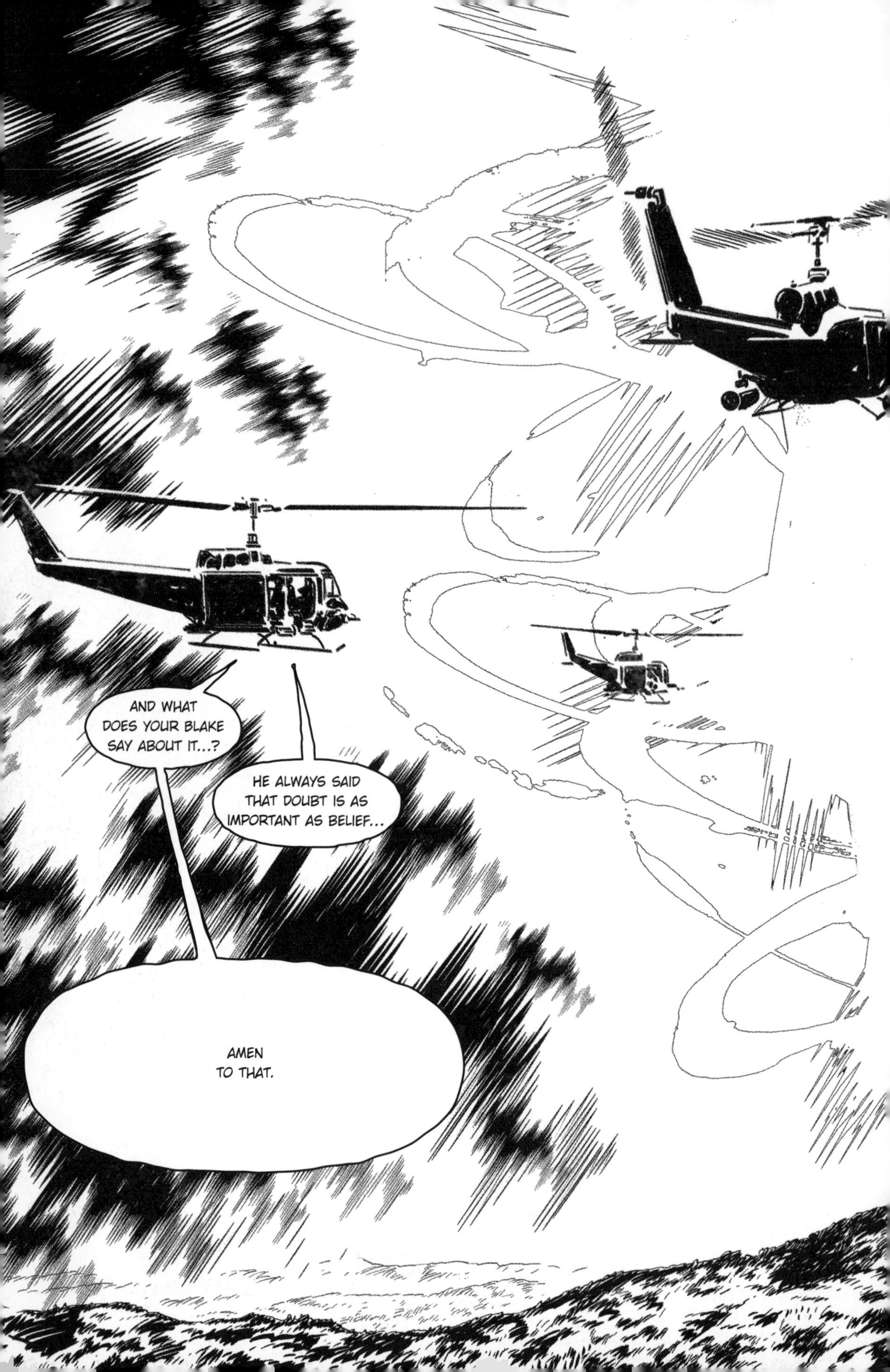
AND WHAT DOES YOUR BLAKE SAY ABOUT IT...?
HE ALWAYS SAID THAT DOUBT IS AS IMPORTANT AS BELIEF...
AMEN TO THAT.

Lesson Seven

Into thine hands, O Lord, I commend my Spirit

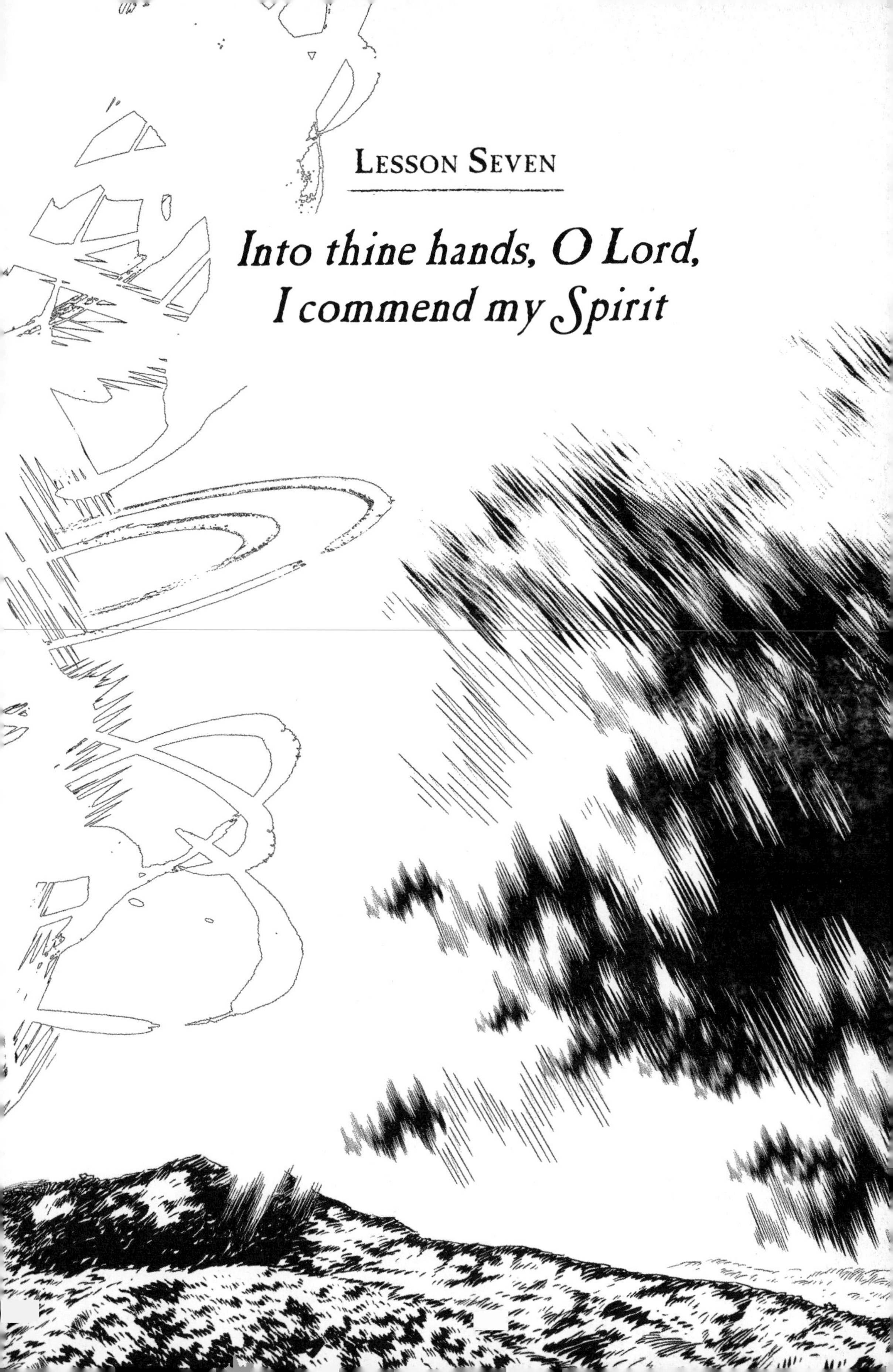

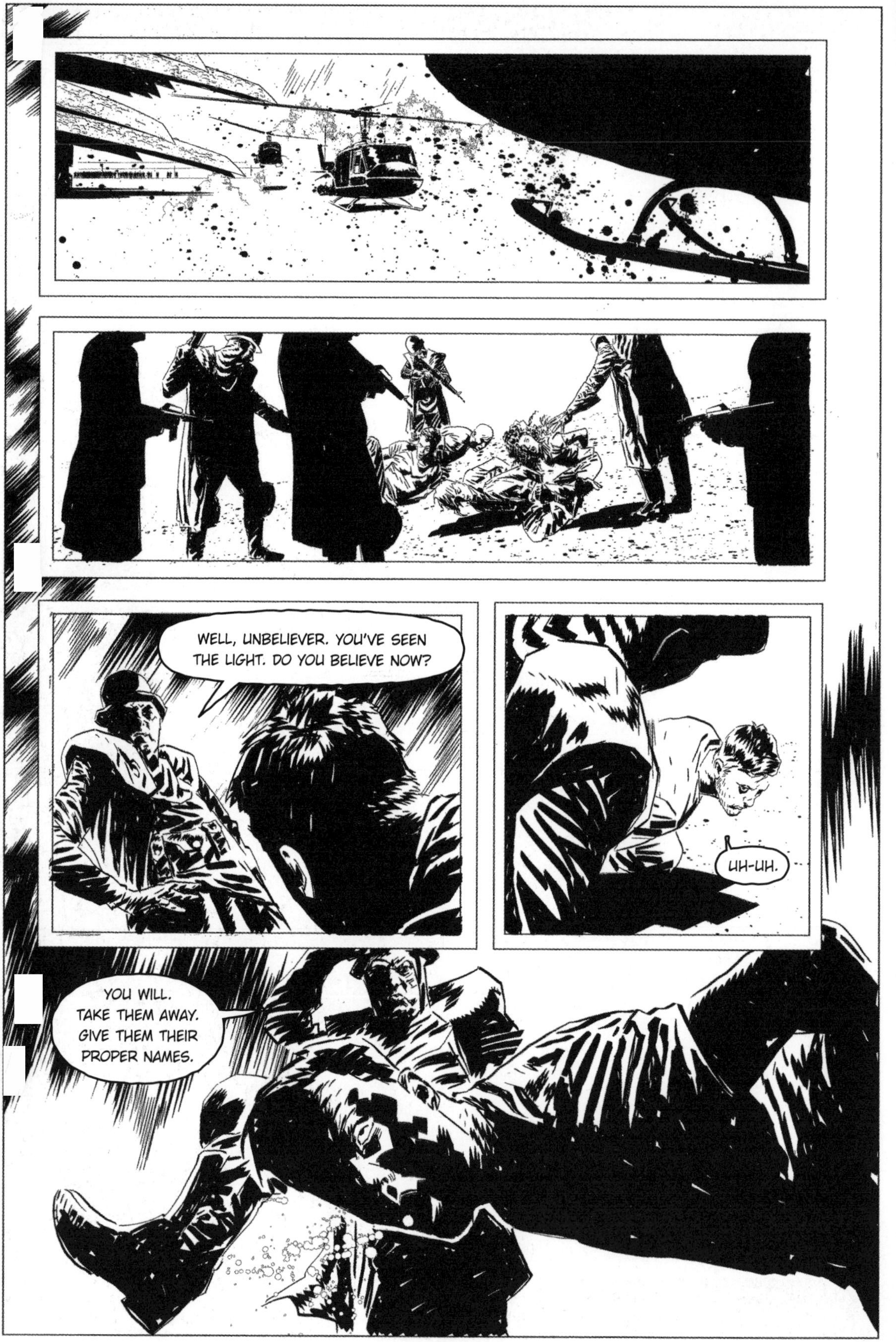
WELL, UNBELIEVER. YOU'VE SEEN THE LIGHT. DO YOU BELIEVE NOW?
UH-UH.
YOU WILL. TAKE THEM AWAY. GIVE THEM THEIR PROPER NAMES.

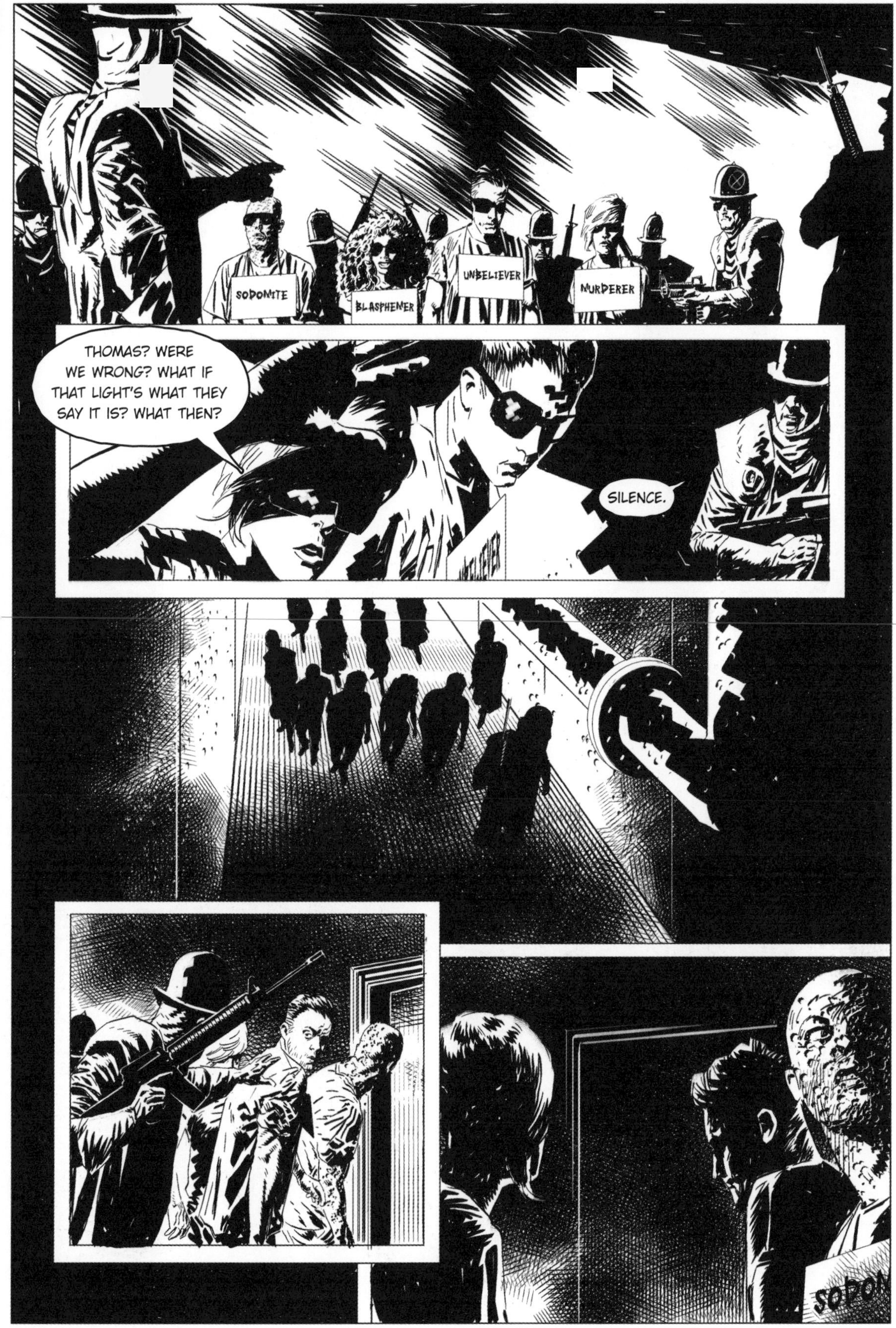
SODOMITE
BLASPHEMER
UNBELIEVER
MURDERER
THOMAS? WERE WE WRONG? WHAT IF THAT LIGHT'S WHAT THEY SAY IT IS? WHAT THEN?
SILENCE.
UNBELIEVER

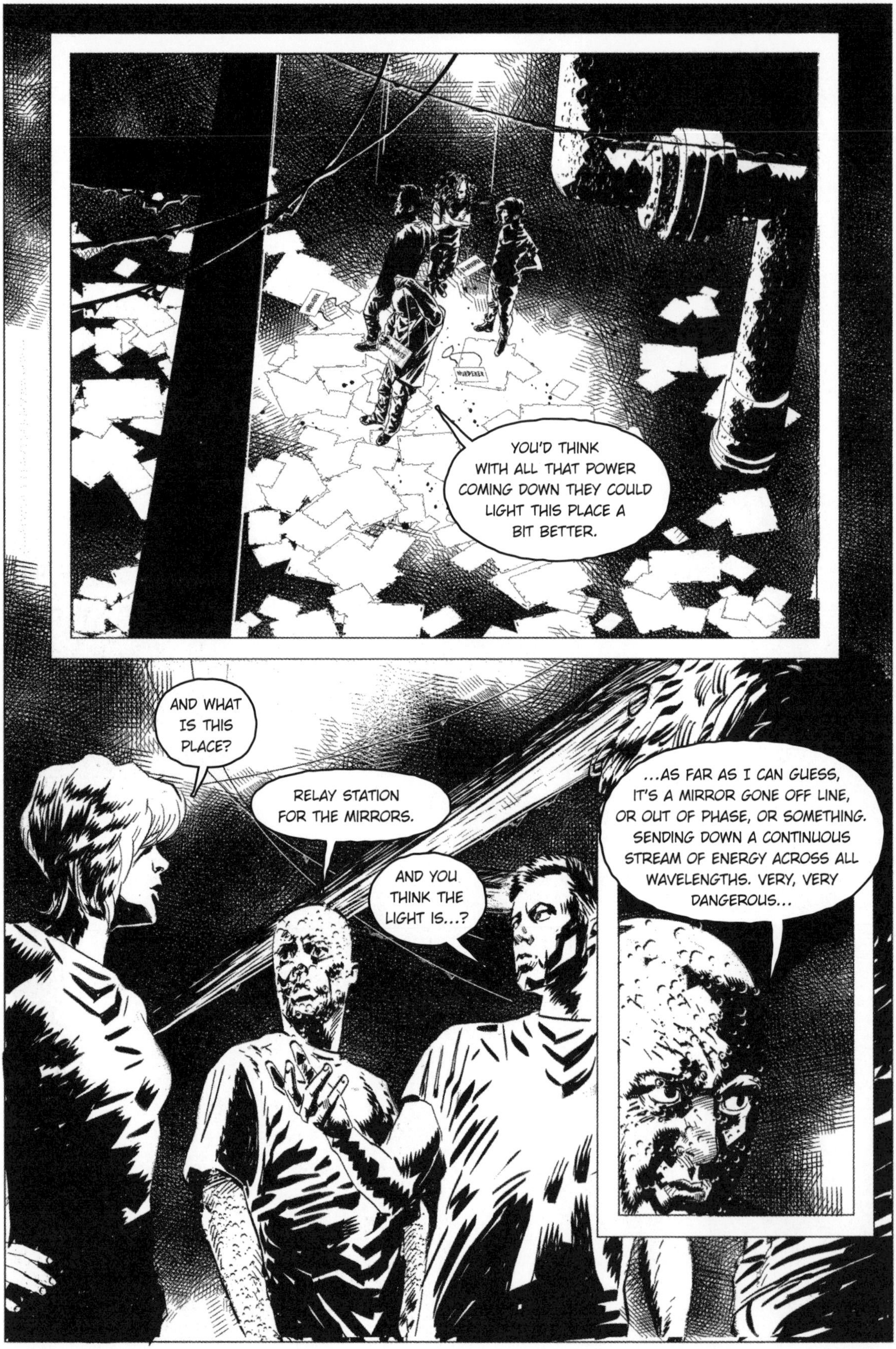
YOU'D THINK WITH ALL THAT POWER COMING DOWN THEY COULD LIGHT THIS PLACE A BIT BETTER.
AND WHAT IS THIS PLACE?
RELAY STATION FOR THE MIRRORS.
AND YOU THINK THE LIGHT IS...?
...AS FAR AS I CAN GUESS, IT'S A MIRROR GONE OFF LINE, OR OUT OF PHASE, OR SOMETHING. SENDING DOWN A CONTINUOUS STREAM OF ENERGY ACROSS ALL WAVELENGTHS. VERY, VERY DANGEROUS...

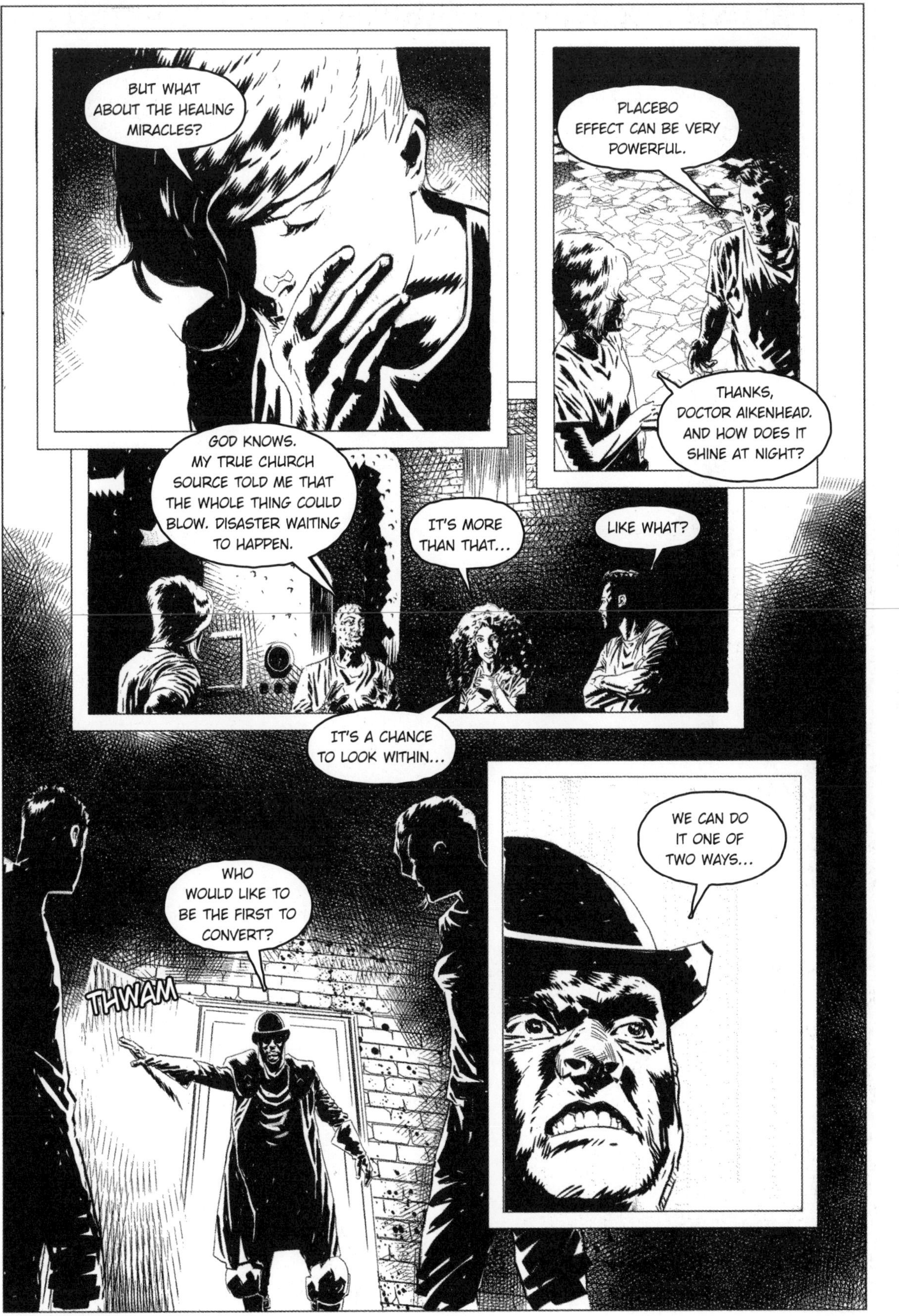
BUT WHAT ABOUT THE HEALING MIRACLES?
PLACEBO EFFECT CAN BE VERY POWERFUL.
THANKS, DOCTOR AIKENHEAD. AND HOW DOES IT SHINE AT NIGHT?
GOD KNOWS. MY TRUE CHURCH SOURCE TOLD ME THAT THE WHOLE THING COULD BLOW. DISASTER WAITING TO HAPPEN.
IT'S MORE THAN THAT...
LIKE WHAT?
IT'S A CHANCE TO LOOK WITHIN...
WHO WOULD LIKE TO BE THE FIRST TO CONVERT?
THWAM
WE CAN DO IT ONE OF TWO WAYS...

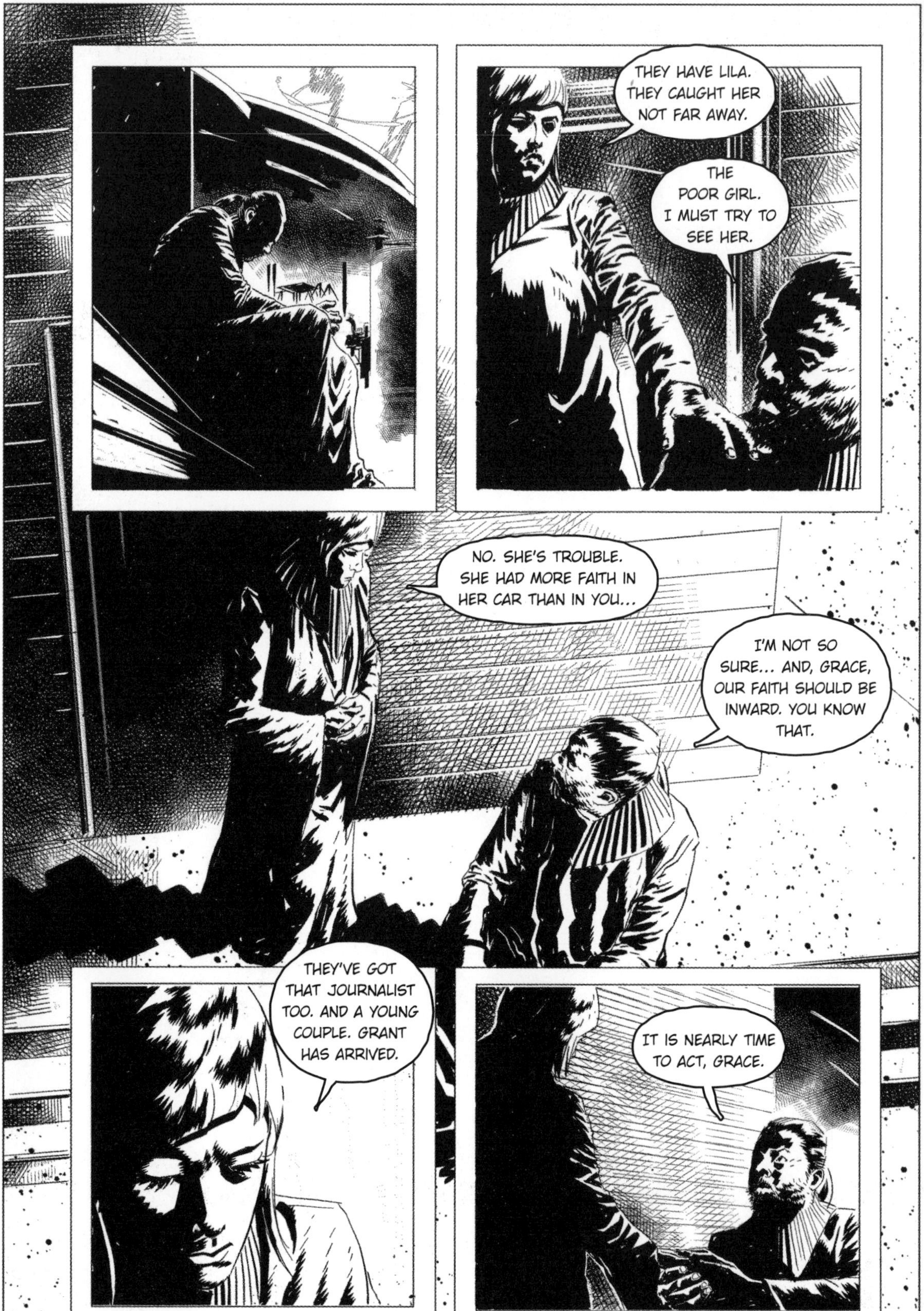
THEY HAVE LILA. THEY CAUGHT HER NOT FAR AWAY.
THE POOR GIRL. I MUST TRY TO SEE HER.
NO. SHE'S TROUBLE. SHE HAD MORE FAITH IN HER CAR THAN IN YOU...
I'M NOT SO SURE... AND, GRACE, OUR FAITH SHOULD BE INWARD. YOU KNOW THAT.
THEY'VE GOT THAT JOURNALIST TOO. AND A YOUNG COUPLE. GRANT HAS ARRIVED.
IT IS NEARLY TIME TO ACT, GRACE.

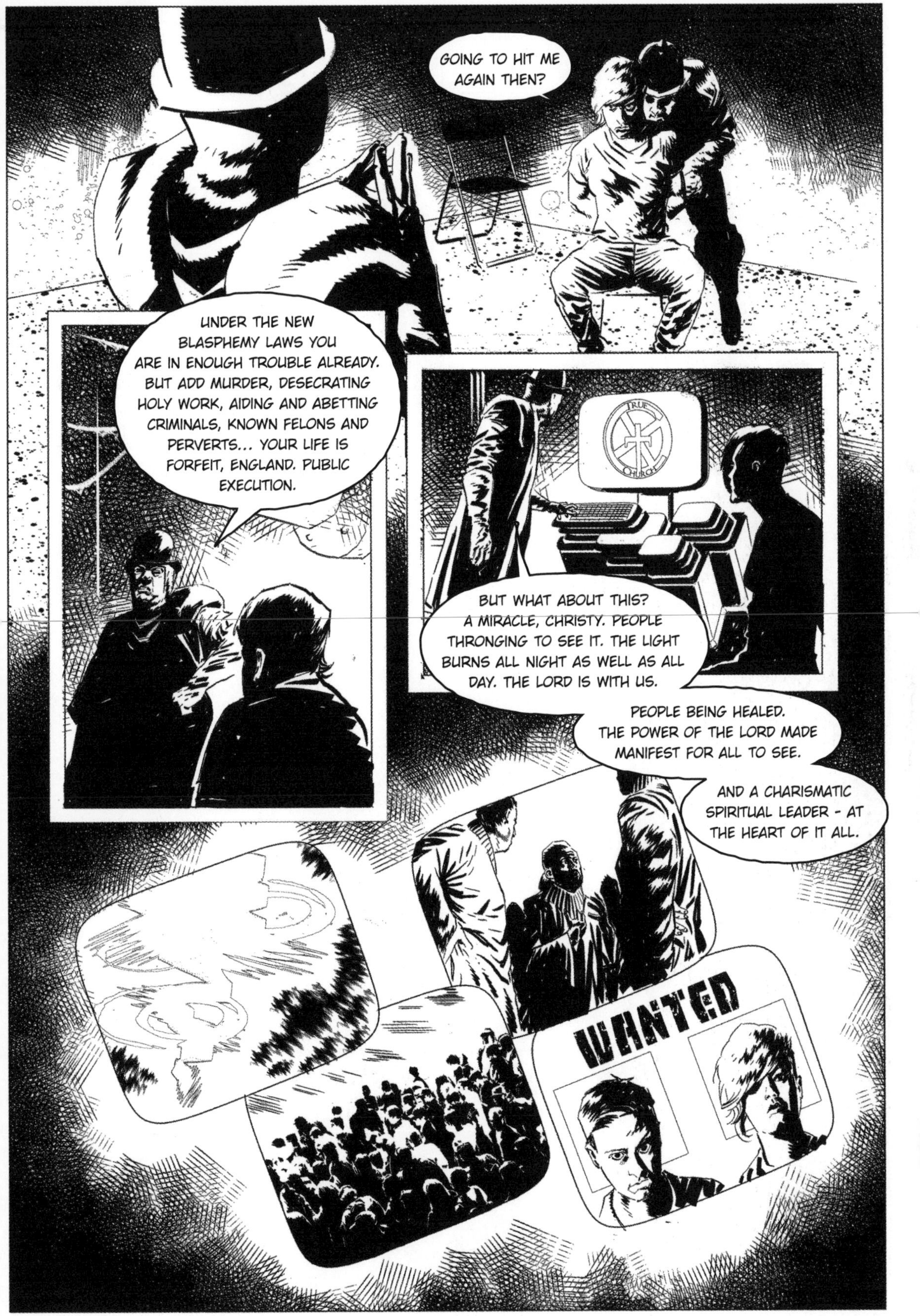
GOING TO HIT ME AGAIN THEN?
UNDER THE NEW BLASPHEMY LAWS YOU ARE IN ENOUGH TROUBLE ALREADY. BUT ADD MURDER, DESECRATING HOLY WORK, AIDING AND ABETTING CRIMINALS, KNOWN FELONS AND PERVERTS... YOUR LIFE IS FORFEIT, ENGLAND. PUBLIC EXECUTION.
TRUE CHURCH
BUT WHAT ABOUT THIS? A MIRACLE, CHRISTY. PEOPLE THRONGING TO SEE IT. THE LIGHT BURNS ALL NIGHT AS WELL AS ALL DAY. THE LORD IS WITH US.
PEOPLE BEING HEALED. THE POWER OF THE LORD MADE MANIFEST FOR ALL TO SEE.
AND A CHARISMATIC SPIRITUAL LEADER - AT THE HEART OF IT ALL.
WANTED

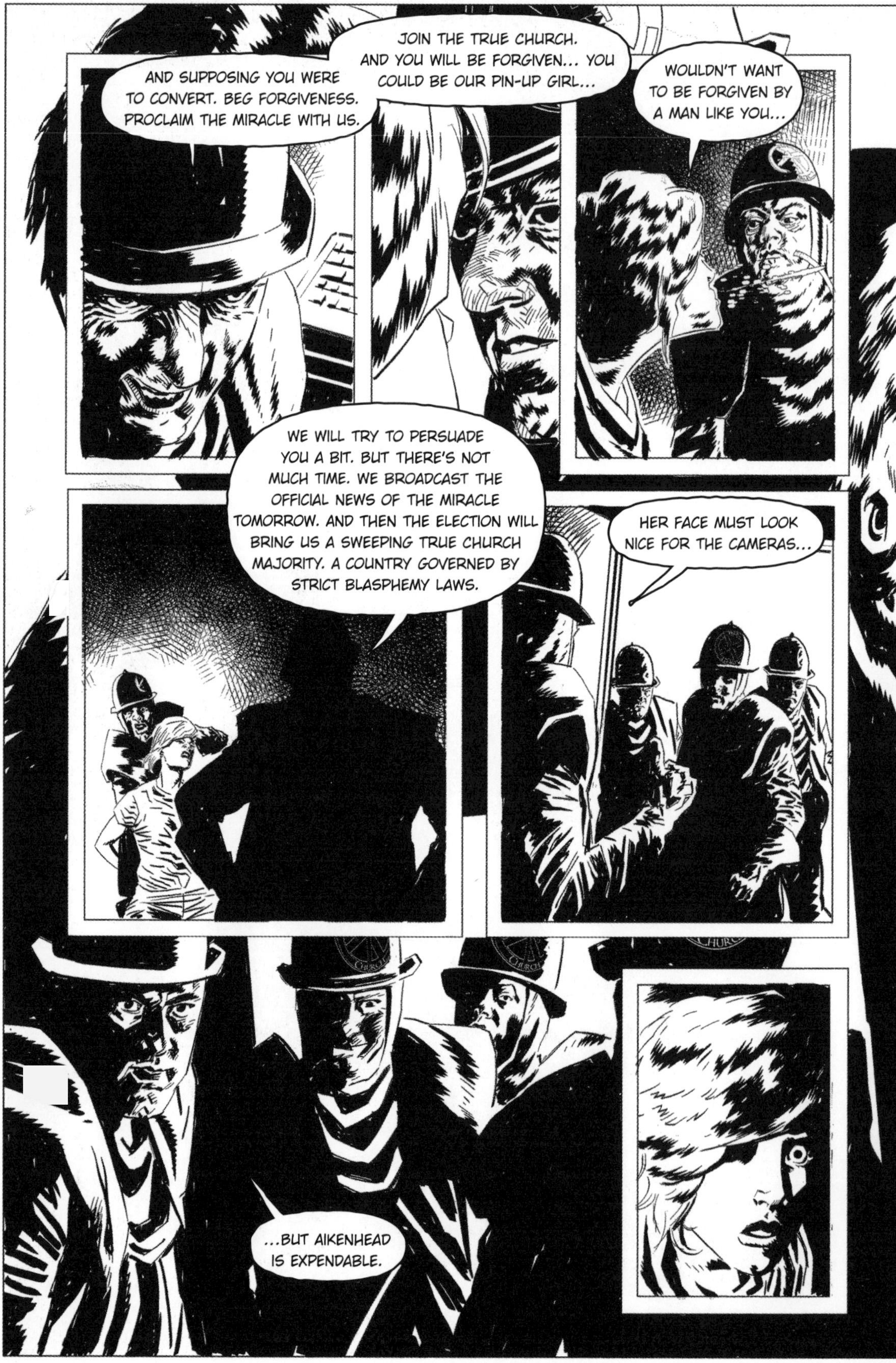
AND SUPPOSING YOU WERE TO CONVERT. BEG FORGIVENESS. PROCLAIM THE MIRACLE WITH US.
JOIN THE TRUE CHURCH. AND YOU WILL BE FORGIVEN... YOU COULD BE OUR PIN-UP GIRL...
WOULDN'T WANT TO BE FORGIVEN BY A MAN LIKE YOU...
WE WILL TRY TO PERSUADE YOU A BIT. BUT THERE'S NOT MUCH TIME. WE BROADCAST THE OFFICIAL NEWS OF THE MIRACLE TOMORROW. AND THEN THE ELECTION WILL BRING US A SWEEPING TRUE CHURCH MAJORITY. A COUNTRY GOVERNED BY STRICT BLASPHEMY LAWS.
HER FACE MUST LOOK NICE FOR THE CAMERAS...
...BUT AIKENHEAD IS EXPENDABLE.

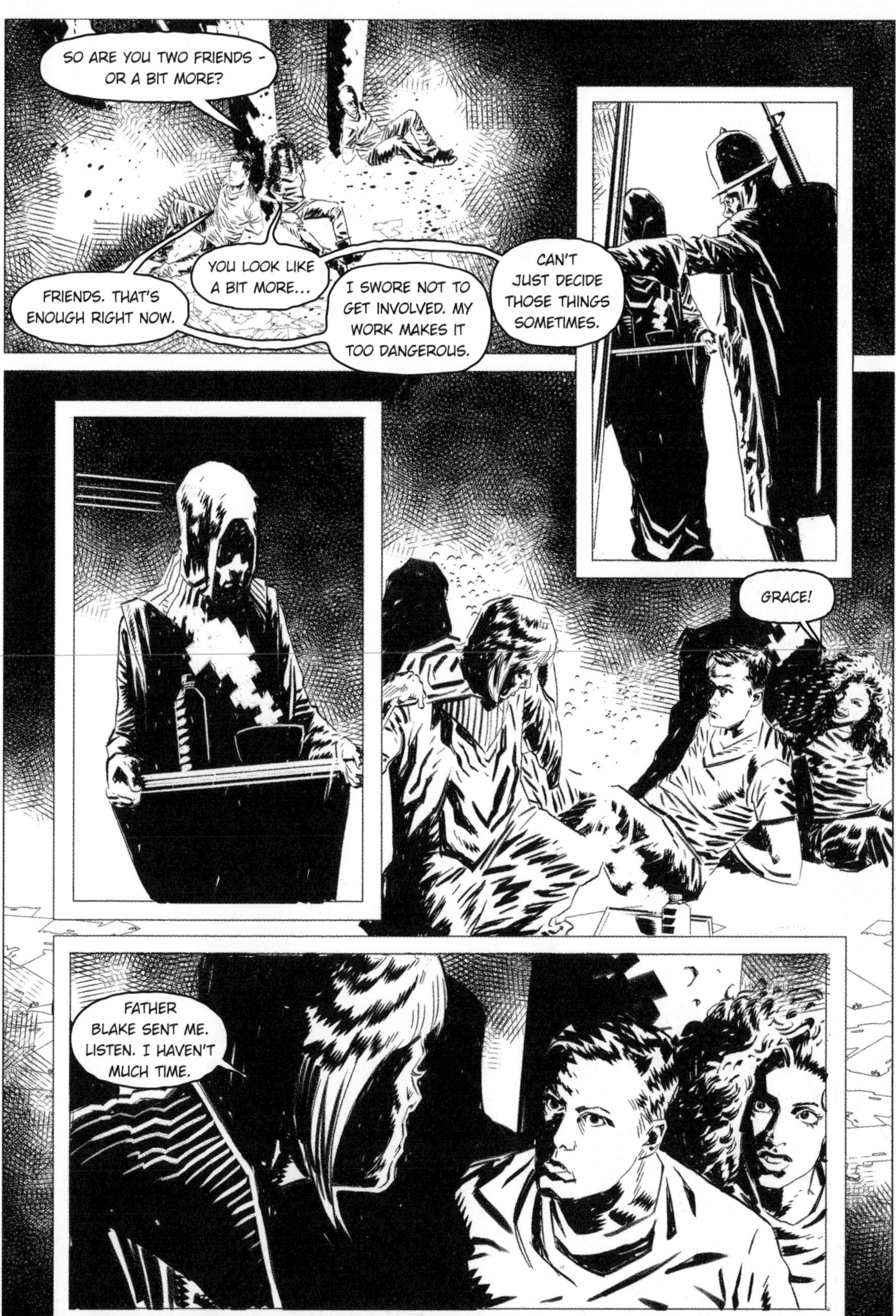
SO ARE YOU TWO FRIENDS - OR A BIT MORE?
FRIENDS. THAT'S ENOUGH RIGHT NOW.
YOU LOOK LIKE A BIT MORE...
I SWORE NOT TO GET INVOLVED. MY WORK MAKES IT TOO DANGEROUS.
CAN'T JUST DECIDE THOSE THINGS SOMETIMES.
GRACE!
FATHER BLAKE SENT ME. LISTEN. I HAVEN'T MUCH TIME.

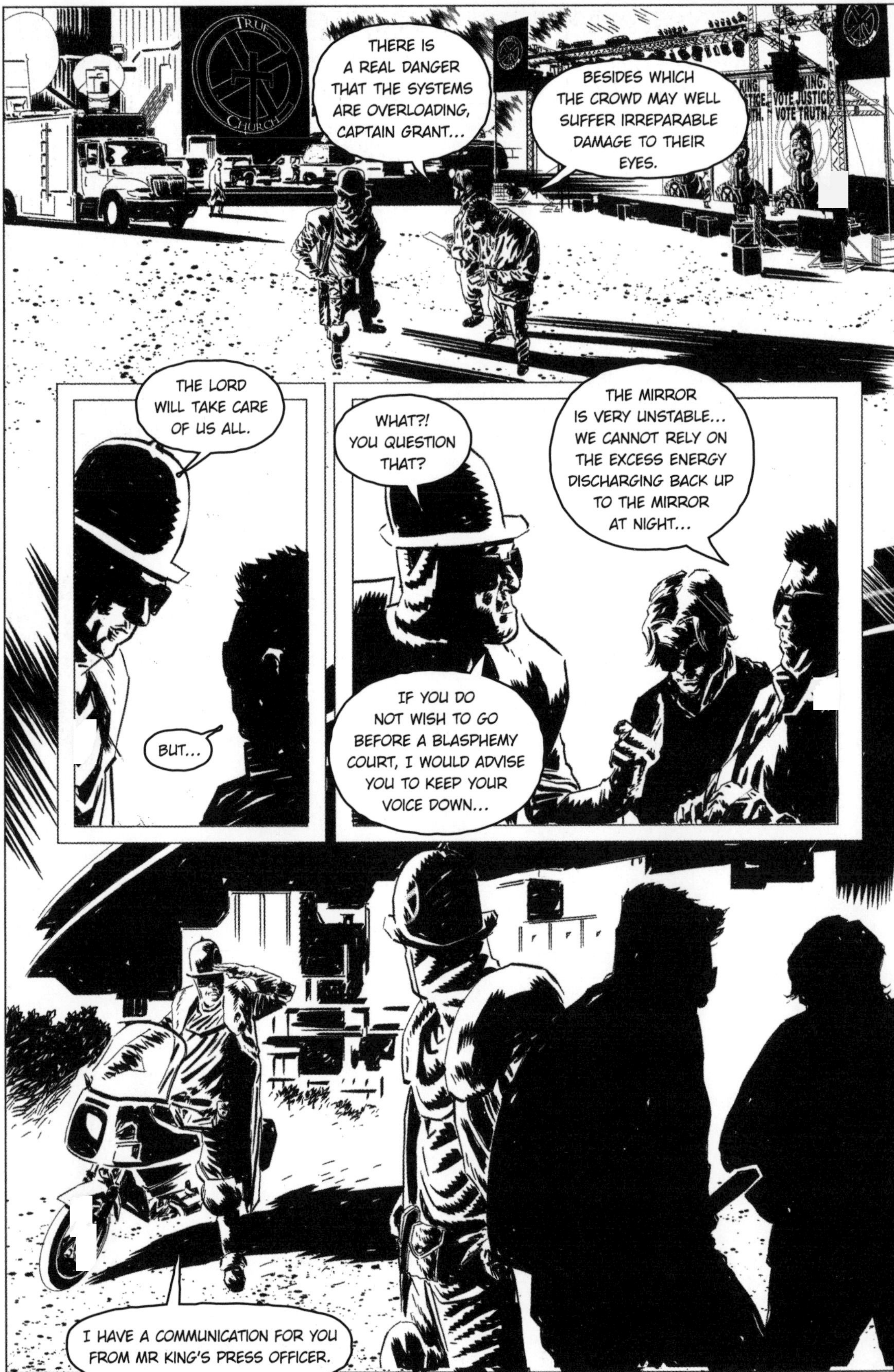

TRUE CHURCH
THERE IS A REAL DANGER THAT THE SYSTEMS ARE OVERLOADING, CAPTAIN GRANT...
BESIDES WHICH THE CROWD MAY WELL SUFFER IRREPARABLE DAMAGE TO THEIR EYES.
VOTE JUSTICE VOTE TRUTH
THE LORD WILL TAKE CARE OF US ALL.
BUT...
WHAT?! YOU QUESTION THAT?
THE MIRROR IS VERY UNSTABLE... WE CANNOT RELY ON THE EXCESS ENERGY DISCHARGING BACK UP TO THE MIRROR AT NIGHT...
IF YOU DO NOT WISH TO GO BEFORE A BLASPHEMY COURT, I WOULD ADVISE YOU TO KEEP YOUR VOICE DOWN...
I HAVE A COMMUNICATION FOR YOU FROM MR KING'S PRESS OFFICER.

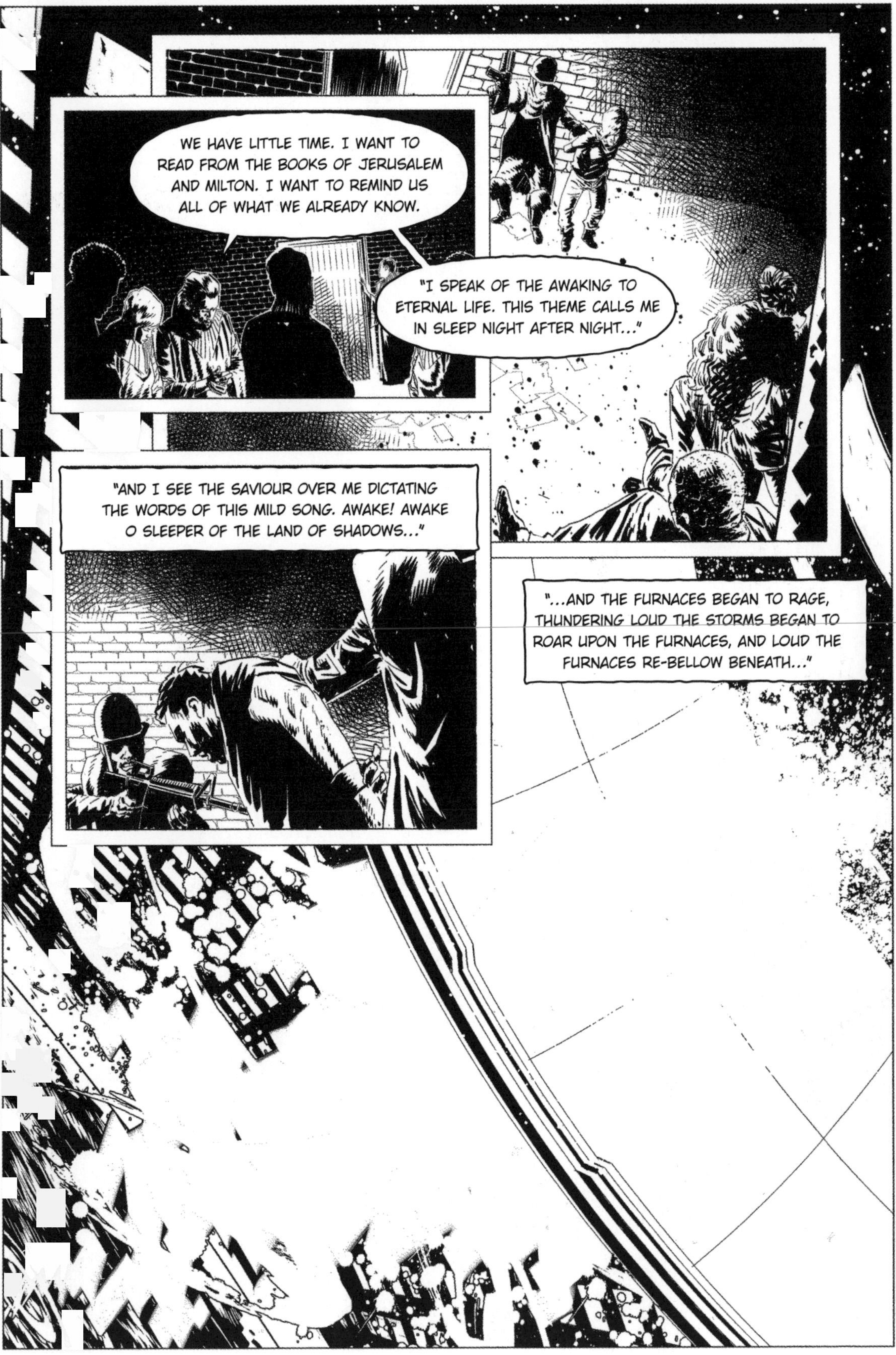
WE HAVE LITTLE TIME. I WANT TO READ FROM THE BOOKS OF JERUSALEM AND MILTON. I WANT TO REMIND US ALL OF WHAT WE ALREADY KNOW.
"I SPEAK OF THE AWAKING TO ETERNAL LIFE. THIS THEME CALLS ME IN SLEEP NIGHT AFTER NIGHT..."
"AND I SEE THE SAVIOUR OVER ME DICTATING THE WORDS OF THIS MILD SONG. AWAKE! AWAKE O SLEEPER OF THE LAND OF SHADOWS..."
"...AND THE FURNACES BEGAN TO RAGE, THUNDERING LOUD THE STORMS BEGAN TO ROAR UPON THE FURNACES, AND LOUD THE FURNACES RE-BELLOW BENEATH..."

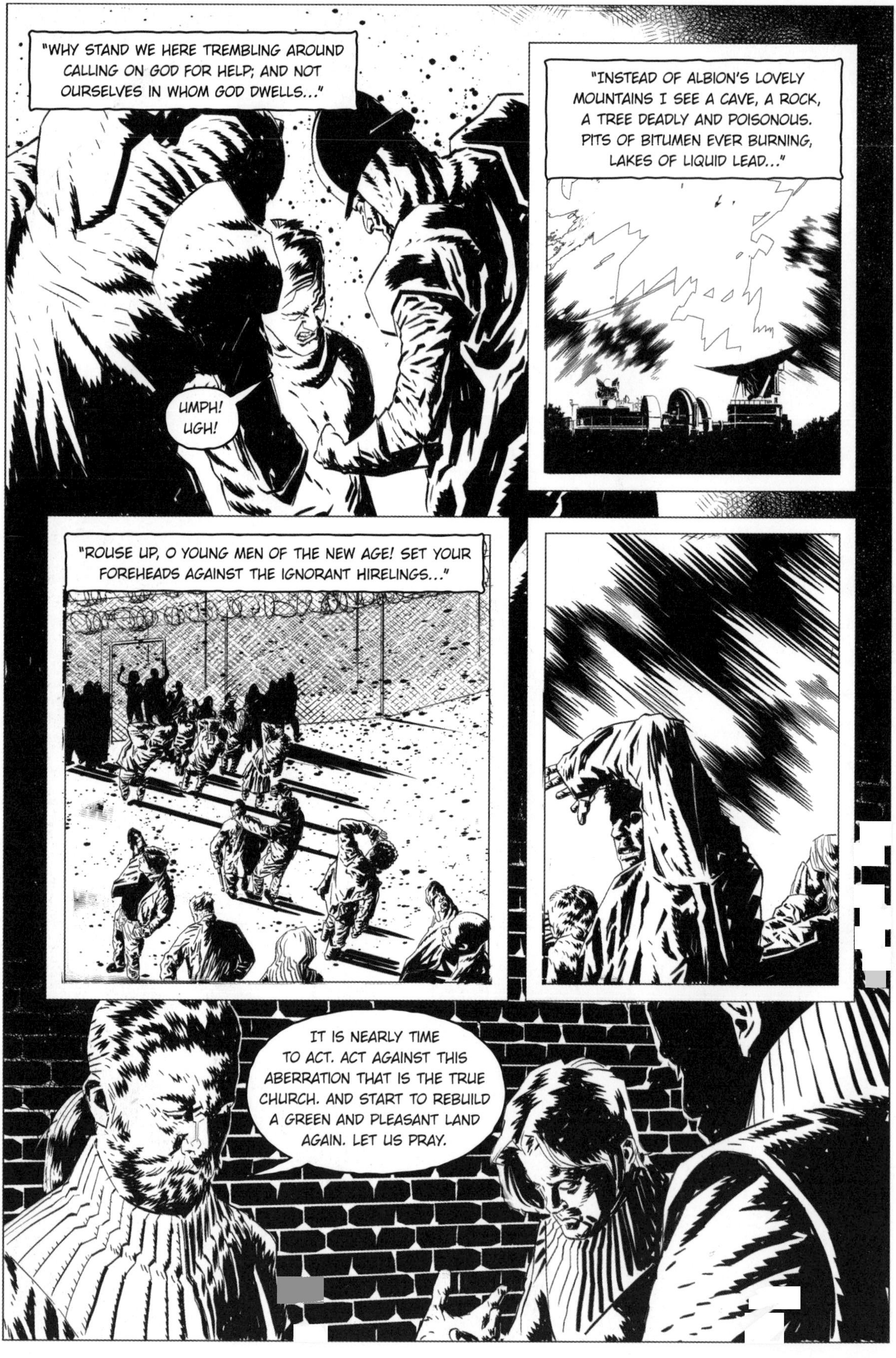
"WHY STAND WE HERE TREMBLING AROUND CALLING ON GOD FOR HELP; AND NOT OURSELVES IN WHOM GOD DWELLS..."
UMPH! UGH!
"INSTEAD OF ALBION'S LOVELY MOUNTAINS I SEE A CAVE, A ROCK, A TREE DEADLY AND POISONOUS. PITS OF BITUMEN EVER BURNING, LAKES OF LIQUID LEAD..."
"ROUSE UP, O YOUNG MEN OF THE NEW AGE! SET YOUR FOREHEADS AGAINST THE IGNORANT HIRELINGS..."
IT IS NEARLY TIME TO ACT. ACT AGAINST THIS ABERRATION THAT IS THE TRUE CHURCH. AND START TO REBUILD A GREEN AND PLEASANT LAND AGAIN. LET US PRAY.

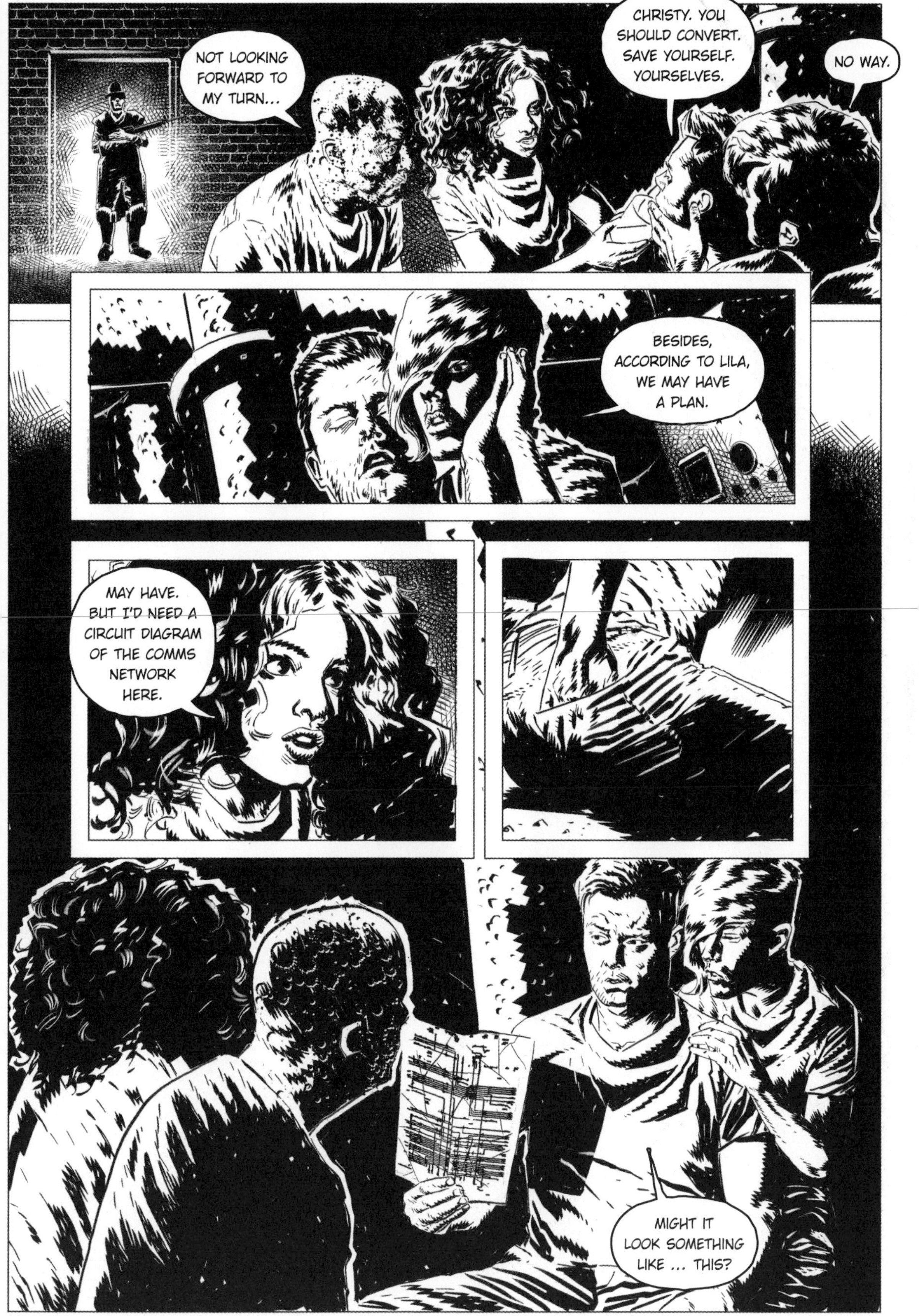
NOT LOOKING FORWARD TO MY TURN...
CHRISTY. YOU SHOULD CONVERT. SAVE YOURSELF. YOURSELVES.
NO WAY.
BESIDES, ACCORDING TO LILA, WE MAY HAVE A PLAN.
MAY HAVE. BUT I'D NEED A CIRCUIT DIAGRAM OF THE COMMS NETWORK HERE.
MIGHT IT LOOK SOMETHING LIKE ... THIS?

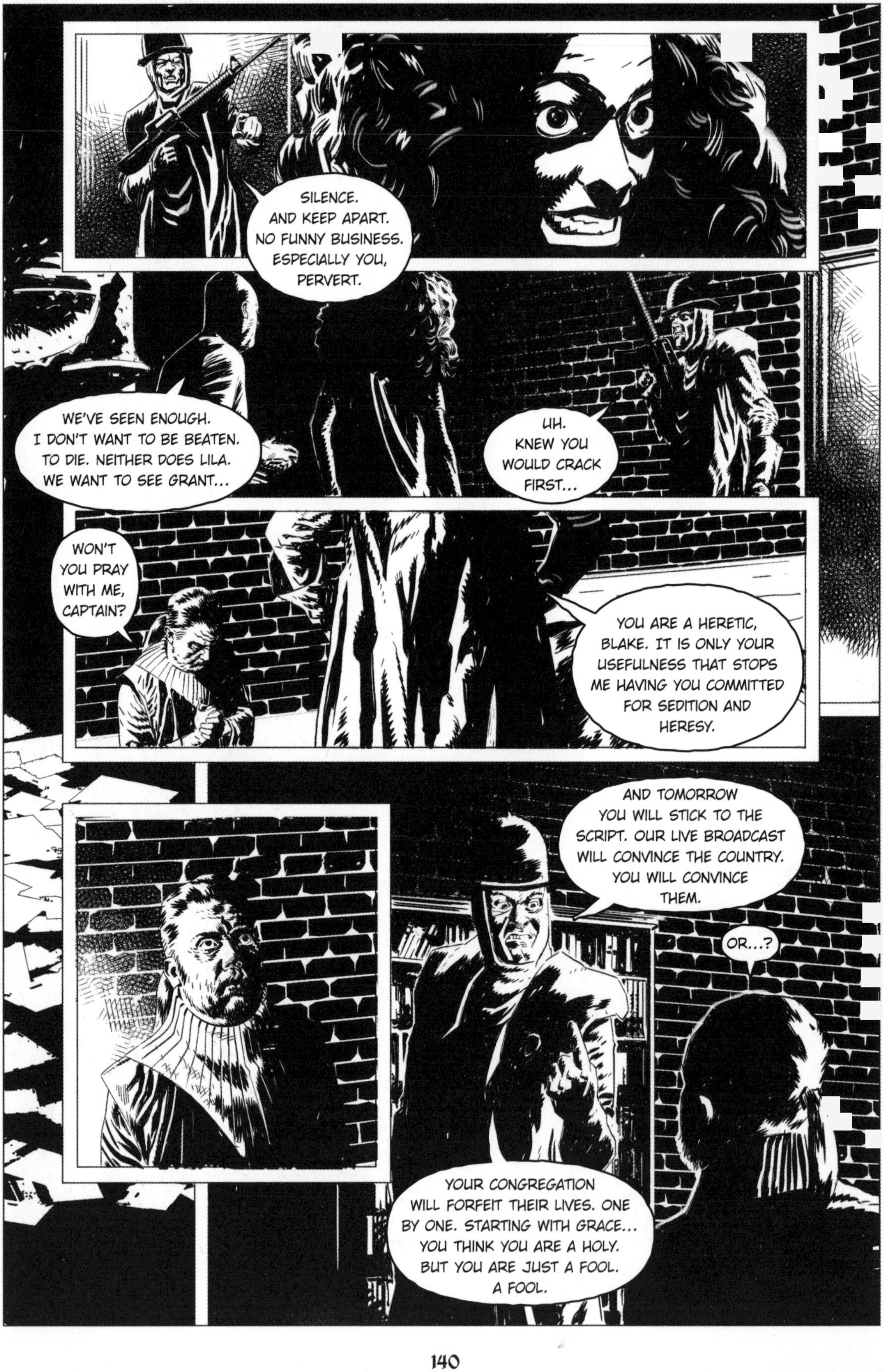
SILENCE. AND KEEP APART. NO FUNNY BUSINESS. ESPECIALLY YOU, PERVERT.
WE'VE SEEN ENOUGH. I DON'T WANT TO BE BEATEN. TO DIE. NEITHER DOES LILA. WE WANT TO SEE GRANT...
UH. KNEW YOU WOULD CRACK FIRST...
WON'T YOU PRAY WITH ME, CAPTAIN?
YOU ARE A HERETIC, BLAKE. IT IS ONLY YOUR USEFULNESS THAT STOPS ME HAVING YOU COMMITTED FOR SEDITION AND HERESY.
AND TOMORROW YOU WILL STICK TO THE SCRIPT. OUR LIVE BROADCAST WILL CONVINCE THE COUNTRY. YOU WILL CONVINCE THEM.
OR...?
YOUR CONGREGATION WILL FORFEIT THEIR LIVES. ONE BY ONE. STARTING WITH GRACE... YOU THINK YOU ARE A HOLY. BUT YOU ARE JUST A FOOL. A FOOL.

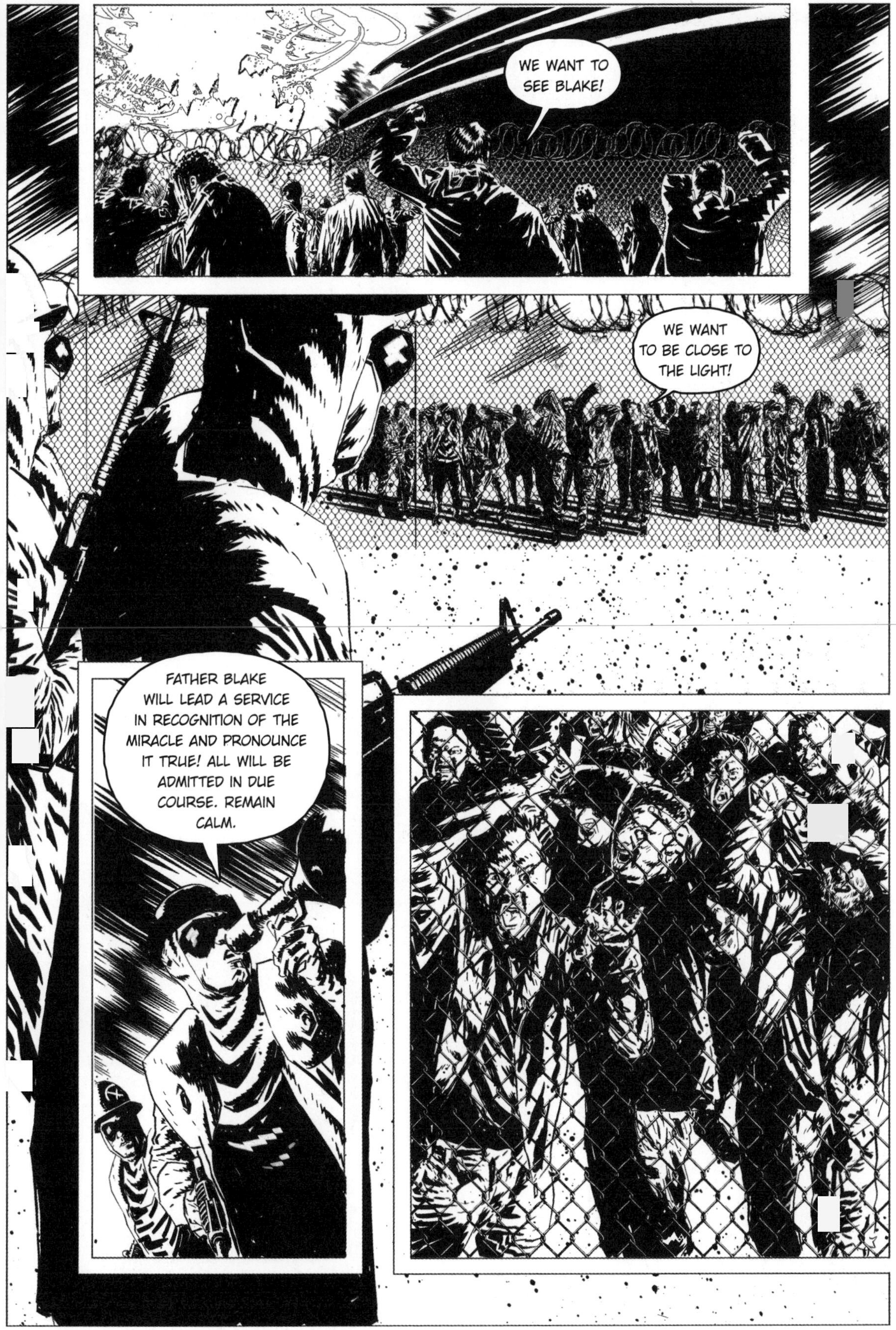
WE WANT TO SEE BLAKE!
WE WANT TO BE CLOSE TO THE LIGHT!
FATHER BLAKE WILL LEAD A SERVICE IN RECOGNITION OF THE MIRACLE AND PRONOUNCE IT TRUE! ALL WILL BE ADMITTED IN DUE COURSE. REMAIN CALM.

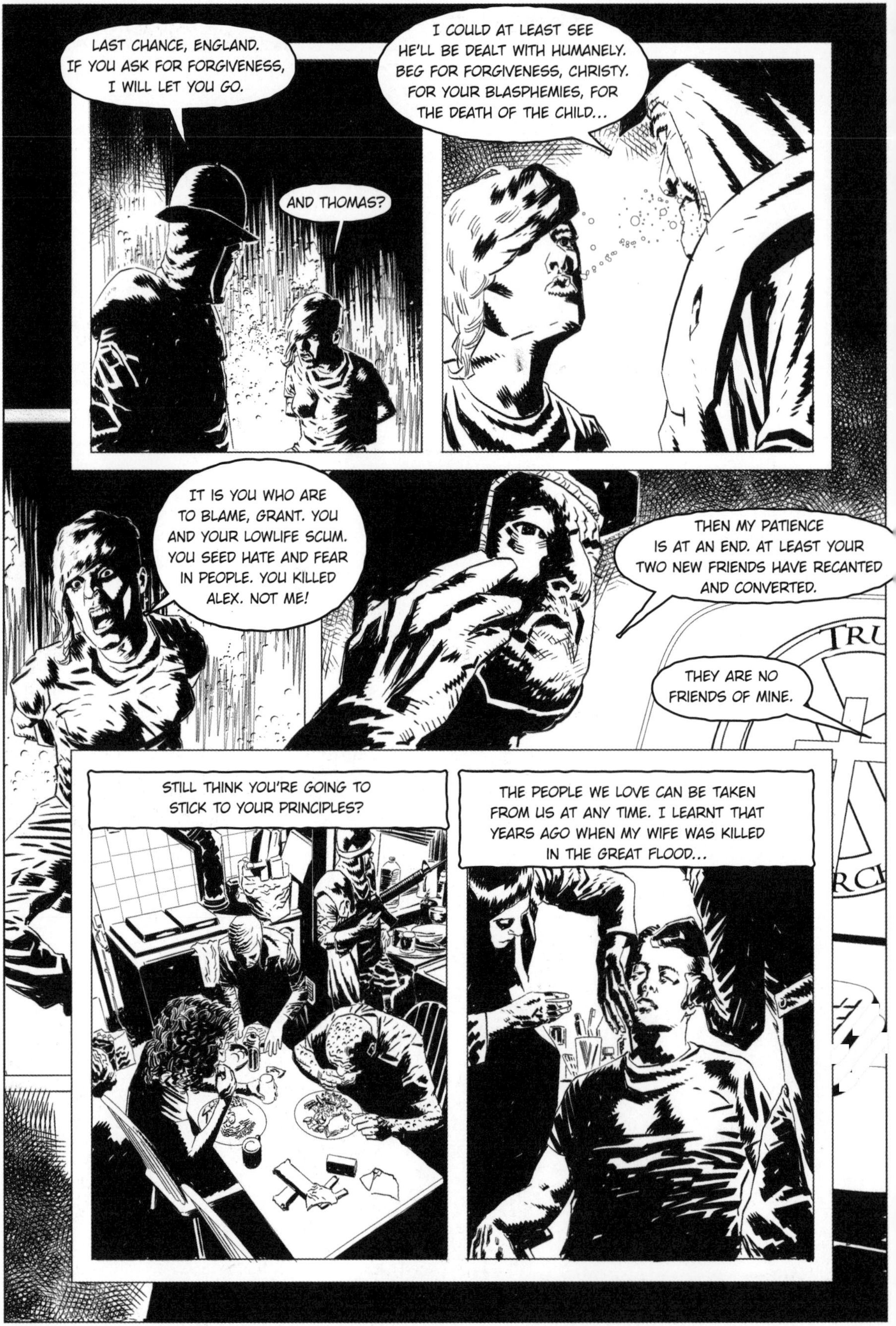
LAST CHANCE, ENGLAND. IF YOU ASK FOR FORGIVENESS, I WILL LET YOU GO.
AND THOMAS?
I COULD AT LEAST SEE HE'LL BE DEALT WITH HUMANELY. BEG FOR FORGIVENESS, CHRISTY. FOR YOUR BLASPHEMIES, FOR THE DEATH OF THE CHILD...
IT IS YOU WHO ARE TO BLAME, GRANT. YOU AND YOUR LOWLIFE SCUM. YOU SEED HATE AND FEAR IN PEOPLE. YOU KILLED ALEX. NOT ME!
THEN MY PATIENCE IS AT AN END. AT LEAST YOUR TWO NEW FRIENDS HAVE RECANTED AND CONVERTED.
THEY ARE NO FRIENDS OF MINE.
STILL THINK YOU'RE GOING TO STICK TO YOUR PRINCIPLES?
THE PEOPLE WE LOVE CAN BE TAKEN FROM US AT ANY TIME. I LEARNT THAT YEARS AGO WHEN MY WIFE WAS KILLED IN THE GREAT FLOOD...

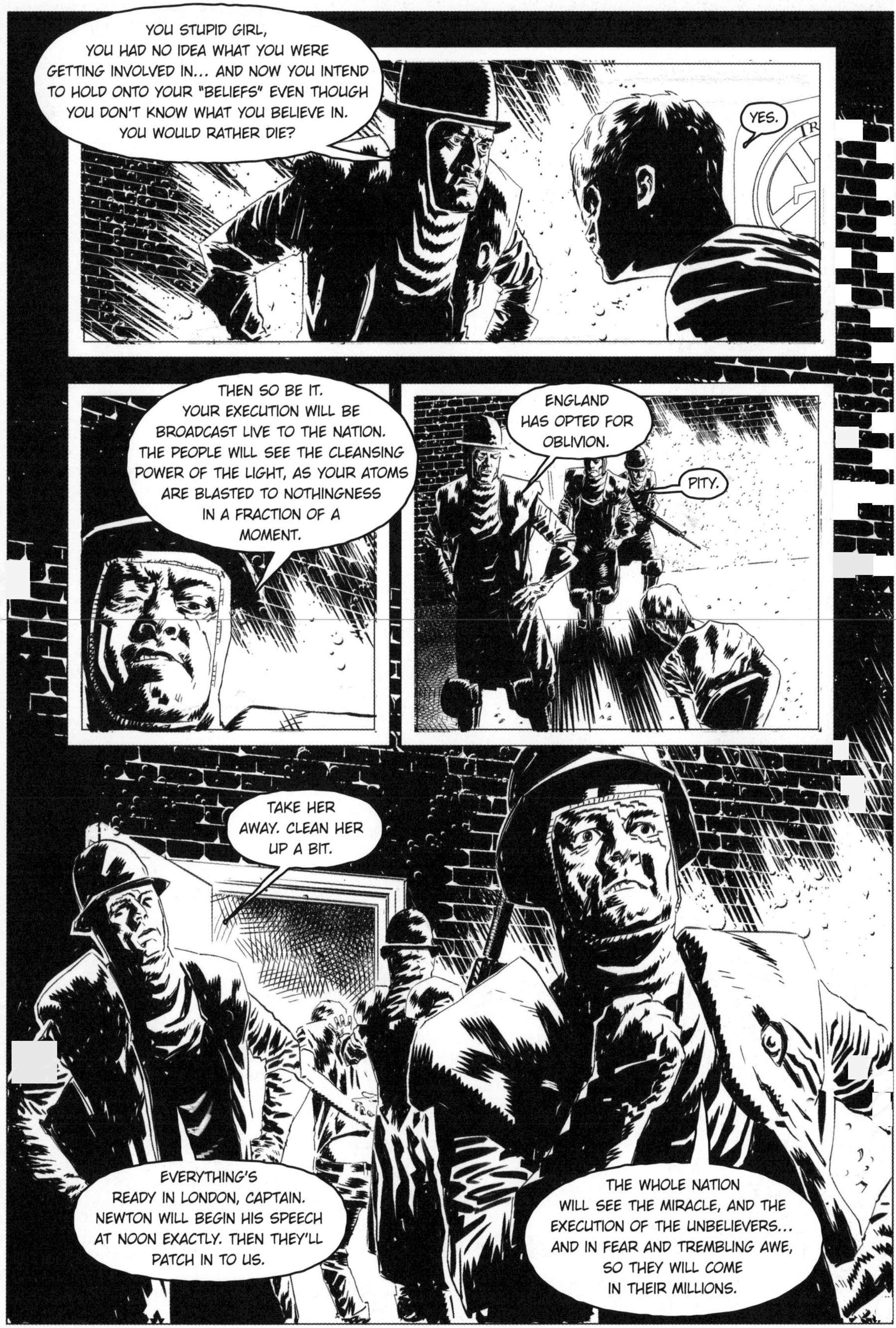
YOU STUPID GIRL, YOU HAD NO IDEA WHAT YOU WERE GETTING INVOLVED IN... AND NOW YOU INTEND TO HOLD ONTO YOUR "BELIEFS" EVEN THOUGH YOU DON'T KNOW WHAT YOU BELIEVE IN. YOU WOULD RATHER DIE?
YES.
THEN SO BE IT. YOUR EXECUTION WILL BE BROADCAST LIVE TO THE NATION. THE PEOPLE WILL SEE THE CLEANSING POWER OF THE LIGHT, AS YOUR ATOMS ARE BLASTED TO NOTHINGNESS IN A FRACTION OF A MOMENT.
ENGLAND HAS OPTED FOR OBLIVION.
PITY.
TAKE HER AWAY. CLEAN HER UP A BIT.
EVERYTHING'S READY IN LONDON, CAPTAIN. NEWTON WILL BEGIN HIS SPEECH AT NOON EXACTLY. THEN THEY'LL PATCH IN TO US.
THE WHOLE NATION WILL SEE THE MIRACLE, AND THE EXECUTION OF THE UNBELIEVERS... AND IN FEAR AND TREMBLING AWE, SO THEY WILL COME IN THEIR MILLIONS.

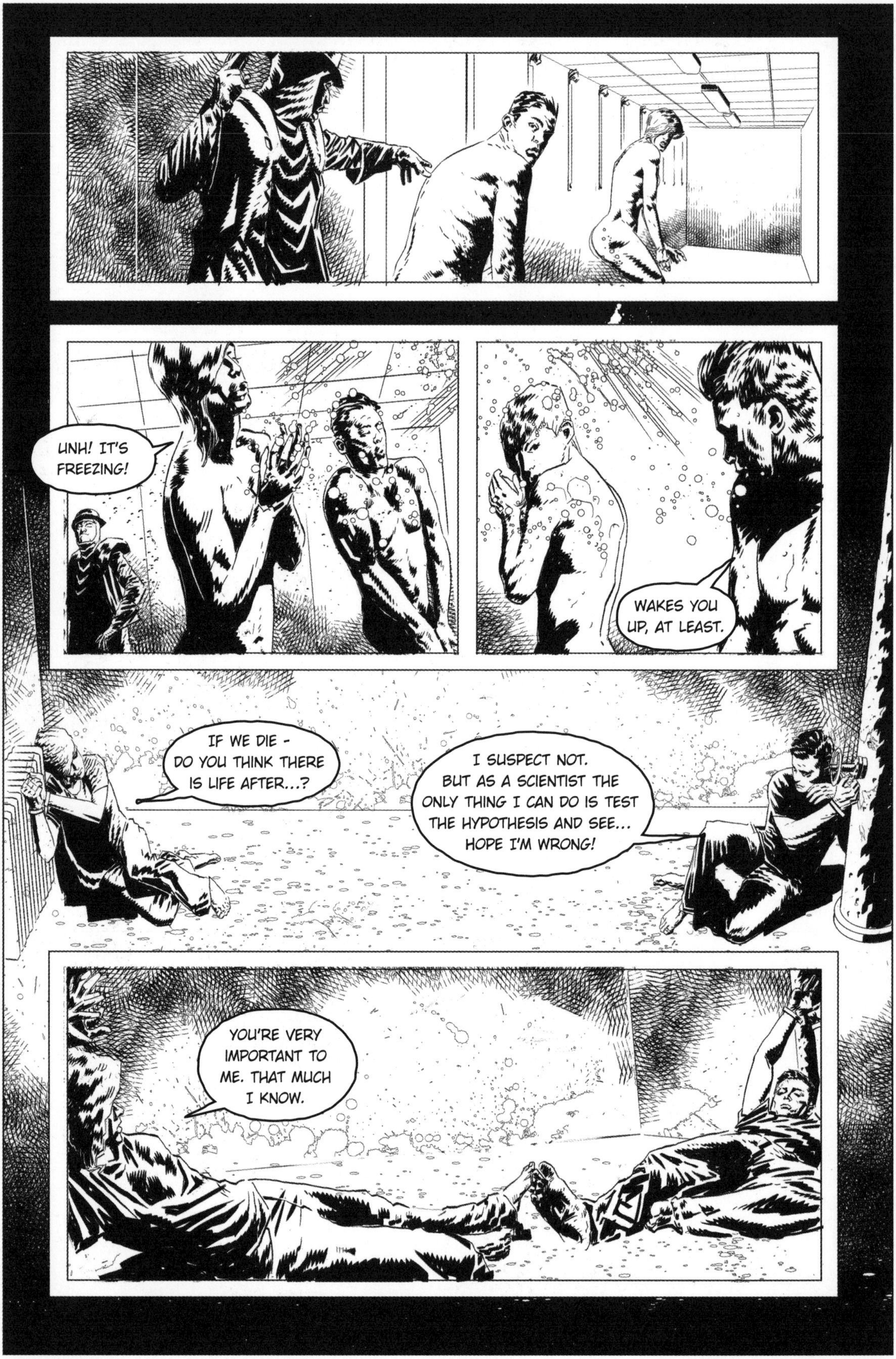
UNH! IT'S FREEZING!
WAKES YOU UP, AT LEAST.
IF WE DIE - DO YOU THINK THERE IS LIFE AFTER...?
I SUSPECT NOT. BUT AS A SCIENTIST THE ONLY THING I CAN DO IS TEST THE HYPOTHESIS AND SEE... HOPE I'M WRONG!
YOU'RE VERY IMPORTANT TO ME. THAT MUCH I KNOW.

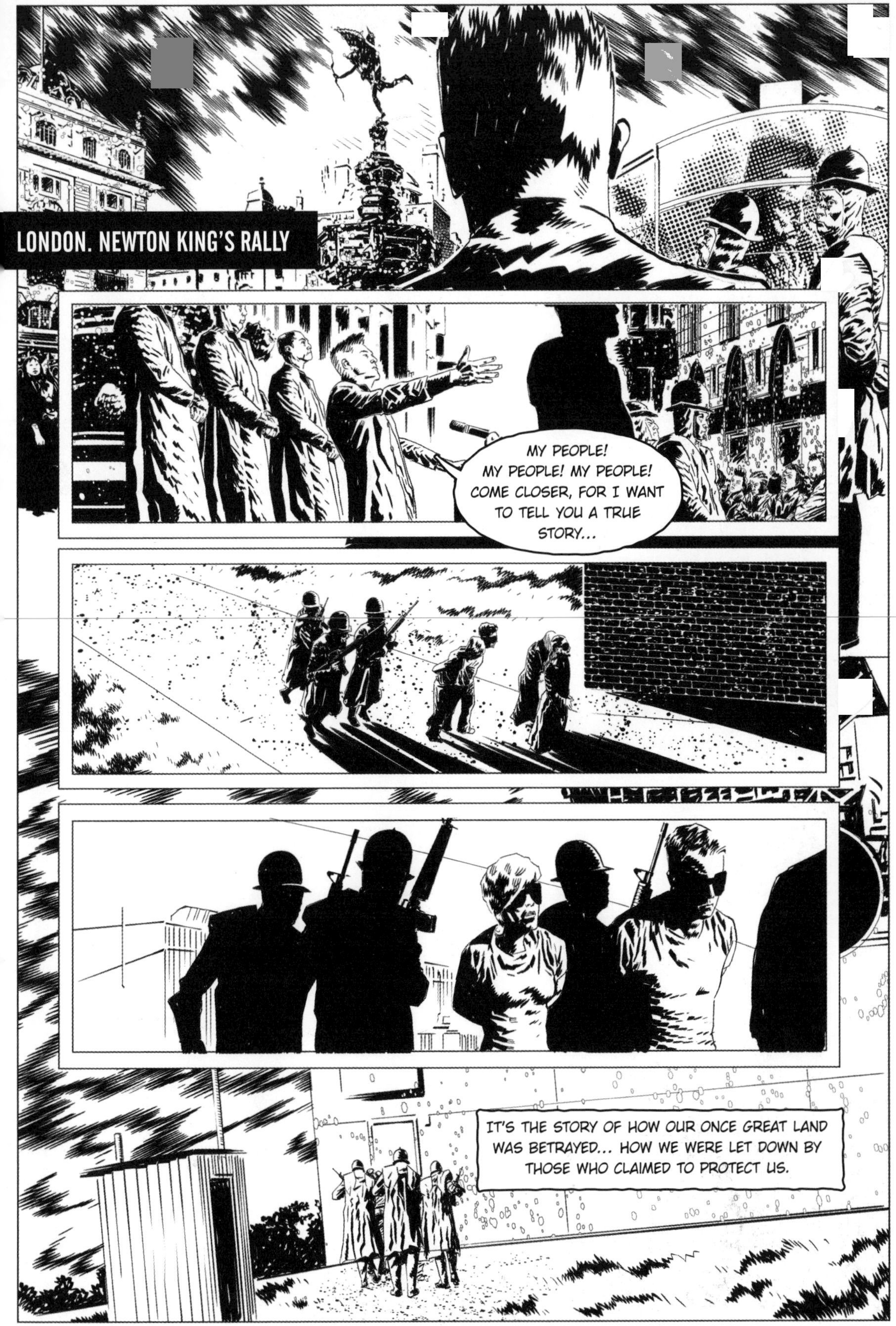
LONDON. NEWTON KING'S RALLY
MY PEOPLE! MY PEOPLE! MY PEOPLE! COME CLOSER, FOR I WANT TO TELL YOU A TRUE STORY...
IT'S THE STORY OF HOW OUR ONCE GREAT LAND WAS BETRAYED... HOW WE WERE LET DOWN BY THOSE WHO CLAIMED TO PROTECT US.

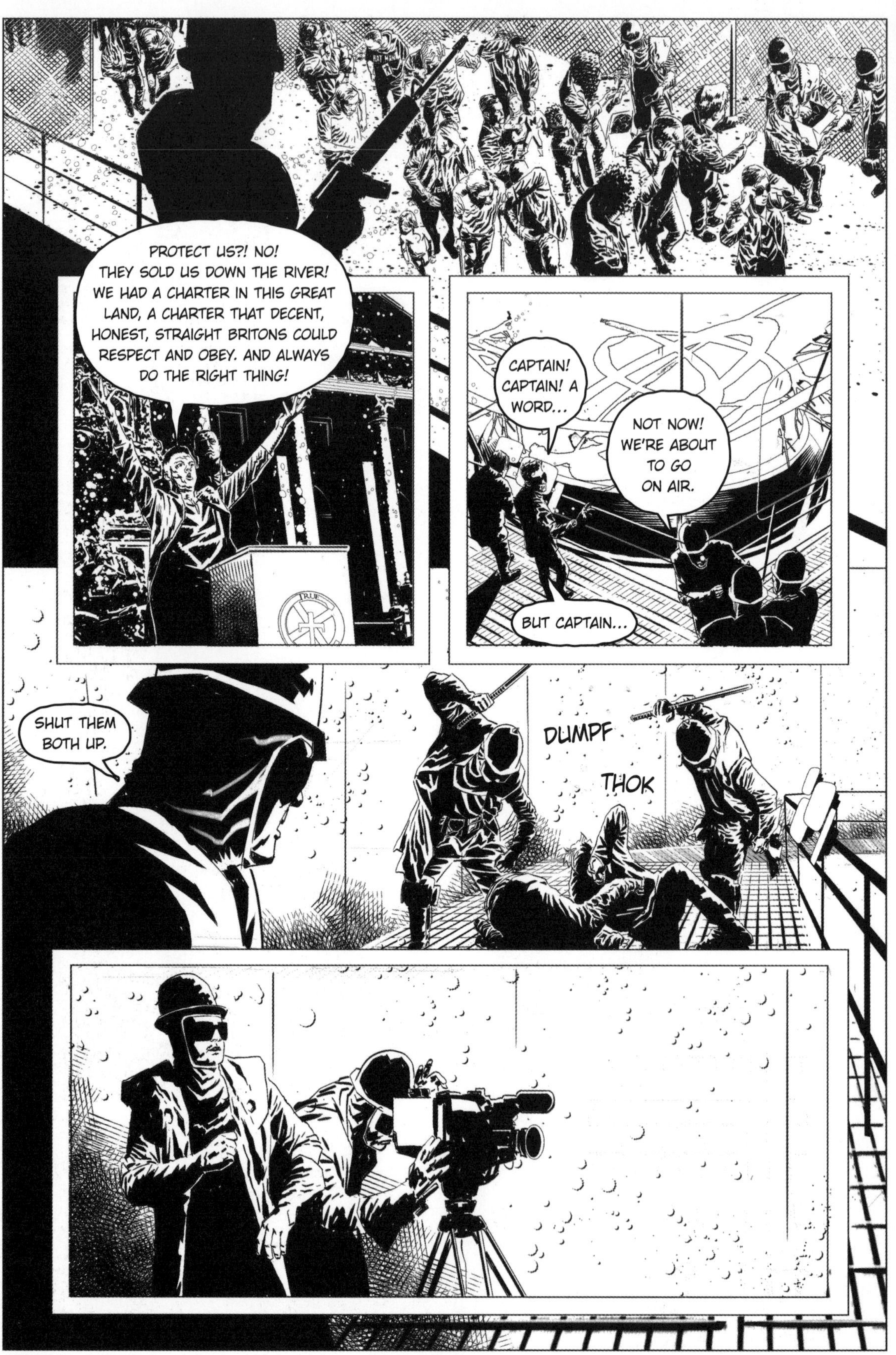

PROTECT US?! NO! THEY SOLD US DOWN THE RIVER! WE HAD A CHARTER IN THIS GREAT LAND, A CHARTER THAT DECENT, HONEST, STRAIGHT BRITONS COULD RESPECT AND OBEY. AND ALWAYS DO THE RIGHT THING!
CAPTAIN! CAPTAIN! A WORD...
NOT NOW! WE'RE ABOUT TO GO ON AIR.
BUT CAPTAIN...
SHUT THEM BOTH UP.
DUMPF
THOK

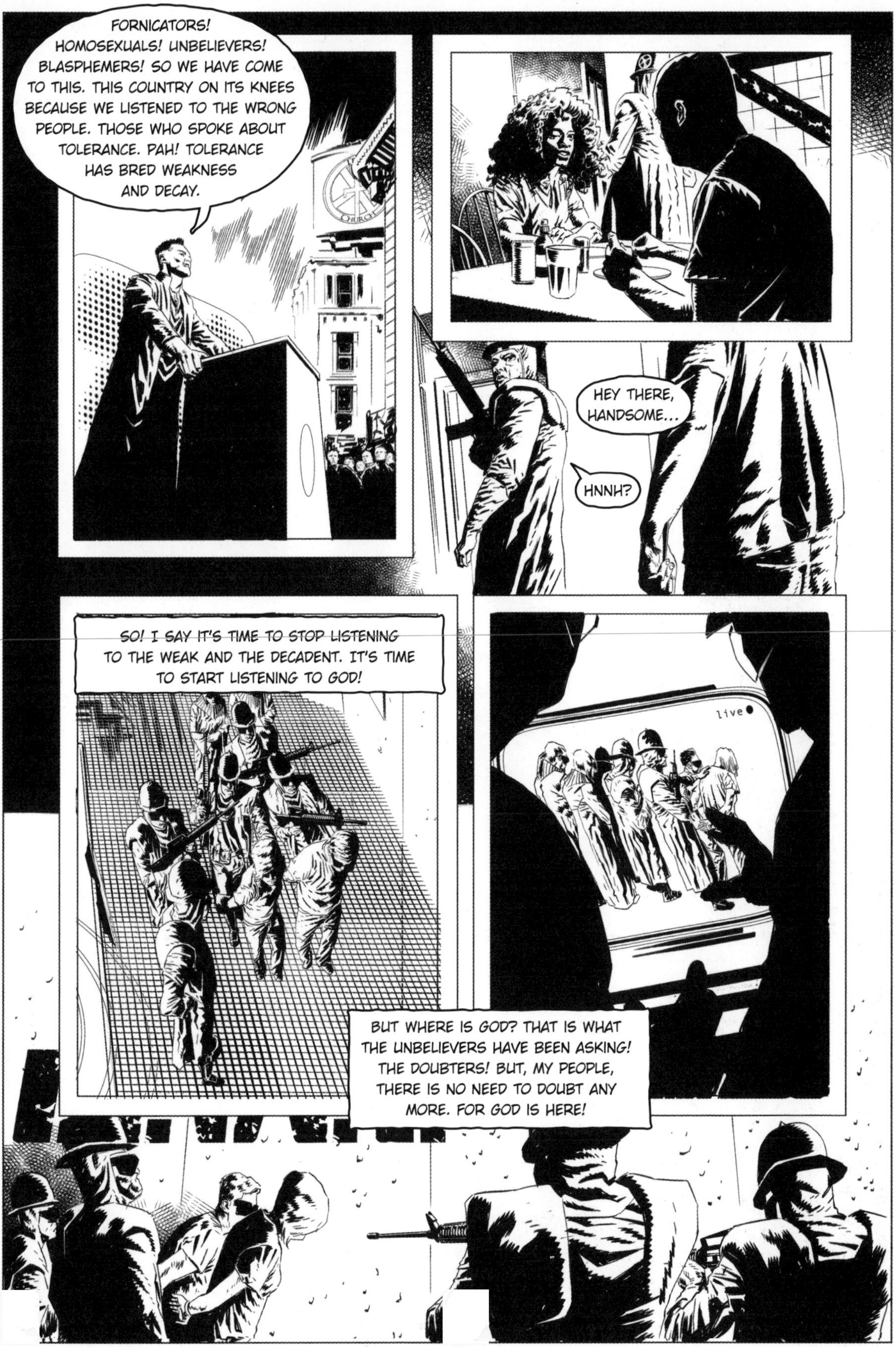
FORNICATORS! HOMOSEXUALS! UNBELIEVERS! BLASPHEMERS! SO WE HAVE COME TO THIS. THIS COUNTRY ON ITS KNEES BECAUSE WE LISTENED TO THE WRONG PEOPLE. THOSE WHO SPOKE ABOUT TOLERANCE. PAH! TOLERANCE HAS BRED WEAKNESS AND DECAY.
HEY THERE, HANDSOME...
HNNH?
SO! I SAY IT'S TIME TO STOP LISTENING TO THE WEAK AND THE DECADENT. IT'S TIME TO START LISTENING TO GOD!
live
BUT WHERE IS GOD? THAT IS WHAT THE UNBELIEVERS HAVE BEEN ASKING! THE DOUBTERS! BUT, MY PEOPLE, THERE IS NO NEED TO DOUBT ANY MORE. FOR GOD IS HERE!

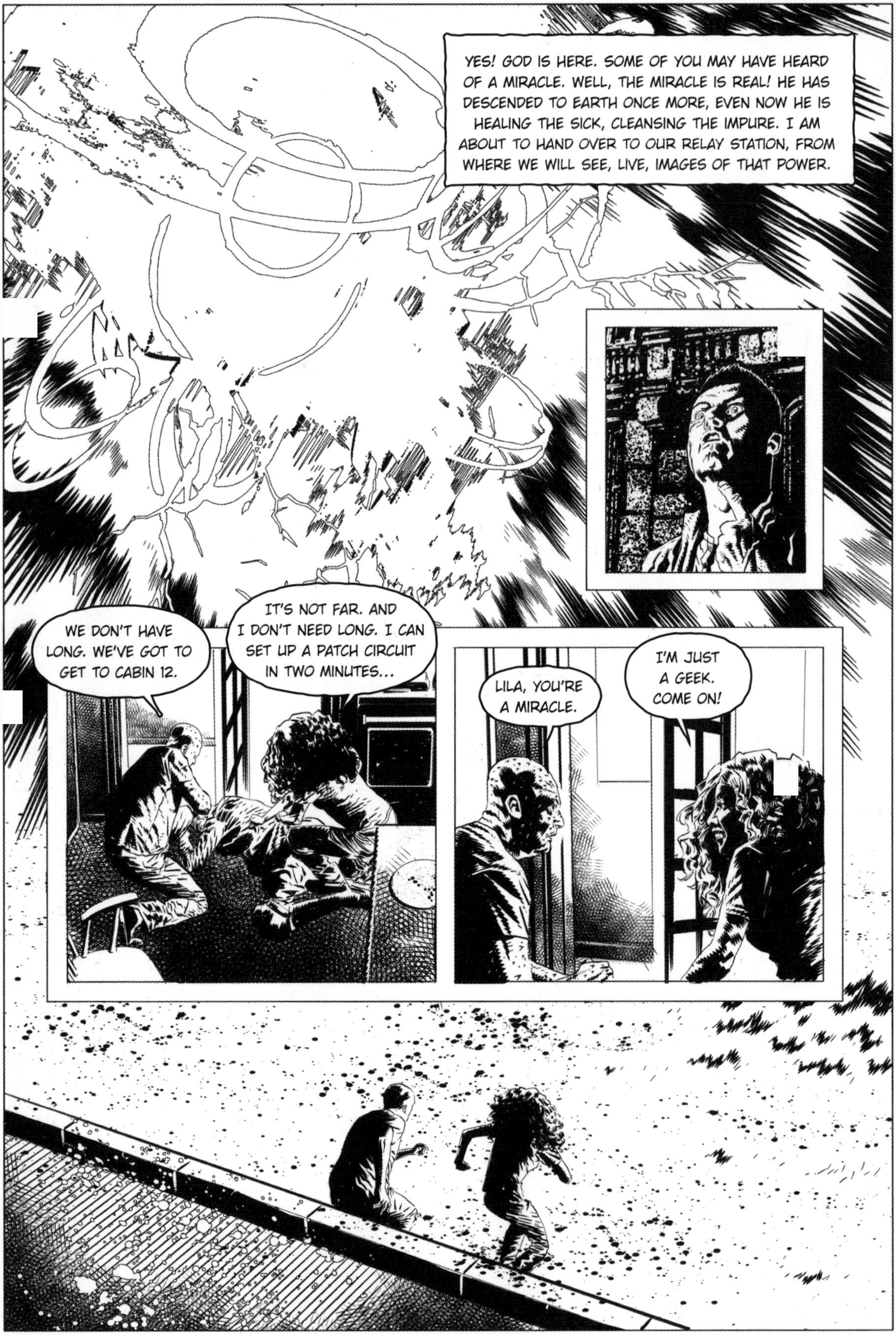
YES! GOD IS HERE. SOME OF YOU MAY HAVE HEARD OF A MIRACLE. WELL, THE MIRACLE IS REAL! HE HAS DESCENDED TO EARTH ONCE MORE, EVEN NOW HE IS HEALING THE SICK, CLEANSING THE IMPURE. I AM ABOUT TO HAND OVER TO OUR RELAY STATION, FROM WHERE WE WILL SEE, LIVE, IMAGES OF THAT POWER.
WE DON'T HAVE LONG. WE'VE GOT TO GET TO CABIN 12.
IT'S NOT FAR. AND I DON'T NEED LONG. I CAN SET UP A PATCH CIRCUIT IN TWO MINUTES...
LILA, YOU'RE A MIRACLE.
I'M JUST A GEEK. COME ON!

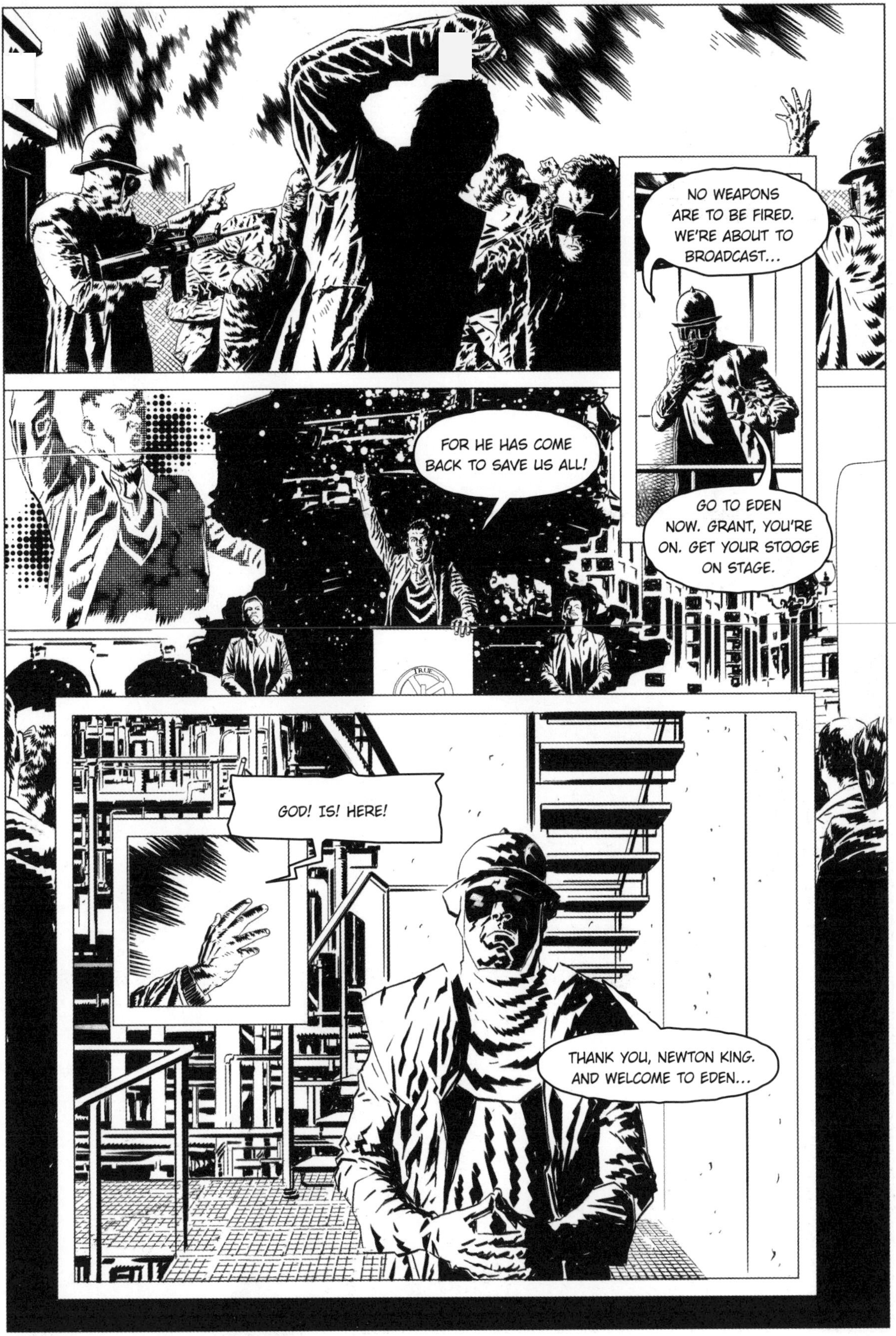
NO WEAPONS ARE TO BE FIRED. WE'RE ABOUT TO BROADCAST...
GO TO EDEN NOW. GRANT, YOU'RE ON. GET YOUR STOOGE ON STAGE.
FOR HE HAS COME BACK TO SAVE US ALL!
GOD! IS! HERE!
THANK YOU, NEWTON KING. AND WELCOME TO EDEN...

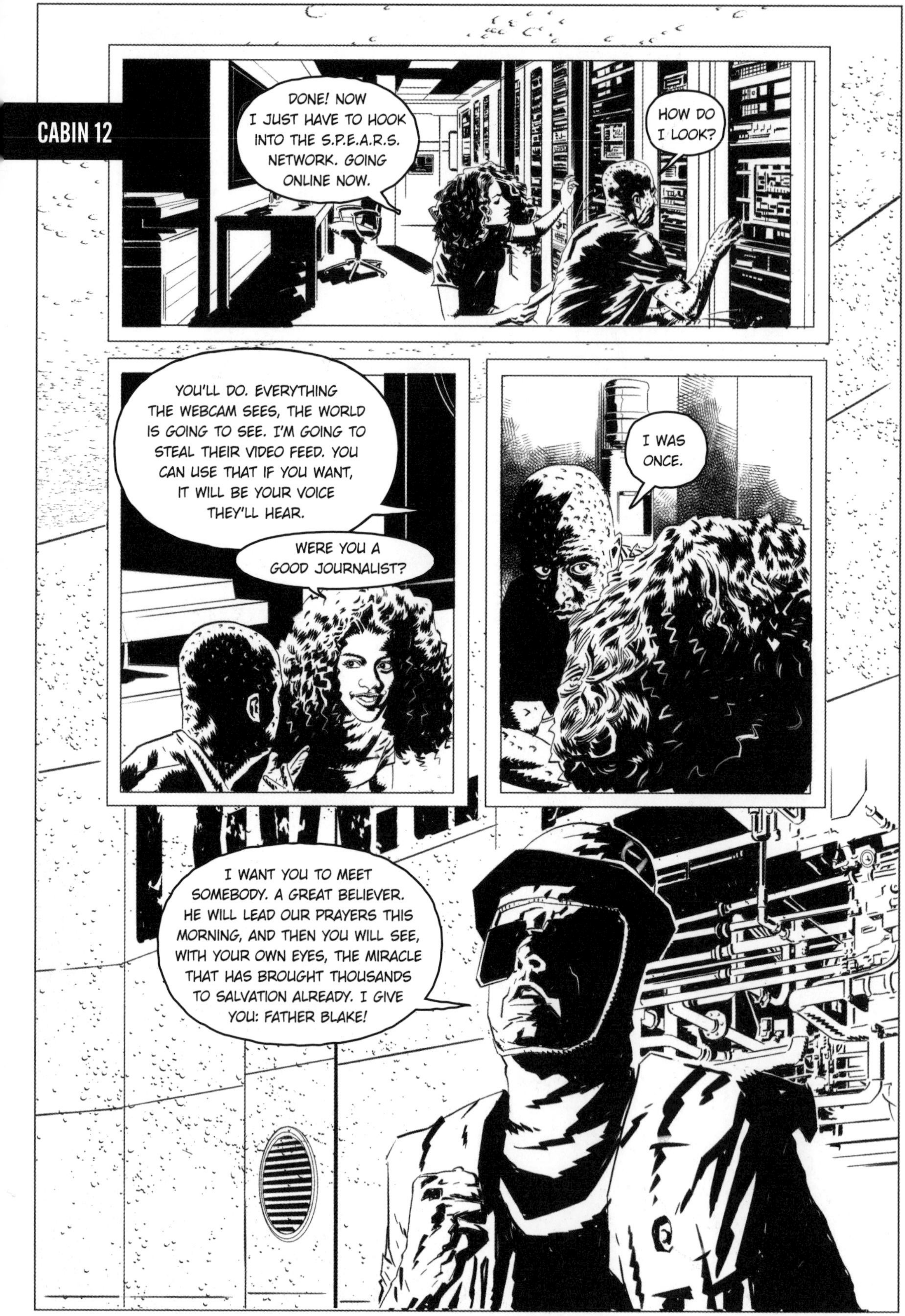
CABIN 12
DONE! NOW I JUST HAVE TO HOOK INTO THE S.P.E.A.R.S. NETWORK. GOING ONLINE NOW.
HOW DO I LOOK?
YOU'LL DO. EVERYTHING THE WEBCAM SEES, THE WORLD IS GOING TO SEE. I'M GOING TO STEAL THEIR VIDEO FEED. YOU CAN USE THAT IF YOU WANT, IT WILL BE YOUR VOICE THEY'LL HEAR.
WERE YOU A GOOD JOURNALIST?
I WAS ONCE.
I WANT YOU TO MEET SOMEBODY. A GREAT BELIEVER. HE WILL LEAD OUR PRAYERS THIS MORNING, AND THEN YOU WILL SEE, WITH YOUR OWN EYES, THE MIRACLE THAT HAS BROUGHT THOUSANDS TO SALVATION ALREADY. I GIVE YOU: FATHER BLAKE!

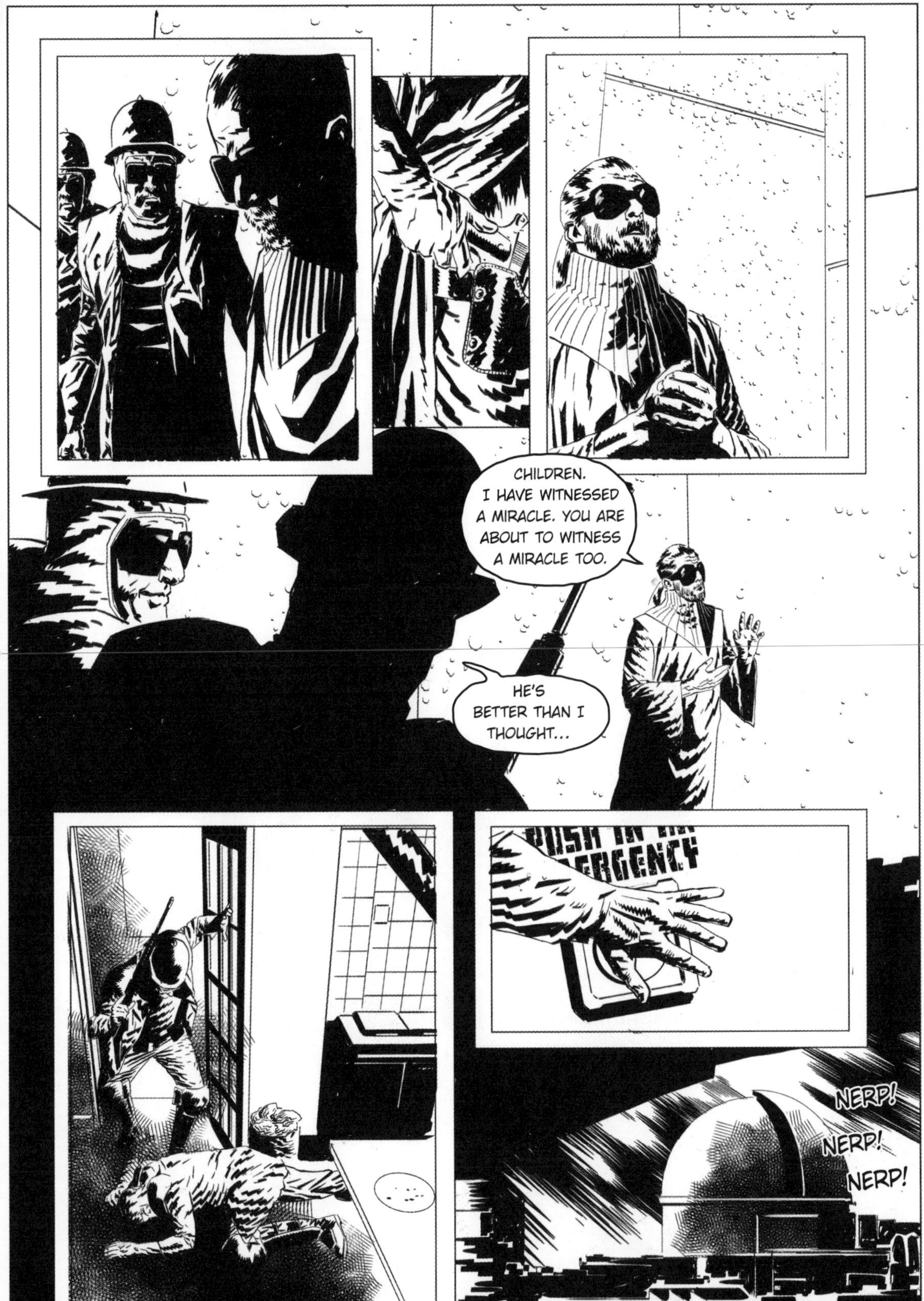
CHILDREN. I HAVE WITNESSED A MIRACLE. YOU ARE ABOUT TO WITNESS A MIRACLE TOO.
HE'S BETTER THAN I THOUGHT...
PUSH IN EMERGENCY
NERP!
NERP!
NERP!

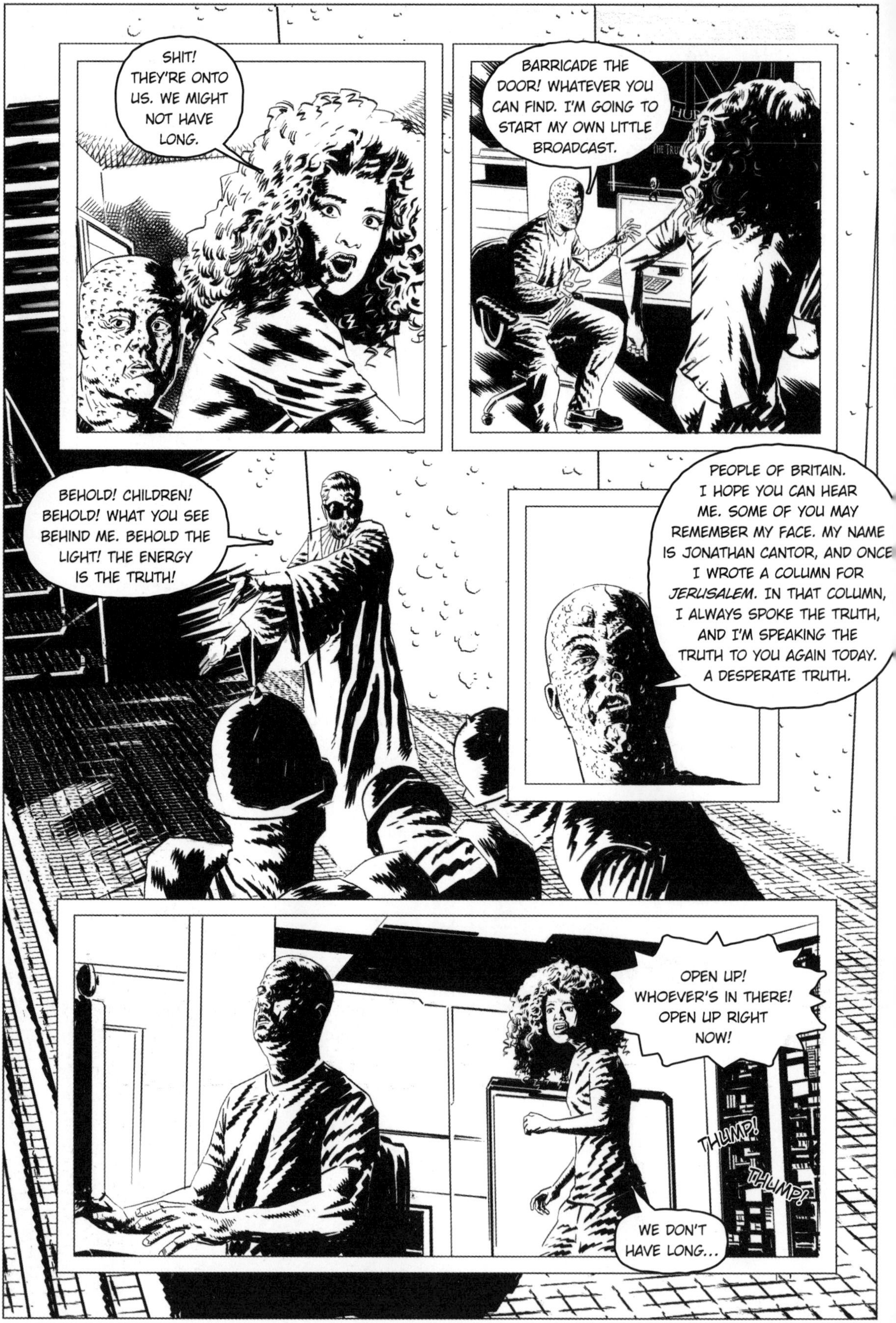
SHIT! THEY'RE ONTO US. WE MIGHT NOT HAVE LONG.
BARRICADE THE DOOR! WHATEVER YOU CAN FIND. I'M GOING TO START MY OWN LITTLE BROADCAST.
BEHOLD! CHILDREN! BEHOLD! WHAT YOU SEE BEHIND ME. BEHOLD THE LIGHT! THE ENERGY IS THE TRUTH!
PEOPLE OF BRITAIN. I HOPE YOU CAN HEAR ME. SOME OF YOU MAY REMEMBER MY FACE. MY NAME IS JONATHAN CANTOR, AND ONCE I WROTE A COLUMN FOR *JERUSALEM*. IN THAT COLUMN, I ALWAYS SPOKE THE TRUTH, AND I'M SPEAKING THE TRUTH TO YOU AGAIN TODAY. A DESPERATE TRUTH.
OPEN UP! WHOEVER'S IN THERE! OPEN UP RIGHT NOW!
THUMP!
THUMP!
WE DON'T HAVE LONG...

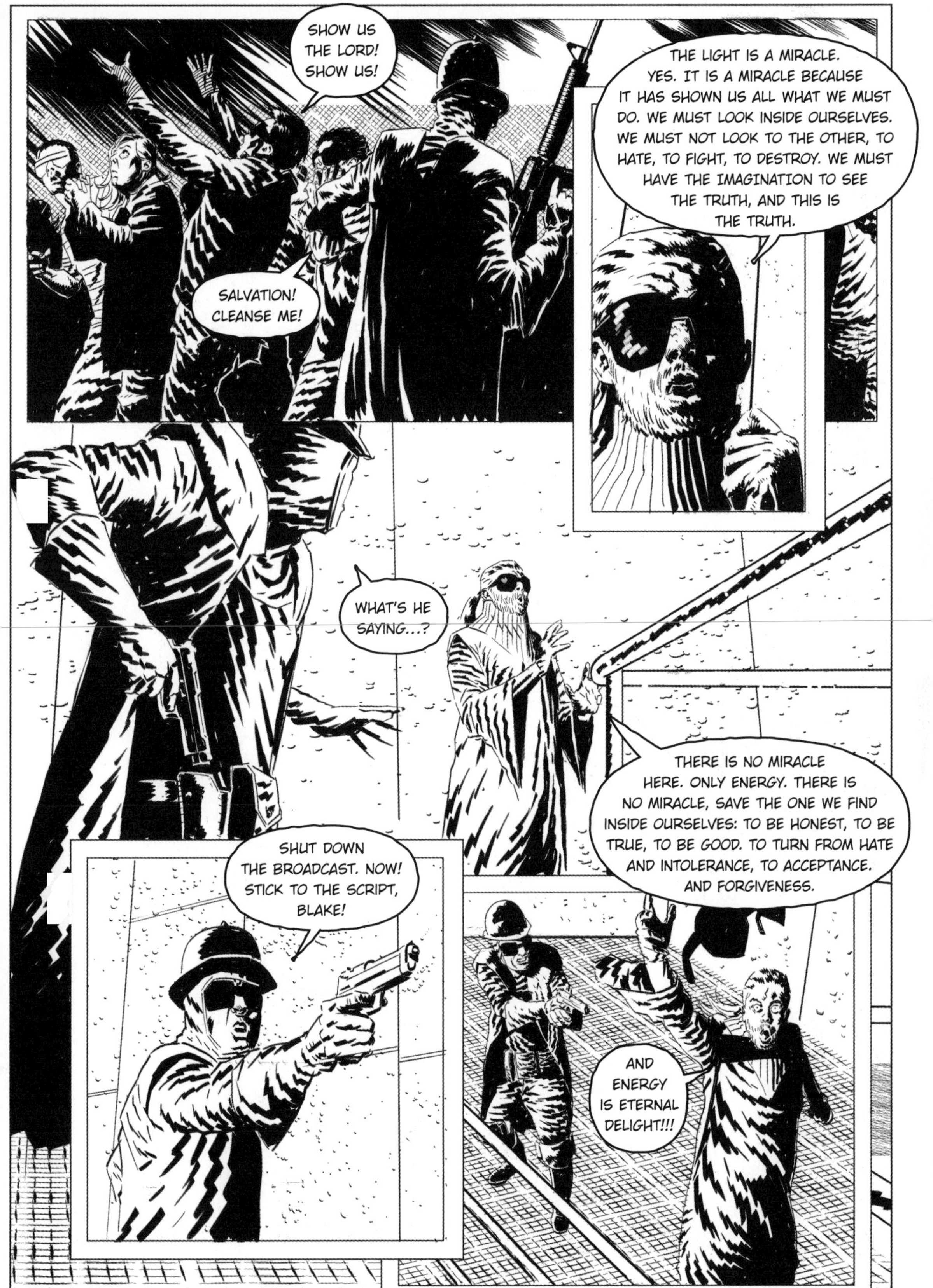
SHOW US THE LORD! SHOW US!
THE LIGHT IS A MIRACLE. YES. IT IS A MIRACLE BECAUSE IT HAS SHOWN US ALL WHAT WE MUST DO. WE MUST LOOK INSIDE OURSELVES. WE MUST NOT LOOK TO THE OTHER, TO HATE, TO FIGHT, TO DESTROY. WE MUST HAVE THE IMAGINATION TO SEE THE TRUTH, AND THIS IS THE TRUTH.
SALVATION! CLEANSE ME!
WHAT'S HE SAYING...?
THERE IS NO MIRACLE HERE. ONLY ENERGY. THERE IS NO MIRACLE, SAVE THE ONE WE FIND INSIDE OURSELVES: TO BE HONEST, TO BE TRUE, TO BE GOOD. TO TURN FROM HATE AND INTOLERANCE, TO ACCEPTANCE. AND FORGIVENESS.
SHUT DOWN THE BROADCAST. NOW! STICK TO THE SCRIPT, BLAKE!
AND ENERGY IS ETERNAL DELIGHT!!!

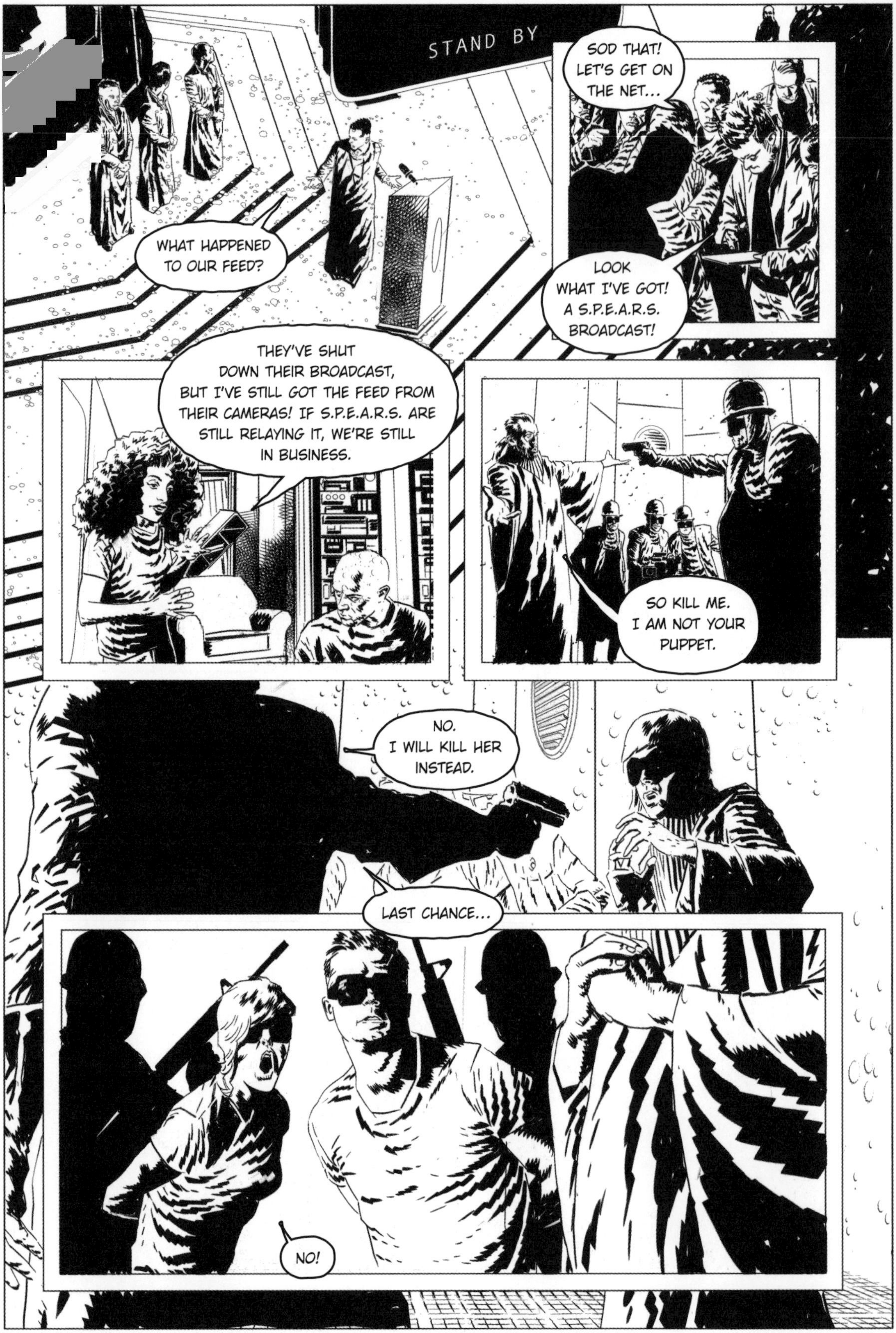
STAND BY
WHAT HAPPENED TO OUR FEED?
SOD THAT! LET'S GET ON THE NET...
LOOK WHAT I'VE GOT! A S.P.E.A.R.S. BROADCAST!
THEY'VE SHUT DOWN THEIR BROADCAST, BUT I'VE STILL GOT THE FEED FROM THEIR CAMERAS! IF S.P.E.A.R.S. ARE STILL RELAYING IT, WE'RE STILL IN BUSINESS.
SO KILL ME. I AM NOT YOUR PUPPET.
NO. I WILL KILL HER INSTEAD.
LAST CHANCE...
NO!

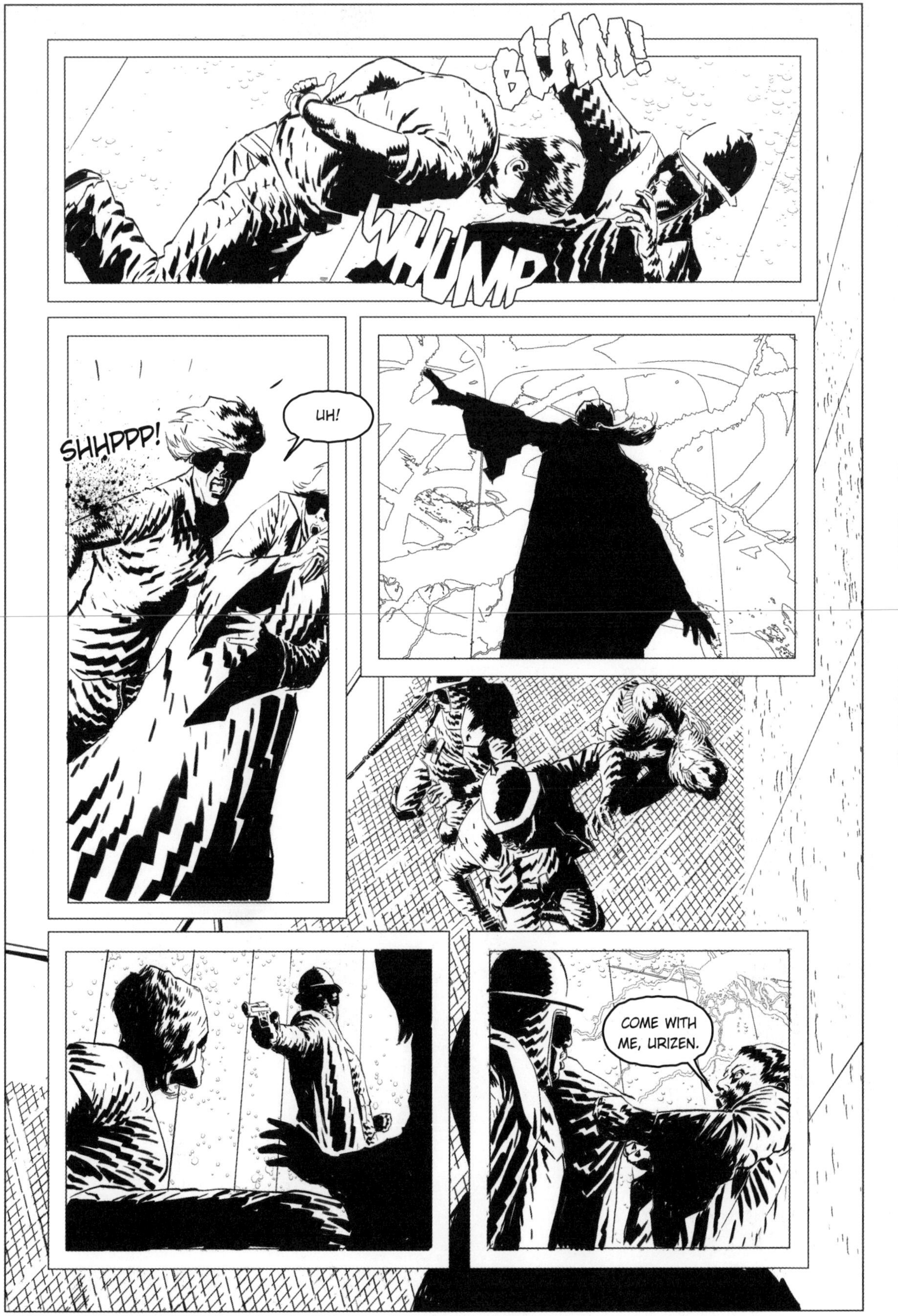
BLAM!
WHUMP
SHHPPP!
UH!
COME WITH ME, URIZEN.

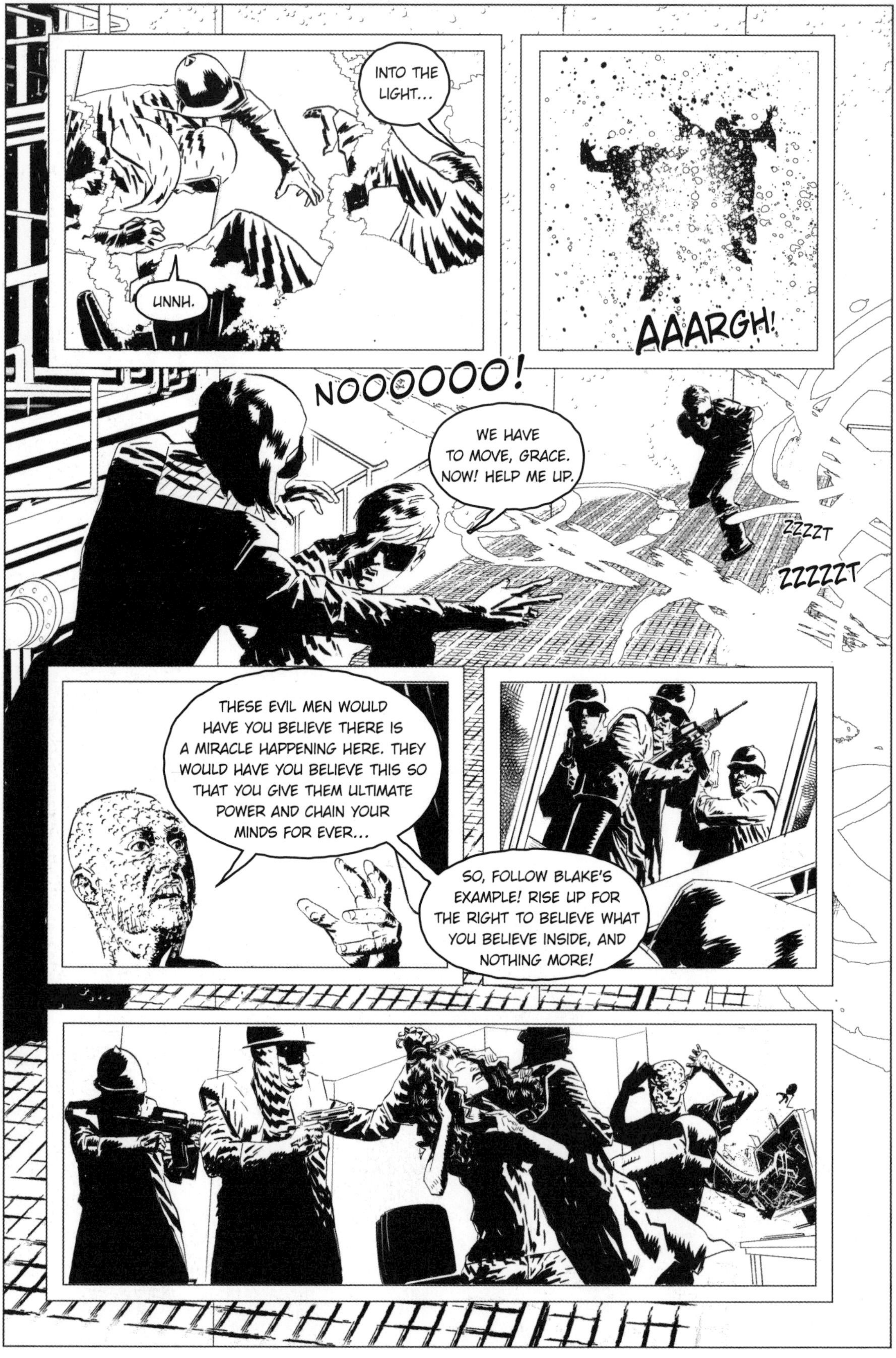
INTO THE LIGHT...
UNNH.
AAARGH!
NOOOOOO!
WE HAVE TO MOVE, GRACE. NOW! HELP ME UP.
ZZZZT
ZZZZZT
THESE EVIL MEN WOULD HAVE YOU BELIEVE THERE IS A MIRACLE HAPPENING HERE. THEY WOULD HAVE YOU BELIEVE THIS SO THAT YOU GIVE THEM ULTIMATE POWER AND CHAIN YOUR MINDS FOR EVER...
SO, FOLLOW BLAKE'S EXAMPLE! RISE UP FOR THE RIGHT TO BELIEVE WHAT YOU BELIEVE INSIDE, AND NOTHING MORE!

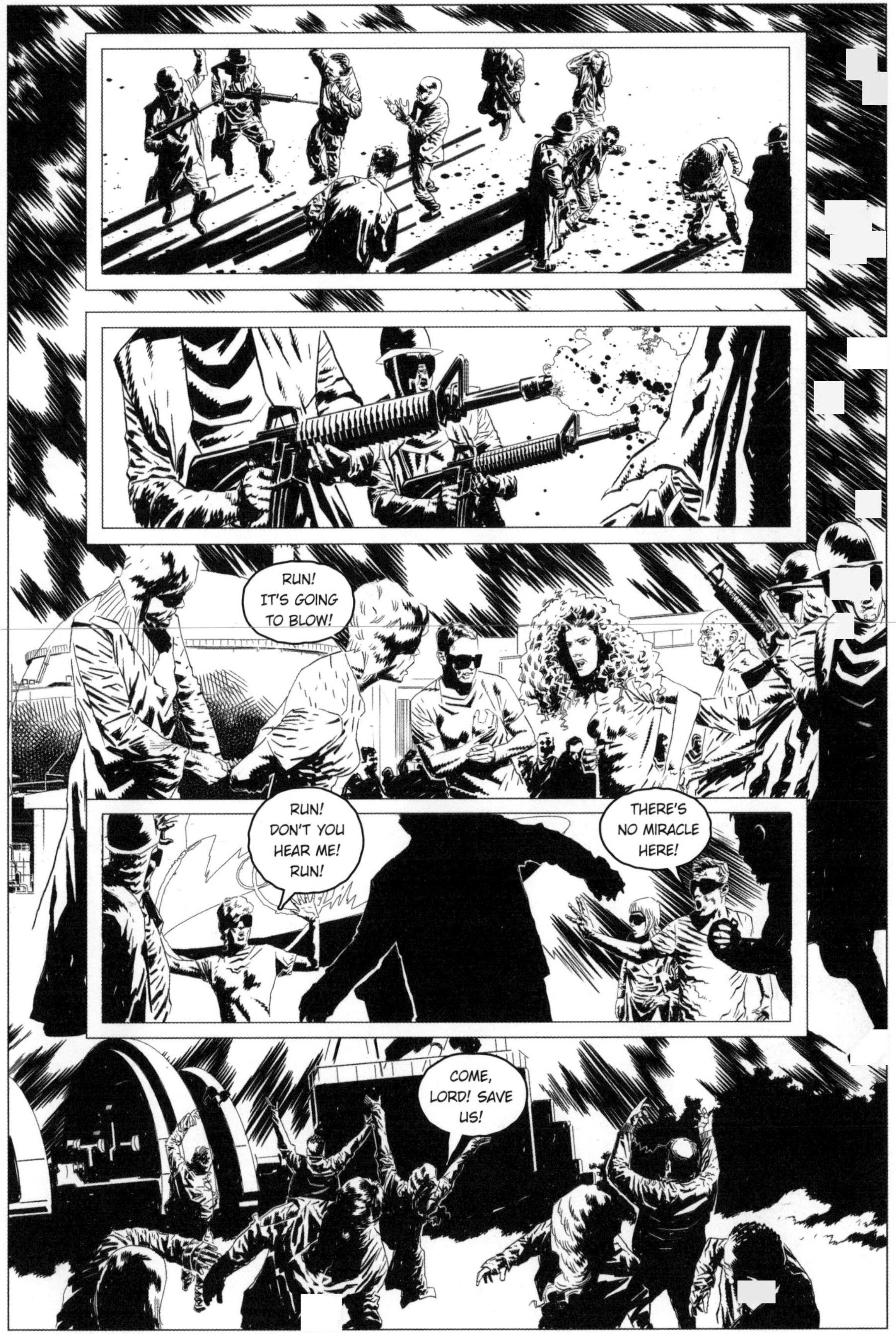
RUN! IT'S GOING TO BLOW!
RUN! DON'T YOU HEAR ME! RUN!
THERE'S NO MIRACLE HERE!
COME, LORD! SAVE US!

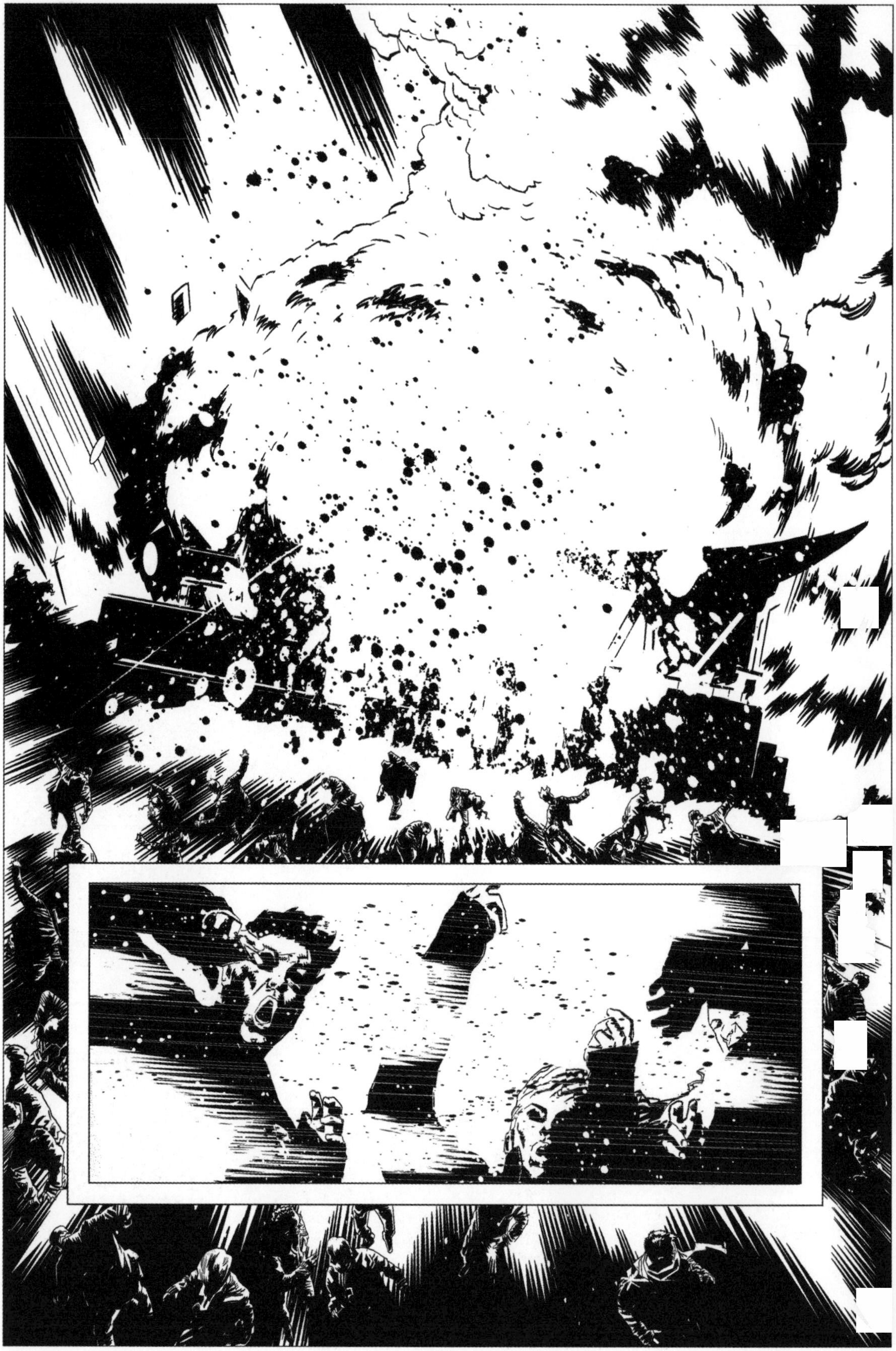

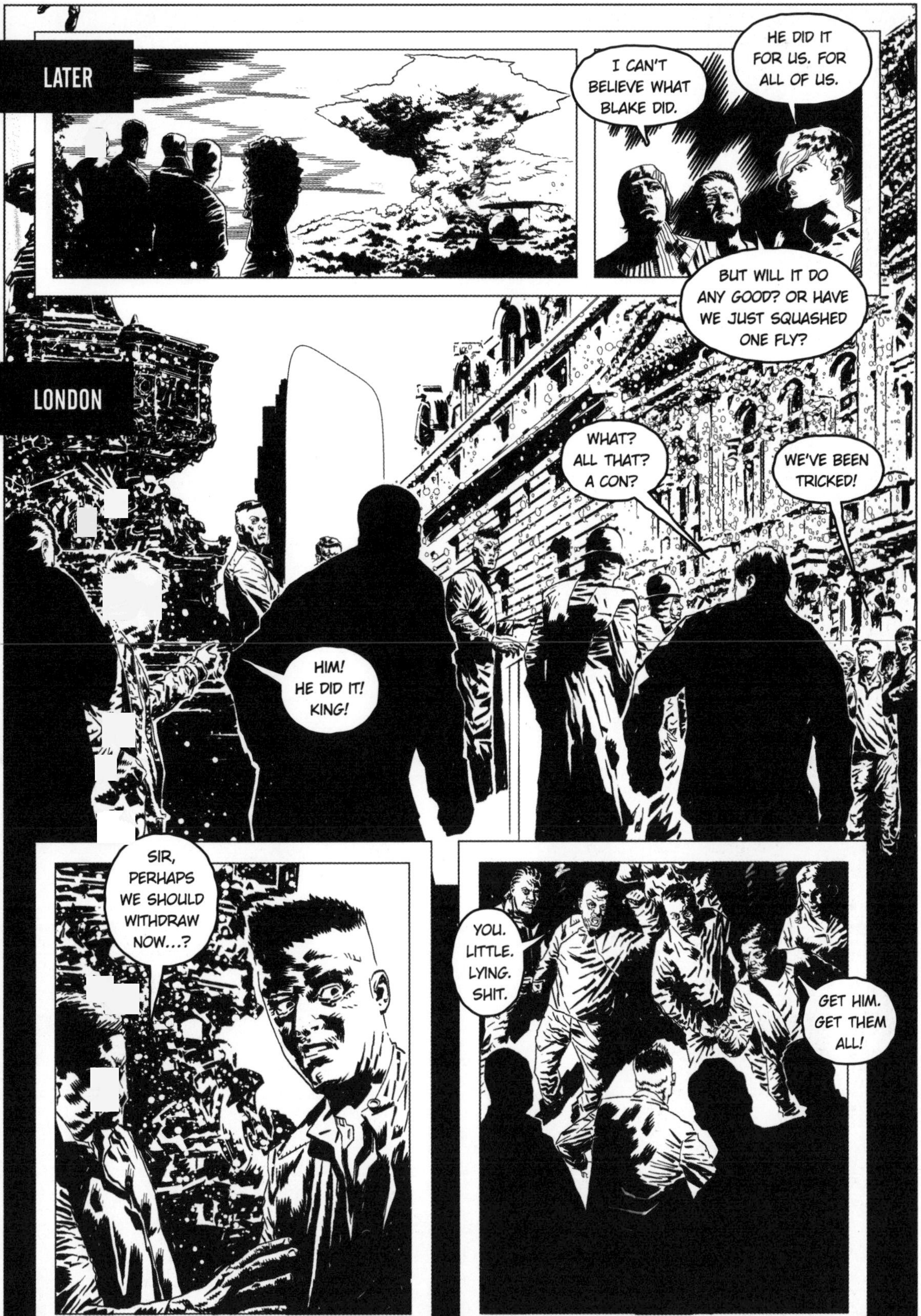

LATER
I CAN'T BELIEVE WHAT BLAKE DID.
HE DID IT FOR US. FOR ALL OF US.
BUT WILL IT DO ANY GOOD? OR HAVE WE JUST SQUASHED ONE FLY?
LONDON
WHAT? ALL THAT? A CON?
WE'VE BEEN TRICKED!
HIM! HE DID IT! KING!
SIR, PERHAPS WE SHOULD WITHDRAW NOW...?
YOU. LITTLE. LYING. SHIT.
GET HIM. GET THEM ALL!

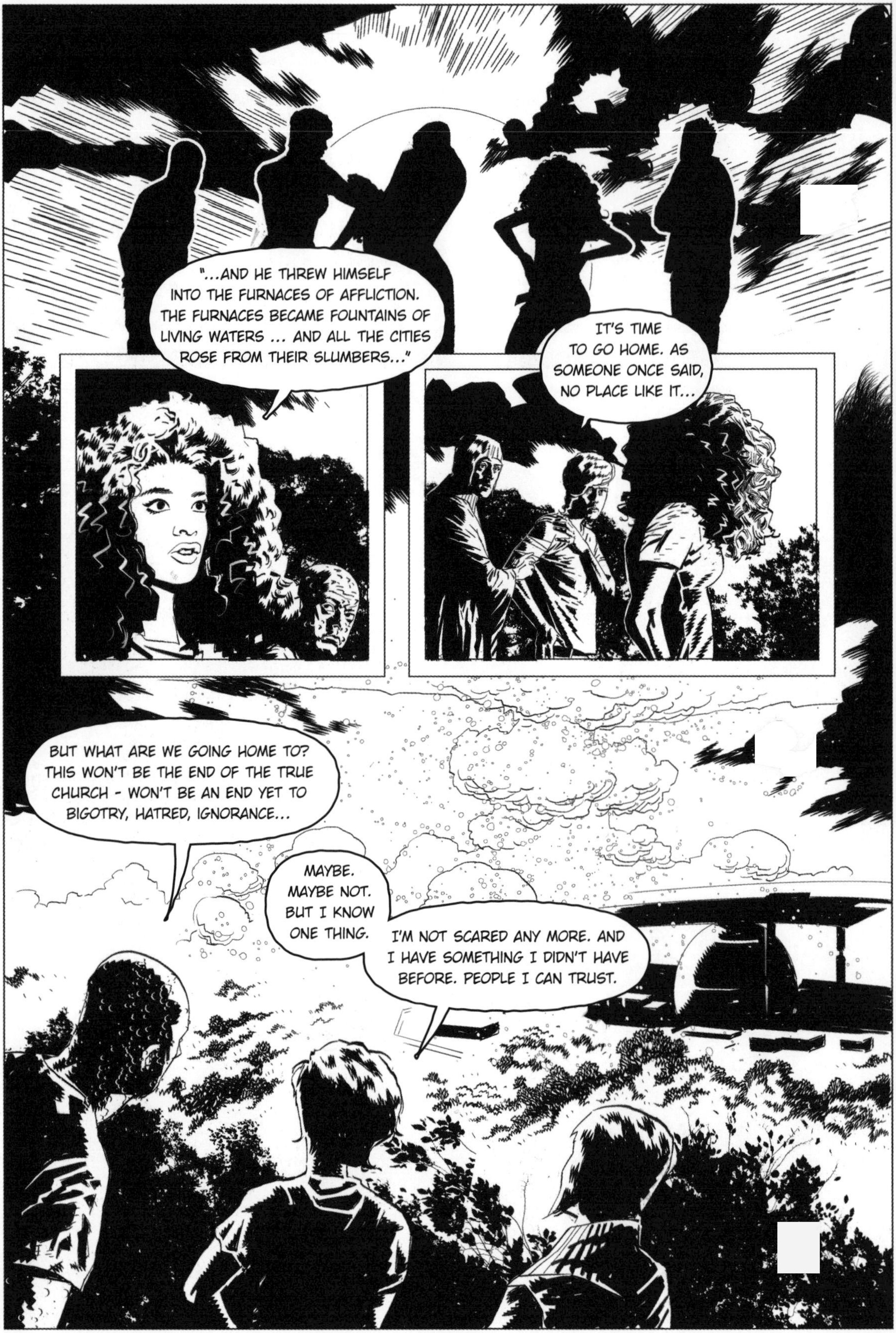
"...AND HE THREW HIMSELF INTO THE FURNACES OF AFFLICTION. THE FURNACES BECAME FOUNTAINS OF LIVING WATERS ... AND ALL THE CITIES ROSE FROM THEIR SLUMBERS..."
IT'S TIME TO GO HOME. AS SOMEONE ONCE SAID, NO PLACE LIKE IT...
BUT WHAT ARE WE GOING HOME TO? THIS WON'T BE THE END OF THE TRUE CHURCH - WON'T BE AN END YET TO BIGOTRY, HATRED, IGNORANCE...
MAYBE. MAYBE NOT. BUT I KNOW ONE THING.
I'M NOT SCARED ANY MORE. AND I HAVE SOMETHING I DIDN'T HAVE BEFORE. PEOPLE I CAN TRUST.

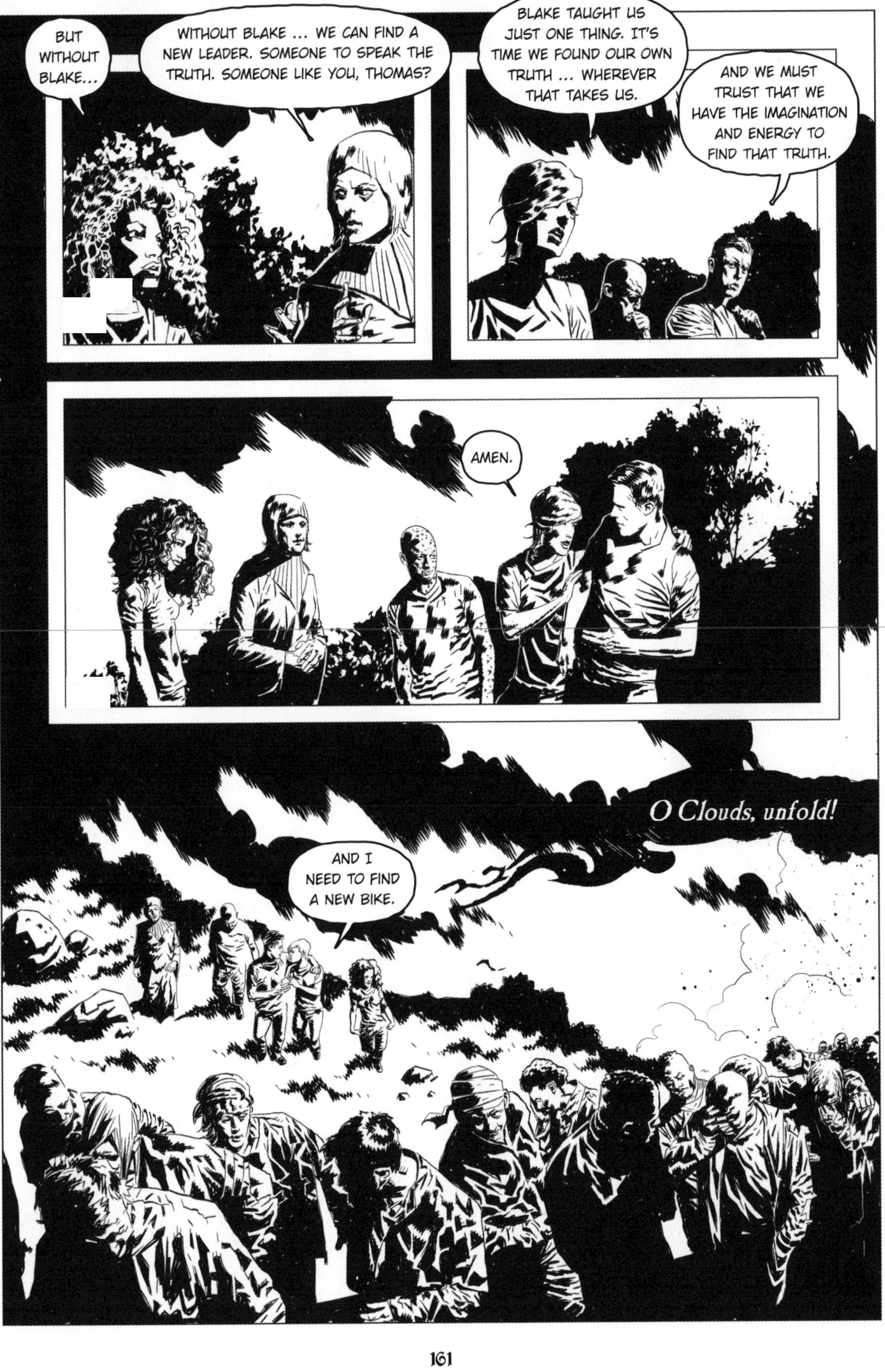
BUT WITHOUT BLAKE...
WITHOUT BLAKE ... WE CAN FIND A NEW LEADER. SOMEONE TO SPEAK THE TRUTH. SOMEONE LIKE YOU, THOMAS?
BLAKE TAUGHT US JUST ONE THING. IT'S TIME WE FOUND OUR OWN TRUTH ... WHEREVER THAT TAKES US.
AND WE MUST TRUST THAT WE HAVE THE IMAGINATION AND ENERGY TO FIND THAT TRUTH.
AMEN.
O Clouds, unfold!
AND I NEED TO FIND A NEW BIKE.

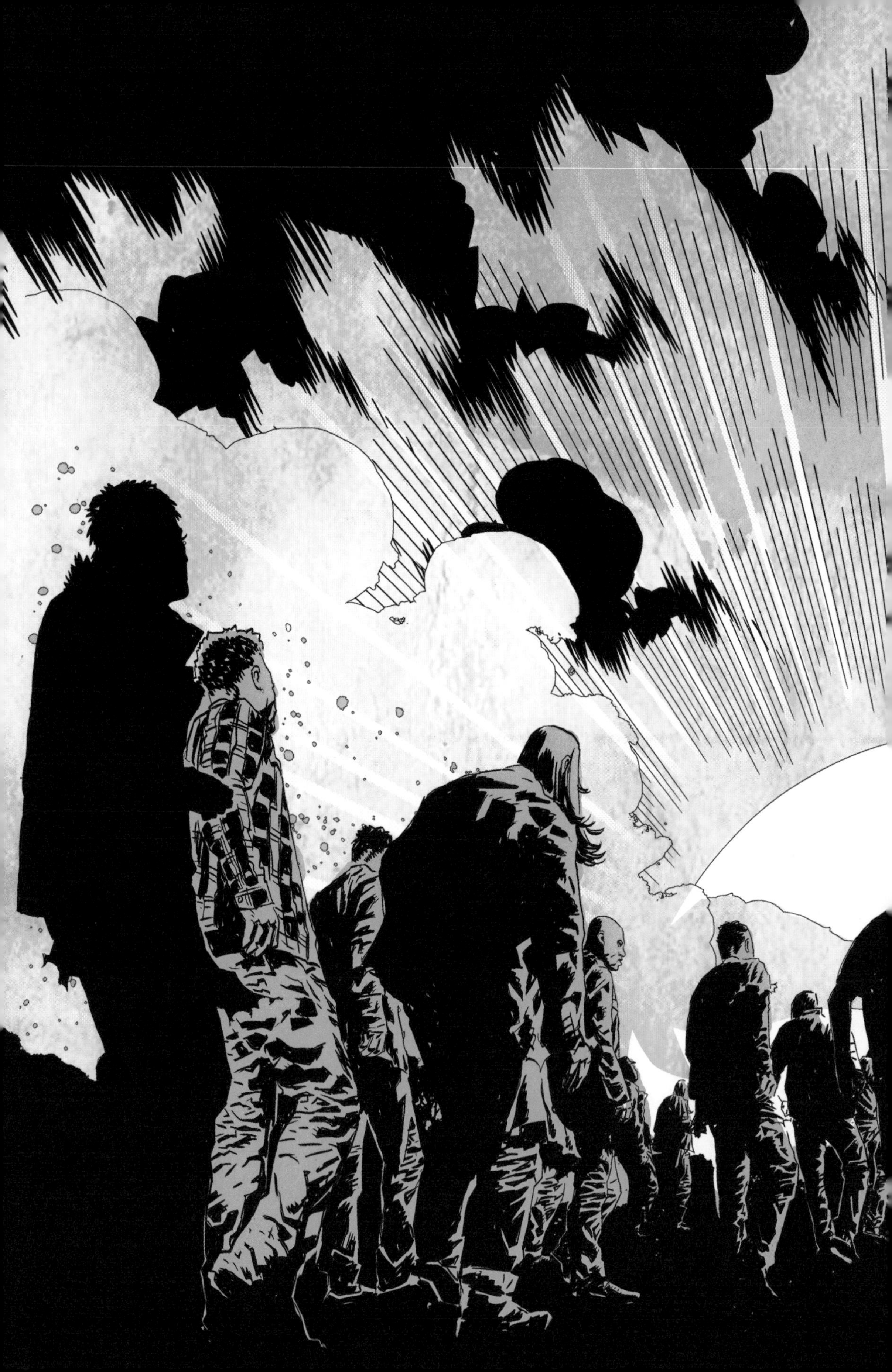

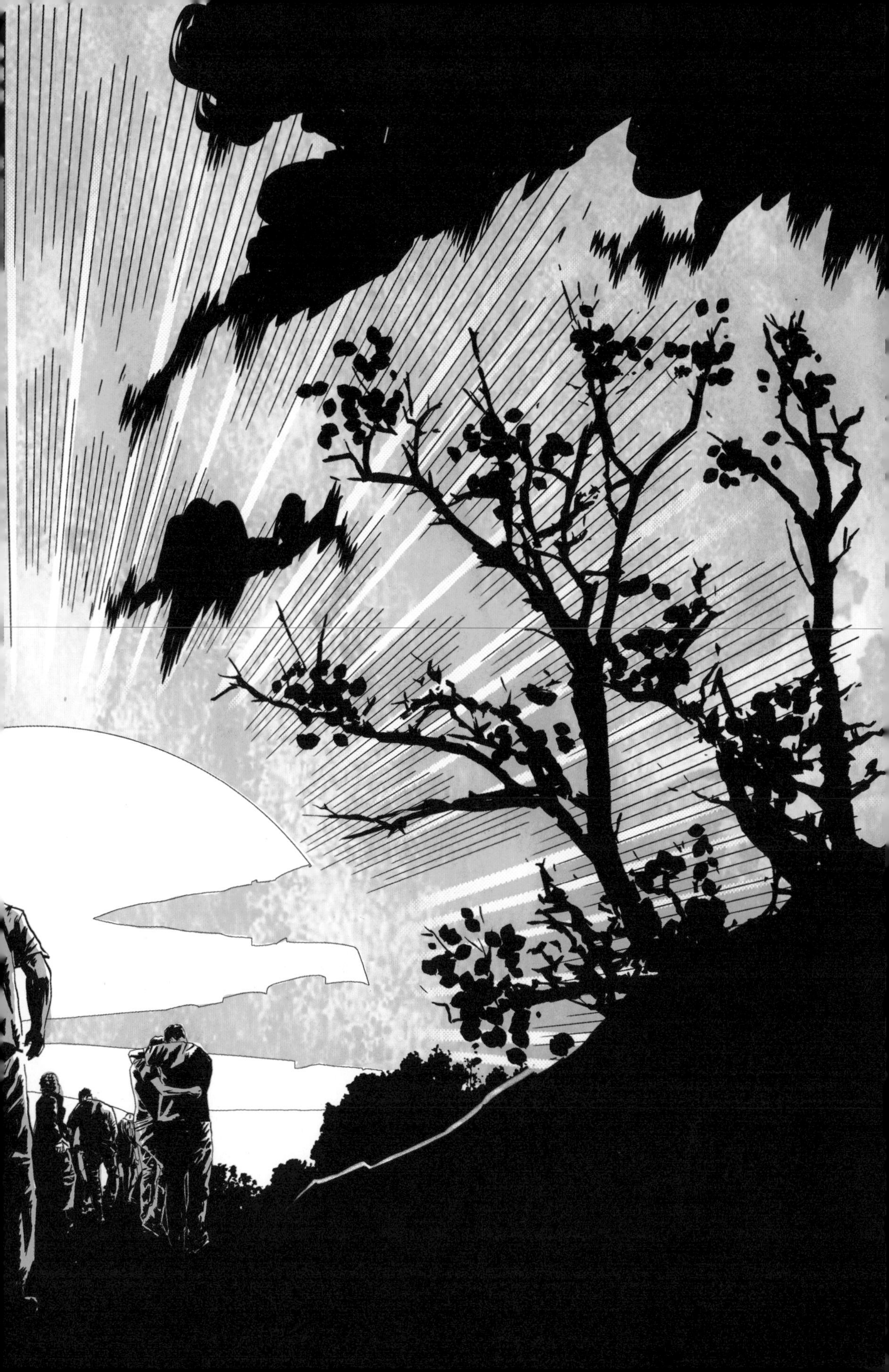

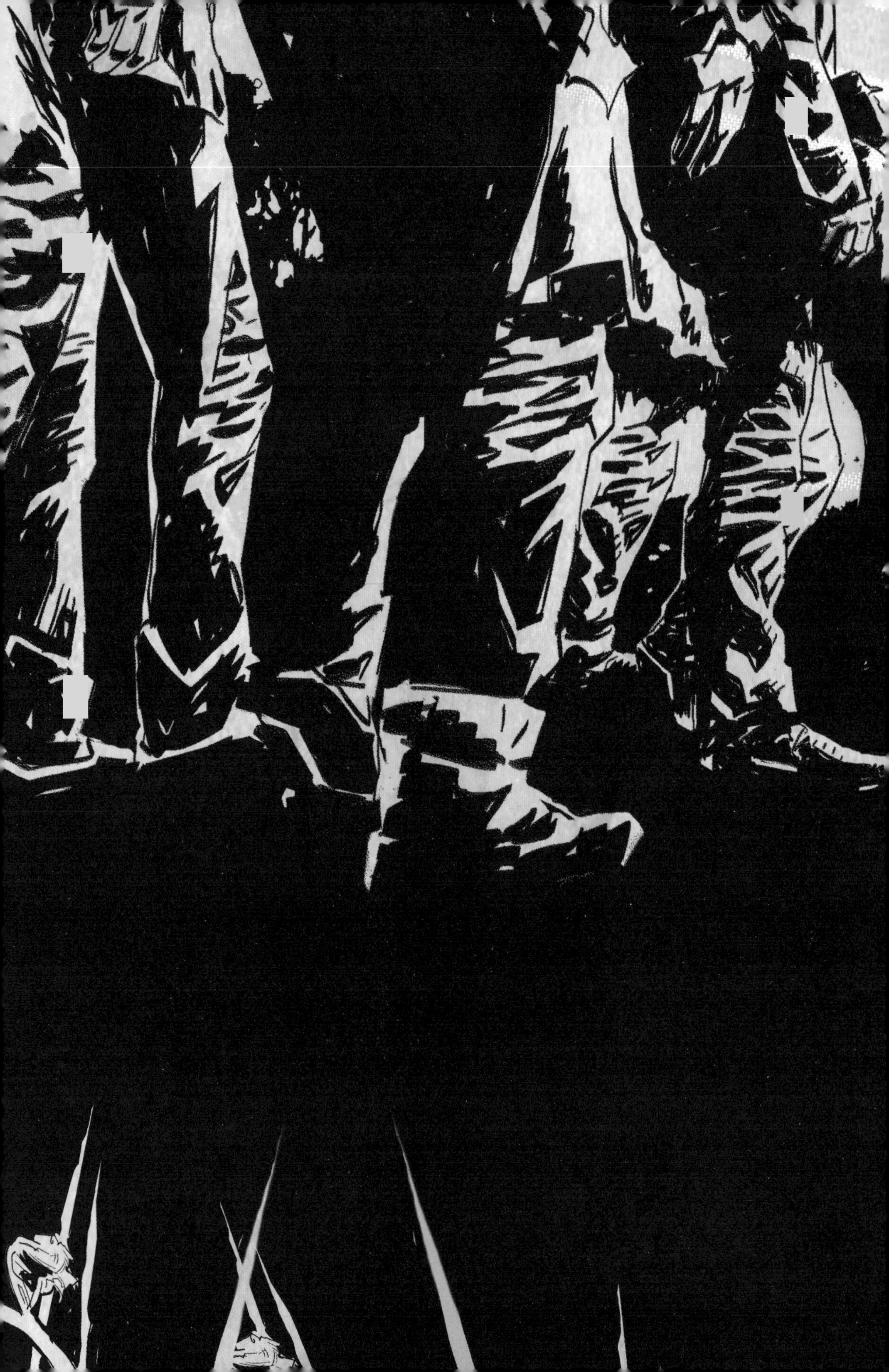

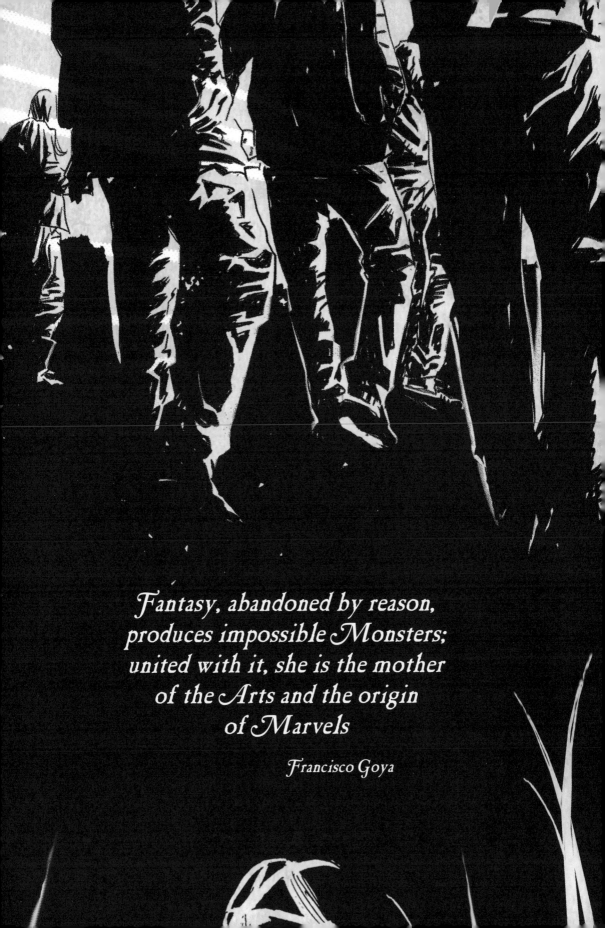

*Fantasy, abandoned by reason,
produces impossible Monsters;
united with it, she is the mother
of the Arts and the origin
of Marvels*

Francisco Goya

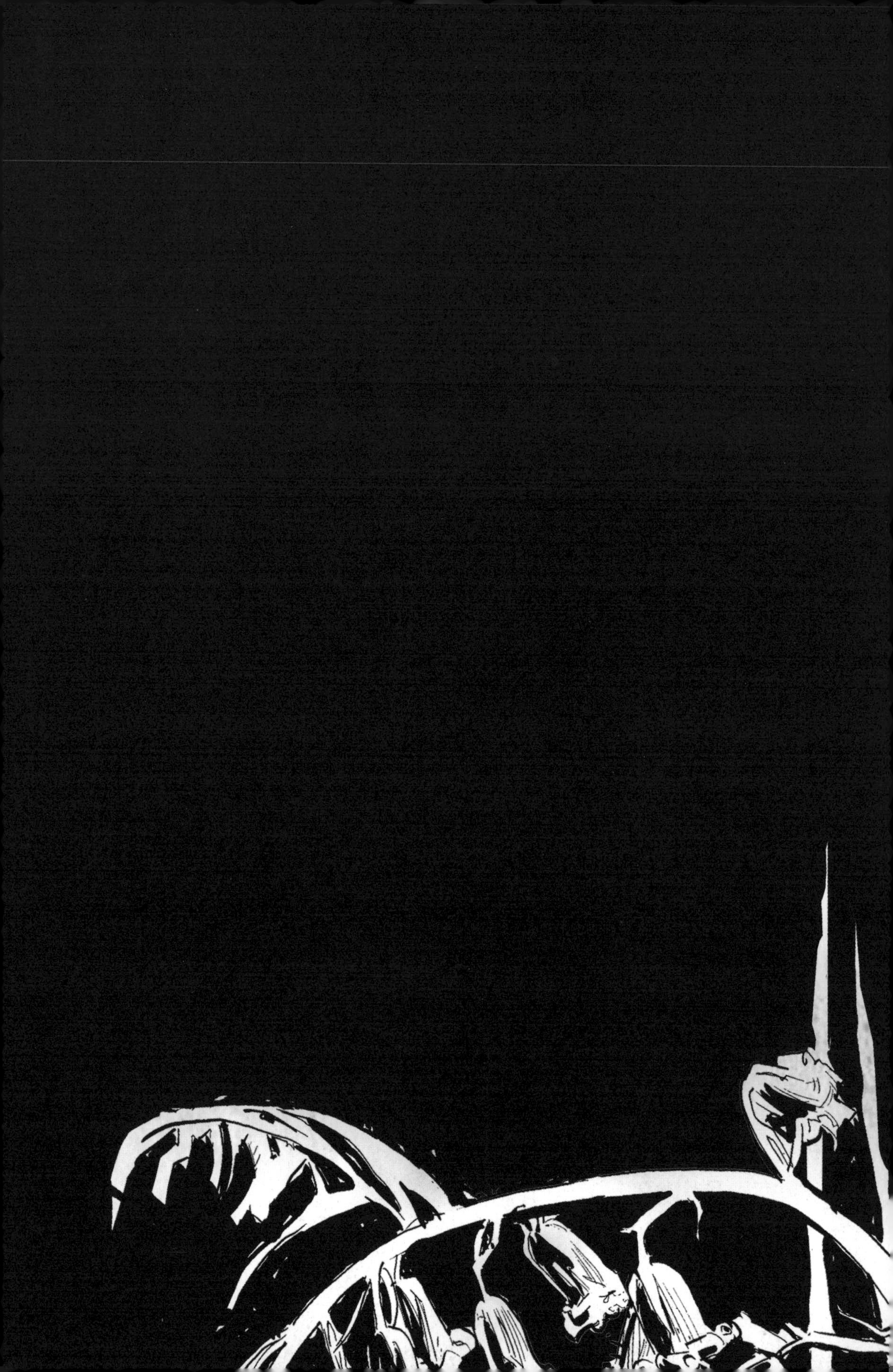

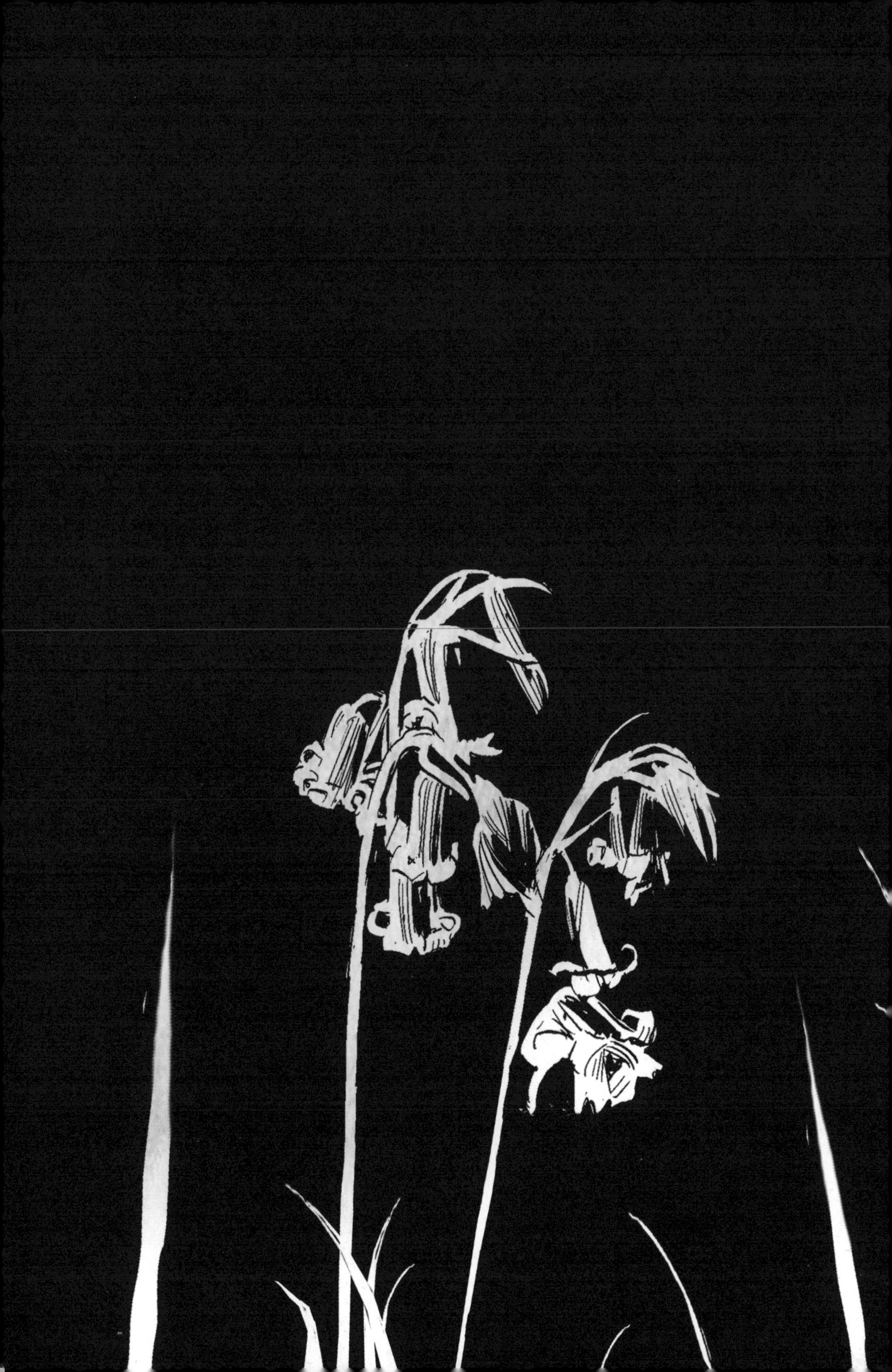

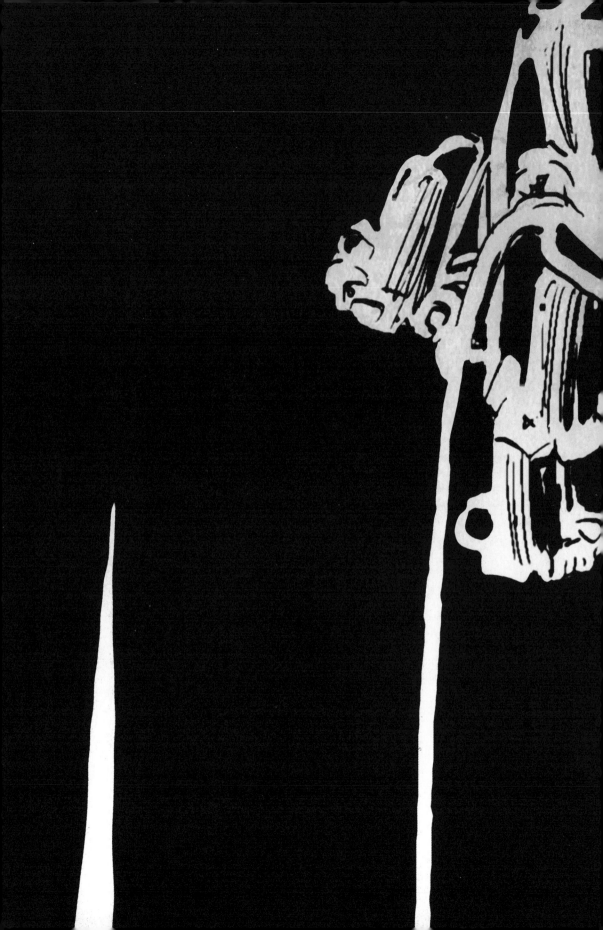

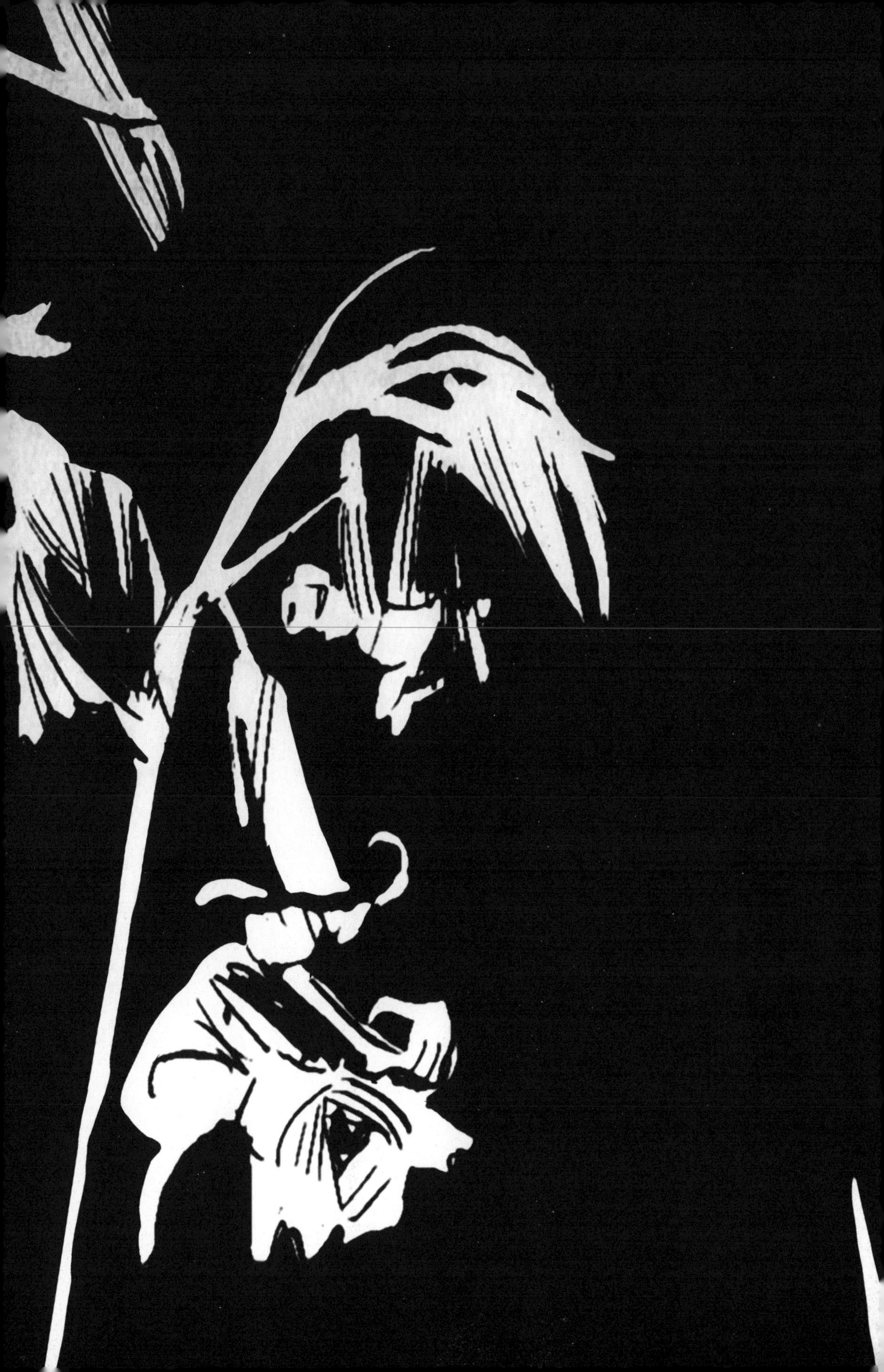

On William Blake
and other influences...

The setting for our mutual childhood was a strangely mixed one. Though our parents had very little disposable money, we grew up in a large, quirky house surrounded by an acre of semi-wild garden. Often left to our own devices, this was the perfect growing medium for eager imaginations as we made expeditions to far-flung places in space and time without ever leaving home.

One of the central objects which stimulated those imaginations was a large, ornate and cloth-spined box on the bookshelf. Printed in gold on that spine were three words: JERUSALEM, WILLIAM BLAKE.

It was many years before we actually knew what the thing was: a rare unbound facsimile of the visionary poet's *Jerusalem* produced by the Trianon Press. This particular copy had once belonged to Blake scholar Joseph Wicksteed, and contained his own personal annotations. To Julian it seemed to have the authority of a family bible. Marcus – being that bit younger – actually believed that "William Blake" was God's true name and that this was the book he'd written.

Wicksteed had given the book to our father just before his death, and Dad kept it in pride of place with his other art books. Unfortunately that was within scrawling reach of two inquisitive boys, and that beautiful spine was once the recipient of some thick blue crayon. Fortunately it came off again, but we were still shamed as teenagers when reminded of what we'd done as we looked at the contents properly for the first time...

And when we did, we were blown away by the imagery, the lettering, the colours; in short, the power of Blake's lines, both drawn and written. His vision of the world – for all its complexity – is one that is very familiar to children prone to flights of imagination. We could easily imagine seeing angels in trees, departing joyful spirits or giant ghostly fleas and both said a hearty amen to Blake's credo: "I must create a system or be enslaved by another man's; I will not reason and compare: my business is to create." And so maybe what Marcus thought – that God had written the book, using the nom de plume "William Blake" – was unwittingly not so far from the truth; Blake believed that it is up to each of us to find our own spirituality.

Another object in the house fired this Blakean vision. A massive oil painting of Blake's *Tyger* hung in the high-ceilinged living room; the beast's eyes glowered down from the wall, untameable, but like some kind of protecting, totemic spirit nonetheless.

Many other influences and memories have gone into *Dark Satanic Mills* – for example, an early visit to the Tate, when Blake's engravings glowed in the semi-darkness of the rooms. Or the rusting old Citroën DS that sat under a massive apple tree in the garden. It broke down fatally one day and was never sent for scrap – instead it became our playground as we hurtled along in it on imagined adventures, and occasionally took our big sister for a taxi ride. Or the fact that Dad – though a pacifist – saw nothing wrong with a little space violence, and bought us Issue One of that ground-breaking comic, *2000 AD*. Bits of Dredd and Strontium Dog also inhabit these pages.

It's fitting that our first published joint project should dig so deep into our childhood. Though, now adults, that mutual imaginative play is still running: whilst researching a film project in New York – and finalizing the text of this book – we saw Barbara Kruger's artwork stamped in massive letters on the roof of a Portakabin near the High Line: BELIEF+DOUBT=SANITY. That very neatly sums up what we want to try and say with *Dark Satanic Mills*.

Marcus & Julian Sedgwick, 2013

Marcus Sedgwick

Marcus Sedgwick was born and raised in East Kent, England. He now divides his time between a small village near Cambridge and the French Alps.

Alongside a sixteen-year career in publishing Marcus established himself as a widely admired writer of YA fiction; he is the winner of many prizes, most notably the Branford-Boase Award for his debut novel *Floodland*, the Booktrust Teenage Prize *My Swordhand is Singing* and the Blue Peter Book Award *Lunatics and Luck*. His books have been shortlisted for over thirty other awards, including the Carnegie Medal (five times), the Edgar Allan Poe Award (twice) and the Guardian Children's Fiction Prize (four times). In 2011 *Revolver* was awarded a Printz Honor.

His latest title is *Doctor Who: She Is Not Invisible*.

He has illustrated some of his books and has provided wood-engravings for a couple of private press books.

Julian Sedgwick

Julian Sedgwick was born in East Kent, England, and studied Oriental Studies and Philosophy at Cambridge University. Since then he has worked variously as a bookseller, writer, painter and therapist. For the last ten years he has also worked in film and documentary-making as a researcher and development screenwriter.

Dark Satanic Mills is the first fruit of a writing collaboration with his brother, Marcus. Other projects, including an original screenplay, are under way. His first book in the Mysterium trilogy is published by Hodder Children's Books.

He lives in the Fens with his wife and two sons, and spends any spare time drawing and trying to master Japanese.

And did those feet in Ancient Time
Walk upon England's mountains green?

John Higgins

Although John Higgins is perhaps best known for his award-winning colouring on *Watchmen*, he has also worked on a huge variety of titles for most of the major comic-book publishers, bringing his skills as an artist and sometimes writer to characters ranging from the eighteenth-century bounty hunter Jonah Hex all the way to the twenty-first century's ultimate lawman Judge Dredd, and pretty much every other major comic character in between.

John also created *Razorjack* — which he wrote, illustrated and initially published — as a personal project that gave him the opportunity to express his darkest fears and to shine a light into the deepest recesses of his mind. He feels that this experience also helped shape the twisted mindset required to co-create and write *The Crimson Corsair* for DC Comics, an ongoing two-page short that appeared in every issue of *Before Watchmen*.

A collected edition of *The Crimson Corsair* by DC Comics and a new edition of *Razorjack* by Titan Books were published in 2013.

Marc Olivent

Marc's previous works include a *Rise of Nightmares* short comic for Sega games and *The Adventures of Daniel S. Wiienstein* for *Mishpacha* magazine.

He lives in Lincoln with his partner and their three-year-old daughter.

And was Jerusalem builded here
Among these Dark Satanic Mills?

First published in Great Britain 2013 by Walker Books Ltd
87 Vauxhall Walk, London SE11 5HJ

1 2 3 4 5 6 7 8 9 10

This book has been typeset in
Caslon Antique Vari and CC WildWords

Printed and bound in China

British Library Cataloguing in Publication Data:
a catalogue record for this book is available
from the British Library

ISBN 978-1-4063-2988-9

www.walker.co.uk